Sweet Lies

Copyright

Opening Quote

Breakin' down and coming undone. It's a roller coaster kinda rush. And I never knew I could feel that much. And that's the way I loved you.

That's the Way I Loved You by Taylor Swift

Chapter One

✗ Alex ✗

This.

This is what I need.

A break from the bullshit that is my family. The constant missions. Training. The dinner table talk of how perfect I am, and how I'm developing into the best leader my family has ever seen.

I don't even want it. I grew up in it. I was forced into my role, but I never wanted it. I never wanted to lead a fucking mafia. No matter how powerful it would make me. How much money I'd have. The women I'd have dropping at my feet.

There's a dark side to the life I grew up in. A sinister side. I can't have feelings. They show weakness. I can't show mercy or feel remorse. Being forced to kill, like I am on a damn near daily fucking basis, feelings will destroy the strongest of souls.

I'm only nineteen years old and every damn day, I'm forced to do more and more illegal things. Run drugs. Guns. Kill those who double cross me. Those who think they can hold out drug money or weapons deal money. I have so many aliases to stay out of trouble, I don't even know who the hell I am anymore.

That's why I'm here. Breathing in the freshly cut grass on the University of Southern California - Los Angeles' campus. UCLA is my escape. My way out. I made an agreement with my dad, Matthew Lucinio, leader of one of the most powerful mafias in the world, that I would major in business as long as he limited his insatiable need to make me into him. No more missions. No more fucking training. Let me concentrate on building my own life.

He hated every fucking second, but I didn't give a single solitary shit. He wants me to take over the mafia so badly, he would agree to anything so long as he had some hope that I'd do what he wanted if he agreed to my terms.

Little does he know I have no intention of taking over. He's grooming the wrong twin. My twin brother, Josh, is the one who wants the reins. But our idiot father refuses to listen to us. So, I decided to force his hand. Now, he has to take Josh seriously. He's the one who knows the operations inside and out. And he's just as good, if not better, than me in missions and training. If I let myself admit to that anyway.

Our father also has no idea I had already intended on majoring in business. I want to own my own company. Trying to tell him that my dreams are beyond the dark walls of the mafia world, though, is like trying to tell an atheist there is a God. Newsflash. I've been through too much shit in my life to believe anything that stupid. God exists? Fucking bullshit.

The more I think about everything my father has put my brother and I through, the more pissed off I become. So, I force myself to calm down as I take in my new home.

UCLA.

A new beginning.

A new turn at life on my own terms and not those of my family.

I take a deep breath and head to my first class of the day. Even though my major is business, I'm still required to take generals. English 101. Whatever the hell that is.

A few minutes later, I walk into a giant lecture hall and stare in complete awe for a moment before I regain my composure. There has to be at least a hundred people in this room. I scan the class for an empty seat and find one near the back. I glance at the clock and realize that I'm close to being late. I don't want to get screamed at by the old guy behind the desk.

Not that I'm intimidated. I don't get intimidated by anyone. I just prefer to make a good impression, and this guy already looks like he's having a tough day. Even though it's just begun. His hair is disheveled, and he looks tired. I hurry to the empty seat and sit.

Sitting next to me is a gorgeous girl with dark brown hair. She's small, but incredibly defined. She has her eyes closed and is breathing out through her nose. I can't help but smile a little. She's obviously not capable of hiding her emotions. I can tell she's nervous as fuck.

I feel this ridiculous overwhelming sense to comfort her in some small way, though. I mentally kick myself and focus my attention forward. Anywhere but on her.

"You smell really good."

I stop with my coffee cup halfway to my lips. Her voice sends shivers all throughout my body. I turn my head to her. "What?"

Her eyes fly open and she covers her mouth as she whips her head around towards me. "I didn't say that out loud. Did I say that out loud?"

Her eyes are a deep blue. I could drown in them if I let myself. Which I absolutely fucking will not. Instead, I give her a cocky smile. "You did say that out loud."

She looks mortified and, for a flicker of a moment, I feel the need to reach out and touch her hair. I choke the urge down and keep my cocky facade in place.

My goal here is not to get involved with anyone. I intend to learn. To grow. Better myself. Women, though I do enjoy them, aren't part of my plan here. Especially women who have the power to make me catch feelings. No way. I'll use one to satisfy an itch. If they do something like fall in love? Not my problem.

But there's no way this girl could satisfy me. I'd crave more and more of her. One time would never be enough.

"I'm so sorry! Sometimes I just blurt things out. My mother used to tell me that if I didn't start thinking about what I say before I say it, I'd be alone and miserable forever." She bites her lip and looks down at her hands. She's playing with her nails, but I can't take my eyes away from her lips. Her very, very kissable lips. My blood rushes straight to my head, and not the one it should be. "She's joking, but sometimes, I believe that."

6

I clear my throat, drop my hands and coffee cup to my lap to cover my growing hard on, and tear my eyes away from her as I face forward. The old guy is getting up. I assume class is about to start.

Good. I need a distraction. A distraction from her infectious smile, gorgeous blue eyes, and perfect fucking tits that are standing at attention in her tight tank top. Though, I'm pretty sure the top wouldn't be tight across any other female's chest in this classroom. This girl just has large breasts that I'm fighting hard to not stare at.

I quietly clear my throat again. "Don't worry about it."

"It's just that I get kind of nervous in settings like this. My heart races, and I have to breathe deeply. I've been here for ten minutes, and breathing deeply isn't working. I mean, it wasn't. Until you sat down. For some reason your scent just instantly calmed me. It was really weird. That's never happened before. And, oh my God. I'm babbling. I promise I'll shut up now."

I smile once more as I glance at her. She's facing forward now, chewing nervously on her bottom lip. A plump bottom lip I'd love to run my tongue across. This is not good. I need to find somewhere else to sit. "Really. Don't worry. I don't mind. I'm flattered."

She looks at me in surprise. "Really? Pretty sure most guys would have fled and found someone less annoying to sit next to."

"I don't think you're annoying." Far from it. Intoxicating is a better word. I really need to find somewhere else to sit.

She smiles widely at me. I force myself to once again focus on the instructor as he begins speaking.

She talks too much. I should be annoyed. Maybe it would help me get myself in check. "You smell like coconut." I keep my voice low.

My body leans into her on his own accord. Fucking asshole. I tried not to say a damn word or lean into her at all. But I couldn't stop the words from flying out of my mouth or my body from touching her. It's like they both have a mind of their own.

I turn my head towards her and catch the smell of her hair. Definitely coconut. I never cared what a woman's hair smelled like before, but everything about her is overwhelming to me. Fucking beautiful. I didn't come here for women. I figured if I blew off steam with one here and there, it would be fine, but I can't stop myself from touching her. I

7

grab a strand of her pretty locks. She inhales sharply as she closes her eyes and leans into my touch.

I smile and force myself to let go as I focus on the lesson. I can't sit next to her again. She's going to break me. The inappropriate thoughts running through my head are going to cause a lot of problems.

"Do you like coconut?" she whispers.

I take a quick glance in her direction before facing forward again. "I didn't until today."

I can see her smile out of the corner of my eye.

Nope.

Definitely making a point to sit next to anyone else from now on.

Chapter Two

✗ Jessa ✗

For the first time since deciding to go to a huge college, I feel relaxed. I feel okay with my decision. Making the choice to come to UCLA was something that took months of agonizing and fighting with myself about. I spent many sleepless nights thinking. Overthinking. And then thinking more. I'm not far away from my parents. Campus is only twenty minutes from home. But I had never been good with change. I'm eighteen now. An adult. And I still hate change like I did as a young kid.

UCLA requires new students to live on campus during their first year. I was not lucky enough to get a room by myself. I have a roommate who I already don't like. She seems like a horrible person. And she's so obviously boy obsessed. She'd been at a party until just an hour ago when she came crashing in like an ape to our dorm room. At least we have our own rooms.

I sigh as I look at my phone and shut off my alarm. Even with how unlucky I am with my roommate, I'm smiling. My face is flushed and hot. I grab my shower caddy and a towel and make my way to the bathroom. My mind drifts to the incredible deep blue eyes of the guy from my class yesterday.

I can't get him out of my head. I could drown in his eyes. Lose myself in his fresh scent. He smells like everything I think calm would be. A smell completely unique to him and impossible to describe. He's tall and muscular. He towers over me and is so well-defined. Yet, he didn't come across as intimidating or scary.

I quickly finish my shower and head back to my room to get ready for the day. It's still blissfully dark and quiet, now that my bitch roommate is sleeping.

I open my laptop to quickly print off the syllabus for today's classes. My entire first year is generals and prerequisites to the good classes. My major is project management. It's a step down from architecture. I get to do nearly everything except all of the crazy math and to scale models. I hate math and scales. But I love drawing. I love coming up with ideas and putting them on paper, then allowing an architect to bring my dreams to life.

I've never wanted to do anything else. My dad is an architect and would love nothing more than for me to become one, too, and take over his business. But I didn't want to. He had learned to respect that. Especially when he noticed my detailed drawings at such a young age. The older I got, the better I got at it. My parents have always been incredibly supportive of me.

After finishing getting dressed, I grab my things for the day and head out. I stop by the coffee shop to get a drink, then I hurry across the campus, enjoying the fact that it's not busy. Most people look like zombies as they make their way to their first class. I may be the only one wide awake and carrying a nice turtle mocha in my hand. I love that there is a coffee shop right in my dorm building.

"It probably isn't a wise idea for a girl like you to be walking around campus by herself," the deep voice I haven't been able to get out of my head reverberates. I lose my grip on my coffee. The owner of the voice that fills my dreams catches it with lightning-fast reflexes. "Didn't mean to startle you."

I can't speak. I can only stare up at him as I lose myself in his eyes. His beautiful, sexy, deep, blue as the ocean eyes.

He smiles a cocky half-smile as he holds my cup out to me. "See something you like?"

I shake my head to snap myself out of my reverie. He's gorgeous. Way too gorgeous to be interested in someone like me.

"Uh… sorry… I guess… I was lost in my own head." I take the cup and hold it up to my face to try and hide my blush as I turn and begin to start walking again.

He falls into step beside me. "So yesterday. In English. I never got the chance to introduce myself. I'm Alex Lang."

"Oh… Yeah, um… I'm Jessa. Holloway." I don't have any idea how the words are coming out, but I can hear how shaky they are.

"Nice to put a name to the beautiful face."

I look up at him in shock. "What?"

He smiles and looks down at the ground. "That was probably forward. I figured you'd be okay with it, though, since the first thing out of your mouth when I sat down was about how good I smell."

I feel myself turning shades of red that I'm positive have no name yet. I'm pretty sure I've just invented them. "Sorry about that."

He shrugs as he looks back up with a smile. "Don't be."

We reach my building, and I sigh. "This is me."

Alex looks up. "Yeah? What class do you have?"

"U.S. Government. With Professor Dukes."

"No shit? Me, too."

I allow myself a grin before I become suddenly shy again. Leave it to Alex to notice.

"What just happened?" His voice. It's so deep. So powerful yet gentle and soothing enough to ease my nerves.

"Nothing. It's just…" I pause and shake my head.

"Just what?"

"I can't find the words without sounding like a complete lovesick fool." I put my hand over my mouth. Seriously. I have got to get this babbling and blurting-things-out-without-thinking thing under control. Alex smiles. "Sorry."

"Don't be."

He gestures to the building. We walk to class, finding a seat near the back. The lights in the room are still off, but there's enough light coming in from the windows to make it light enough to see.

Alex sits next to me and drops his backpack on the ground. After a moment of silence, he sighs heavily and turns to me. I smile shyly at him. "What?"

"I had every intention of making sure I sit as far away from you as possible." He catches a strand of my hair between his fingers, and my heart catches in my throat as I frown. I knew a guy like him could never see anything in a girl like me.

"Sorry." I can't look at him, so I look down at my lap. He twists the strand of hair around his finger and tugs.

"I came here with the intention of sticking to my studies and staying away from women. But something about you..." I look up at him, unsure where he's going with this. "I've never not been able to stop thinking about a woman before. But yesterday, you were all that was on my mind. This morning when I woke up, all I could think about was you."

I smile softly and lower my eyes, looking at him through my lashes. "Me, too."

He lets go of my hair. I hear him exhale. Like he's relieved. My heart spikes again as he rests his leg comfortably against mine. It feels so natural that all I can do is revel in the feeling.

Throughout class, Alex finds small ways to touch me or lean into me. He smiles discreetly at me when he catches me glancing at him. Near the end of class, I'm fighting from jumping into his arms and never letting him go. I don't have any idea what the professor has even talked about for most of class because all I can think about is Alex's hands, or legs, or arms. Every time he touches me, it's like electricity shoots through my entire body.

"Now, onto this project that many of you expressed excitement about. I warn you. It will not be easy."

I perk up at his words and am suddenly all ears. After reading the syllabus, this project sounds so exciting. I've already come up with ideas.

"You will choose one person to work with. You must create an entire city, and a government. And the class must vote for the best city. Whichever team wins will get an extra twenty points added to their final exam."

I'm nearly vibrating with excitement as the professor continues. "Pick your partners. I want names before you leave. Which is right now."

I'm just about to turn to Alex when the guy next to him grabs his attention. "Hey, I'm Seth. Want to partner up?"

My heart sinks.

"No thanks, man. Already got a partner." I can feel my eyes light up as I smile, hopeful he's talking about me. He says nothing, though, as he gathers his stuff.

"Whatever, dude." Seth turns away. The guy next to me grabs my arm. I turn to him and try to pull my arm away, but he tightens his grip. My heart starts racing as blood rushes to my ears.

"Hey, sexy thing. Name's Grant. Looks like you and I are partners on this."

Before I can say a word, Alex stands and pulls me against him and away from Grant. "Touch her again, I'll break your fucking hand. She's already got a partner."

"Alright. Fuck." Grant gathers his stuff and scurries away. I let out a breath I didn't know I was holding as Alex's strong arms wrap possessively around me. My racing heart begins to calm, and I take a deep breath.

"You okay?"

"I… think so. He grabbed my arm and wouldn't let go." Alex gently takes my hand and looks over my arm. I watch his expression darken, so I look down at my arm. There are red marks where Grant grabbed me. "Damn."

"He even so much as looks at you, I swear I'll kill him."

I put my hand on his chest. "Can we just get out of here?"

"Absolutely."

He helps me gather my stuff, then takes my hand. My world is right again so quickly, my head actually spins. He makes me feel safe. Invincible.

Alex leads me up to Professor Dukes. "Ms. Holloway. I have you partnered with Grant Sanders."

"Excuse me?" Alex asks.

I look up at Alex. Fear begins to overtake me and I start shaking. "Alex." My voice comes out nearly inaudible. Something about that guy makes me so uneasy that the thought of being partnered with him makes me feel like I want to run home and never return to college. Ever.

13

"Professor Dukes, Jessa already informed Grant she didn't want to partner with him. He was upset. and now he's trying to force her to."

"Hmm… Is this true, Ms. Holloway?"

I nod. "I don't want to be partners with him." My lip quivers. I bite it, refusing to let myself cry.

"I assume the two of you had intended to be partners?"

"Yes, sir," Alex says.

"Very well. There was a student who was absent today. I'll put Mr. Sanders with him."

"Thank you, sir." Alex leads me out into the hallway. "Still okay?"

I nod, but I'm not. I'm doing everything I can to calm my breathing. As soon as we're outside, I pull him to the side of the building and throw myself in his arms as I start crying. Not like I've ever thrown myself at a man I barely know, but Alex is safe. I feel it with every fiber of my being.

"He tried to…" I grip his shirt and sob. "Make me! Why? Why would he do that?"

Alex hugs me tighter. "Shh… It's okay. I won't let him touch you. Don't worry about him."

He sways with me and runs his fingers through my hair until I'm calm enough to let him go. I don't know how long he stays with me hugging me, but very suddenly, I'm overcome with embarrassment and shame.

"I'm sorry. You probably think I'm a crazy person." I wipe my eyes.

"I don't think that at all, Jessa." He pulls me close to him again. "What's your schedule like for the rest of the day?"

I pull back and dig for my schedule. When I find it, I hand it to him so I can compose myself.

"We have statistics together."

I smile up at him. "I really hate math."

He grins and puts his arms over my shoulders as we start walking to our next class. "Well, lucky for you, I'm amazing at it."

"Lucky for me, indeed."

Alex and I find a seat together once we reach our class. He immediately takes my hand in his when we sit. He doesn't let go the entire class. He'll never know how grateful I am for that.

14

I spend the rest of the day with Alex in a coffee shop on campus. We talk. We laugh. We talk about each other's family. We're both only children. We both love football. We're both competitive board game players. We're competitive in general. We both love the beach and find the crashing of the waves against the shore peaceful and relaxing.

We're enjoying each other so much that we lose track of time. The sun has long ago set on us when we realize how long we've been sitting here.

"Wow. Didn't mean to keep you out all day," Alex says.

"It's okay. No homework. And honestly, my roommate is a mole rat."

Alex laughs. "A mole rat? Not a pig, or a cow? Tell me you don't live in a barn. I'll have to make up my couch for you to save you from such a terrible living situation."

I smile as we leave the coffee shop hand in hand. "Nope. A mole rat. Pigs are too cute. I love them. And cows aren't nearly as obnoxious. She's disgusting." I shiver a little. Alex puts his arm across my shoulders and rubs my arm. I can't help but snuggle into him.

"Tell me about this roommate."

"Oh my God. She's awful. We met a couple days ago when she moved in. I had already moved in. She was upset I took the room in the back. She's incredibly rude. And so noisy. She's gone out drinking both nights she's been here. She gets back at like five in the morning and crashes around. I like that she's gone at night, but until she leaves? She's really terrible. Loud music. She's messy. I really hate messes. Awful."

"I have no roommates. I'm pretty lucky I could afford to get a suite to myself."

I look up at him. "Seriously? You're so lucky. I'm here on a scholarship because of my grades. My parents are paying for my room and board, and I get a monthly allowance, but they want me to learn life lessons. Make my own way in life. They want me to concentrate on school, so I have no job, but I have to budget everything with what I'm given."

"I can respect that, though. Everyone should be able to make their own way in life. No matter where they come from, or how much their parents make."

"I don't think it's possible for you to be any more perfect."

Alex laughs. The sound comes out a sensuous, deep hum. I shiver again, but not from the cold.

I look up at the building in front of us and sigh. "I guess this is the end of the night. This is me."

"Want me to walk you up?"

"I do, but if my roommate is there, I'll be thoroughly embarrassed at the state of my living arrangements."

He smiles and leans down, lightly brushing his lips across mine. I close my eyes and smile.

"I'd like to kiss you, but I don't want to scare you away by moving too fast." He straightens up and cups my cheek. I lean into him.

"I'll see you in class tomorrow?"

"I'll be there," he whispers.

I smile and force my feet to move. He waits for me to get inside my dorm before he waves and walks away. I feel like I'm floating to my room.

I'm very happy to see my roommate isn't home. The only good thing about her is that I get a quiet night of sleep since she's never here after like nine at night.

I get ready for bed and curl up under my covers. Alex's handsomely chiseled face makes its way into my mind and stays there all through the night.

Chapter Three

⚔ Jessa ⚔

(Two Days Later)

I put my pillow over my head and scream. Loudly. I kick my feet and throw a literal tantrum, throwing my pillow across the room, still screaming. The music coming from the common room in our dorm is so loud, my scream would never be heard over it anyway. Even if I didn't have the damn pillow over my face.

I look at my phone. Alex had put his number in my phone the day we spent all day at the coffee shop and told me to call or text him whenever, but the idea of texting him at four in the morning is just cruel so I throw my phone instead as I get up and make my way out of my room with my shower caddy.

"Come to join us, party virgin?" my roommate asks.

"What? No! I'm not... Ugh!" I stomp my foot. I don't care how childish I'm being. I hate her. This is the second night she's taken her away-party home. "Can you just keep it down?"

She folds her arms over her chest. "No. Stop being such a stick in the mud."

"Are you kidding? It's four in the morning!"

She shrugs and turns away from me, climbing into someone's lap on the couch. Grant? Gross. So gross.

My roommate, Marrisa, is a perfectly beautiful woman. She's very California. Tan. Blonde. Blue eyes. She's taller than I am and slim. Men fall at her feet. Which is ironic because she also falls at theirs.

My eyes fall on the TV and the wall behind it. I gasp. What the hell happened? The wall. It's covered in… Star Wars wallpaper? She's… obsessed with deep space?

I can't. I can't do this anymore. I storm back to my room as Marissa starts making out heavily with Grant and people start trickling out of our room.

I give up. I'm up. I may as well attempt the statistics problems I've been putting off.

I sit on my bed and take out my book. It doesn't take long before my frustration level hits an all-time high, and I shove everything off my bed. I hate math. I don't understand it. I can't do it. There's no point in it. It's not even relevant to my major.

At least the music stopped. Doesn't help my mood, though. Angry and frustrated tears sting my eyes as I get dressed. Afterwards, I pick up all of my things and stuff them into my bag. I haven't slept. I haven't even eaten because everything I buy Marissa thinks is hers.

My phone vibrates with a text message as I am storming out of my bedroom.

Alex: Good morning, peanut. Ready to put the rest of our government class to shame?

I smile and slow down to type out my response.

"You heading to class? I'll walk with you," Grant says sleepily from the couch.

I stop, phone in my hand. Everything about him freaks me the hell out. He simply doesn't take no for an answer. He's so entitled. It's scary, honestly

Jessa: Can you come up to my room instead? Please? I'll explain when you're here. Room 871.

I look at Grant. He's grabbing his shirt. "Not a chance."

I nearly sprint to my room. I don't like him. Not even because he grabbed my arm and caused it to bruise. Or even because he's so arrogant

18

and cocky. It's something else. Something far deeper and sinister. I lock my door and run my hand over my bruised arm.

Alex: Be there in a few minutes. Hang tight, sweetheart.

I pace back and forth as I wait. A heavy knock hits my door, and I jump.

"Come on, Jessa. We're gonna be late, and I need coffee to kill this fucking hangover."

"Go away, Grant. I'm not going anywhere with you."

"Stop being a bitch. We're going to the same place. Just walk with me."

Jessa: Please hurry. I doubt the door is locked. I'm in my room.

Grant tries to open the door. When he realizes it's locked, he slams his fist into it. I jump and let out a squeak. "You're being ridiculous. Open the door!" he bellows.

Alex: On my way up.

"Go away! I don't want to go anywhere with you!" I yell.

He pounds on the door again. "Quit embarrassing me! Let's just go!"

"Jess? Where are you, baby?" Alex. Thank fucking God.

"Great. Called the fucking calvary, huh?" Grant growls.

"Alex!" I yell.

"You have two seconds to back the fuck away from her door." Alex's voice sounds dangerous.

"Or what?" Grant asks with what sounds to me like a smirk.

"Or you're going to get hurt. Leave. She's made it clear she wants nothing to do with you."

There's silence, and then I hear a door slam. A few moments later, there's a light knock on my door. "It's okay, peanut. It's me."

I unlock the door. For the second time since I've met him, I throw myself at him. He wraps me in his arms and backs me into my room, closing the door behind him.

"I don't understand his obsession with me."

"What happened, honey?"

I take a deep breath and sit on my bed. Reading me, he sits next to me and keeps me in his arms. "Last night, my stupid roommate, Marissa, came back and threw another loud party. Second one in a row. I didn't get any sleep. I haven't slept in two days. I've barely eaten in two days because everything I buy and label she takes." I sniffle. "So I went out there at like four in the morning and asked her to keep it down. But she ignored me and started making out with Grant on the couch. I came back here to my room and tried to do homework. She finally turned off the music, but I still couldn't understand anything I was looking at. So I gave up, got dressed, and was leaving. Grant was up and said he'd walk with me. That's when I texted you and came back here. He followed and started pounding on my door and calling me a bitch."

"Because you wouldn't go to class with him?"

"He won't take no for an answer. And he really scares me, Alex."

"I know, honey." Alex pulls me closer to his side. "First thing we do is get you something to eat. How about a bagel from the coffee shop? Their breakfast ones are surprisingly good." His hand rubs my arm soothingly. I nod, and he stands, pulling me up with him. "Why didn't you call earlier? You could've come by my place."

I smile softly as he leads me to the coffee shop in my dorm and orders for both of us. We sit at a table. "Don't you think it's a little early for boy girl sleepovers?"

"Funny." He grins, knowing I'm joking. On a serious note, why didn't you call me? You could've slept on my couch. And you've been downplaying your roommate situation."

"Have not!"

"Jess, you told me she parties all night, but at other places. And that she's a bitch when she's there and when she gets back. You mentioned nothing about her taking all your food, or that she's brought the party home. Explains why you looked so tired yesterday. And today."

I've learned over the past couple of days that Alex is annoyingly perceptive. And he can read people like no one I've ever met.

"I didn't want to bother you so early in the morning. Not fair to you."

"I told you to call me whenever. I meant that."

I smile as we finish our breakfast. He takes my hand, and we make our way to our government class. We take the same seats we had before and wait for class to start.

"So, what homework were you struggling with? Anything I can help with?"

"It wasn't exactly homework. I was trying to do some problems for statistics. I wanted to try and figure it out, but I can't. It's only our second day in that class and I already know I'm going to fail. I don't understand it."

"I will not let you fail. Math is like my second language. I'll get you through it, peanut."

I chuckle. "Peanut? Why peanut?"

He looks down at me and grins. I melt into his gaze. "Because you're half my size and incredibly cute. Small. Like a peanut."

"Adorable. I should probably start calling you Hulk, then."

He laughs. "Try again. I may be big and tough, but not to that extreme. And I'm not green."

"Hmm… Wolverine?"

"Nope."

I think for a moment and then smile slyly. "I've got it."

He narrows his eyes. "Why are you looking at me like that?"

"Human Torch. Because you swoop in when needed and are so hot."

I lean into him a moment as he laughs. "Not a chance in hell."

I'm just about to retort when I see Grant making his way up to where we're sitting. He flops into the chair next to me and grumbles. "Hey."

He rests his leg against mine, and I stop breathing, gripping Alex's leg in fear. Alex leans into my ear. "Stand up, baby. Switch me places."

He kisses my ear, and despite the incredible fear I feel towards Grant, I shiver in delight at Alex's warm lips on me.

I do as I'm told and stand. He gently moves me by him and sits next to Grant. "Ugh, here we go," Grant grumbles.

"First, you grab her arm and leave bruises. Second, you try to force her into being your partner for our project, even though I told you she has one. Third, you try to force her to walk to class with you, even though she said no. And fourth, you scare the hell out of her by, again, trying to force her to do something she doesn't want to and pounding the shit out of her door. So tell me, do you know the meaning of no? Or is this a lesson I need to teach you?"

"Dude. You talk like she's your possession. Women aren't possessions. Asshole."

21

Alex chuckles darkly. "Here's what's going to happen. You're going to find a new seat tomorrow. You're going to leave Jessa alone. You aren't going to talk to her. At all. You so much as breathe in her direction, you face me. And I am one scary motherfucker."

I swallow hard and shiver. I don't know why I don't feel fearful of Alex, but he's undeniably intimidating.

"You don't scare me. And I think Jessa can talk to me without her bodyguard running interference."

"I'm far more than her bodyguard. But hey. You can think whatever you want. Truth is, she *is* mine. She'll never be yours. And as long as she's mine, she'll never have to face you or anything else on her own. So, it looks like you'll be dealing with me. Do what I say, and you'll be fine. Fuck up. Well, you'll wish you never laid eyes on her."

Professor Dukes starts class, and I take Alex's hand. It's a rather comforting feeling knowing I have him on my side.

I have no doubt in my mind that having him as an enemy is a very bad decision.

Chapter Four

 Alex

(Two Months Later)

It's been nearly two months since Jessa crashed through my walls and things couldn't be any more perfect. My decision to stay out of mafia life has been the second best one I've ever made. The first was choosing to talk to Jessa after our first day of class.

She's an amazing woman. Unlike anyone I've ever met. She's easy to talk to. I love being with her. When I'm not with her, I miss her like crazy.

I haven't spent a single day without her since I met her, and I truly like her more and more with each day.

I smile as my phone starts ringing. Not bothering to look at the caller ID, I pick it up. "Hey, beautiful."

"Aww… Thanks. No one's ever called me beautiful before," a deep male voice says in my ear instead of the sultry sweet one of the woman who has overtaken every thought I possess.

"God, you're an asshole," I say to Ryan Crane, my best friend.

"I get that a lot."

"What do you want, Ry? Jess should be on her way over with her statistics homework."

"How's that going? You told her the truth yet?"

I had lied to her about my last name and my family. I enrolled using my true name, but the university is under strict orders to use Alex Lang for my classes. The only ones who knew my true identity are the Dean and the admissions director. I specifically asked it to be this way because I want a completely separate identity from that of my family. I want to make my own way.

"No. And you know my reasons. I don't want her anywhere near my family."

"You know this isn't going to end well. What happens if things become serious? You're eventually going to have to tell her. You can't protect her from your family if she has no idea who your family is."

"Well, I'll cross that bridge when I get to it. What do you want?"

"Uh, I have a job. One of my guys' sister is in some trouble. Gang member boyfriend. Latinos, I think."

"What's the trouble?"

"He's got her running drugs. Problem is one of her buyers beat the hell out of her. Put her in the hospital. She didn't meet her deadline."

"And you think the boyfriend is going to go after her."

"I don't think. I know. I sent my guy with a couple others out to LA. When they got to the hospital, she'd been moved to the ICU. Boyfriend was admitted to her room and beat the hell out of her again. He may have succeeded in killing her had her monitors not started going fucking crazy."

"Wow. You got surveillance on him?"

"That's where I need you. I found him, but I'm spread pretty thin. I'm flying out, but I can't spare the extra men."

"I'll get you some guys. I'll have Gavin meet you at the airport. He'll grab my team and you can brief them at your hotel."

"Thanks, man."

"Sure."

Ryan is the leader of the Crane Mafia, a very large and very dangerous mafia. Bigger than even my family's mafia. He took over for his father a couple of years ago and turned it legit and has grown it larger than it already was. He's only twenty-five.

First time I met him, I was still a teenager. My dad had started a war with his dad. The two of us became fast friends. Mostly because he saw himself in me and spared my life. The only reason he took over as early as he did is because one of my dad's guards shot his dad. It was because of Ryan and me that a truce was called, though our dads still hate each other to this day

"Let me know if you need me, but not tonight. I'm gonna try to convince Jessa to stay."

"Roommate giving her shit again?"

"Yeah. She needs a fucking break." I hear a light knock on my door. "She's here now, Ry. I'll check in tomorrow."

"Sounds good. Thanks, Alex."

"Anytime."

I hang up with him and text Gavin Vandenberg, one of my best friends, marching orders to meet Ryan at the airport and get him whatever he needs. I put my phone away as I open the door. My eyes fall on Jessa and drink in. "You are a sight for sore eyes, baby."

"It's kind of chilly out there."

"Late October in LA. It's either hot or cold. Never any in between."

I let her in and take her jacket. She looks exhausted as she collapses on my couch.

"I can't get over how quiet it is here. I'd give anything for this."

I sit down next to her. "Anything, huh?"

She smiles and curls up into my side. I put my arm around her. "Anything."

There's another knock on the door. Jessa sighs as she sits back up.

"Takeout," I say with a grin as I stand. She perks up as I answer the door. I pay the delivery driver and tip him handsomely. He gives me a huge smile as I close the door.

"Casa Bianca?" she asks hopefully.

"I wouldn't order elsewhere, Jess."

"Bianco?"

"Baby. Would I order you anything different?"

She smiles widely and follows me as I take the food to the kitchen. I grab plates and forks and turn to see her with her eyes closed inhaling the scent of the pizza.

I put everything on the counter and take her face in my hands. I lean down to kiss her. My tongue darts across her lips. She melts into me, her lips molding to mine as they open for me. I tighten my arms around her and slip my tongue inside her warm and waiting mouth. Her small hands splay across my stomach and bunch my shirt into their grip.

She moans and wraps her arms around my neck. I back her against the counter and press further against her. My cock is hard as fuck and I know she feels it, but I can't seem to stop. She tastes so good. I slip my hand under her shirt and run my hand along her beautiful soft mounds. Her nipples immediately harden. She presses against me, deepening the kiss. I wrap my arms tightly around her with a groan and slide them down to her ass.

Perfect.

Round.

Just enough to get a good grip on. Which I do without hesitation. I tug her closer. My dick strains against my jeans. Our tongues fuse together, like they were made for one another. I can't get enough of her, bur fuck. I have to stop before I take this too far. I don't know how ready she is for that step, but it's something we should probably discuss before I take it there.

I pull away slowly and kiss her softly with a smile. I release my grip on her leisurely as her eyes flutter open. Her grip on my shirt loosens slightly as she comes back to herself. She looks up at me and blushes as she looks down to her hands where my shirt is bunched into her fists. Her blush darkens, and she bites her lip.

"That... was..." She trails off and doesn't look up.

I run my fingers through her hair and kiss her forehead. "Incredible. And something I can't wait to explore more of."

She smiles shyly. I step around her to my refrigerator. I take out a Pepsi for myself and a Mountain Dew for her as she slips out of my grasp and makes her way to the bar seats behind me. I take a second to compose myself before I close the door and turn back to her. She's sitting at the counter, a nervous smile on her face.

"You got breaded mushrooms and garlic bread." She says the words softly and doesn't look at me. I reach around her to put our sodas down, then hug her from behind and kiss her cheek.

She smiles at me, and I sit next to her as we dig into our food. When we've gotten our fill and I've put everything away, I turn to her with every intention of talking about our next steps and where she sees this going. But she looks almost sad. And incredibly tired.

"Talk to me."

"It's nothing." She doesn't meet my eyes.

"Jess. It's me. Come on. What's going on?"

She sighs heavily. "I'm just so tired. Fifteen credits is weighing on me. Even though they aren't hard classes, I just can't keep up because I'm so tired."

"Is Marissa getting worse?"

She looks at me, and I can see something more than just sadness and exhaustion. "She's dating Grant. He's there all the time. And they're... loud. There's no way anyone could mistake what's going on in her room."

I narrow my eyes. "How long has that been going on?" I ask, keeping my voice calm and level, even though I'm pissed off this has been happening. She looks down. "Jess. Honey, I can't do anything for you if you don't talk to me."

She takes a deep breath. "I didn't want you to be upset or get into trouble or anything."

I can't help but chuckle. "Don't worry about me. I can take care of myself, baby."

"A month." She doesn't say anything. Just stands up and walks over to my sitting room.

I follow and take her hand, stopping her in her tracks. "I've got somewhere else in mind. Somewhere more cozy." I lead her down the hall to another private and small sitting room near my bedroom. "Ignore the throw pillows. My mom had to have some kind of say over decorations."

"'Gangsta rap made me do it.' Really? She bought that?"

"I swear. She definitely tries far too hard, but I didn't have the heart to tell her no. She bought it because I like to listen to Eminem from time to time." I move the pillows off the couch and sit, waiting for her to join me.

"He's not classified as Gangsta rap. Is he?"

I smile. "No."

"I didn't think so." She laughs as she sits and curls up next to me. God, I fucking love when she does that.

27

I wrap her in my arms and flip on the TV. "NCIS?" I ask.

"Sure." I find her favorite show, and she relaxes against me. I kiss the top of her head and let her burrow into my side. When she's comfortable, she puts her arm around my waist.

"You know. It's the weekend. Why don't you stay here? She'll probably have loud parties all weekend. If you were here, you'd be able to sleep. And we can work on that statistics homework."

"If you're trying to convince me by telling me all the good things about staying here, you don't need to. I pretty much want to move in at this point. I'd take a cardboard box under a bridge to living with her."

I chuckle and hug her a bit tighter. My heart starts racing as I realize I want that. I want her to move in. It's only been two months, but I want her with me all the time. I want to touch her whenever I want. I want to be assured she's getting sleep, eating, and above all else, safe. Especially knowing Grant is dating Marissa. There's no doubt in my mind that it has to do with Jessa. He wants to be close.

"Then get your stuff. Move in. Not like there isn't enough room."

She looks up at me. "Really? You... You'd let me move in here?"

"Why not? Gets you away from them. And you know I like having you around." She focuses her attention on the TV and is silent for so long that I am pretty convinced I fucked things up somehow. "Honey, I don't mean to pressure you." I run my fingers through her hair.

"Maybe we could see how this weekend goes first?"

I look down at her. My heart actually skips a fucking beat. "You mean..."

She nods. "I'll have to get some stuff, but... I'll stay if it's okay."

I tilt her chin up so I can kiss her long and passionately. I fight myself from pulling her into my lap. I can't be responsible for my actions if her ass is against my dick like that. "Tomorrow, peanut. Tonight, you need to sleep."

"Where will I be sleeping?"

I want to tell her I want her with me, but I don't want to push her. I clear my throat. "Uh... Wherever you want. You can sleep here. You'll fit. Or you can take a couch or recliner in the other room. Or... um... There's my room, too." I glance down at her just to see how she takes the suggestion.

"Can I think about it?"

"Take your time, sweetheart. Actually, let me get a t-shirt for you for the night." I untangle myself from her and stand up. As I am returning, my phone rings. "Ryan," I mutter when I see his name on my screen. I hit the answer button, but say nothing as I turn the corner to my sitting room. I hand Jessa the t-shirt.

"You can change in here. I have to take this call." She takes the t-shirt, smiles at me, and nods. I walk out of the room and put my phone to my ear. "What." It comes out a low growl.

"I wouldn't call and interrupt your night if it wasn't important."

I sigh and rub my forehead. "I know. What happened?"

"I got some intel. I've been looking for the higher ups for that gang, and I found them. They have a meeting tomorrow."

"When?"

"One. In the afternoon. Brazen as fuck. I know. But they'll all be there. It's my best chance at making sure they don't go after my guy's sister."

I lean against the counter. I don't need to ask the question I'm about to, but I do it anyway. "What do you need from me, Ry?"

"Your guys, obviously. I have a few of my own, but I could use you. And before you say anything about being pulled back in, I wouldn't ask if I could do this on my own. You know that. But I'm stretched so fucking thin right now. I need as many guys as I can get, and I trust you. He went after my guy's family, man. You know I don't take that shit lightly."

Family means everything to Ryan. It's what he stands on. He never would have taken over the Crane Mafia as quickly as he did if not for his dad being injured. He'll never admit it, but it's only been three years. He's done a lot but he doesn't have full control over it yet. He still gets a lot of help from his brothers and his dad. If he says he's stretched thin, he means it.

"I know. Look. Jessa is here for the weekend. I'll help you, but we have to hit quick. And I'll need your shower. I'm not bringing that shit near her."

"Understood. I'll have a pair of jeans and a shirt for you so you don't have to walk out with a bag."

"Thanks. Text me the meet up point. I'll meet you there."

"Done. And hey. Have a good night." I hear the tease in his voice.

"Asshole." He laughs and hangs up.

I shake my head and text orders for Gavin to pull some guys and contact Ryan before I put my phone away. I walk back to the sitting room. I raise an eyebrow when I don't see Jessa. I glance around the room, half expecting to see her hiding in a corner giggling or something. When I don't see her, my heart beats a little faster.

I turn off the TV and light as I leave the room. The bathroom door is still open, so I know she's not in there. I would have seen her come down the hall to the living room. My breath comes out a little quicker as I quietly push the cracked door to my bedroom open.

Jessa is dead asleep in my t-shirt on my bed. My mouth goes dry. She's wearing panties underneath, but they do very little to hide what's underneath. I swallow hard and let out a low groan. I don't want to wake my girl.

After stripping down to my boxer briefs I gently crawl into bed. She stirs, and I pause. When she quits moving, I lay down next to her. I'd like to pull her against me and wrap her in my arms, but she needs sleep. I really don't want to wake her.

But Jessa feels me next to her. She doesn't open her eyes, but she wraps her arm around my waist and rests her head in the crook of my arm when I wrap it around her. I rest my hand on her ass. She's back asleep within minutes, her leg between mine and every part of her pressed against me.

I groan again already knowing I'm going to dream about everything I want to do to her. Like lick her hardened nipples. Massage her supple mounds. Stick my hand between her legs and bring her insurmountable amounts of pleasure while I drop a finger inside her. With the thoughts of everything I want to do with her invading my mind, I fall into a peaceful and deep sleep.

Chapter Five

⚔ Alex ⚔

Waking up beside Jessa with my arms wrapped around her, my hand on her perfectly full ass, and my face buried in her coconut infused hair is my new favorite thing in the world. I stay as still as possible for as long as I can praying to a God I don't believe in to never let this moment end.

She stirs, and I hold my breath, tightening my grip. She nuzzles closer into me.

"Why are you holding your breath?" she says softly.

I chuckle, but it comes out more like a low hum from deep within that vibrates throughout my chest. "Because I like being like this. I don't want it to end."

"Me either."

I hold her a little while longer until my phone rings. I sigh and reach over her to see who it is. Ryan. If I don't answer, he'll know to text, so I put the phone back down, but I know I need to get up. It's already ten in the morning. I'll need to get ready soon. I give her ass a squeeze.

"I hate to do this to you, but I have to get up. I have to help a friend out."

"Oh. Sure. Okay." She looks up at me.

I smile. "You're so beautiful in the morning," I say into her hair as I kiss her head. She blushes. I kiss her softly on the lips before climbing out of bed. "I need a quick shower. Then I can make breakfast if you want."

"You cook, too? Geez. You're the full package, aren't you?"

I raise an eyebrow as her eyes travel over my body, pausing on my semi hard cock. My boxer briefs do nothing to hide it. Her eyes don't leave it, and I feel it hardening.

"Just you wait. I'm sure you'll enjoy the package I have to offer," I say teasingly. I smile wider when she blushes.

To her credit, though, her blue eyes darken, and she doesn't quit looking at the full on tent I've created in my underwear. She licks her lips. "Can't wait."

I nearly choke. "Make that a cold shower." I shake my head and grin at her as she giggles. I turn quickly, grabbing my phone. It vibrates in my hand as I walk to the bathroom. I look down.

Ryan: Time change. An hour. I'll explain when you get here.

"Fuck." I make a beeline for my bedroom again. I love my bedroom. There's a large floor to ceiling window that spans the entire length of the room. The walls are a dark gray. The room isn't large, and my king size bed takes up almost all of it. I wouldn't have it any other way.

"I'm sorry, baby. I gotta go now." I grab a pair of dark blue jeans and a black t-shirt with some black SWAT boots and quickly get dressed.

"Is everything okay?"

I lean down to kiss her softly. "It's fine, peanut. I'm sorry I have to leave you. I'll be a couple of hours."

"Okay." She smiles, and I kiss her again. I hurry out of the room and to my car, rushing to the meeting point. I arrive just at eleven and jump out of my car. As soon as I reach Ryan, he hands me a gun and bulletproof vest.

"I figured you wouldn't be able to grab gear without raising suspicion."

"Thanks, man. I hated leaving her. She's going through a lot."

"I won't keep you. We'll be done quick."

I put my vest on. He hands me a shoulder holster for my gun and leg holster for my second. When I'm geared up, he hands me my earpiece.

"So, what happened?" I ask.

"Intel I got. My guys said they're planning another strike on my guy's sister. We need to take them out now."

"What's your plan?"

"I have your guys watching the place. You, me, and my three guys are going in. There's seven of them and five of us. We're outnumbered, and I do not like that. We go in fast, hard, and we don't miss. That's why I need you. You're just as good in a raid as I am."

I sigh. He's right. I am good. I've been doing this a long fucking time. His dad had him out when he was a kid. My dad did the same thing as his. Only, I think I may have been out there at a younger age than him. My father is far more assholish. At least he actually loves his kids.

"I'm doing this because you're like my brother, Ryan. I hate everything about this life."

"I know. So do I. But we're taking out bad guys here. Keep that in the forefront of your mind. It'll get you through. The world will be better off without these dicksnorters in it."

I shake my head and chuckle. Ryan Crane has always had a way with words. "Alright," I say. "Let's do this."

We duck through a couple yards and jump a fence until we get to a rundown house.

"We go through the back," Ryan says. "My guys through the front. On my count. Three…. Two…. One…. Enter…," he whispers into our earpieces.

Ryan busts through the door, and I follow close behind. A guy comes around the corner, and I shoot. Ryan shoots someone else. "Two down," he says.

Ryan and I move through the house with practiced ease. I hear Ryan's guys call out that they took three more out. "Stay down here," he says to his crew. "Clear it. Alex and I are going up."

I follow him up the stairs. We clear rooms as we go until we finally reach the last one. Ryan nods, and I bust down the door.

We're immediately met with a hail of gunfire. We both take cover behind the wall. After a few seconds, the shooting stops. I meet Ryan's eyes. He nods again. Staying low, I slide into the room shooting to give him cover. Ryan slips in behind me and shoots one of the guys.

"We're missing one," I say. I stand as Ryan and I make our way through the room. Finding no one, we turn to leave when all of the sudden, I'm speared out of nowhere. I fall to the ground with hands around my neck. "Fuck!"

Still holding my gun, I shoot my attacker in the stomach. He slumps on top of me and Ryan shoves him off.

"Fuck me, I hate this fucking job," I growl.

"You good?"

"Just help me up."

He reaches down a hand and pulls me to my feet. I look over and see the guy still moving, so I shoot him in the head.

"That's seven," I say. "Can we get the ever living fuck out of here now? I need a fucking shower."

Ryan laughs and pats me on the shoulder. I'm covered in blood. "Thanks, Alex. I'm glad I can count on you."

"Anytime, Ry. I'll get a cleanup crew to deal with this."

"One less thing for me. I can get my guys back to the hospital."

I shoot a quick text to Gavin to get a crew in here to clean up. "I have to get back to Jess. I didn't give her any explanation, and I don't want her there on her own. She needs rest after the bullshit with her roommate. I know for a damn fact that girl isn't resting right now."

"Well, let's get you a shower and that blood cleaned off you."

XXX

I jump out of the shower, dry off, and quickly get dressed. Ryan is waiting for me in the bedroom of his penthouse.

"Thanks for the shower."

"No problem. You tell Jessa the truth yet?"

"Not fucking happening. Let it go."

He holds up his hands and smirks at me. I glare as my phone starts ringing. I check the caller ID and smile at Jessa's name as I answer.

"Miss me?" I ask.

"Alex! Help!" Jessa screams.

"Jessa?" My heart stops beating. Ryan looks at me quizzically. "Jessa, honey. Talk to me!"

She screams again. "Alex! Alex, help!"

"Jess, where are you?" I'm already running out the door. Ryan is on my heels. Jessa screams again. Thank God his penthouse isn't far from campus.

"Shut up, bitch!" a male voice yells.

"Grant? Is that Grant? What the fuck? Jessa, where are you, baby?"

"Help!" she screams again.

I jump in the passenger seat of my car. Ryan takes off. "I'm coming, baby. Where are you? Tell me where you are!"

"Oh my God! Grant! What are you doing?" a female voice yells. It has to be Marissa.

"Mind your own fucking business!" Grant yells back.

I hear the tell-tale sound of a slap and another scream. A door slams and Jessa's screams become muffled. It had to have been dropped outside her bedroom door. Which means she has to be in her dorm room.

"Marissa! Pick up the fucking phone! Marissa!" I'm yelling into the phone as I look at Ryan. I'm completely panicked. He expertly flies through the L.A. traffic.

"H-hello?"

"Marissa?" My voice is hardly recognizable to myself. I fight to steady my breathing. My heart rate is out of fucking control.

"Y-yes? Yes," she whispers.

"Marissa, it's Alex. Jessa's boyfriend. Tell me what's going on."

Marissa starts crying. "He has her. I'm so sorry, Alex. I'm so, so sorry."

"Marissa, stop it. Stay strong for me. Where are you?"

"Our dorm. He t-took her to her r-room."

"Okay. I'm coming, Marissa." I can hear Jessa's screams becoming louder. The air completely rushes out of my lungs. I look at Ryan. "Go fucking faster."

"Tell me where I'm going."

"Her dorm." Ryan pulls onto the UCLA campus moments later and speeds towards the dorms. "On the left," I tell him. "Marissa? Talk to me, honey."

Marissa screams. "Stop!"

"Bitch!" Grant yells. I hear crashing, like someone is being thrown against something.

"Marissa!" Jessa screams. I hear more crashing and Jessa screams again.

"I called Gavin and Damon. They should be right behind us," Ryan says as he whips into a parking spot. We jump out of the car.

"Marissa?" I yell into the phone. "Jess? Talk to me!" Ryan and I run to her building. We sprint into the building and pound up the stairs. I glance behind me and see Damon and Gavin have caught up.

"Stop fighting me!" Grant yells. "Stop!"

Jessa screams again and there's more crashing and crying. "Let go! Alex! Please! Help me!" Jessa cries.

"He's not going to save you this time, you fucking whore!" Grant yells at her.

"I'm coming, baby!" I yell into the phone, hoping like fuck she hears me. That they both hear me, so he backs the fuck off. She screams again.

"What the fuck, boss?" Damon asks.

Her scream is loud enough that we all hear it in the hall. People are starting to come outside of their rooms, curious as to what's going on. We reach the door to her dorm. I'm fucking pissed that it's locked.

"Bust it down," I growl. I stand back and with Gavin, kick the door in. We've gained an even larger audience. More students are coming out of their rooms, but I don't care. She needs me.

"Where is she?" Gavin asks.

"Her room. In the back," I answer.

We all make our way to the back of the dorm room and see Grant holding Jessa facedown on the ground. He's trying to remove her bra. Her shirt is lying next to her, tattered and torn. Rage turns my blood to ice. I reach down and grab a fistful of his hair and rip him off her.

"Please help me," she cries.

I haul Grant against my chest, one arm tight against his neck. He gags. No air is getting to his lungs. I don't give a single fuck. I tighten my grip against his windpipe, tugging his hair until I know it's painful. I'm sure he'd scream, but he needs to be able to breathe to do that. He's never fucking breathing again.

"Deal with her. We got him," Ryan commands. Ryan tries to pull Grant from my grip, but I don't let go. "I got it. Take care of her."

Ryan's voice is the calm to my rage. I'm radiating anger, but I finally listen to him and release Grant. Ryan shoves him out of the room into Damon and Gavin's arms.

"He's done," I growl to Gavin. I'm doing everything I can to control myself. I don't need to tell Gavin what I mean when I say those words. He knows. And if he didn't, he'd get it by the fire filling my eyes.

"Yes, sir," Gavin says with a dark smirk.

I kneel down next to Jessa. She's scratched up. Her lip is cut. I can see he hit her. Marissa is curled up in the corner of the room near the door crying.

"I'm so sorry... So, so sorry...," Marissa sobs.

"Are you hurt, Marissa?" I ask. I wrap Jessa in my arms. She's starting to hyperventilate. I hold her as tightly as I can in my lap.

"I'm sorry," Marissa whispers.

I watch Marissa as I hug Jessa tightly. I kiss her neck and whisper to her. "It's okay, baby. I'm here. I'm right here. You don't have to worry about him again. You're safe."

"I'm so sorry," Marissa whispers. There's a crash in the common room and Marissa screams. Jessa jumps.

"It's okay, baby. Shh.... You're safe," I whisper in Jessa's ear. Marissa covers her ears, like she's trying to block out her own screams. She's in shock. I need to deal with that right fucking now. "Marissa, listen to me. Look at me. I need your help." She looks at me, still screaming. "I need you to go get Gavin for me. He's out by the door guarding it."

She nearly chokes as she stops screaming. She starts gasping. "No!" she cries as her eyes widen. "No! Please don't make me."

"Marissa! Stop!" I yell. She jumps but focuses on me. "If I let Jessa go, she's going to hyperventilate to death. You have to get Gavin. Please, Marissa. I promise you'll be safe. I won't let anything happen to you. Please. Please trust me and help me." The distraction will help her, too, but I don't tell her that.

She nods and shakily gets to her feet. She swipes at her eyes, even though the tears still fall from them. She stays close to the wall like it's her only protection and walks slowly out of the room. As long as she's focusing on anything other than her own rising panic, she'll get through this.

"Alex," Jessa whispers. "I... c-can't... b-breathe."

"I know, baby. I know. Just focus. Focus on me. I need you to feel me breathing and breathe with me."

I don't need to tell anyone in my crew where to be. What to do. They know what needs to happen without me having to give the command, so I know Gavin is guarding the dorm while Damon and Ryan deal with Grant.

I need Grant's phone. Mine is broken. I stepped on it after I dropped it while I was ripping Grant off Jessa. Jessa's is shattered at my feet. I'm pretty sure Ryan or I stepped on it. Marissa's looks to be in pieces as well. Only hers has blood on it. Judging from the blood that had been gushing from Grant's temple, I would bet my fortune that she hit him with it. Fucking hard.

Jessa's breathing begins to regulate as I continue kissing her neck and whispering to her. "That's it, peanut. Good girl. Keep breathing, honey." I keep my own breathing steady for her. Gavin comes in with his arm wrapped around a terrified and shaking Marissa. "Phones," I say to him. "For all three of us."

"On it," he says. We'll all have new phones by the end of the day.

"Get Doctor Freeman here," I continue. "I want both girls checked."

"Already called him," he responds.

"Good. Go wait for him," I say as I run my hand through Jessa's hair. He tries to let Marissa go, but she clings to him and cries into his arm.

"Please! Please, don't go," Marissa pleads. Gavin looks at me completely unsure what to do. It's not often he's unsure of his next actions. Gavin, like me, is always very sure of himself.

"Go," I say. "Leave her with me. Close the door behind you."

He nods and pries Marissa off him. He looks her straight in the eyes. "You're safe with him. Okay? I'll be right outside. No one is getting in here." She cries as she nods. He gently pushes her towards me. She hesitantly sits next to me when I hold an arm out.

"You're safe," I say. "Both of you. I promise."

I hold Jessa in my lap and Marissa close to my side. After a long while, they both are calm and breathing.

"I was just going for a walk," Jessa says quietly. She talks into my chest. "He grabbed me. He had a knife. I didn't scream until he dragged me in here because he dropped the knife. I tried to call you and run, but he grabbed me."

There's a knock on the door and both Jessa and Marissa cling to me. "It's okay," I say. "I promise. It's just the doctor."

Gavin opens the door and lets Doctor Freeman in. He closes the door behind them and stands outside, guarding us. No one is getting in here.

"Mr. Lang," Doctor Freeman begins. "What do we have here?"

I shoot the doctor a look of mild surprise, and he winks. Good. He's been briefed about my alias. "We had an incident," I begin. "Jessa's stalker and Marissa's now ex-boyfriend attacked Jessa. I don't really know what happened exactly, but it sounded like Marissa tried to help, and he shoved her into the dresser. They both need to be looked at."

"Understood," Doctor Freeman says.

I kiss Jessa on the head. "Honey, let Doc look at you. Please."

She shivers but releases her grip on my shirt. Doctor Freeman helps her onto the bed and starts his exam. Marissa refuses to let me go.

"Tell me what happened, Marissa."

She grips me harder. "I was in my room. I heard the door slam. I thought Grant was back with coffee. And then I heard screaming. I ran out of my room and saw Jessa. Grant… He had her hair. He slapped her. She started screaming for you. Her phone was in her hand. I was confused. I didn't realize she'd called you. I almost thought you were here or behind them." Marissa sniffles and wipes her tears.

"It's okay, honey. What happened next?"

"I… I asked what he was doing. He shoved me away. I tried to get Jessa away from him, but he shoved me away again and slapped me. I hit the wall really hard and fell. He slammed her door. She was crying and… screaming. And I heard you yelling for me. She dropped her phone when he shoved her into her room. I heard… her… fall against something or get shoved. I opened the door and hit him with my phone in the head." She sobs a few times before continuing. I hug her tighter. "He shoved me and slapped me so hard that he knocked me out for a few minutes. When I came to again he… had her on the floor, Alex. He was going to…." She breaks down again. "It's my fault! I'm so stupid. I knew he liked her, and I

39

knew he wanted her. I knew he was just trying to get to her through me, and I let him!"

"Marissa, stop it. You can't blame yourself for what he did."

"I can't stay here alone. What if he comes back?" she asks.

"He won't. He's been dealt with," I say.

"You don't know he won't come back," she cries. "What if he tries to kill us?"

I can't tell her he won't be bothering either of them anymore because he's dead. My crew and Ryan will make it look like he ran away or something. I sigh and look up at Gavin as I rub her shoulder.

"I'll stay a few days. Okay? Just until you feel safe and trust me when I say he won't be coming back," I say. Jessa moves over on the bed, and the doctor helps Marissa up. I stand with her and move next to Jessa. She leans her head against my stomach. I put an arm around her.

"I'm so sorry. I just wanted to go for a walk," Jessa whispers.

"I know, peanut. You don't have to worry about him anymore. He won't bother you again." She nods against my abs. A few minutes later, the doctor finishes with Marissa.

"Both girls are okay," Doctor Freeman says. "A little banged up. Marissa here has a concussion. Keep a close eye on her. Any severe dizziness, sudden painful headache, or blindness, call me right away and meet me at Cedar. Nausea is expected, but again. If it's severe, bring her in."

"Thanks, Doc," I say.

"Anytime. Keep Marissa away from bright lights for the next few days. Laptops and phone screens will make her sick. Reading a lot. She'll need to be out of classes for at least a week. Jessa is good. She'll have a few bruises. I'd suggest she not try classes for a week either. I'll check in tomorrow." He leaves with a reassuring smile. Gavin looks at me.

"Go to my place. Grab enough clothes for a few days for me. Necessities," I command.

"It's an all girl's dorm," Gavin says. "We can visit, but we can't stay here."

Fuck. I hadn't thought of that. "Then go help Marissa get some things together. We'll go to my place for a few days."

"You've only got one bedroom," Gavin says.

"And two sitting rooms. We'll figure it out. Move," I say, not in the mood to argue with someone I consider my brother. Family.

I help Jessa get everything she needs to stay with me as Gavin obeys my command. I know neither of them have anything to worry about, but I'm not leaving Jessa alone. Call me a bleeding heart, but Marissa being so scared is something I can't leave alone either. No matter how much of a bitch she has been to Jessa.

I had a feeling when I left this morning that I shouldn't have. Lesson learned. I'm never not trusting my instincts again.

Chapter Six

✕ Jessa ✕

(Two Months Later)

It's been nearly two months since Grant attacked me and Marissa, and I'm completely terrified to walk anywhere on my own. I'm so afraid that Grant is going to come out from his hiding place and finish the job he started. There's no doubt in my mind what his true intentions were.

Marissa and I have become incredibly close. It happened very quickly. She stopped partying all together and started really focusing on school. I'm so glad that we gave each other the chance to redeem ourselves in each other's eyes. We've become each other's fiercest protectors.

I'm pretty sure Alex is getting fed up with me, though. He seems incredibly irritable. He disappears on me for hours at a time. He has a constant headache when I'm around. He finds reasons why I can't stay the night or weekends with him, even though he had wanted me to move in with him. He seems so tired in classes that he barely pays attention. I'm struggling in statistics, and I know I've been leaning on him a lot for help. He gets really frustrated with me when I don't understand.

I sigh and stare hard at my statistics book while I chew on the end of my pencil. I have ten problems to get through tonight. I'm trying to do it on my own.

"Okay, Jess. Focus. I know you can do this. A card is drawn randomly from a deck of ordinary playing cards. You win a hundred dollars if the card is a spade or an ace. What is the probability that you will win the game?" I look through my notes. I can do this. I start mumbling to myself. "What do I know? I know there are fifty-two cards. I know a suit is thirteen cards. I know there are four aces. I know one of those aces is a spade. Good. You got this, Jessa."

My phone vibrates. I see a text from Alex. My heart skips a beat just like it always does when I see his name, but I debate whether I should look at it. After a brief war with myself, I give in.

Alex: You coming over? Don't you need stat help?

I glare at the phone. Not even a hi? How was your day, peanut?

Jessa: No. I'll do it on my own. You've been busy, and you're probably sick of helping me.

Alex: If I was sick of helping you, I wouldn't have asked if you were coming over.

I huff and go back to my problem, intent on doing it on my own.

"Okay. So, I have a chance at getting eighteen cards. No. Wait. The ace. I can't count that twice. Can I count that twice?" I look through my notes trying to find anything to help me, but I find nothing. I look up at a knock on my door.

"Jess?" Marissa calls softly.

I sigh. "Yeah?" I answer. Marissa opens the door looking like she's about to cry. "What happened? Are you okay?"

She shakes her head and sits on my bed. "It's Gavin…"

"Gavin?" I furrow my brows. Ever since Grant attacked, the two have gone on several dates.

She nods and sniffles, then hands me her phone. Gavin's face fills the screen. Only he isn't alone. His arms are wrapped around another woman, and she's kissing him. With her tongue. Gavin's caption leaves no room for doubt.

"Me and sexy new girl," Marissa says with a sniffle as if she's read it over and over. She starts sobbing as my phone vibrates.

I sit up and hug her as I look at my phone. Another text.

Alex: Fine. I'm staying out with the guys. See you in class.

"You weren't even home?" I whisper, glaring at my phone.

Marissa looks at me. "What?"

"Nothing. Just Alex. He's not even home, but he just invited me to his house."

Marissa wipes her eyes. "Guys are stupid."

"Yeah," I agree. And right now, I kind of do. "So, what happened with Gavin? I thought you were close with him now."

She shrugs sadly. "We… had a fight. He's just been gone so much. And he's so secretive about it all!"

I bite my lip but say nothing because Alex has been the same way. He disappears a lot and never explains why. I know Gavin is his best friend. They have a lot of the same classes. I know whatever is going on with Alex also involves Gavin. I'm sure their friend Damon is with them a lot, too. They seem inseparable.

"His dad is in investment banking or something. He owns his own firm. It's a super good job. Gavin doesn't want to take over for his father. I asked him why. I told him that we could get our own place together. He'd make good money. He's getting a business degree."

I wince. "Maybe that wasn't the best thing to say," I say quietly.

"Yeah… I know that now…," she says sadly. She looks at my open book and grimaces. "That doesn't look fun."

I chuckle. "It really isn't. I don't understand anything. I can't grasp it at all."

"Finals are coming up."

"Yeah. I'm going to fail it. Alex helps me with my homework, but the tests? I'm barely getting by. If I fail the final, I'll fail the class." I chew on my lip.

Marissa hugs me. "I think you know enough to get by."

I sigh, thinking about the easy problem in front of me. I can't understand them. "I really don't think so. But thanks for trying to cheer me up."

She hugs me again. "Thanks for distracting me."

I shut my book when she pulls away. "You're going to watch a movie with me. Because I give up on all of that." I frown at my mess of homework.

Marissa jumps off the bed. "I'll get the junk food!"

44

I smile as she rushes out to our small kitchen. I take another look at my notes, then put it all away. I'm surprisingly okay with the fact that I will have to take the stupid class again. It's unfortunate, but maybe next time I can get a tutor or something.

I shake my head. No statistics tonight. No Alex. No Gavin. No Grant and thinking of where he disappeared to. Just me, Marissa, and Dwayne "The Rock" Johnson. A lot of him.

✗✗✗

Alex: Woke up late. Be a few minutes.

I sigh at the text. It's the next morning and I'm waiting for Alex in the coffee shop in my dorm. He had taken to walking to every class with me, even the ones we didn't have together. I really love that he cares enough about me to understand my fear of walking to my classes alone, but that wasn't everything. What I really love is the time with him. Precious time that seemed to be few and far between recently. I sigh again as I type out my reply.

Jessa: I'll just meet you there.

I gather my stuff and grab my coffee. I don't want to walk by myself, but something is going on with him, and I am tired of him being so secretive.

Alex: Don't be ridiculous. I'll be there. Just a few minutes late.

I keep my phone in my hand, nervous at the walk on my own. Every shadow, every person walking by me is suspect. My heart is beating erratically, but I force my feet to keep moving. I can do this. I'm strong. Grant won't be me. Not like that. I've worked so hard to get here.

Jessa: Just forget it. I'll meet you there. I'm being stupid making you walk with me anyway.

I hurry along the sidewalk. When I get to the building my class is in, I nearly run to the room. It's only when I find my seat that I relax.

I take a few calming breaths, then take out the statistics homework I haven't finished. I need the distraction. I'm having a difficult time catching my breath. Not have an anxiety attack. Not showing my insanity to the world. I try so hard to hide it.

After a few minutes, my heart rate has slowed some, but I've gotten nowhere with the homework. Alex chooses that moment to walk into the classroom. He glares at me as he takes his seat next to me. We're the only two people in the room at this hour.

"Did it ever occur to you that maybe I like walking with you to your classes? That maybe I enjoy the time with my girlfriend?" He starts talking out his stuff for class, and I'm stunned into silence. He looks at me. "Did you finish your statistics homework?" he asks. The edge that had been in his voice is still there. I bite my lip and look down at my book as I shake my head. Alex follows my gaze.

"I tried," I say quietly. "I'm still trying. I feel so stupid because I don't get this."

He looks at my notes. "You're on the right track." His voice is far more soothing than it was. "Set it up as fractions. You have fifty-two cards. That's your bottom number. And then everything else you figured out. Those are your top numbers. Make sense so far?"

I take a breath and try to forget about the morning. My anger towards him. His shortness with me. "So…, thirteen over fifty-two for the spades. Four over fifty-two for the aces. And one over fifty-two for the ace of spades."

"Good girl. One step at a time. Now what do you do?"

"Um…" I sniffle and try really hard to focus. "Add everything?"

"Close. What about that one ace?"

"Well… Aren't we already counting it?"

"We are."

"So… we shouldn't count it twice." I start to erase it from my notebook, but Alex grabs my hand.

"You can't pretend the ace doesn't exist, baby. What do we do with something that we know exists, but that we don't need?"

"Um… we… subtract it off?"

"That's my girl," he says proudly.

I smile at the praise. "So, I would add the thirteen and the four. And I would subtract one."

"Good girl."

"And I come up with sixteen over fifty-two. That's my answer?"

"Almost. What do we do to fractions? We always have to make sure they're what?"

"Make it the smallest it can be?"

"Yep."

"So, the odds of winning the game would be four over thirteen."

"You have a four in thirteen chance of winning."

I smile as I circle my answer. Alex digs in his backpack and hands me his notebook. "What's this?" I ask. "What are you doing?"

"You're on question one of ten, Jess. You don't have time to finish. Just copy mine."

I give him his notebook back and shake my head. "I can't do that. I'm the one who didn't do it. I'll face the consequences."

He pushes it back to me. "You didn't finish because I haven't been there to help you. Just copy it. We'll go over it together later." I look down at it, and Alex sighs. He takes my hand in his. "Honey, look at me."

I do as I'm told. Alex rubs his thumb back and forth across my knuckles. I don't want to ask what I'm about to because it hurts me. Alex is the first man I've ever been with. He's my first boyfriend. I lost my virginity to him. Even after four months, I can see him in my future.

"Did I do something to upset you and make you distant?" I ask. "I know I'm being annoying with not being able to walk anywhere on my own and function like a normal adult. I'm just sca -"

"Honey. Stop. Stop, baby. I'm not annoyed at you. I'm sorry I've been acting like an asshole. There's been a lot of... family drama. I've been dealing with a lot of shit. I'm sorry, baby. I am."

I smile, relieved I didn't do anything wrong. "Is it wrong I'm glad? I thought you were sick of me and my neediness shit."

He reaches up and palms my cheek as he leans down to kiss me. "Not a chance in hell, peanut. And I don't think you're needy either." His lips meet mine in another sweet kiss as other people start filing into the classroom. He pulls away and kisses my forehead. "It's just a presentation today. Copy that, and I promise we'll go over it later."

"I don't know what the point is. If I fail the final, I'll fail the class. And I'm going to fail the final. I try so hard, but I don't understand." I look down hopelessly at Alex's notebook.

"I won't let you fail, Jess. I'll study with you all fucking day and night until you understand if that's what it takes. Now, do what I told you to."

I sigh as I start copying. "This feels so wrong." I keep my voice low so only he can hear me. He drapes his arm over the back of my chair and plays with the ends of my hair.

"I said I would help you through, and I meant it."

I smile and shake my head as he continues playing with and tugging at my hair. His fingers lightly graze my neck. He sends shivers throughout my body, but I don't think he has any idea. Any idea at all.

✕✕✕

Later that night, at Alex's place, I let out an exasperated growl. Alex laughs as my phone goes off. I look at the caller ID and sigh.

"It's my mom," I say. "I've been ignoring her for a week."

"Take the call. It'll give you a break from this." He gestures to the statistics problems in front of us as I answer the phone.

"Hi, mom."

"Hi, sweetheart. I haven't heard from you in days," she says. I lean back against the couch and pull Alex by his shirt back to me. He chuckles and puts his arm around me. I love that he understands my silent plea as he pulls me close.

"Finals are coming up. I'm doing everything I can to not fail statistics."

"You've never failed a class in your life. I'm not worried. When will you be home?"

"Oh... um... It looks like probably Wednesday next week." I feel Alex tense next to me.

"Well, we can't wait. We miss you like crazy."

I smile. "I love you, too, mom." After a few more minutes of chatting, I hang up and take a deep breath. I look up at him and smile as I kiss his chin before I climb into his lap, straddling him as I face him. I put my arms around his neck as his find their way around my waist.

"What are you doing?" he asks.

"I've been thinking about something for a while now."

"Yeah? What's that?"

I push down on him and wiggle. He groans and I feel him respond underneath me. I smile, trying not to hesitate. "Well, my parents are expecting me home for Christmas. I didn't go home for Thanksgiving because of everything with Grant and being so scared. I didn't want my parents to know what happened or see how jumpy I was." I smile softly as I look down at his chest. "Maybe you could come home with me?"

I look up at him through my lashes. He reaches up to tuck some of my long hair behind my ear. He snakes his hand to the back of my head and guides me to his lips. He kisses my nose and tugs my hair so my lips meet his. His kiss is sweet and warm and sets me on fire. Just like it always does.

"You want me to meet your parents?"

I drop my gaze again and bite my lip. "Is that not something you want? Is it too soon? I don't know how this all works… I've only ever been with you."

"I don't mind meeting your parents. But I can't do Christmas Day. It's… a very big day in my family. Dinner party and showing off."

"Oh." I look down, slightly disappointed.

"Not to say I can't swing by every other day if you want me to. You don't live that far away from here. It would be like a forty minute drive for me."

"You mean…?" I look up at him hopefully.

He grins. "I'd love to meet your parents."

I smile brightly and plunge ahead, getting a little braver. "Maybe you could stay a night or two…" I trace his shoulder and focus on my finger.

He chuckles and drops his hands to my ass. "Well, where would I sleep?"

His tone is teasing as he pushes me down gently. I feel his length between my legs. I close my eyes, focusing on how hard he is; how amazing that makes me feel. Always makes me feel.

"Maybe… you could sleep in my room?" He grins and moves himself a little against me, letting me feel him even more. "God…"

"You honestly think your parents would let me sleep with their precious little girl?" He moves his hips against me.

I grip his shoulders and close my eyes, losing myself in the feel of him like I always do. My eyes flutter closed. "Yes…" I press harder against him, letting his dick relieve some of the pressure he's built between my legs. My eyes snap open quickly when he flexes his cock. I clear my throat. "Yeah. They will. They trust me."

"You, maybe. I doubt they'd trust me." He leans forward and kisses me. "Especially since all I can think about right now is making you scream my name."

He stands with me still wrapped around him, and I squeal. He grins again as he kisses me and walks to his bedroom. He kicks the door closed and drops me on his bed, climbing in next to me. Without missing a single beat, he kisses down my jawline and neck as he wraps me tightly in his arms. His tongue flicks across the sensitive flesh. He kisses it again as he gently sucks it.

"Mmm…," I moan. I can't form words. The feel of his lips, his breath against my skin… It's all so intoxicating. My thoughts are filled with only him and his actions.

He kisses my cheek and lips, sliding his tongue inside my mouth and meeting mine in the most intimate of dances. I wrap my legs around his waist. He runs his hand down my side to my ass. He lifts my hips so I can feel his incredibly hard length against my center once more. I moan into his mouth as I tighten my legs around him.

"Christ, Jessa," he murmurs against my lips with a smile. "I lose complete control with you."

I can't help the burst of laughter that escapes my lips. "That's such a lie. Even when you think you've lost control, you haven't." Alex is the most in control person I've met in my whole life.

His sexy grin grows wider. Before I know what's happening, clothes are flying. Moans are getting louder. The touches get more teasing; erotic. The goosebumps freckling my skin become more prevalent. The kisses are far more heated.

I'm on fire for him. I feel like a literal inferno is raging underneath my skin. It's me who loses control. I crave him. All of him. I'll take whatever he gives me as long as I have him. Alex and I are fireworks. A fiery explosion of color.

Alex positions himself between my legs and quickly rolls on a condom. I'm always amazed at how quick he is at it. Efficient. His mouth crashes down on my nipple at the same time his incredible sized cock slams into me. I arch into him. My nails dig into his shoulders, and my mouth forms a perfect 'O' as my eyes flutter closed. No sound comes out because I can only focus on what's happening with my body.

"Jessa, fuck," Alex groans against my nipple as he kneads the other one and tugs it. He starts thrusting. "So tight for me."

I pant against his shoulder as I move with him. I try to get him to go faster. I spread my legs wider, so he'll sink deeper, but he grips my hip with his other hand and controls my pace. I tighten my legs around him and clench, but Alex isn't having it. He'll give me everything I desire and more, but he'll do it at his pace. Ironically, he seems to know what pace I need, even when I don't.

Except for this time.

"Alex, I need you." I try to get him to thrust faster.

He grins against my chest. "You have me." He kisses across my breasts, still slowly thrusting.

"Alex," I nearly whine. "You know what I mean. More... Faster. Harder. Anything."

He nips the nipple he's just reached as his hand drops to the one his mouth just left. I gasp as he rolls one nipple between his thumb and forefinger; the other with his tongue. I shiver and tremble underneath him, silently begging him to let go and give me all I want from him.

He nips my nipple and looks up at me as he shifts. He kisses up to my neck, never stopping the torturing, slow, deep thrusts. "I know what you want, baby. But it's far from what you need." His lips crash to mine as he wraps his arms around me.

He thrusts harder and deeper but doesn't give me the fast. Little by little, I feel all of the tension I've built up over the past weeks fading with each and every thrust. I get tighter and tighter around him. More and more breathless. He kisses and licks his way down to my neck. He hums, and I savor each sensation running through my body.

Alex pounds hard into my pussy as he breathes against my neck, moaning and holding me as tightly as I am him. But the pace never changes. He shifts his hips from side to side, hitting that perfect spot every single time, but he continues the slow ministrations. Both of our breathing becomes more erratic, but the thrusts are steady. I meet each one.

"Mmm... Alex...," I moan into his shoulder as he buries himself inside me balls deep with each thrust.

My grip on him becomes tighter as my pussy clenches for him, squeezing his dick. Alex kisses up my jaw to my lips. He lets out quiet groans to my moans and almost silent grunts to my panting. Our eyes meet while his hand travels down my body and between us. Without looking away or stopping the delectable movement inside me, he sets his thumb against my clit. He rubs in smooth circles. A jolt of electricity seems to travel through my clit all throughout my body until I'm jerking into him. My pussy uncontrollably clenches and pulses around him.

"Jessa, fuck, baby," Alex rumbles against my lips. His blue eyes are dark and full of need. He takes my breath away.

Inside me, his dick thickens, making me tighten even more. He continues thrusting slow and deep, but he's rubbing my clit fast and furiously with the perfect amount of pressure. The contrast in speed is doing unexplainable things to me. Once again, I thought I needed one thing, and Alex knew far better. As he takes me to the edge only he knows how to, I feel myself falling.

"Oh my God, Alex," I whisper.

"Come, baby. Come for me," he commands against my lips right before he takes them with his.

"Mmm!" I moan into the kiss and give him everything he wants. I tighten so hard around him and hold him closer to me with my legs. I come with a scream into his mouth as my body slams into his.

"Mmm…," Alex grunts as he releases at the same time I do. I can't feel his come, but I can feel the warmth through the thin cover sheathing his cock. He pulls away from the kiss slowly with a cocky grin I've come to love so much.

I giggle and blush. "God, Alex."

He leans down and kisses my neck. "Fuck, peanut," he rumbles low, sending vibrations through me that make me moan. "How does it always get better and better with you, baby?"

I blush even more as I untangle my legs from around his waist. He slowly pulls out, gripping his dick and the base of the condom. Neither of us are ready for accidental pregnancy. While there is always a risk, even though I'm on the pill and he always uses condoms, we both are very careful about it.

I watch as Alex's naked body makes its way off the bed and out of the bedroom to dispose of the condom. He comes back moments later with a warm cloth. As he always does, he helps me to clean up. He's so gentle and tender that I can't help but fall more and more in love with him.

It might be too soon for those words. I won't utter them. At least I'll try not to, but I feel it. I've felt it for a long time. Alex captivated me from the very second he entered my world. I didn't even need to see him to know there was something about him I want. Something I crave. Something I can't live without. It's like he's the completion of the complication that is me. The calm to my storm. The sane to my crazy.

I smile as he wraps me tightly in his arms. One of my favorite things to do after we ravish each other is to cuddle. I sink further and further into Alex's embrace until I'm so comfortable and content that nothing else in the world matters. Nothing can penetrate my bubble. Not with Alex by my side.

Chapter Seven

⚔ Alex ⚔

Seeing a sleepy Jessa walk into my kitchen wearing my t-shirt and a sexy as fuck pair of pink panties may very well be my undoing. I pause with my orange juice halfway to my lips as she sits down at one of the barstools and slides my phone across the counter to me.

"Your phone is mean," she says.

I raise an eyebrow and chuckle. "Mean?"

"It won't shut up."

I put my orange juice on the counter and grab my phone just as it starts ringing again. I sigh as I look at the caller ID.

My brother.

I kiss Jessa on the head and walk back to my room, not missing her swiping my orange juice. I laugh. When I get to my room, I sit on the bed and answer the phone.

"What, Josh?"

"About fucking time. Fuck, man. I've been calling you for twenty minutes."

I put my head in my hand. This can't be good. Josh is my twin brother. He knows better than to keep calling unless it's important.

"Okay. So? What? You know after the other night I said I'm done. I have finals."

"I know. I do. But dad has a mission tonight, and he's going to ask for you. Just fair warning."

"I'm not doing it. I'm busy with more important things. He fucking promised me he'd leave me alone until I graduated."

"I tried to tell him I'd take your place. But you know what he said."

"That you aren't good enough. Like he always says."

"You got it."

I sigh heavily, feeling an immediate headache. "Okay. Here's what's going to happen. You're my twin. You're just as good as I am. Go in my place. Pretend you're me."

"What? No. He's our father. He'll know right away I'm not you."

"Make him believe it. You're the one who wants to take over. Not me. When it's done and over and he congratulates me like he always does, I'll flat out tell him it was you."

"You can't do that. You know what he'll fucking do."

"What? Hit us? We aren't fucking kids anymore, Josh. You want the boss position, you have to do what needs to be done to take it. He thinks you aren't up to my standards, J. So. We make him see that you are."

"He's been taking you on missions since you were twelve. He only lets me go when he wants to fucking say I messed something up. No fucking way I'll pass as you."

"Josh, you and I train together. I know what you're capable of. I've seen it. You've been on missions. You can do this. Please do this for me. It's finals, and I promised Jessa that I'd help her study for the statistics final. I've been letting her down for the past month. Maybe longer because of this bullshit. Help me out here."

He sighs. He's the only one in my family who knows anything about Jessa. We tell each other everything. And since Jessa has become an incredibly important part of my life, I couldn't keep that from my twin. Thank God I know I can trust him not to say anything to our parents about her.

"Fine. I'll do it. But you owe me for this."

"It'll go a hell of a long way in getting you in boss position, Josh. Convincing him that you're the one who should take over."

"You're right. I know. But it doesn't make this shit easier."

"No different than training. How many times have you bested me? You're good. You may not have ever led a mission, but you're ready for this, J. Trust me."

"So what do we do? You act like you'll be there?"

"Dad will call. I'll tell him I'll meet him there. I'll text you the location. Get your gear ready. Take the car I take."

"The black Camaro with tinted windows."

"Yep. Put your gear in the trunk. That's where I keep mine. Don't forget a second Glock. You know I always have one in a shoulder holster and one strapped to my thigh."

"And then I show up."

"You show up pretending to be me. Wear all black, just like we both would. Make sure you have a vest with you. Don't show up with it on like you would. Do not take any other earpiece other than number one. That's mine. Anyone else takes it, doesn't matter who it is, make them give it to you. If you don't, it's a dead giveaway."

He chuckles because he knows how possessive I am with my gear. I've gone toe to toe with my father over it. "Got it."

"You'll lead Team Two, just like I would. He'll have you go in the back entrance."

"And I go in first. Just like you would."

"You got this."

"I do. I can do this. I want to lead. Now's my chance to prove myself."

"Fucking right." I hear a beep and look at my phone. "Dad's calling. I'll text you."

"Okay."

Josh hangs up, and I switch over to my dad. This needs to be quick. I miss my girlfriend.

"What?" I growl as irritated as possible.

"Is that anyway to talk to your father?"

"Since I know what you're about to say, I'll say yes. It fucking is."

"Look. Last mission. I have Josh in training until you're done fucking around with college. He's running with me more and more. But he's not ready for this yet. This is big. I need you."

I smile to myself and make a dramatic show of sighing in exasperation. "He's ready. You just won't give him the chance. He's run plenty of missions with me and you. You fucking know it. But fine. What's this last mission? And I fucking mean last. I'm done. You agreed. You want me to even consider taking over, you leave me alone to do this."

"Last mission. Thirteen gang members impeded on our turf. They took over part of my drug trade. I need them out. We're meeting at the Hawthorne Mall and walking the rest of the way."

I shake my head. It doesn't sound fucking big at all. He's just being his typical asshole self. "Time."

"Midnight."

"Fine. I'll be there. Anyone touches my earpiece, I'll shoot them. Please let it be you." I hang up the phone before he has a chance to respond, then text Josh the details... including the bit about shooting our father if he takes my earpiece.

Josh: Shoot our father? Don't fucking tempt me.

Alex: You're telling me. I'll see you tomorrow.

I hate that I'm going to have to leave Jessa for a couple of hours, but it's better than disappearing on her again. I'm done with that shit.

I walk back out to the kitchen and see Jessa has curled up on the couch with her book on her lap. She's mumbling to herself and is deep in concentration.

"You look cute as hell sitting there like that." I sit next to her and she automatically curls up at my side. I could get used to this.

Her.

She smiles and looks at me. "So..., can I ask you something?"

"Anything." I pull her tighter to my side and kiss her head.

"Marissa saw this picture on Gavin's Facebook." She brings the picture up on her phone. I immediately recognize it. It's from the other night at a club we had gone to.

I sigh. "Gavin is an asshole sometimes, sweetheart. He's a good guy. Really. I'd trust him with my life, but he doesn't take bullshit. Marissa started to interject herself into shit that she really shouldn't be. Like Gavin's finances and getting a house with him. They're not exactly exclusive. Neither of them have had any conversations about anything more than having fun. So, when Marissa started talking about things that I haven't even talked to you about, it pissed him off. They broke up. We went out. He got really drunk. I took him home. That girl was just some random girl at the club. I doubt they'll even see each other again. Hell, he probably took the picture down as soon as he saw it when he woke up."

She's quiet for a few moments before she sighs. "She was really upset."

"Which upset you because you girls have gotten really close."

She nods. "I just feel bad. She really likes him. Still."

"Like I said. He's a good guy. He'll treat his woman like a Queen until she pisses him off. And he is a player. He doesn't usually date a girl. He might for a couple weeks, but then he's done. Actually, I thought Marissa was going to last a while. He seems to really like her." I pause with a smile. "Still."

She leans against my shoulder. "I hope I never have to deal with that."

I reach up and capture her chin. I gently guide her face up so she's looking at me. "I'm not like that, Jess. If things aren't working out for us, we'll talk about it as a couple and move forward. Gavin just… isn't used to relationships and how they work. He's never been in one. I don't really know where those two will end up, but we'll have to wait and see. Because I do know that he does really like her. It might just take him a while to actually admit that to himself."

She smiles softly. "Promise to never hurt me like that?"

"Well, I'm pretty sure she hurt him first, but I do promise not to hurt you like that, baby." I push out all thoughts about the web of lies I've spun around her to think about another day. Instead, I capture her lips with mine. She opens for me with no hesitation. Only want. Need. The same need for me that I always have for her.

I lift her into my lap. She straddles me like it's the most natural thing in the world. My hands immediately gravitate to her ass. I allow them to run up her back and underneath her t-shirt. She inhales sharply. My hands hit the sides of her perfect, soft, and full tits.

She presses herself down and rubs herself over my hard cock. Unable to take the tease, I reach over to the drawer in my end table next to the couch and tug it open. I've never been so grateful for throwing an extra condom in there just in case. I'm prepared for any situation, sex included.

I tear it open with my teeth as she watches in fascination. She always watches what I do with wonder. It's sexy as hell. I grin and push her panties aside with one hand at the same time I'm pushing my sweats down with the other. I roll the condom over my already hard shaft. Her eyes widen as I sink into her with a low moan.

"Holy fuck, baby." I let my head fall back against the couch as I wrap my arms around her, pulling her close and tight.

Jessa wraps her arms around my shoulders and leans down to kiss me as she starts moving rapidly. I let her take what she needs as I tangle my tongue with hers in our very own made up passionate and fiery dance. I meet her thrust for thrust, moan for moan, and stroke for stroke.

"Alex, yes!" She throws her head back and rides me hard and fast, taking my cock as deeply into her tight pussy as she can, then spreading her legs to take me even deeper.

"Christ," I groan when I'm seated so deeply inside her that my eyes roll back. "Fuck."

I pound into her pussy as hard as she's bouncing on my cock and let my hands slide down to grip her thighs. I slide my hands underneath her panties and grip her ass as I nip her lip and moan again. She's slamming down on me so hard, I'd be afraid she's hurting herself if she weren't moaning in pleasure. Her pussy squeezes my cock and pulses around me.

I look down at where we're connected and damn near come watching her pussy take my dick. Jessa tightens her grip around my shoulders as she kisses my neck. I nip hers and suck lightly before I kiss it.

"Fuck, Jess. You're so tight," I whisper.

"I'm gonna come…," she moans against my neck right before she licks it. She kisses it again.

I grin. "I know. Come for me, beautiful. All over me."

She blushes and hides her face in my neck. She comes with a low moan and breathes my name. She'll never admit it, but she loves when I talk dirty to her. She also loves the hard, quick sex sometimes. Just enough to get us both off and relieve the tension.

"Oh, Alex… Yes…" Her thighs tremble as she gives me her release.

"My God, Jess," I rumble against her neck as I come. My dick jerks inside her as I fill the condom. I slow my thrusts and ride us both through.

We haven't been together for that long, but my girl knows just how to right my world and relieve tension.

Holy fuck, I'm falling in love with her.

XXX

The next afternoon, after walking Jessa to her drawing class, I jump out of my car in front of my family's estate. We live in a large house that's been in our family for generations. It's old but well taken care of.

I hate this place.

I hate everything about this house. But that could be because it holds absolutely no happy memories for me. Even memories of my mother hugging me or playing hide and seek with Josh are marred with memories of my father ruining it. He'd always tell mom not to coddle us when he caught her hugging us. When Josh and I were caught playing together, he'd beat us. There was never a time to play. Only time to train.

My dad always blamed Josh for distracting me. Taking me away from training time. Even though he was expected to do as much damn training as me. My job was and is to take over the Lucinio mafia. Not be distracted by such silly fucking things as being a child.

I growl as I slam the car door shut. I'm pissed. I'm seething with anger at even being put into this position. I shouldn't have to be here. I should be studying. I should be waiting for my girl to finish class. We should be deciding what to do for dinner as we work on statistics.

Right as I'm entering the house, Josh meets me at the door and shoves me back outside, closing the door behind him.

"What happened?" I ask. I'm not even surprised at this point. Josh shoving me outside to talk to me before the onslaught is common practice.

"He's doing it again. He's trying to psych me out. Saying how you're so much better than me. And what a perfect mission it was that you led."

This has been our father's m.o. since the two of us were born. He's always saying Josh isn't good enough. He's not as good as me. He's a distraction. I grab Josh's arm, pull him to me, and hug him. I do it because he needs it. He needs to know in this moment that someone is fucking proud of him.

"It was a perfect mission, right?" I ask. I already know the answer. "I wasn't the one there, man. You were."

"He won't care. He'll find something I did wrong as soon as he finds out it was me."

"Josh, I'll be there. I'll be right there with you." I sway a little with him.

He tightens his grip on me. His arms shake a little. "Why does he constantly try and put a wedge between us?"

"Because he's a horrible father. As soon as you take over, you can do whatever the hell you want. He can't stop you."

"He'll never let me take over. Ever."

I push him back, so I can look in his eyes. "Then let him give me control. I'll just abdicate and give you the fucking throne anyway. Either way, the Lucinio mafia belongs to you, J." I smile encouragingly at him. He smiles and nods, visibly taking a few deep breaths to calm down. After a few more moments, he relaxes and collects himself. I smile and grasp his shoulder. "Ready to go in there?" I ask.

"Ready."

"Let's get this over with."

We walk in together, meeting our father in his office. He immediately stands and hugs me, ignoring Josh completely. What a fucking asshole.

"My boy!" our father says.

"Dad." I push him away and sit next to Josh in one of the leather chairs in the office. Josh stares down at his hands.

"Great mission last night. Great mission. Everyone was dealt with and disposed of. We have our territory and our business back."

"Great. But -" I start.

"I can't tell you how proud of you I am," he continues.

"Thanks, but -"

"You're going to make a hell of a leader when the time comes," he says, cutting me off.

"I don't want it. You know I don't," I say.

"Nonsense. The power and money that comes along with the Lucinio name is something anyone would want. And it's yours," dad says.

"No. It's Josh's. You have another fucking son, you know. I don't want to run it. He does."

"We've talked about this over and over. The mafia belongs to you. You're the oldest. You're the one on the important missions."

My level of anger rises with every word out of his mouth. Finally, it explodes. I stand and put both hands on his desk, shoving his laptop and lamp off it.

"Are you not hearing me? I... Don't... Want... It! Josh was born to do this! Why are you completely ignoring what either of us are telling you? Why are you forcing this on me when you know I don't fucking want it."

My dad stands to his full five feet ten inch height and fury flashes across his blue eyes. He has dark brown hair, and he's muscular. Josh and I get our looks and our build from him. For a second, I'm a scared little kid again. And then I remember I'm not a kid. I'm an adult. And I have four inches and a whole lot more muscle than he does to my advantage. I stand to my full height and stare him down.

"Do not back talk to me, boy," he says.

"Or what? You gonna try to hit me? Sorry dad. I'm not fucking ten anymore." His eyes flick to Josh, who is cowering behind me. "You think you can take it out on him because you can't intimidate me anymore? Just like when we were kids. But here's the difference. We aren't. You touch Josh, you deal with me. He might hesitate to pull the trigger because deep down, there's some part of him who wants you to love him and be proud. I won't hesitate because I don't give a fucking shit about you. And you're perfect fucking mission? I wasn't there. That was all Josh."

"What?"

"Yeah, dad. The son you keep saying isn't ready. The one you keep taking on small missions and saying is still in training. He's been going with me on missions since we were fucking twelve. I told you he's ready. I told you he was born for this. I told you he's better in training than I am. That he fucking bests me at every damn turn. But you just can't hear that, can you?"

"Bullshit."

"It was me," Josh says quietly. "Alex was busy. He tried to tell you."

"Next mission, you both will be there." His hard gaze meets mine.

"No. I told you, I'm fucking done," I growl.

"Both of you. No excuses." Dad glares and growls right back.

"I said, no," I say with narrowed eyes.

"You'll be there, Alex," he commands with a slightly upturned smile. My heart suddenly starts beating faster. Whatever he's about to say, he knows he has me. "Or I'll shoot him."

He glares at Josh. My racing heart stops beating as our father walks out of the office without another word. Josh inhales sharply, like he's breathing for the first time in fuck knows how long. I plop down in the chair and rub my temples. My headache has grown exponentially. I can barely see.

"Now what do we do?" Josh asks, his voice shaking. He's scared. I know my brother. He knows as well as I do that our father would do it.

"I'll figure it out, Josh. I've always protected you. I'm not stopping now."

I really have always protected him. Despite being the favorite son, I took the brunt of the beatings. I made him run and hide. I'd do it all over again, too. If it comes down to his life or mine, it'll be mine my father takes. Not his. Never his.

XXX

(One Week Later)

I throw the rest of my gear in my trunk as Josh appears at my side. It's pitch black out, and I just went through another fucking mission that I didn't want to.

"I have no chance of taking over. He won't let me," Josh says.

"You're right, but nothing's changed. I don't want this. He gives me control, I give it to you. End of story."

"It's not that simple. You know that."

I close the trunk and look at him. "Yeah. It really is. I want a life away from this. I don't want Jessa involved in this." I keep my voice low as I watch my father. He turns towards us, and I glare viciously.

"He won't let you abdicate to me. He'll never give this up to me."

"Shh," I hiss. Reading me, Josh stops talking.

Our dad stops near us, and Josh nearly leaps out of his skin when our dad pats him on the back. "You're becoming more and more ready as the days go by. It's possible you'll be able to go on missions on your own soon," dad says.

Josh nods and steps closer to me. "Th-thanks, dad," Josh says.

"Of course we'll need to make sure you're flawless like your brother here before we let that happen. You'll have to train harder. Mistakes aren't an option."

"I understand," Josh says.

"He's flawless already. And he trains enough," I growl as I stick up for Josh.

"He's getting there, Alex," dad says. He walks away, and Josh releases the breath he'd been holding.

"Don't listen to him. You know how good you are and how capable," I say.

"Yeah."

I pull my brother into a hug. After a few moments, I release him, and he smiles. He pats me on the back and heads for the SUV he drove here in. I jump in my Camaro and take off. It's late. Jessa is alone in my bed, and I can't wait to see my girl.

A few minutes later, after I've parked the Camaro and jumped in my own car, I hit the freeway. There isn't a lot of traffic in L.A. at this hour.

Two in the morning. If I'm being honest, I love this time of the morning. No one around. Just me and the salty ocean air as I whip through the streets. I love this place. L.A. is the perfect place to get lost. It's big enough to swallow anyone who doesn't want to be found.

Chapter Eight

 Jessa

(Eight Months Later)

Beginning my second year of college is a lot more exciting than I thought it would be. Even though I'm still taking a lot of generals, I'm not forced to live in the dorms.

Which means I can live with Alex.

"So?" Alex slips his arms around my waist and bends to kiss my neck. "What do you think? Want to lease it with me?"

We're standing in a penthouse suite near campus. It's completely gorgeous. My dream. But it doesn't stop the frown and sigh as I pull away. "I love it, Alex."

Alex folds his arms over his chest and looks at me with furrowed brows. "I didn't mean to move too fast. I thought you'd be up for this since you spent most of your time at my dorm anyway. And during the summer, I was mostly with you at your parent's."

I smile, though a little sadly. "It's not that. I do want to move in with you."

"But?"

I turn away from the window overlooking the city. Alex is standing behind me. "I can't afford this place. My dad said he'd give me the money that he would be paying if I stayed in the dorms, but even with that and what he gives me per month, I can't budget enough to pay half. I can't even come close to half for a single month."

Alex smiles and then gently takes my face between his large hands. He leans down to kiss me. I close my eyes as he runs his fingers through my hair. Kissing Alex is my addiction. Fuck it. *He's* my addiction. He's my drug.

After a few moments, Alex pulls away. I giggle as he playfully licks my lip. "How about I pay the rent?" he asks.

"Alex…, that's not fair."

"You can pay for groceries. And utilities. You really don't have to. I can afford everything, but I know you. You'll feel bad if you aren't contributing in some way. Even though you walking around in my t-shirt and letting me kiss off that cake batter lip gloss you wear is enough for me."

He bends to lick my lip again, and I giggle once more as he sexily and sweetly bites it. "This place is so expensive. Maybe we could find a cheaper apartment."

Alex kisses me and then lets me go as he sighs heavily and looks out the window. "Jess, there's a reason I like this place. More than just because of its proximity to campus. More than just because I knew you'd like it. Hell, more than just the view."

I slip my arms around him from behind and kiss his back as I hug him. He puts his arms over mine and leans into me. "I'm listening."

He takes a deep breath and lets it out as he turns to me. He takes both of my hands in his and kisses them. "It's because it's a secure building. It's one of the first of its kind. You need a key fob to get in. Facial recognition technology. In order to get up here, you need a specific access code and keycard. Palm and retina scan to get inside."

My heart skips a beat. "That… seems like overkill, Alex."

He smiles softly and pushes some hair behind my ear. "I understand why you'd think that." He lets me go and stalks to the kitchen.

I watch him lean on the counter, a haunted expression on his face. I furrow my eyebrows. "Alex? What's wrong?"

"Baby, do you trust me?"

I crease my eyebrows, unsure where he's going with this. "You know I trust you. What kind of question is that?"

"An important one. Because what I'm about to say and ask from you is going to force you to put a great deal of trust in me with very little information for you."

I cross my arms over my chest and watch him. "Okay." He straightens and beckons me to him. I obey, but walk towards him slowly, increasingly more confused as this conversation continues. "Alex, just tell me what's going on. You're not acting like yourself."

As soon as I reach him, he grabs my hips and picks me up, setting me on the counter in front of him. He gently spreads my legs, then steps between them. "You know I love you, right?"

"Yes."

"I want to protect you. Make sure you're safe. You believe that, too, right?"

"Alex, yes. Just tell -" He puts a finger up to my lips, cutting me off. My heart beats faster, but not because of his touch. He's freaking me out.

"Jessa. I love you. My top priority is to make sure you're safe. Apartments that would be in your price range don't offer the amount of security that this building does."

I take a deep breath and let the words I've been thinking since this conversation began tumble out of my mouth. "Alex, you're scaring me."

"I know. I don't mean to, but I can't tell you anything else." He pulls me against him and wraps his arms around my waist as he kisses me. When he pulls away, he looks deeply into my eyes. "I need you to trust me. I know it scares you. I know I'm not giving you a lot to go on. But I've always made sure your safety came first. You know that. I've never given you a reason not to trust me, and you know how much I love you and how important your trust in me is." He kisses me again. He keeps looking deeply into my eyes. There's no deceit. No lies. Just love.

Finally, I sigh and nod. "Okay."

"Okay?"

"Okay. I trust you. I don't like being put into a position where I don't know what's happening, but if you think this is best and this is what puts you at ease, then I'll trust you."

He picks me up. I wrap my legs around his waist and my arms around his shoulders and squeal as he spins me around. "I love you, baby." He sets me down as I kiss him.

"Well, Mr. Lang? Ms. Holloway? What do you think? Did I give you enough time to discuss?"

I look up at Alex and smile before I turn towards the real estate agent. Alex puts his arm around my waist. "We'll take it, Ms. Ridges," Alex says.

"We love it."

She smiles and claps happily. "I knew it! I knew you'd love it!"

She hands Alex some paperwork. He walks to the counter and flips to the end. He signs the paperwork and then adds account information. He flips to a page before that and hands me the pen.

"Seals the deal." He gives me a sexy, killer smile as I take the pen and sign.

"I guess that means we're in this for the long haul." I look up at him as Ms. Ridges takes the paperwork and packs it away. We lock eyes, and I couldn't break away if I tried.

Ms. Ridges clears her throat. "We'll need to go to security to get everything with them dealt with. They'll get you your key fob and access."

"Right." Alex kisses me and takes my hand. This is a huge step for us. I'm not sure what this will bring, but I know I can't wait.

✗✗✗

(Four Months Later)

"I just... want..." Marissa huffs out a sigh. "I just want a chance with him. No one has really compared to him. I just don't feel a connection with anyone." Her eyes fall to her hands.

She looks so miserable that my heart hurts, but I'm beyond confused. I glance at Alex. I can't see his face as he stirs something delicious smelling over the stove. His back muscles are tense and rigid. I can tell he's stirring a little more furiously than he probably needs to.

I clear my throat. "Didn't you just say last week that you hate him? You saw another image of him with a different girl on his Facebook or

68

something? Well, one of like a hundred." I jump when something in the kitchen clangs. I look over at Alex. His back is still to me, but he's gripping the counter in front of the sink.

She shrugs with a sad sigh as she nibbles her lip. "I really just miss him, Jess."

Before I can retort, I hear a knock on our door. Alex glances at me over his shoulder. I meet his gaze with a small shrug. I have no clue who it could be, but I'm not expecting anyone other than Marissa tonight.

I'm not too concerned about it being someone we don't know, though, because part of the security features this building has to offer is a twenty-four hour manned security desk. They have a list we've provided them with people we've approved to be sent right up. They don't need to go through a security check because they're trusted.

Feeling Alex's eyes on my back, though, I stand on my tiptoes and peek through the peephole. I tilt my head when I see Gavin and start to feel super uneasy. Alex didn't mention he was coming by, but with Marissa here, I'm not sure how things are going to play out.

I rub my chest as I open the door slowly. Gavin is grinning on the other side of the door. I'd never tell Marissa, but I have gotten kind of close to Gavin over the past several months. He's really a great guy, as Alex said he is. Not only that, he's like family to Alex. After hearing his side of the entire situation, I can't really blame him for leaving, but I wish they would have talked it out. So much time has gone by. Gavin is bitter. Marissa can't decide if she loves or hates him.

Gavin's smile falls from his lips as he looks at me. "You okay? What's wrong?" His eyes have fallen to the hand rubbing my chest.

I sigh and drop it as I shake my head. "Nothing... What are you doing here?" I ask, keeping the door closed enough that he can't really see around me and inside.

Gavin raises an eyebrow. "You invited me. You texted me a little while ago and said Alex is making pasta. Which you know is my favorite."

It's my turn to furrow my brows. I shake my head, confused. "I never invited you. I mean, not that I mind." I huff out a sigh. "I don't know what I'm trying to say."

Gavin laughs. "Jess. I have the text." He takes out his phone and pulls up my texts with him. "See? Your name. And my response."

I just shake my head again because it is my texts with him. But I never sent that, nor did I see any kind of response to it. I close my eyes and let out a frustrated groan when I figure it out. "Marissa," I whisper.

"What? Jess, what the hell's going on? Are you going to let me in?"

"I…" I sigh. "Marissa's here," I whisper.

Gavin is quiet for a second before it dawns on him. "She took your phone and texted me."

I look up at him before looking over my shoulder to Marissa. She's sitting at the table with her head down. Alex is watching me intently, chewing his lip with a furious glare that would make me tremble in fear if I didn't know it's not intended for me. He continues stirring his sauce, but his eyes never leave the door.

"Part of me really wants you both to work it out," I say quietly. "The other part completely understands why you walked. I'm very torn."

Gavin closes his eyes and lets his head fall back as he shakes his head. His entire six foot two, muscular frame is tense. He reaches up and pinches the bridge of his nose as he opens his eyes and looks down at me. I chew the inside of my cheek.

"It's not your fault, Jess. Come here." He pulls me in for a hug, and I melt in relief. I don't know why, but I was honestly thinking he'd blame me for this. "She's tried reaching out before. I've told her a few times we're done. I didn't think she'd use you to get to me."

I let out a breath and shake my head. "Me either. Maybe old Marissa." I look up at him hesitantly. "She has changed. A lot. She's really become responsible and serious about school and her future. And I think she was being sincere when she said she misses you."

Gavin drops his arms and breathes out a sigh. "I'll talk to her, Jess. But I'm not promising anything. She gave off the wrong vibes. I know what my bank account says. I don't need someone who only likes me because of how many zeros follow my name. And that's basically what I got out of her."

I nod. "I know. It was wrong. But…" I chew my cheek a little more. "Maybe… people change…?" I give him a slow shrug. "I mean, how she got you here… that wasn't right. But maybe she thought it was the only way and really wants to apologize."

"You have a real knack for seeing the best in people, Jessa," he says quietly. "It's something you need to be careful with. Lots will take advantage of that."

I step back with a soft smile. I know he's right. It's not something I haven't heard before. I'm too nice. Too trusting. It's something I'm working on little by little.

Gavin takes a visible deep breath. And within seconds, the super cocky facade he puts up for literally everyone other than the people he isn't close to is tactfully put back in place. No more vulnerable. No more angry. No more confused. Just Gavin. Heir to millions and Alex Lang's best friend. It's a sight to watch.

Gavin stands to his full height and squares his shoulders. He strides past me. I close the door behind him. His back shows no tension. The arrogant way in which he carries himself is at the forefront of all of the other emotions I saw. The ones I'm sure he didn't think he'd let slip in there.

"What's up, man?" Gavin asks Alex as he pats him on the back and sniffs the sauce he's stirring. "Smells fucking incredible."

Alex chuckles and glances over his shoulder at Marissa. He says nothing at all. Just shakes his head. Anyone close to him, though, would see the muscle in his jaw ticking. I reach them both just as Alex turns off the burner.

"It's ready," he says, low enough for only us to hear. "This is going to be bad. And I'm not at all in support of it."

Gavin chuckles. "It's all Marissa, Alex," Gavin says just as low. "She texted from Jess's phone inviting me over here. We're just going to talk. Nothing more. I think after almost a year, I owe her that."

Alex growls low as he looks at him. "Fuck… that… You don't owe her fucking anything."

Gavin smiles and gives Alex's arm a squeeze. He winks at me and heads for the table. He sits right next to Marissa. Her eyes snap to his as he grins. "Hey, Marissa."

Alex just shakes his head and huffs out a breath. He tosses the wooden spoon he's holding into the sink. He bends and opens the oven. He pulls out garlic bread and sets the pan on a cooling rack. I watch him for a few moments. Alex is very efficient. Even if he is radiating fury.

"How come you didn't tell me Marissa had been contacting Gavin?" I finally ask him, keeping my voice low.

He doesn't look at me. He continues tossing the salad he's made. "Because it wasn't your business, baby. I don't ask you for every detail you talk about with Marissa. I don't think I should have to tell you everything I talk about with him."

I bite my lip and nod slowly as I hug myself. The conversation is very over. And he's right. He doesn't ask me for details on conversations I have. It's not fair for me to do it to him. But ever since we moved in here, I haven't quite been able to get past Alex's reasoning for wanting such a secure place and asking me to trust him on why. And he's not been forthcoming about it.

I know he expects me to trust that he's doing the right thing, but I'm beginning to realize that there are things I question. Like where he gets the money to afford something like this on his own. Why he tends to disappear a lot and show up without explanation as to the reason he's so moody and quiet. Where his headaches come from. It's hard to blind trust someone. Especially when worry prevails over it all.

I sigh quietly as I help him take platters and plates to the table. Marissa and Gavin are talking in hushed tones, though Alex and I could still hear them in the kitchen a little bit. As we both sit down, though, it's hard to miss their words.

"Riss, I still don't think you're getting it," Gavin says patiently. He leans back in his chair and scrubs his hands down his face before looking back at her again. "Listen. Honesty here. That's what you want. So, I'll give it to you. I do like you. I did feel some kind of a connection with you. I don't know what the fuck it was. I won't go as far as saying it was love. But it was there. And it's something I've never felt before and haven't since. I still feel it. But it takes a back burner to the fact that I felt, and still feel, that all you were and are after is money and how much of it my last name brings."

Marissa's eyes widen. "Gavin, I… don't…" She shakes her head and sniffles. "Maybe then. I'll be honest with you and say that, but it's not how I feel now. I've spent this whole time trying to get over you and being unable to. That connection you say you felt and still do? I feel it, too."

Alex scoffs as he starts dishing up. I drop a hand on his thigh and try to silently communicate that it's none of our business. Something he just told me a few minutes ago. I feel like he understands because he lets out a low growl. He puts food on everyone's plates, including Marissa's, and then drops his hand over mine and squeezes it.

The silence lingers on as we all eat in silence. No one says a single word until I quietly stand and start clearing the plates. I have no doubt that Alex wants to stay and support the man he thinks of as his brother, so I say nothing when he doesn't move. The glare he's leveled at Marissa stays plastered to his face.

"Do you think we could try again?" Marissa nearly whispers as I take her plate and Gavin's.

Gavin sighs and glances at Alex. "I don't know, Marissa."

Alex growls and stands. He starts helping me clean the table. When we have everything in the kitchen, he helps me with the dishes as the two talk quietly behind us. Alex and I work in silence. I can feel his tension coming off him in waves. It's obvious he doesn't want Marissa in Gavin's life. He doesn't trust her in mine but tolerates her for my sake.

Truth be told, Marissa is my only friend. The only other two I have are Gavin and Damon, both Alex's friends, and both like family to him. It's good for me to have someone separate from them. Alex said it helps keep me independent and my own person. Honestly, I believe he's correct. I love being around him and Gavin and Damon most of the time, but I do like doing something outside of the group sometimes. It helps make me realize I'm my own person. Alex is good about helping me keep that in mind.

Alex sighs as his phone chimes in his pocket. Gavin and Marissa move to the living room as Alex takes out his phone. I look up at him and finish drying the last dish.

Something dark crosses his eyes. He leans down and kisses me. "I'm sorry, baby. I can't stay. Damon texted. He's needing some help."

"Oh. Is he okay?"

Alex smiles. "Nothing bad. Just needs some help with his homework. He's struggling in one of his classes."

I smile. "Always the one who swoops in and helps. I'm sure he'll do just fine with you tutoring him."

He kisses me with a grin and hunger in his blue eyes. "I shouldn't be long." He glances behind him. "Keep an eye on them, huh? Don't let Gavin do anything stupid."

I can't help but giggle quietly. "Like… get back together with Marissa?"

He taps my ass with a wink but says nothing as he heads for the door. He puts his shoes on and grabs his keys before disappearing out the door. I dry my hands and steady myself as I drop the towel over the drain rack to dry.

I walk to the living room and curl up on an oversized chair to watch whatever movie Gavin and Marissa put in. Not like they're watching it anyway. They're still talking. I can't help but be amazed at how peaceful it is. No raised voices at all.

I settle into the chair and focus on the movie because it's better than wishing Alex were here. I love being around him, but what I love more is that he told me where he was going and didn't just disappear this time. He might not realize how much that means to me, but considering how worried I've been about him, just those simple words have gone a long way in easing my mind.

And building more and more of the trust in him that we both desire.

Chapter Nine

⚔ Alex ⚔

"I don't think you're understanding what I'm trying to tell you." Josh is pacing back and forth in front of me as I sit on the bed in his room.

I sigh. I told Jessa I was coming to help Damon. And then texted both Damon and Gavin to cover the lie for me if she asks. I'm sick of lying to my girl, but I have very little other choice. And when my brother texts me 911, and that is literally all it said, there's no way I'm not going to run to him if I need to.

"Josh. You gotta relax. All we know is that he knows I don't live on campus, and that I may or may not be living with a girl."

Josh glares at me. "He's going to put surveillance on you."

"Yep."

He stares at me like I've lost my mind. Maybe I have. "How are you not at all concerned about this?"

I smile. "Because there's something you're missing about our father."

"Yeah? What's that?" He crosses his arms over his broad chest.

Josh and I are twins in every single aspect. The only place we truly differ is our muscle tone. Josh is a little bigger. He's always spent far more time in the gym than me. Not to say I'm not muscular. I am. I have a body a lot of men would kill for. Josh just has more.

"He needs us, J. Why do you think he's so agreeable to both of us? You wanting to be more involved in the mafia? Me stepping away? Last year, we taught him a lesson. We stuck to what we wanted to do. Despite his threat to kill you. He feared that if he kept that shit up, we'd both walk. And then he has no one to carry on his legacy."

"So…, he thinks if he keeps me out, I'll just walk away. But that makes no sense because he doesn't want me to take control."

I shrug as he sits next to me. "If he keeps you out, he knows we'll both walk. He won't be able to give it to me or you. He's afraid we'll both start our own and take him out. He's trying a new tactic. Be agreeable. Give us both what we want." I sling an arm over his shoulders.

He winces from the recent beatdown, but it's the deep hurt across his face as he nods that gets me. "I just don't understand why he hates me so much. Why he doesn't want me to take over."

"Because he's not fucking well. He's sick. To him, I was born first. I take over. He doesn't need you. He doesn't need a second son. It's stupid as hell. But you know how he is. I'm trying to do this the dignified way. Get him to give me control so I can turn around and give it to you. It'll save a lot of hassle for both of us if I just walk and force him to hand it over. And you know that no matter what happens, this is yours. Not mine."

He nods as he hangs his head. "Just once I'd like him to look at me like he looks at you. With that pride and admiration. Instead of hatred and resentment."

I carefully give his shoulder a squeeze, avoiding the bruise from the pistol whip he took from one of the guards.. "Misplaced anger and resentment. He has every reason to be proud of you. If he'd look at your accomplishments."

Josh sniffles, and my heart almost fucking shatters. Our dad has been horrible to him his entire life. I've always protected him the best I could. And now here he is, trying to protect me.

The entire reason I'm here is because he found out some shit that freaked him out. He heard our father talking about putting a tail on me to see what the hell I'm up to at the University. He thinks I'm chasing pussy. I knew it was coming. It's the entire reason I moved us into one of Ryan's buildings. It's the most secure building in the city. Probably even more so than any of the Government buildings. I knew it would only be a matter of time before he found out about me and Jessa.

The other reason he called me over, though, is because he woke up naked in his bed with no fucking recollection on how he got here. The only thing he remembers is getting into it with dad about leaving me alone. He remembers guards holding him back while another punched him in the stomach, pistol whipped his shoulder, then his head. He's got a goose egg of a bump on the side of his head from it.

"Josh. Look at me." He does. The pain behind his eyes is nearly unbearable. "Please don't let him get to you. Use your anger at the way he treats you against him. Use it to fuel you. It's what I do."

He just shakes his head. "What about Jessa? What are we going to do about her?"

"He's not going to do anything. If he does, then we'll fix it. Together. Just like we always do."

"Are you sure we just want to ignore this?"

I sigh and drop my arm. I rest my elbows on my knees and lean forward. "We aren't totally ignoring him."

"Then what are you going to do, Alex? This could potentially be really bad. Fuck what happens to me. I can take a few hits. But if he goes after her…"

I look at him. "Listen. All he knows is that I'm sharing a place with a girl. Jessa and I don't have any classes together except our math class. We go to campus together. We come home together. We made sure our class times were as close as we could be so we could spend as much time together as we can. But he doesn't know that. For all he knows, she's a girl in one of my classes that I'm helping out."

"If he asks me what I know, you want me to say that?"

"Tell him she had a crappy living situation. I felt bad so I let her move in with me. The penthouse has two levels. Four bedrooms. It wouldn't be a stretch to get a roommate to share it with."

"Maybe you should get Gavin or Damon to move in with you. He thinks you all work for him and we're all friends. Fuck. Family even. Might help it be more believable. Have more than one roommate in a four bedroom. Especially two of them being guy friends. "

I think a second, then nod. "Actually, that's not a bad idea. Jessa's friend, Marissa, has a terrible roommate. Messy as fuck. Loud. And she couldn't get a suite this year."

"Wait a second. So, she's basically in a two bed room? Like a hotel or some shit?"

"Exactly. I can talk to Jess. See if maybe she wants to move upstairs and let Marissa and Gavin stay downstairs. The bedroom up there is bigger anyway, but Jessa thought it was overkill to have a bedroom half the size of the entire penthouse."

"So, Gavin and Marissa are dating again, right?"

"Much to my dismay. I fucking hate that girl. Something about her just rubs me the wrong way. Not even because of the way she was with Jess. She just seems shady as fuck. It would give me a way to keep an eye on her. Damon can help me out. Protect Gavin and Jessa that way."

"There's your four people."

I smile at him and gently pat his back as I get up. "Thanks for the idea. Good job, little bro." I give him a teasing grin.

He laughs. "Never gonna let me live that down, are you?"

"Not a fucking chance." I head for the door, then stop as I turn back to him. "Josh, you know I'll always be here for you. Right? I'll never stop protecting you."

I feel like he needs to know that. That he needs those words to get him through. He refuses to leave this house. He feels like it would show weakness. Like he's running away. He won't ever do that. He won't ever show our father anything that can be construed as anything less than a strength.

It's also because he won't leave our mother alone. We've spent years trying to get her to leave, but she won't. It took us both a while to realize the true reach our father has. It wasn't until he started opening up to us about how big our mafia actually is. How powerful. I don't blame her for wanting to tread lightly. Hell. It's the reason Josh and I haven't just killed the fucker. It would cause an upheaval we probably wouldn't walk away from.

"Yeah. I know." He gives me a shaky smile.

I walk back to him. I pull him up into a hug. "Trust me."

"I do."

I give him a last squeeze before he pulls away and lays down. I've noticed he's been fighting to stay awake most of the time I've been here. He has a concussion for sure. I'll be making it a point to check in on him. And not just me. Gavin and Damon will be here, too.

I glance back at Josh before I leave the room. He's already asleep. I'm happy he's okay, but I'm pissed the fuck off at our father. Lucky for him, he's not fucking home. If he were, I can't say I wouldn't say fuck the consequences and blow his brains out of the back of his head.

✘✘✘

The drive back to the penthouse in the LA traffic is fucking long. It's the middle of the night on a Saturday. I'd wonder why the hell there's so much traffic but I know the answer. Saturday's are always busy. People coming and going from clubs and concerts.

I hit my brakes and groan as I hit more slow traffic. It's hot tonight. I am not at all in the mood for traffic.

I sigh and call Gavin. "Hey, Alex. What's up?"

"I don't know, man. I just left the house. Fucking traffic. I just want to be home."

"What did Josh say?"

"He said my dad found out I moved off campus. I knew he would find out. It's why I chose the building I did. But he also said that the fucker has seen Jessa."

"That... doesn't sound good."

"I honestly don't know. I don't think it's a good idea to take chances, though. Josh seemed really concerned."

"I trust Josh. His instincts have never led any of us wrong before. I don't think it's a good idea to brush aside his concerns. He's around your dad every day."

I rub my forehead. "Yeah. I know."

We're both silent a moment before Gavin sighs. "He fucked him up again?"

"Yeah, but Josh won't leave. He won't leave mom. He won't let dad see his walking as any kind of weakness. I know where he's coming from. It's why I struck this fucking deal with him. Make him think I'm still in when I'm working so fucking hard against him."

"I get it, bro. What do you want to do?"

"I don't want Jessa to know any of this. I don't want her near this shit. I want to figure out a way to protect Josh. Get rid of our father. None of anything I can actually do. Except keep Jessa out of it. That I can do."

"I know, man. But I think we need to do something. We can't just hope he doesn't make any kind of move. You and I both know better than that."

"I agree. Josh and I came up with a plan. I don't know if you'd be up for it."

"You know I go where you go."

"I know you like your apartment, but I think it would be a good idea to move into the penthouse. And before you argue with me, allow me to give you more ammo to use against me."

Gavin laughs, and I smile. "I'm listening."

"Jessa told me Marissa's living with that messy as hell goth chick? She said something about not being able to sleep because the girl watches her at night."

"Yeah. And the most recent thing is her science project. She told me that tonight when we were talking."

"Do I even want to know?"

"Probably not. But if I have to know, so do you. Since the first day of classes, goth girl has had a cheeseburger sitting on a paper plate by the window."

I look at my phone and choke back a gag. "It's been four months. We're nearly to Christmas."

"Yeah. The fruit flies are bad, but she's convinced the mold is toxic. She was coughing pretty bad. Even at dinner when we are all quiet. I thought she came down with a cold or something. As soon as she told me, something snapped. I can't let her go back to that shit. I took her home with me after I tucked Jessa into bed. She fell asleep watching the movie we had on."

I pause and rub my temple as I drive slowly. "Well, you know how I feel about her, but not even I'm that big of an asshole. Obviously, she needs to get out of there. I'd say let her stay at your place and you move in with me, but this is about Jessa."

Gavin sighs. "Yeah. I'm not to the point of moving in with her, but I'd do anything you need me to for Jessa. You really think Jessa's going to go for this, though? Marissa, maybe. But me?"

"Jessa's safety is my number one priority. I moved us to that building because of the security it provides. I don't have to worry about her being home. But I'll be honest. I don't want her to be alone. And not just because of my father." I growl low. This slow moving traffic is going to make me turn into a demon.

"Care to elaborate?"

"Remember Grant?"

"Yeah. That dude's body will never be found."

I don't doubt it. I have a very good crew with unlimited resources, and Gavin is not a fucking Saint. "Remember Jessa's reaction? The full-on panic?"

"Yeah, Marissa wasn't that much better."

"Jessa's attacks are getting more frequent. She doesn't tell me, but I know her. I can tell. She's adamant she doesn't have attacks. But when she's upset or stressed with school, she has these small ones. It doesn't take much to calm her down, but they're happening. She loses focus. Looks around the room. Bites the sleeve of her sweater. Tugs it between her fingers. Tugs her hair. Rubs her chest."

"She was rubbing her chest when I showed up last night. I knew something was up right away. You don't want her to be alone if we have to be out just in case she needs something."

"Knew there was a reason I liked you."

"Speaking of how great I am and completely changing the subject, I found us a hacker. Good guy. Name is Lance Engle. He's in one of my electives. He's majoring in computer science or some shit, but he's really fucking good."

"I forgot I asked you."

"Rounds out the team. And I trust him. Ran him through some tests. He didn't bat an eye."

I smile. I don't need a hacker. But I prefer to always be prepared if I ever do need one. "We can talk about that later. I do want him set up on monitoring us, though. Aliases and everything. Clearing shit out if we ever leave anything and end up in the system. Erasing us."

"On it, boss."

"About moving in, though. What do you think?"

"I think we need to play this smart. I'm going to need a reason to leave my apartment."

"Fuck. Maybe I should just tell her."

"I'll think of something. You tell her, you'd have to tell her everything. You're opening Pandora's box. I don't think lying is the best option, but in this case? I think you're right. Until Josh takes over the Lucinio Mafia, she doesn't need to know. Way too much danger."

He's right. When Josh takes over, the danger to her won't be so great. Right now, mafia life is not something I want my girl anywhere near. And I'll protect her from it at all costs.

(Three Days Later)

A few days later, after dinner, the four of us are sitting in the penthouse living room. Gavin meets my eyes. Time to begin this shitshow.

"Marissa," I begin after clearing my throat. "Gavin said that you were having more issues with your roommate. Something about a science project?"

"Oh no! Marissa, what happened? You didn't mention anything," Jessa says.

Marissa coughs. It's dry and looks like it hurts. I narrow my eyes. I've suspected she's faking this entire thing, but it's hard to fake a cough like that.

"It's fine. Really." She smiles softly.

Gavin slips an arm around her. "I don't think it's fine, Riss. And I still think you need to be seen. I told you that last night."

"I don't have insurance. I can't afford to be seen," she whispers.

I lean back in my chair. Something is happening right now that I'm not aware of. I don't like surprises. Gavin looks just as shocked as me. Marissa looks completely shaken and Jessa won't meet my eyes. I narrow my eyes. I've done my homework on her. Her dad makes quite a bit. So much that she doesn't need to take out loans to cover any of her tuition. She's about the same financially as Jessa is.

"Jess?" She has never been able to keep anything from me. "What am I missing? What happened?" I look at her.

"What happened?" Gavin asks Marissa. "What don't I know?"

Marissa takes Jessa's hand. It's an unusual gesture. One that throws me off even more. Jessa takes a deep breath and looks at me. "There was a reason Marissa asked me to go shopping with her today. Just us," she says quietly.

"It's um… because my parents don't approve of my major. They don't like that I plan to major in art. They think it's useless." Marissa starts crying.

Gavin doesn't hesitate. He pulls her onto his lap and hugs her. "Shh… Hey. I got you. I got you, baby."

"I… needed some personal… um… things, and I have no money."

She starts sobbing. Both Gavin and I look at Jessa. She looks down at her hands. "They froze her accounts. She'll be able to finish this semester because the tuition has been paid but won't be able to finish college. Unless she gets a job and can work out a payment arrangement. It's… why… she was living in the budget dorms. Her parents wouldn't pay for her to have a suite."

Gavin and I look at each other in total astonishment. This is even better than we planned. I'm going to have to look into all of this to make sure Marissa is telling the truth, but she just made it so I don't need to lie to Jessa. At least not as we were about to. Fuck knows I've told my girl enough untrue shit.

"Marissa needed some clothing and… other things. So, I bought them for her." Jessa continues watching her hands as she picks her nail.

"We get it. She has her period. Needed tampons and underwear," I say. Jessa chuckles. Marissa hiccups through her tears. I smile. "Okay. Here's what we're going to do. First thing is we're getting Marissa to a hospital. Mold is nothing to fuck with. You may have a respiratory infection."

Marissa turns to me, her eyes watery. "Did you not hear me? I can't afford it." Her voice is barely above a whisper. I thought it was because she was embarrassed to speak, but I think it's more because of the mold issues and cough. I don't think she can talk louder without it hurting.

"But I can," I say with a shrug. "I'm not spending time arguing with you. Dr. Freeman can meet us there. You can see him. Second is your living arrangement. You can't stay there anymore. It's making you sick."

"Maybe she could stay with Gavin." Jessa says the words softly as she looks at Gavin. I know she's hesitant to suggest it. They've only just gotten back together.

Gavin jumps in, saving me yet again. "I'd love to say yes, but my lease is up. Landlord doesn't like me much, so he isn't renewing. I have to look for a place myself. I mean, we could look for a place together, baby, but I wouldn't be able to put you on the lease without income."

"Jessa and I will move upstairs." I say to Gavin before looking at Jessa. Jessa smiles at me, and it's all it takes for me to know she knows where I'm going with this. "Four bedrooms. They can have one down here."

Jessa nods. "I'd love that."

"You're really okay with that?" Marissa whispers hopefully, her eyes bouncing between the both of us. "I'll get a job. And help as much as I can."

"Riss, don't. Alex can handle it on his own. And I make enough to cover whatever I need to," Gavin says.

"I can't finish school. I have to do something with my time." She sniffles as she plays with the hem of her shirt.

"Which leads me to number three. Tuition," I say.

"Alex…" Jessa looks at me with tears of happiness as she moves from the couch to my lap. She kisses me. I smile.

"What? How? You can't do that." Marissa shakes her head. Her voice cracks even more than it already has.

"I know you can cover it, Alex, but let me take care of it. I make plenty," Gavin cuts in.

"Gavin… I can't ask you to do that." Marissa is near tears again.

"You aren't. I offered. I invest most of my money as it is. Just consider this an investment in you," Gavin says.

"You… I… don't want you to think it's about money again…" Her eyes fall.

Either she's an incredible actress, which is my bet, or Jessa is right and she's turning over a new leaf. I can't put my finger on her. I believe some things that come out of her mouth, but definitely not others. I won't tell Jessa, but her being here allows me to keep my eye on her, too. I won't let her fuck Gavin, me, or Jessa over. I don't trust that she won't.

"I've seen your art, Marissa. I know how good you are. I know how much you love creating your art. I think you have an incredibly bright future ahead of you. I'm not about to let this throw a fucking damper on it."

Jessa sniffles and nuzzles into my neck. I kiss the top of her head as I pull up Doctor Freeman's contact information and wait for him to pick up.

"Mr. Lang. Good evening. What can I do for you?"

"Doctor. Gavin's girlfriend, Marissa, has had a fairly long-term exposure to mold. She's got a pretty dry cough that looks like it hurts. Any chance you could meet us at Cedar?"

"I can treat her just as well where you are. Save you a trip."

"Fair enough." I give him the address.

"I'll be there as soon as I can. I'm going to stop and get some antibiotics. She'll need a specific regimen if she has an infection, depending how far she's progressed."

"Thanks, Doc." I hang up.

As Gavin hugs Marissa and I hold Jessa, I've never been so relieved at how things worked out. I'm not at all certain what the hell my dad's game is, but he's never been particularly smart. I've always been able to outmaneuver him. Josh has always been my wingman. We've always been smarter than him.

He seems to think he can put a wedge between us, but our bond has always been stronger than he thinks. With Josh and I working together and Gavin, and soon Damon, staying here with Jessa and Marissa, my dad will never get close to Jessa to manipulate me.

If that's what his game even is.

Either way, he doesn't know that I know he's watching. That I am and will always be one step ahead of him.

Chapter Ten

✗ Josh ✗

I spent the morning after Alex left fighting a headache and pacing back and forth in my room. Much like I'm doing now. Alex is right. We don't know our dad's plan. I shouldn't be so nervous until we do know. I need to be calm and rational. I usually am. I didn't get to where I am with my training or running missions with Alex by being irrational.

But lately, my thoughts are so fucking jumbled. One second, I'm just as fucking ruthless and dominating as he is. Other times, I have to fight myself to remember that Alex is my brother. He's on my side. Not my damn competition. I know our father is going to give him control. But this mafia is mine. It belongs to me. I'll fight whoever the hell I have to for it.

I growl and run a hand through my hair. I tug. "Fuck! Stop it, Josh. You know the plan. It's always been the fucking plan. Alex would never betray you."

It's a thought that's been creeping into my head more and more. What if he doesn't think I'm good enough? Weak? What if he doesn't like my plans to make our mafia legit? What if he decides to run it himself and not give me control? What if he's really working with our father?

I growl at myself again. These thoughts are dangerous. Fucking detrimental. I know better than what my brain is telling me. Maybe what I need to do is work some of this nervous energy off. Head to the gym.

Run.

I nod decisively and walk to the basement where the gym is after quickly changing into sweats and a t-shirt. This is my absolute safe place. It's the one room no one ever comes to. My father rarely does. This is the one place I have control. Everything about it. It's mine. My equipment. My design. Mine.

I immediately hit the rowing machine. It's my favorite. I feel like I'm getting a full body workout, and I love the burn I feel afterwards. It's almost like my muscles actually live for that feeling. Breathe for it.

I close my eyes and let myself feel. I let the workout wash away my worries until all I can feel and think about is the burn. The soothing ache.

And then it all ends.

I can feel his presence before I even open my eyes.

The entire last near hour has been for nothing.

I drop the ropes and sigh as I open my eyes. "Father," I growl.

"It seems every time I decide to come down here, something has been added. Or changes have been made."

"Because it's mine. Why exactly *are* you down here? You hate this place." The very fucking reason that I love it so much.

After looking around a few moments, calculating, he finally meets my glare with one of his own. "Your mother said dinner is ready. She told me to come find you." He turns to leave without another word.

I growl as I get up. My mother has never been the problem in this house. She's always loved us the best she could. It's not her fault that our father has beat her into submission. She'd do anything he told her to just so he'll keep his fists to himself. So she doesn't end up in the hospital. Again.

After quickly showering, changing, and getting to the kitchen, I hug my mother and kiss the back of her head. My mom is really rather pretty. She's slim. She's not tall, but not too short. She still has a full head of gorgeous brunette hair. Her eyes are just as much piercing blue as mine and Alex's.

"Hi, mom. Need any help?"

"Yes, sweetheart. Take the bread basket out. It's the last thing. They just came out of the oven."

I smile as she hands me the basket. "Sure thing."

She smiles and reaches up to cup my face as I turn. "You remind me so much of my brother. I wish you'd gotten to meet him."

My eyes soften. She's told us stories over the years of her brother. But she always stopped talking whenever my father entered the room. I was curious about it for a long time. Until one day, not thinking I'd heard her, she mumbled something about thinking dad had been the one to kill him. I wouldn't be surprised at all, and why she shut her mouth so quickly suddenly made a lot of sense.

But the fact that she sees him in me quiets the doubts that constantly run through my mind. She has told me what a powerful man he was. How kind he was. Strong. Intelligent. How his moral compass was always pointing the right direction, even though he was far from an angel. Comparing me to a man she thinks so highly of is the greatest compliment she could ever give me.

I kiss her forehead before turning. She follows me as I bring the bread out to the dining room. The incredibly stiff, formal dining room that absolutely no one in this house is truly comfortable in. Except my father.

I take my place next to my mother, who sits to my father's right. No one is allowed to sit in Alex's seat, to the left of my father, even if he's not here. That's where the heir sits, and I'm not even close. I'm surprised my father lets me sit at the table at all. I wouldn't put it past him to make me sit on the floor and eat like a dog.

"Josh. I haven't heard from Alex in a few days. How is he?" dad asks.

"Fine." Don't ask about me. Ask about the favorite son. I fight back a sneer and a glare, choosing to focus instead on my dinner.

"I hear he has a girlfriend. A gorgeous little brunette."

I nearly choke, but I cover it and look at him. I've learned a thing or two about shutting emotions off from watching Alex. I give nothing away. The last I heard, he knew about Jessa but never put two and two together that she's Alex's girlfriend.

"Does he?" mom asks, a slight hint of excitement in her voice. "Alex never brings any of his girlfriends home. Is that true, Josh?" She looks up at me, a hint of smile playing at her lips. "He tells you everything."

I smile softly at my mother. Time to lie my ass off. "No. He met a girl in his math class. She was having issues with a roommate and Alex felt bad. She couldn't study or anything because her roommate sucked so bad." I keep my eyes on mom but watch dad. He'd never know, though. I refuse to look his way.

"Poor thing," my mom says, her smile turning into a frown.

I see my dad is watching me intently. I've studied my brother. Watched him. I not only know how to hide emotions, but also how to lie without giving anything away. My father will never understand just how much his bastard son has learned.

"What was this roommate like?" Dad fishes.

Looking at him for the first time, I continue my lie. "A partier. So, his friend couldn't get shit done. She started falling behind. Alex just got that penthouse. It has four bedrooms, so he asked if she wanted a room. Plenty of space." I give a shrug for good measure as I take a bite of my food. I don't break eye contact, though. It would be a dead giveaway to the lie, and I'm not fucking stupid.

"Is she renting? Hopefully, my boy knows nothing should ever be free." He's trying to bait me. Alex warned me he would. He's trying to get information.

"Well, he's so smart, right, dad? I'm sure the great Alex wouldn't let you down." I play into him because that's what he wants. He wants me to show that jealousy for my brother. He wants to see that wedge slowly anchored between us. "He has two other people there, too."

"Oh, really?" Dad continues fishing.

I hold the smirk as I keep my eyes on his. It's obvious he didn't know that. I watch him absorb the lie. He fucking loves getting information. But what he loves even more is getting information that he thinks the person he's fishing it from lets inadvertently slip. I didn't let it slip at all. I gave him a sliver to chew on.

"Yep. Gavin and Damon moved in with him. They're all going to the same university. May as well, right?" I go back to eating as he rolls the information over in his head.

He considers Gavin and Damon part of the Lucinio Mafia. He has no fucking clue that they have and always will run with Alex. As soon as I take over, they'll be on my side. Not his. It's been the plan since we were all old enough to make one.

Dad glares as he stabs a piece of meat. I smile inwardly, extremely satisfied with myself. At least Alex and Jessa will be safe from his bullshit for a little while longer. Though, I still don't know why he gives a shit. I intend to find out, though.

"I didn't send that boy to school just so he could party my money away."

"Leave the boy alone. He's just having fun," mom says, defending her son. She always defends us. At least tries to.

"I didn't ask for your opinion, Rebekkah. Shut your mouth, or I'll shut it for you," dad bites out. Mom bites her lip and looks down at her plate.

I stand. I've had enough of him fucking with her. It's time someone defended her for once. Alex and I were never able to really do it before. But we're both a lot bigger now. I'm so fucking sick and tired of him disrespecting her. Talking down to her.

"Why don't you pick on someone who has a chance against you." I growl the words through clenched teeth.

"Josh. Don't." She whispers the words and puts a small, frail hand on my wrist. Dad stands up. I pull away and meet him, standing toe to toe and putting myself between him and her.

"You best remember what I'm capable of, boy," dad growls.

"And you best not disrespect my mother," I growl right back. To anyone else, we'd probably sound like two fucking bears fighting for territory or something.

Mom stands and gets between us, pushing us both apart. Not at all the plan. I'm supposed to be protecting her. "Both of you. Stop it. Enough. There's no need to fight."

She tries to push us both away from each, but neither of us budge. Before I can move her behind me again, dad shoves mom away. She screams and hits the edge of the table with her head. He drags her up by her hair and away from me just as I'm reaching down to help her up.

Protect her. That's my goal.

My fucking job. No one else here is going to do it.

"Matthew, please!" she shrieks as she tries to pull away.

He punches her in the mouth, and I see red. And not from the blood that flies from her mouth when I hear the sickening cracking of bone. He throws her into a wall just as I'm reaching for her once more. She cries and screams as he bends for her again. She cowers, holding her hands up like she'll be able to fend him off. His eyes never leave mine.

I lose it.

I'm not fucking missing getting a hold of her again. I'm faster than him.

I run for him and shove him off with a tackle any linebacker would be proud of. He goes flying backwards and crashes into the table. "Get off her! Get the fuck away from her!"

Putting my body between her and him once more. With superhuman speed, though, he recovers. He grabs me around the throat as my eyes blur. Something is wrong. I'm slower than usual. I feel weaker. Maybe it's the residual effects of the concussion. He spins me and shoves me. I stumble backwards and crash into the table as my dad reaches for my mom again. I rush him, grab his wrist before he can, and wrench it back. He turns to me and lands a fist to my jaw.

"Josh!" Mom reaches for me, but my dad kicks her in the ribs. She cries and folds herself into a heap on the ground.

He turns away from me, and I rush him again. But his guards are running into the room. Before they can get to me, like I know they will, I land a hard punch, smashing into my dad's face and relishing at the sickening sound of breaking bones.

"Get off her!" I scream again, reading my fist for a second punch. Two guards grab me and pull me away. I kick my feet out and connect with my dad's stomach and ribs as they lift me clear off the ground. "Run! Mom, run!" I command.

The guards drag me back, but I break free, shoving my dad to the ground so my mom can get away. Have the fighting chance that I'm not going to. The guards grab me again. Another one knees me in the stomach. I double over and cough, trying to catch my breath.

"Mom, run!" I command again, my eyes on her. My mom starts to crawl away and then attempts to use the wall to get up.

One of the four guards surrounding me punches me in the stomach and then the ribs.

I fight to get away because I'm not fucking so weak that I'll ever give up, but he punches me in the face. I feel my eye immediately swell; the blood instantly ooze.

My dad gets up and grabs my mom.

"No! Get off her!" I scream. I get punched in the mouth and then kicked in the ribs again. Hard. Harder than the first time. I drop to my knees. The guards haul me back up and tighten their grip on my arms. I struggle, trying to get to my mom. Protect her. My dad pulls her against him by her hair. She cries and screams. "No! Please!"

"Shut up!" He screams at me as he slaps her. She falls to the floor onto her knees crying in pain. I'm sure her jaw is broken.

"Mom!"

I'm older. Wiser. I'm more muscular than Alex now. But it means nothing. Fighting with the guards has sapped my strength. The little I had to begin with. There's a guard on each side of me holding me by the arm. There's another one in front of me who's punched me a couple more times since dad slapped mom back to the ground.

I'm weaker, but I still refuse to give up. Giving up is how a person fucking dies. I won't let these assholes kill me. I use the guards holding me as leverage and kick the guard in front of me in the balls. He drops to the ground howling in pain.

"You want to act big and tough? Shoot your mouth off?" Dad is talking to me, looking right at me, but he slaps my mom again.

"No!" I wrench my arms free with the last bit of strength I have and run to my mother. She's crying and cowering on the floor. She's curled up in a fetal position, trying to protect herself. Her head. Face. Vital organs.

I'm supposed to be protecting her, but as soon as I reach her, my dad quickly stands and kicks me in the ribs. I nearly collapse from the pain, but I grab my mom anyway. I shield her the best I can.

I have to get her out of here. Away from him.

But a guard grabs me and puts his arm tightly around my neck, halting my movements and hauling me away from her.

My dad kneels in front of me. My mom isn't moving, but she's bleeding on the floor from her head. My heart squeezes in my chest. I'm watching her fucking die. I feel it. And it's my fault. I can't get to her. I can't protect her. I'm a fucking failure. She's dying because of me.

The guards arm tightens around my neck. I can't get away from him. I have no more adrenaline. No more strength. I haven't recovered fully from the last time. I'm slowly starting to lose consciousness.

"You'll never be your brother, Josh," dad says as he kneels to the floor with the guard as my knees buckle. "You'll never be able to stand up to me. You may as well quit trying now. Because every time you fall out of line, I'll take it out on her." His eyes never leave mine, but he points to my mother lying in a heap on the floor. "You'll never beat me."

I hiss when I feel a prick at my neck. Before I can try and investigate where it came from, I see his fist flying towards my face. There's nothing I can do to stop it.

I don't know if it's his fist or the fact I'm being choked out, but everything goes black.

✗✗✗

Fuck. When the hell did my bed get so fucking hard? I need a new one. Now.

I try to sit up to order one and groan as dizziness and nausea overtake me. I am forced to lay back down.

"Oh, shit…" This is not good. It can't be good.

I keep my eyes closed, willing the room to stop spinning.

This is absolutely not good.

Am I hung over? I don't remember going out. I don't remember drinking anything.

Think, Josh. What do you remember?

I roll to my side.

Pain.

Everywhere.

It radiates in every direction, and the contents of my stomach threaten to make an appearance once more.

"Oh… Fucking hell." And that's exactly what this feels like.

The last thing I remember is the gym. Did I fall off a machine?

No.

That doesn't seem right.

Dinner. I was at dinner. I ate. My dad asked questions about Alex.

And then…?

My mom… My mom!

I snap my eyes open. One of them is swollen shut. The other one has dried blood all over it.

I sit up fast, ignoring the dizziness and waves of nausea. I look for my mom, realizing all at once that I'm lying on the dining room floor.

Everything hits me. I remember it all.

The fight.

My mom.

I force myself to my feet, grimacing at the pain. The nausea and dizziness overwhelms me.

Instantaneously, I hit my knees and vomit on the floor. There's no holding back. Everything in my stomach comes up at once. My throat hurts. My head fucking feels like it's exploding.

"Fuck."

Through all the pain and puking, I notice one thing. She's not here. My mom isn't here. I can only think of one person I can call to help me. Hopefully, he'll come. Hopefully, he doesn't blame me for this. I'm already blaming myself.

I take out my phone as I slowly sit back on my knees. I make my way to the wall, not daring to crawl or walk. I just inch my way and collapse against it. The effort has completely stolen my breath.

Alex. I need my brother.

"Hello." His voice is filled with sleep. I woke him up. I don't even know what time it is.

"Alex…" My eyes are getting heavy again. I fight to stay awake. "He did something to mom. I… tried."

"What?"

"Mom. He did… something." I try to shake the cobwebs away and form a cohesive sentence.

"I don't know what's going on, but I'm on my way."

"I tried to save her."

"I'm on my way, okay? What happened?"

The dizziness. Nausea. Fuck the nausea. I lean over and throw up again.

"Shit. Shit! Stay with me, Josh. I'm on the way."

94

Mom. What the hell did he do with her? I push myself back up. "Fuck. Alex. He has her somewhere."

"Just stay with me, bro. Try to keep talking. Tell me what happened."

What the hell did he do with her? I fight another wave of nausea and my eyes grow heavy. My memory is getting hazy. "I tried to save her."

My arm. I have no control over it. I feel it dropping to the ground, but I can't stop it. Why did I call Alex? What the fuck was I babbling about? My mind blanks as everything once again goes black.

Chapter Eleven

☒ Alex ☒

As soon as I saw Josh's name come up on my caller ID at three in the morning, I knew instinctively something was very wrong. I hadn't been able to sleep when Jessa and I went to bed because my chest was actually hurting. Something just didn't feel right. I couldn't tell if I was having a heart attack or if something was happening to my twin.

I was about to call Josh when he called me. I didn't want to wake Jessa, so I had made my way to the couch long before the call.

While I was talking to Josh, though, I was silently making my way through the bedroom and throwing clothes on. Jessa didn't move, and I thanked the stars for that. I didn't want to explain to her where I was going at three in the morning in such a fucking hurry.

I quietly close the door to the bedroom behind me and nearly run to the room Gavin and Marissa claimed as their own.

I have the phone up to my ear still, but Josh hasn't responded to me. "Josh! Come on, answer me, man."

Silence. I'm pretty sure he passed out. I have no fucking idea what's going on.

I walk over to Gavin and Marissa's bed and gently shake Gavin awake, praying like hell he doesn't try to punch me. If someone tried waking me up like this, I'd shoot them without a second thought. Especially if my girl was naked next to me like Marissa is next to him.

"Mmm... What...?"

I kneel down and whisper. I don't need or want to explain to Marissa what's going on if she wakes up. "Get up. Let's go. Hurry up."

He obeys and quickly gets out of the bed, careful not to wake up the naked woman sleeping next to him. Fuck. Marissa naked. Not something I wanted to see. I'd rather deal with naked Gavin over that shit. I pull the blanket up over her, covering her so I don't throw up. Gavin grabs his jeans and throws them on as he's following me out of the room.

He closes the door behind him and follows me out to the living room. "Ignore what you saw."

"Traumatized for life. Never getting hard again. But I don't care. I've seen naked women before, and I know what naked men look like. Look, something happened." I turn to him. "I don't know what, but Josh called. I think he passed out. Kept saying something about trying to save my mom and how he took her."

"Who?"

"Fuck if I know. The assumption is my father." I grab my keys.

"Wait a sec. I'll grab my shirt."

"No. I need you here. I want you with Jessa and Marissa. If I'm not here when they wake up, make something up. I'll call Ryan."

He nods, satisfied I'll have good backup. "I'll take care of it. I'll text you the excuse if I need one."

I nod as I run out the door. As soon as I reach my car, I jump in and waste no time peeling out of the garage. I immediately call Ryan. "Come on. Pick up, Ry."

"What?"

"You still in LA?" I ask, hurriedly. Ryan had come to LA for a concert. I'm hoping he hasn't left yet.

"Why?" He grunts and sounds cranky.

"My brother just called. My dad did something. I don't know what. He said something about trying to save my mom, then I think he passed out. I'm driving about a hundred and twenty trying to get there. I could use you."

"Yeah. I'm on the way. Your crew meeting you?"

"No. I have Gavin with Jessa. Gav just moved in with his girlfriend. Long story. I'll explain later. I sent Damon to Tulsa. My dad has something going on there that sounds shady as fuck. I need intel. And I haven't worked with the new guy yet. Don't want him in on this. And I don't have time to wake up anyone else."

"So, you're going into an unknown situation just us. Alex, are you fucking crazy?"

"It's my family, Ryan."

"Fuck. I know. Don't you fucking go in there until I get there. Understand me?"

"Yeah. I got it."

"Alex. I mean it. We aren't going in half fucking cocked. Wait for me. I'll bring people."

"I said I got it." I hang up and race through the streets, barely slowly when I hit the 405.

I don't know what we're going to walk into, but I trust Ryan. He's right. We can't go in half-cocked. Especially where my father is concerned. He's always been mean and unpredictable, but lately… Lately it's almost like he's crossing into crazy, and that scares me.

I force myself to stop outside the gates to the house. I don't want to. Everything in me wants to make sure Josh and my mom are okay. I force my breathing to slow down and call Josh. I've been trying since I hung up with Ryan, but Josh isn't answering. Neither is my mother. I've tried her, too. My dad's phone goes straight to voicemail.

"Fuck. Hurry the fuck up, Crane."

As if on cue, a black car flies up the street in front of me. He cuts his lights, and I drive up to the gate, letting us in. Ryan follows me, and the gates close behind us. We pull up to the front of the house, and I jump out. I open my trunk and grab my vest and gun. Ryan and two other guys that jump out of his vehicle follow me as we head to the house. I let us in, disabling the alarm as Ryan closes the door.

"What's the plan? What are we doing?" he asks.

"Shoot first. Ask questions later." I start for the stairs, but Ryan holds me back.

"No. We treat this like a mission. How many guards?" He's whispering. His guys stay close but keep their eyes on a swivel.

I growl as I glare, but keep my voice low. "We don't have time for this. Josh and my mom could be dying."

"How… many… guards?" He speaks slowly and deliberately. Commandingly.

I take a steadying breath and hold it. He's right. I need to reign in my emotions. I exhale the breath. "If my dad is here, six. They'll be around the house. If not, none. He only cares about himself. Doesn't care about anyone else here."

"You think he's here or not?"

I listen for a moment, and my eyes carefully scan the dark entryway. "No. If he were here, we'd have already been confronted with a guard. There were none outside. No SUVs parked out there. He has them with him."

Ryan nods. "We clear the bottom floor. Just like we normally would."

"Basement first." I say. "Josh's gym is down there. A bathroom and shower. Guest bedroom."

"Now you're thinking. Put everything else away. We clear. We act."

I nod as we silently make our way to the basement. We clear it as the other two say upstairs, keeping watch. Josh isn't down here, and neither is my mother.

We work together to clear out each room on the main floor. When we get to the dining room, I see Josh. He's against the wall but slumped to his side.

"Shit…" Ryan covers me as I rush to Josh's side. The other two cover us both. Josh is lying in his own vomit, and he looks like he got his face stomped on.

"Holy hell. Josh. Come on. Wake up, buddy." I try to keep my voice low, but it's not as low as I'd like it. Ryan and I both hear footsteps.

"Take him. We have to go," he whispers.

I lift Josh and put him in a fireman's carry over my shoulders. "I'm sorry, man. I hope you don't have broken bones."

"On me," Ryan commands us all. "Let's move."

"Upstairs. Josh's room is the third door."

Ryan heads for the stairs cautiously, scanning everywhere. The footsteps fade out as we make our way as swiftly as possible up the stairs.

Ryan gets us to Josh's room, and we close ourselves in. The two guards stand inside the room but by the door. We don't want to alert anyone, but we want protection. I drop Josh in one of his chairs and use the flashlight on my phone to get a better look at him.

"He needs a doctor," I say.

"Call someone. And then we eliminate the threat before your doctor gets here. Hurry up."

I take out my phone and call Doctor Freeman. He picks up quickly. "Alex? What happened?" he asks groggily.

Having a doctor on my payroll is a necessity. I really lucked out when I found this one. He's discreet, fast, and he's never let me down.

"Sorry to wake you. Get to my house. Josh is down. Looks like he got beat up bad. Call me when you get here. I'll let you in."

"Don't worry about waking me. My job is to help when you need me. Just Josh is injured? Anyone else?"

I pause a moment to collect myself. "Count on my mom being injured. I haven't found her yet."

"Yes, sir. Twenty minutes."

I hang up and turn back to Josh as Ryan stands next to the door talking to his guards. It's cracked slightly so they can hear. I don't want to shake Josh too much or aggravate any of his injuries, so I gently take his face in my hand. "Josh. Josh. Come on. Wake up." I'd shake him, but I don't dare. He's still breathing so I know he's just passed out, but I have no clue what his injuries are and how severe. "Josh."

"Mmmhmm…"

"That's it. Come on, bro. Get up."

"Mmm…" His eyes flutter as he turns his head to look at me.

"That's it. Wake up."

"Alex?"

"I'm here. What happened, man?" He tries to stand up. "No. Stay sitting down. Doc is on the way."

"Alex. We have to clear the rest of the house," Ryan says quietly.

I take a deep breath and nod. We have to find whoever belonged to those footsteps. "Stay here. Okay? Don't move. Try to stay awake. I'll be back."

"Okay," he whispers. He closes his eyes.

"Josh. No. Get up. Come on." I pull him up and make him stand. "Shower. Come on. I need you, bro. Stay with me."

He shakes his head and nearly falls back on the chair. "Shit. I -"

"Fight through it. I can't do this without you, Josh. I need my brother." I sling his arm over my shoulder and hurry to the bathroom. I turn on the water, making it lukewarm. He has to come to, but I don't want to shock his system. "Come on, Josh. Get out of your clothes. I need you."

He's messed up, but he's breaking through the fog. I help him out of his clothes and get him in the shower.

"Ahhh! Fuck! Fuck!" he bellows at the chill.

"I have to clear the house. Finish up," I command.

Josh stands against the wall catching his breath as the water hits him. After a few seconds he waves me away and steps under the spray, using the wall for support. I make my way out to the room.

Ryan motions for me to go first. "We need to find your mom. Guard is still downstairs."

I nod as I lead him through each room, leaving my parent's for last. We silently enter the room, searching it for anyone. My coward dad isn't there, but my mom is. She's laying in the bed, curled in a protective ball. I rush to her as Ryan, once again, takes his place at the door with his guards.

"Mom!" I whisper as I ever so gently brush her hair from her face.

She's completely naked.

Fucking naked.

What the ever living hell did he do to her? I can see the scratches and bruises all over her body. I don't even need any light. It's dark as fuck in here, and I can see the bruises clearly. They're that prominent.

"Mom. Wake up. Please?" I hug her bone thin body to my chest as I reach for the blanket. She's shivering. Her body is freezing cold, and the blanket is stuck. I can't get it out from under her without lifting her. I don't want to move her.

"Ryan! Help me." I hiss the words out as loudly as I dare. Ryan hesitantly looks over at me before looking back out the door. After a second, he hurries to the side of the bed and yanks the blanket out from where it's tucked under the mattress.

"We have to go. Cover her up and leave her. We have to clear the house."

"Fuck off. I'm not leaving her alone. I can't wake her up, dude." I'm starting to panic. I feel it. I'm good at controlling everything including emotions. But when it comes to my mom, I just realized now that I can't. My mom is everything to me. She always has been. I'd do anything to protect her.

"Alex. Listen. I know how much she means to you. But you can't protect her if we get ambushed. She's breathing. Cover her. Leave her. We have to clear the house. Move." Ryan's commanding tone breaks me out of my own head. He's right. Again. In order to protect her and Josh, we have to eliminate whatever threat is lurking in this house.

I grab the blanket and cover my mother. I kiss her on the cheek. She groans. "I'll be back," I whisper.

I kiss her on the cheek again and let her go. I stand and meet Ryan and the guards at the door. He motions me to follow. We stealthily walk down the stairs and continue our methodical search. When we reach the kitchen, we see a light on. Ryan puts a hand up and peeks around the corner as I stop behind him.

He looks at me with a wicked grin. "He's sitting there fucking reading a paper and drinking coffee," he whispers.

"Easy kill, but we need to know where the fuck my dad is. He isn't answering."

"Flank him. I'll take left. You take right." He nods to the two guards. "Stay alert. Cover us. We take him fast and by surprise."

I nod and follow him. His two guards get in position to cover us as we both move quickly and flank my father's douche of a guard.

"What the hell?" The guard reaches for his gun as he quickly gets up and backs away.

Ryan and I raise our guns to his head. "I wouldn't fucking do that," I growl.

"Christ. Alex? What the fuck, man?" He looks at me confused as fuck as to what's going on.

I move like the wind and put him in a sleeper hold as Ryan keeps his gun on him. I keep my grip loose enough so he can talk, but tight enough so that he can't move.

"Answer the questions or I break your neck," I rumble. "Question one. What the hell happened to Josh and my mother?"

"Josh went crazy. Went after your dad. Your mom stepped in."

"Hmm…" I tighten my grip around his neck with one arm and punch him in the ribs with the other.

"Ahh! Fuck, man!" He flails to get away but quickly gives up when he realizes how futile it is.

"Try again. They're both in bad shape. What happened?"

"We had to step in! Josh was about to kill your dad!"

I punch his other side, and he screams. I hear a satisfying crack. "How many more ribs you want broken?"

"Okay! Okay. Your dad was laying into your mom. We had to hold Josh back."

"The truth. Much better." I punch him in the ribs again because I fucking can. I break another one, and he howls in pain. He nearly collapses, but I haul him back against me. He fights to breathe. "Question two. Where the fuck is he?"

The guard doesn't answer. He continues to fight for breath. I let him drop to the floor. He grips his ribs and hits his knees. "Shit. Holy shit," he whimpers.

"I'd answer if I were you." Ryan kicks him in the stomach. He doubles over, coughing up blood on the floor.

"Where the fuck is he?" I ask again.

"He left. Went to Mexico."

"What? Why?" I furrow my brows and glance at Ryan.

"He said he needs a break."

Ryan looks at me. I know he's thinking what I am. Something doesn't make sense. There's something my dad doesn't want me to know. Something he's keeping very fucking secret.

I kick the guard in the back of the head. He falls forward gasping for breath. He coughs up more blood. I kick him in the ribs. He starts crying. I kick him again and he turns to his side, hissing and holding his ribs.

Unable to stop myself from standing by and watching or taking part in what they did to Josh and my mom, I kick him in the face. He rolls onto his back, still crying. I kneel down next to him. Ryan keeps his gun trained on the guard's head.

"Maybe you'll tell me the truth now. Why Mexico?"

"He's... new... shit..." He leans his head back and continues crying in pain.

I slap him. "Why the fuck Mexico?"

"Drugs. New drugs."

"He's getting involved with the cartel?" My heart slams into my throat.

"Yes... Fuck... Yes, okay?" He tries to turn away from me, but I yank him by his hair and slap him in the side of the head. He cries more.

"Where's he shipping?"

"I don't... know." He gasps as he coughs up blood on himself.

I stand and kick him in the ribs again. He can't even scream anymore. "Last chance. Where's he shipping?"

"Montana! Montana... Three Forks."

"Is he fucking crazy? The cartel?" Ryan asks in as much disbelief as I feel.

"He's gotten more brazen. I never thought he'd get involved with the damn cartel."

"Doesn't he know how much danger that puts his wife and kids in?"

"He doesn't care about us. Never has. It's always about him and the money." I kick the guard again and then kneel down once more. I grab his hair and make him look at me. "How long is his trip?"

"Month... to..." He spits up blood and gurgles on it like he's choking. "To make sure the... plan in place... is solid."

"Fuck me. What the fuck is wrong with him?" I stand up and shoot the guard in the head without a backward glance as Ryan and I walk out of the room. My phone rings. I look at the caller ID. "Doc. You here?"

"At the gate."

"Code is 1051. Gate will close behind you. Park next to my car. I'll meet you at the front door." I hang up as Ryan and I walk to the door. The guards follow, still covering us just in case anything jumps out at us. We can't be too careful.

"The fucking cartel."

"He knows better. I don't know what his game is. Montana?"

"There's a huge drug trade in Montana. I know it runs all over the damn place, but Montana and Minnesota are connected. They run up from

Mexico straight up I35 and across to Montana through North Dakota via I94. They call it Drug Corridor. I have no factions anywhere up there. I'm not big enough yet to take on the fucking cartel."

"We're going to have to team up."

"How? You don't have control. You move a team that big, he'll know."

"Doesn't matter. I'll use this against him."

"How? Fuck. Alex, stop." He grabs my arm and forces me to face him as I open the front door. Doctor Freeman is just showing up. "How? Tell me. I'm all for it, but how?"

"He'll have contacts in the cartel. I have trusted people in his inner circle. He obviously didn't tell me because he knows I'll stop him. He doesn't know that a lot of the guards he keeps close work for me. He has leverage on all of them. He doesn't pay them. I do. With his money. And all of that leverage? I have ways to counteract all of the damage he could cause. He has nothing. He doesn't know how much power I have already without even having control. Which means, he has no fucking clue how much power Josh has because this is all for him. We can't take him out, but we're working on it."

Doctor Freeman follows us up the stairs as I talk. I don't have to tell him to keep everything he hears completely confidential. He knows.

"You think you can get information? Enough that we can take them out?" Ryan asks.

"At least enough that we can take out this line of them. We need to figure out their path. We have to hit them where it hurts."

"Take out their route?"

I nod as we get to my mother's room. Ryan stays outside the door. His guards have remained downstairs. I turn to Doctor Freeman. "She's cut up. Bruised. She's breathing, but she's in bad shape, and she isn't wearing any clothes. I want her checked for sexual assault. I think he sodomized her. She's truly fucked up."

I open the door and let him in. He sucks in a sharp breath when I turn on the lamp next to the bed. "Shit. What about Josh?"

"Bad shape but less. I'll check on him now. Take care of her first. If something happened to him and he's worse, I'll have Ryan come to get you." He nods as he turns to my mom. I leave the room, and Ryan and I head for Josh's. "If we take the route, control it, they'll find another way for sure, but they'll go after my dick father."

"Alex, they'll go after your entire fucking family!" Ryan spits out in shock.

"Let them."

Ryan stops me again and takes a deep breath before he starts talking again. "If you want to do this, you think about it real fucking hard. You go after them, you'll start a goddamn war. You better have precautions in place because they'll come for your mother, Josh, and your pretty fucking girlfriend. You have to send whoever you care about away, because they'll take this right to your fucking doorstep."

"Then that's what I'll do, Ryan. I'm not letting him get us involved with the fucking cartel. We can't come back from that."

"Then figure out a way to back out of whatever fucking deal he makes with them. Because they'll keep coming for you. Your mom, Jessa, you, and your brother will never be safe from them." He glances at Josh's door. "I'll stand guard while you talk to Josh."

He lets me go and steps back so I can walk into Josh's room. Josh is sitting on his bed in boxers. He looks up at me. The defeat in his eyes slams straight into my chest.

"He really fucked me up. I don't know what he did with mom. I tried to protect her. I failed."

I sit next to him. "Mom is in her bedroom, Josh. I have a doctor here. She's pretty fucked up, too. What the hell happened?"

He takes a deep breath and winces in pain. "Where's dad?"

"Mexico. He ran because he's a fucking coward. He knew I'd go after him." Josh hangs his head in defeat. "Josh. You have to tell me what happened. What the fuck did he do?"

Josh shrugs. I can see the tears forming in his eyes. "He asked about Jessa. Just like I said he would. He doesn't know her name, but I told him what you said to. She's a friend you're helping. I told him you had Damon and Gavin living there, too."

"You told him I turned it into a party house?"

"Just like you said. He said he isn't paying for you to go to school so you can party. And he was very interested in the tidbit about Gavin and Damon living there."

"Just like we thought."

He nods slowly, then lays on his bed. I stand so he can get comfortable, then sit next to him. "Mom said something," he begins. "I don't really remember what, but he told her to shut her mouth. I got pissed. I'm so tired of him being disrespectful to her." He reaches for his blanket. I scan over his body while I help to cover him. "Sorry. I'm cold."

"Don't be sorry. For anything."

He gives me a shaky, watery smile. "Mom tried to get between us, but he shoved her. She hit her head on the table. He shoved her into the wall. He hit her, punched her. I tried to stop him." He tries to fight the tears. I reach for his hand because I don't know what else to do. I'd hug him, but I don't want to hurt him. He takes it as the tears fall. "Guards came in. Held me back. I got away a couple of times. Got a few good hits in on dad. But the guards pulled me off. Beat the hell out of me. I couldn't shove them off. Dad told me to stop fighting him. Every time I step out of line, he'll beat mom. I don't know if he knocked me out or if the guard choking me out put me to sleep. But when I came to, I didn't even know where the fuck I was. I felt hungover. Still fucking do."

"You probably have another concussion. Looks like they got some head shots in on you."

He shrugs. "Ultimately, I couldn't save her. I didn't know where she was. I didn't even know where I was. All I could think of was to call you. I failed. I knew you wouldn't."

I look at him in disbelief. This isn't the Josh I know. The Josh I know has grown into a confident, tough as nails motherfucker. The past year or so, though, he has moments like this. Moments where he's so damn down on himself, it scares me.

"Josh, are you kidding?" He needs to build back up. I see why he feels like he does, but I'm not going to let him think he failed anyone. Not after what he just told me. "You fought off guards and got overpowered. You had no help. There's no fucking way the same thing wouldn't have happened to me. You did everything you could. You fought a hell of a fucking battle, bro. I'm proud of you."

I look up as the doctor walks in. I get up and let him do his work, but I don't miss the slight bit of confidence slipping back and filling the cracks in Josh's broken armor.

Not many things get to me. Fuck with my family, though…

My father is a fucking dead man.

Chapter Twelve

✕ Jessa ✕

For the first time since Alex and I moved into this penthouse, I wake up to a cold bed. We're usually so wrapped up in each other that when one of us move, the other will definitely wake up. I didn't realize how used to it I had become until right now waking up with his arms not right around me.

I sigh and sit on the edge of the bed as I rub my chest. I take a few deep breaths, trying to ease the discomfort.

Still rubbing my chest, I get up and make my way to the living room. Gavin is laying on the couch, and I raise an eyebrow. Alex is nowhere to be seen. Continuing to rub my chest, I decide on a glass of milk. I'm hoping it will ease what I've decided has to be acid reflux.

The refrigerator door closing wakes Gavin. He grunts and sits up, rubbing his face and looking at his phone. I sit at the table with my milk. "Fighting with Marissa?"

He looks at me. "What? No." He shakes his head and stands up. He walks to the fridge. "No. Just couldn't sleep, and I didn't want to keep Marissa awake." He grabs some orange juice and sits across from me.

"What is it with you and Alex? You're both obsessed with orange juice."

He laughs. "It's healthy. Lots of benefits, and it doesn't taste like shit."

I smile as I drink my milk. The uneasiness doesn't subside though. "Where's Alex?" I set my milk down and lift the collar of Alex's t-shirt up to my nose. Usually his scent makes everything better.

"He just needed to help his mom with something. It's close to Christmas, you know? Last minute stuff." He smiles reassuringly, and I nod. My throat feels like it's closing up. Gavin stands and reaches for my hand. I look at him in bewilderment. "You can trust me. You've known me long enough. Alex warned me about what's going on right now. You need a distraction. I have an idea."

I take his hand, but have no idea what he's talking about. "It's just acid reflux. I'll be fine."

Gavin simply nods and smiles as he pulls me to my feet. "I'm not going to argue with you. Go get your swimsuit on. I'll grab Marissa. And I'll make mimosas."

"What's a mimosa?"

He grins. "Champagne and orange juice. But I make it better and without alcohol."

I can't help but laugh. "So… just orange juice?"

"Nope. Trust me. Go get dressed. Meet us upstairs at the pool."

I sigh and do as I'm told.

A few minutes later, I'm making my way to the pool when the door opens. Alex walks in and locks eyes with me. "Hey, baby." He looks upset. Sad, even. I launch myself at him, sensing he needs me as much as I need him. "Mmm… Baby." He lifts me up, and I wrap my legs around his waist. He buries his head in my hair and kisses my neck. "I needed this."

"I could tell." I bury my own head in his neck and breathe him in. I'm instantly okay again. The acid reflux is gone. The discomfort is gone. For this moment, it's just me and him.

"Heading to the pool?" he asks.

"Gavin said I needed a distraction. He said something about mimosas."

"He makes damn good ones." He slowly puts me down but doesn't let me go. "Jessa, um…"

He takes a deep breath and looks over my head, like he's trying to steady himself. I reach up and run my fingers through his soft stubble. He looks back down at me and pulls me closer to him. He bends and meets my lips with his.

I don't know what's going on. I don't know what happened. What I do know is everything that Alex is going through, whatever it is, I feel it in his kiss. There's intensity. Sadness. Hurt. Anger. And then there's passion. Kindness. Sweetness.

His lips don't leave mine as he runs his hands down to my thighs and lifts me. I wrap my legs around his waist, and he carries me to our bedroom. He kicks the door shut behind us and walks us to the bed. His lips sear my soul as he falls on top of me.

"Alex!" His hand finds the string on the back of my bikini top and he pulls, freeing my breasts. I don't even have time to gasp before he takes one in his hand and the other in his mouth. I arch into him and run my fingers through his hair. "Holy shit. Alex…, fuck…" Heat pools almost immediately in my core. Alex pushes himself down on me, and I feel his erection straining against his jeans.

"I need you," he whispers against my skin as he sucks. Hard. He tugs and twists the other one. "Make me forget."

His words cut straight through my heart. I wrap my arms around him as he rolls over onto his back, taking me with him. He tangles his fingers in my hair with one hand. He wraps his other arm around me even tighter than it was. He holds me close against his body and crashes his lips to mine. If I didn't feel it happening, I'd never believe it, but Alex is trembling.

So, with no more words, I let Alex take everything he needs from me. Whatever it takes to calm his tumultuous emotions; the battle raging behind his eyes. His tongue darts in and out of my mouth and dances with mine. Little by little, Alex becomes slightly less tense, and I love that I can do that for him.

Alex grips my ass and kisses down my jaw. He unties the bottoms of my bikini and tosses them as he nips my neck. I gasp and close my eyes, loving the feel of him. His lips and tongue. His hands and skin.

He shifts me off him as he sits up. I watch him as he pulls off his t-shirt and jeans. He lays back down and guides me back on top of him.

Only this time, I'm straddling his face instead of his hips. My eyes widen when I realize what he wants.

He says nothing as he gently pushes me down so I'm on my hands and knees. His arms wrap around my waist and pulls me down until I'm positioned perfectly over his mouth. He wastes no time thrusting his tongue into me.

"Oh my God…," I moan. My thighs are already trembling, but I need him just as much.

As he makes a meal of me, I do my best to stay sane long enough to take his hard length in my hand. I start stroking him as I lick and suck his tip. A bead of come has already formed at his tip, and I eagerly lick it before taking him in my mouth and sucking at the same furious pace he's licking me.

"Fuck…," Alex groans. The deepness of his voice vibrates through my pussy and makes me jerk into him and clench down on his tongue.

But his tongue never stops twisting and swirling inside me, or finding that spot that makes my eyes roll back in my head. And since I completely forgot what I was doing, Alex reminds me by thrusting his dick into my mouth, fucking it much like his tongue is doing to my pussy. Each time his tip touches the back of my throat, I swallow.

He sucks as he licks, and my brain short circuits. My pussy pulses and gets wetter and wetter. I grind down on his tongue uncontrollably as I stroke and suck him frantically. I moan, sending vibrations through his dick. His dick jerks in my mouth.

As retaliation, he growls into my pussy and sets his thumb against my clit.

And I'm done.

"Alex!" I scream around his dick. My walls collapse around his tongue, and I come so hard, I think I black out.

"Fuck, Jess!" Alex shoots jets of his come down my throat as his fingers dig into my hips. I swallow every drop as he licks me clean.

Several minutes later, after we've both come down, I shift and collapse against Alex's side. He kisses my forehead softly as he holds me tightly. My head starts spinning with so much love for him, I'm not sure I'm even on the planet anymore. I don't know what happened to put him so far on edge, but I don't need to. All that matters is I was able to help him. Bring him down like he does me.

Alex has become my whole life.

Chapter Thirteen

⚔ Alex ⚔

(Seven Months Later)

"Hey! Earth to Alex. What the fuck, man? We have shit to do," Ryan says, snapping his fingers in front of my face.

"I'm sorry. I just don't like leaving Jess alone."

"She's got Damon and Gavin, and she's nowhere near here. She's got the police department looking out for her thanks to my brother. New York is a good place to get lost."

I nod and try to focus. He's right. His brother is a cop. He's watching out for her. She has my brothers. And we do have shit to do. We need to end this bullshit drug cartel partnership once and for all.

So, here we are. Sitting in Small Town, Montana, in the middle of July. Three Forks. What the fuck kind of name is that for a town anyway?

I'd much rather be in New York with Jessa. I sent her there on a week-long vacation with Marissa. Gavin and Damon are there for protection, but to Jessa and Marissa, Damon is there because he wanted to see the Statue of Liberty, and Gavin is there because of Marissa. I told

Jessa I couldn't go because I had to escort my mother to Canada to meet my father, and to keep her company while he's in meetings.

"Alex! Fucking focus!" Ryan smacks me in the back of the head.

I wince and sigh. "I hate fucking lying to her, Ry."

"Deal with her later, or you and I won't be getting out of this alive. I need you here. Body and mind. Focus. Salvador is in there."

Demetrio Salvador. Kingpin of this cartel. I've done everything I could to fuck with shipments the last seven months since finding out my dad had partnered with the cartel. Finally, Salvador decided he himself needed to show up for this one. To make sure it all ran smoothly.

Ryan and I couldn't have been any more happy about it if we tried. This was the end goal. Get Salvador here so we could take him out along with everyone he has here. It's the only way we knew for certain to get out of this partnership with no repercussions. And the only way to get him to show his ugly face was to make it seem like everyone on his team was incompetent.

Of course the only thing that didn't come out exactly as we had wanted it to is that Josh isn't here. He hasn't gotten a beatdown since the one that nearly killed him and my mother, but he's gotten quiet. Things seem off. He's fine for quite a bit, but then he just retreats into himself with no warning or explanation for it.

He knows what's going on with all of this because I told him, but he's not here because he's fallen into one of those quiet moods. This time, though, it seems to come with some kind of cramping and nausea. I've wondered if he's falling into depression or something, but as soon as I bring it up, he tells me to back off.

Doesn't mean I don't wish he were here for this. We could use him and his skills right now.

"There are fifteen guards on the outside patrolling the perimeter today. Two guards at each door. That's nineteen. He's upped his security," I say.

"We expected that. That's why we pulled as many people as we did."

"If he upped it out here, no way he didn't up it in there." I point to the large house down the hill in front of us.

"Again. That's why we pulled as many people as we did. We need to overpower them. We do that with numbers."

I nod and take a deep breath, pushing Jessa and Josh out of my mind. I have to do this. Otherwise we'll never be out from under them. I refuse to let Josh take over while we are under the thumb of the cartel. This may be our only chance. The only chance to save my family.

"You think your dad has any idea you pulled thirty of his best guys?" Ryan asks with a smirk.

"Nope. He wants me to take over so damn bad that he already gave me a lot of control. More than I already have secretly. Regardless, everyone is under strict orders to keep this quiet. I said it's a secret mission. Those that are here want nothing to do with the cartel or my fucking father. They all want Josh to take over, so they're all on board. And the head guys of the factions I called them in from don't dare disobey my orders. I have a pretty damn ruthless reputation. Just like you do."

"Nineteen and just as powerful as me."

"I'm twenty-two, you dick," I say with a grin, knowing he's fucking with me. "How many people are in the house? Do we know?"

Ryan raises an eyebrow. "Who the fuck do you think you're talking to? Of course we know how many are in the house. He upped it to seventeen."

"So we have thirty-six people."

"Thirty-seven counting Salvador. My surveillance says he's in the back of the house in the basement. He's in the theater."

"Of course there's a theater."

"We're in Three Forks fucking Montana. Other than riding horses, what else is there to do?"

"Oh, I don't know. Branding cattle. Breaking a wild stallion. Bailing hay. Chasing a tumbleweed." I smirk at him.

He laughs. "Secret ambitions to be a cattle rancher in Montana, Lucinio?"

"If it means getting away from all this mafia bullshit, then fuck yes."

The sun continues to set, and Ryan and our entire team stay hidden in strategic locations around the property. We intend to go in when it's pitch black out. In this part of Montana, there's no street or building lights. Pitch black happens a lot sooner here than in LA.

Finally, the time to strike comes. Ryan and I move in and communicate with our team through satellite fed earpieces. "Phase one initiates in three... two... one," Ryan says.

We stealthily find our targets... each guard patrolling the perimeter of the property. We stay out of view and drop the guards patrolling the property. We each have silencers on our guns, so the attack is quiet and alerts no one since we all shoot at exactly the same time.

I watch the two guards stationed at the front door. "Phase two initiates in three... two... one," I say quietly to our team.

Two of our team members throw a smoke bomb in the front and the back of the house away from the guards. The bombs go off within feet of them. As predicted, one member of each set of guards guarding each door of the house slink away to investigate. Our team throws a second smoke bomb on the opposite side of the house from the first one. The second guard guarding the door leaves to investigate. I can't help but chuckle because these guys are so fucking predictable.

"Phase three in three... two... one," I command. Each member of our team silently shoots our four targets. Within seconds, all nineteen guards are dead.

"Phase four," Ryan whispers "Alex, you in position?" I move my team to the front door, staying away from windows.

"Team one in position," I respond.

"Phase four in three... two... one," Ryan whispers.

We kick in the door and enter the house. My team takes out a couple guards on our way up the stairs. We quickly and quietly clear out the upstairs, taking out two more of the seventeen guards in the house.

"Team one is clear. Four guards down. Moving down," I say.

"Team two is clear. Eight guards down. Twelve total including your four," Ryan responds.

"That leaves five guarding Salvador. Our surveillance team still on lookout?" I ask as I lead my team down to the first floor landing.

"Always. Why?"

"Just a hunch." We meet Ryan at the bottom of the stairs.

"It's too quiet," Ryan says.

"Way too quiet," I agree.

"Team three has eyes out," one of Ryan's guys says. "You guys are good to go. Clear the house. Anyone comes out, we'll know."

"Let's move," Ryan commands.

I follow Ryan down the stairs, my AR-15 at the ready. The rest of our team follows. We end up in a wide open room with no doors or windows. It looks a lot like a man cave, complete with deer antlers and prized animal heads.

I blink a few times, confused. "Um… Clear?"

"This isn't the theater. The theater is in the back." Ryan moves quickly to the back of the house. He pauses at the door and signals me to the side. He holds up three fingers and counts down. When he gets to one, he opens the door, and I go in first, staying low.

"Empty? What the fuck? How did he get out?" I ask.

"I don't know. There has to be a passageway."

"A passageway? Of course there's a passageway. How did we not know this place has a goddamn passageway?" I kick a recliner, completely infuriated.

"Team three, be on the lookout. Five guards and Salvador are MIA," Ryan commands.

"We got them. Southside!" a voice yells. Ryan and I take off running up the stairs. We get to the door just as two black SUVs speed by us.

"Fuck!" I start taking off after the SUVs but Ryan pulls me back as a hail of gunfire rains down on us. He throws me down on the ground and dives next to me, as do some of the other guards.

"Got 'em! Get out of the vehicle! Get the fuck out of the vehicle!" another guard yells in my ear over the earpieces. Ryan and I glance at each other as we get up. We cautiously leave the house and see the two SUVs surrounded by six of our own vehicles.

"Get out of the vehicle now! Right now!" one of our team members yell. They all have their guns drawn.

The rest of us join, taking cover behind our own SUVs. "They won't be coming out," I chuckle.

"Then we take them out. Forcibly," Ryan says dangerously.

I nod. Staying low, we move in teams to the vehicles, quickly overtaking them. "Doors now!"

Like a well-oiled machine, we open the doors to the vehicle in unison and pull everyone out before anyone has a chance to do anything.

"On the ground! Now!' I yell. We shove everyone face down into the dirt. "Where's Salvador?"

"Right here, sir," one of my guys says.

"Shoot everyone else. Cuff him. Leave him to me," I command. The team do as they're told. Everyone is shot execution-style where they lay. Ryan pulls Salvador up by his graying hair, and then kicks him in the knees. He crumples hard to the ground. Ryan and another guard hold him up but on his knees. I kneel in front of him.

"Mr. Demetrio Salvador. It's nice to finally meet you face to face. Tell me. What kind of partnership did my idiot father enter into with you?"

"Fuck you."

I shoot him a cocky grin and look at Ryan. "That wasn't very nice, was it Mr. Crane?"

"Nope. Not nice at all."

Fear flashes across Demetrio's face. "Cr-Crane?"

"Mmhmm. See, Matthew Lucinio doesn't have the authority to enter into partnerships with anyone. I do." It's a lie, but he doesn't need to know that. As far as he knows, I'm the leader. Or at least closer to it than the man he's working with. I punch Salvador in the face. He spits blood. "And since I'm really smart, I partnered with one of the most powerful men in the world."

"Do what you want. I'm not afraid." He's putting on a brave face, but he's scared.

"A failure to this extreme has to just eat you up, huh?" I say with another cocky grin.

"He'll come for you. Both of you."

"Your boss? You trying to scare me?" I laugh. "I'm fucking flattered you think you could lie to me."

"You don't have a boss. You think we're fucking stupid?" Ryan asks, laughing as well.

"Just kill me." He spits in my face. I close my eyes and feel the rage burning low in my stomach as I wipe off the spit. I open my eyes, glaring. My voice is so dangerously low that I send shivers up my own spine.

"Clean-up crew. Deal with this mess out here." I stand. Slowly. "Get… him… up." I walk past Ryan and into the house, knowing he'll follow. I wipe off the spit with the sleeve of my black shirt.

Ryan and his other guard drag Demetrio inside and follow me to the kitchen where I take out a butcher's knife. I look at it, then turn my venomous glare to him. "What kind of deal did you enter into with my father?"

"If you're the leader, you'd know," he says as sassily as possible.

I look at Ryan. He grabs a chair and sits Demetrio down. He removes the cuffs only to cuff him to the chair. I use the knife to cut his arm with a wicked gleam in my eye.

"Ahhh! Arrrrgh!" Demetrio screams.

"What was the deal?" I ask again when he's through howling. He stays quiet as he pants. I cut across his stomach. He screams again.

"Pretty sharp knife," Ryan smirks.

I grin. "Incredibly. I don't think I'll have any issue slitting his throat."

"Now, now. Give him a chance. What do you say, Mr. Salvador?" Ryan asks, playing the good guy role in this entire fucktapade.

"Fuck… you…," Demetrio says, gasping.

"He has very poor manners," Ryan chuckles darkly.

"I think he needs to be taught some." I make another slash across his stomach. Deeper this time.

"Ahhhhh! Ahhhhh! Arrrggghhhh!"

"What… was… the… deal?" Ryan jerks Demetrio's head back by his hair.

"Security! For our guys… during delivery… He… failed. Missing… Arrrggghhh…," he groans through gritted teeth. "Missing shipments."

"He was stealing?" I ask.

"Yes… yes."

"So, I didn't have to waste time fucking with deliveries. He was already stealing some. That's why you're here. To take out my guys that would have been arriving today with your delivery." I smile sardonically when he glares up at me. "Guess you don't have to worry about that anymore." I slit Demetrio's throat. He gargles, and his eyes roll back in his head. Ryan lets Demetrio's head fall as he stops breathing. "I can't believe it. This is where he was getting all the extra drugs."

"You suspected."

"Suspecting and knowing. Two different things."

"There's no one above Demetrio. We checked."

"Yeah, I know, but his whole group wasn't here."

"No. But we know where they are. And this guy isn't that far up the cartel food chain to warrant an appearance by the big guy. He's not going to come after us. Especially since we're going to make this look like a gang war. That's why you sent the girls away for the week. Remember? So we can clean up your father's mess."

"How the hell could he think for one second that this was a good idea?"

"Obviously, he's irrational."

I look at him as we walk out of the house. I point to one of my guys. "Burn it down. I want nothing left. Send a message."

"Yes, sir. We'll take care of it."

Ryan and I climb into an SUV and take off. "At least your mom and brother are safe," he says.

"And Jessa. I know they would've somehow gone after her."

"Everyone is safe. We clean the rest of this up and move on. Boss is taken out. By the end of the week, so will the henchmen."

"You don't think they'll run?"

"Doesn't matter. We have surveillance on them. And I have contacts in the ATF and ICE. They aren't going anywhere."

I smile and shake my head. "You should've seen the fear that crossed his face when I said your name."

"I've become pretty well known for being a ruthless killer. No prisoners. What they don't know is that most of my missions are in conjunction with law enforcement."

"I know. One of the few who know."

He grins as he pulls into the hotel we're staying in. The Lewis and Clark. How fucking fitting. "Get a good night's sleep, Lucinio. It's going to be a busy fucking week."

We both head to our rooms. After I get cleaned up and changed, I fall into bed. This is the reason I want nothing to do with mafia life. Being away for weeks. Constantly having to protect my family from new evils. It's exhausting.

Josh is the one who wants this life. Granted, he wants it to be legal. But he likes traveling. He likes the business aspect of what we do. He loves seeing other parts of the world. He's the protector. He never tires of it.

I hate all of it. I want to settle down. Run Lucinio Tech, my baby that's already grown, thanks in large part to Ryan and his help and influence. I want everything in my life to be normal. On the right side of the law.

My father turned me into an emotionless killing machine at a very young age. I don't want to be that anymore.

I smile a little as my thoughts turn to Jessa. She's the one who taught me there's good in the world. That I'm capable of feeling more than just lust for a woman. It's because of her that I can see a future with a family of my own. It's because of her that I'm able to feel love at all.

Chapter Fourteen

✗ Josh ✗

(Three Months Later)

"It was sloppy. You didn't wait for my signal. You didn't clear the bottom floor, and it caused one of our guys to get hurt. You made me nearly shoot one of our other guys. Our target almost got away because you couldn't subdue him. You're lucky we had one at the door. You hesitated on every single shot. How the hell do you expect me to let you take over with that many mistakes? You'll never come close to Alex."

I glare down at the ground while my father rants and raves at me. I'm sitting in his office, as I have been for the past three hours, just taking the berating.

"You're careless. It's your fault we are down one of our best men. You're not ready to take over. Every mission you fuck up makes me more and more sure of my decision. This mafia will never belong to you. I'd rather die than give you control. We'd all be dead within the week with you at the helm."

"Dad, I left Jonas-"

"Shut up. Just shut your mouth. You have a lot of work to do if you want to prove yourself. You need to start doing what it takes, Josh. Stop fucking around." I clench my firsts together as my dad finally collapses in his chair. "I don't want to hear another word. Get the fuck out of my office. I don't want to see your pathetic excuse of a face anymore."

I glare at him as I leave without a word. I head straight for the garage and jump in my car.

My silver BMW is like a safe haven. Just like my gym.

I peel out of the garage and screech down the driveway. My tires are squealing as I hit the street. I fly down the road, slamming on the brakes when I hit a stop sign. I hit the button on my dash for my top to come down while I wait for the traffic. As soon as I see a clearing, I slam my foot down on the gas pedal, whipping around traffic until I hit the traffic jammed freeway. "Ugh… fuck!"

I pound on the steering wheel. I need the speed. The wind in my hair and against my face. Not a fucking L.A. traffic jam!

I eye an exit and immediately get off the freeway as soon as I come up on it. After a few turns, I hit a deserted dirt road and take off, kicking up an immense amount of dust. I only slow when there's so much dust that I can't see anymore.

After a few minutes, I reach the end of the road and park my car. My gym and my car might be the places I run to when I need to get out of my head.

But this?

This is home.

This cliff above the ocean blue Pacific is my place to regroup. My place to relax. To calm the hell down. It's my place to allow my mind to get right.

Even with the support of my brother, it's hard to keep my head above the water sometimes. Constantly being yelled at, told how much I suck, and how I'll never live up to Alex eventually takes its toll. I fight harder and harder every day to not succumb to his level of crazy. To not let him beat me down. To not let the fog in my mind drown everything else in me that tells me to keep fighting. To keep being me.

I breathe in the salty ocean air and close my eyes as I take out my phone. I realize how much I rely on Alex to get me through sometimes, but

I feel like he's my voice of reason. He's able to cut through the chatter when I can't. He sets me straight.

I breathe in again and again, but the voices telling me my father is right about how much of a fuck up I am don't calm. I've tried to leave Alex alone, to fight my own battles, but I need Alex today. I need my brother.

I sit on the ground, dangling my feet over the edge of the cliff and dial Alex's number. I'm hoping he's not too busy for me. Now that he's in his third year of college, he's gotten really hard to get a hold of. I rub my neck and scratch at the latest bug bite I feel. I pull my hand away, knowing mom hates when I scratch at it.

"Hey, little bro. What's up?" Alex answers.

"Fuck you. It's only a few minutes." I growl the words and am instantly sorry, but I'm pissed. I hate when he calls me his little brother, ven though I know he's joking, and today I'm not in the fucking mood.

"Whoa. Hey. I was kidding. What's going on? What happened?"

"Are you sure you have a minute? I shouldn't have bothered you."

"Josh, you're my brother. I have time for you. Always."

"Just don't want Jessa to catch you."

"She's in class. Don't worry about it. I'd just go into another room anyway. Tell me what's going on. How did the mission last night go?"

I sigh and rub my temple above my eye. "Fan-fucking-tastic," I grunt. Alex is quiet as I gather my thoughts. Finally, I take a breath. "Dad just spent three hours telling me everything I did wrong. How I'll never be you. How you wouldn't fuck up like I did. Basically, how he'd rather die than give me control."

"Well, first of all, what happened on the mission? Walk me through it."

"Well, I had my team positioned at the back door. One of my guys sneezed under a fucking open window. Dude pops his head out the window and sees all of us. Starts screaming for backup. So, I told dad I had to go in. We'd been compromised." I close my eyes and breathe in the ocean air. "Dad said I went in before his signal."

"I don't care what he said right now. One thing at a time. Walk me through the mission." He knows how to get me to focus.

I nod. "Okay. After we went in, my guys took out three guards in the kitchen. There were four in the house. Our target was supposed to be upstairs. Dad's team was to clear the downstairs. My team was the kill team. We were supposed to go up. I left Jonas at the bottom of the stairs just in case. Like a precaution."

"Very smart."

I smile at Alex's praise. "We got upstairs and cleared it. We got to our target and took out the guard. But our target wasn't in the room. He was hiding in his closet. When one of my guys opened the door, he took off. I was clearing the bathroom. He got through my guys. So, I chased him. Yelled to Jonas that he was coming his way. I expected a shot when our target hit the stairs, so I held back. Only the shot never came. I yelled for Jonas and got no answer."

"Hmm…"

"My thoughts exactly. I ran down the stairs after our target. Dad caught up to him as he got to the front door. His guard at the door shot the target."

"What happened with Jonas?"

"I talked to him. He said dad came around the corner and nearly shot him. Got pissed off and sent him to help clear the downstairs."

"So, he pulled your guy."

"Yep. We went home, and after I woke up, he called me into his office. Berated me for three hours. Told me it was my fault Jonas nearly got killed. He said the mission nearly fell apart. It was all my fault. One of the guys fell down the basement stairs. He said that was my fault. It never would've happened if you were there. I'll never be you. I'll never take -"

"Josh. Josh. Listen. He's fucking with your head. You did the right thing. You followed your instincts. Put a guy at the bottom of the stairs to avoid crossfire if your target got away. I've never done that. That was ingenious on your part. And he would've been there just as you intended if dad hadn't interfered."

I nod, watching the sun set. I'm starting to feel slightly calmer. "Yeah."

"Your job was kill team. Your job was to clear upstairs and take out your target. As well as any guards that were upstairs. He didn't give you a second team to clear upstairs, right?"

"Right. He said I was supposed to clear downstairs, too, but the plan was that his team was doing that while mine was upstairs. He said I should be able to do it all on my own."

"He's never done that. He's never cleared the entire house on his own with his team. Neither have I. You should've had a team to clear upstairs and downstairs so you could concentrate on your target. He set you up to fail, Josh. And he's pissed off because you didn't. He sabotaged you by repositioning your guy and by giving you less resources than he would've given me or himself."

I sigh. I will never understand why he hates me so much. "I… Why? I just don't understand what I ever did."

"Nothing. You've done nothing. It's not your fault he's a fucking asshole. No one understands what the hell goes on in his head. Just keep fighting. Never stop fighting him. Never quit standing up for yourself."

"The last time I did that, he nearly put mom in the hospital, then disappeared for two months." I rub my head as it starts to cloud and take deep breaths focusing on Alex's voice.

"And you spent the last damn near year beating yourself up for it. He had to get guards to protect himself against *you*. He has nothing on you, Josh. Nothing. He knows that. That's why he's doing this. You have to fight it. You'll take over. And then you can do whatever the fuck you want with him."

"I should just kill him now."

"Dude, I wish I could say that's the way to go. If we could get away with it, it would have been done long ago. But he's respected throughout the mafia circle. You kill him, it causes unrest. It causes other leaders to look at you like some power hungry son who killed his father for control."

I growl low because I hate that he's right.

"We'll get through this, Josh. Just keep fighting. Know that you're better than him, and that he fears you. He knows you'll be a better leader than him. That scares him."

"Doesn't seem like it."

"You have to look at all of the shit he's done up until this point. Everything. The sabotage. Berating and lecturing you. Trying to pit us against each other. Leveraging your love for mom against you. It's because he's *afraid* of you. He knows you're better than him."

"You're better than him, too."

"You're right. But he doesn't see it that way. To him, I'm just like him. But you? You're a threat. You can take his mafia to a level he's only dreamed of. He knows that. And he hates it because it's proof that you are levels above him."

"You really think so?"

"I know so. Everything you said just proves it."

I smile for the first time all day.

Alex.

Always knows how to calm me. Get me out of my head. Bring me back from the brink of falling into the fog. "Thank you, Alex."

"No matter where I am, I'll always be here for you. Remember that. Understand me?"

I smile again and chuckle. "Understood, big brother."

Alex laughs. "Good, good. Listen, Jessa is about done with class. But if you still have stuff you need to talk out, I'm here for you. Just let me drop her off, and we can meet up."

"No. It's okay. Be with Jessa. I'm okay."

"Are you sure? I got the time."

"It's okay. Really. I'm up at the cliff. I think I'm going to jump, then head out. Maybe grab a pizza."

"Okay. But if you need me, Josh, call. I mean it."

"I will. I promise." We hang up, and I stand, stripping down to my underwear.

I put my clothes neatly next to my car and grin like a fool. I've made this jump hundreds of times, both with Alex and on my own. There's nothing in the world like sailing through the air. Feeling weightless for a few moments before hitting the cold water. That sting removing everything else from my head except the cold as fuck water.

Without giving it a second thought, I run towards the edge of the cliff. The adrenaline makes my heart beat faster. I don't stop when I reach the edge like any sane person would. Instead, I leap off it.

There's nothing but air underneath me now. Nothing but the breeze surrounding me. As I fall towards the water, my stress seems to suspend itself above me. I feel everything lift off me.

I hit the water, and the rest of my worries and cares wash away as I resurface. I float on my back for a little while, letting the calm water do what it's meant to. Calm me. Center me.

I'll be okay. I can get through this. Just like Alex said. I just have to keep in mind that the old man is afraid of me and my abilities. I'm better than him. Smarter. He's jealous.

I can do this. I can beat him at his own game. And I'm not alone. I have Alex. The two of us? We're strong apart. But we're unstoppable together.

Chapter Fifteen

⚔ Alex ⚔

"I know, man. I'm sorry it's even gotten to this point," Damon says as he hangs his head.

"You should've come to me. Long before this shit."

Damon and I are sitting in pool chairs next to the pool on the rooftop of the penthouse. He's just dropped news on me that I can't even process. I sigh and rub my temple as I lean back and close my eyes. The California sun beats down on my chest, and I let it relax me.

"Tell me again what happened?"

"My girlfriend needed help. Got in deep with her now ex-boss. I paid him off. Got her the fuck out," he begins.

"And she's a stripper."

He sighs. "Yeah. It's how Tia was getting through school. She did what she had to do to be able to get her education. Alex, I've known her for years. She's a good girl. Just got in with some bad people. Her boss kept putting her in situations she couldn't say no to."

"Who you paid off instead of coming to me and using resources you have available to you."

"I didn't want them to keep coming for her. Tia was really scared. Is. She is really scared."

"Damon. I fix problems. We fix problems. It's what we fucking do. We've done this since we were kids. You blew your entire life savings on this girl when all you had to do was call me and Gavin. And look where it got you. She's going to get kicked out of school if her tuition isn't caught up. Evicted if her rent isn't paid." I take a deep breath and open my eyes.

Damon flops back on the pool chair and crosses his arms over his chest. "I can help her with school. I just need help getting caught up on her rent."

"And the car that's being repossessed. The credit cards you've maxed out. Dude, what the fuck? I pay you well for every single mission. How the hell did you go through so much money?"

"I helped pay for her medical bills after she was attacked by one of the men her boss was pushing on her. It's lucky I arrived to pick her up after her shift ended or fuck knows what he would have done to her. I knocked his ass out then got her the fuck out. Headed straight to the hospital." He shakes his head and sits up.

"Why? Why didn't you come to me? I could've helped you."

"Because I didn't want you to think of me as unable to handle shit. I didn't want you or anyone to think less of me." He looks down at his hands.

"Fuck, Damon. You're like my fucking brother. To me and Gavin. Fuck. Even Josh. We grew up together. If you can't turn to us, who the hell do you think you'd be able to turn to?" I lean forward and sigh, going back to rubbing my temple. "How much do you need?"

"Fuck. I don't know. I don't want money. I just need help figuring this shit out."

I turn to glare at him. "Damon. Come on. What about your girl? What do you need to fix this?"

"I haven't gotten that far yet. I don't know. She's in class right now. I'm in over my head." He keeps his gaze fixed on the pool.

I turn so I'm facing him fully. "You're already staying here. Tia can stay here with you. I'll talk to Jessa, but she won't care. To be completely honest, it's better that way. I don't want you moving out to protect her. Which she obviously needs. Keeping her here kills two birds with one stone. My dad is fucking psychotic."

He looks at me and raises an eyebrow. "Josh tell you something I don't know about? I talked to him this morning. He never said anything."

"No. Nothing recently. But I am not taking chances. He finds out about what she means to me, and he'll use her for leverage against me. We both know he would."

"To force you to take over?"

"To force me to take over and keep me from giving control to Josh."

"I still say we kill him. Solve all of our problems."

"And add onto them exponentially. Josh and I take him out and Josh takes control, every mafia on his side would come after us."

"So, we take them out, too."

I laugh. "I appreciate the vote of confidence, but mafias don't work like that. You know better." I stand up and pat his shoulder. "Go get your girl. Tell me what you need. We'll take care of it. You know we take care of family."

I give him a supportive smile and head inside to find Jessa. She's not in the bedroom, so I head downstairs. I find her curled up on the couch with a textbook.

She smiles up at me. "Hey."

I smile back at her and kneel in front of her, repositioning her so I am between her legs. I lean down and kiss her core over her sexy booty shorts. She inhales sharply, and I kiss her again. "You're so beautiful." I run my hand up her leg and teasingly rub a knuckle over her warm center as I kiss her neck. She's wearing sexy bootie shorts. I doubt she's wearing panties underneath.

"Alex…," she whispers.

My lips meet hers. I sit next to her and pull her in my lap. She takes off her shirt. Out of the corner of my eye, I see Damon come around the corner and stop. He quietly backs up while I unhook Jessa's bra and toss it on the floor. He leaves the penthouse, silently closing the door behind him, not bothering us in the slightest.

Jessa rubs herself against me as she kisses me. My cock instantly responds to her. "Fuck, baby."

I kiss down to her nipples and take one of them in my mouth. She groans as she dry humps me until I'm so close to coming, I have to still her before I make a mess of my shorts. Jessa reaches down and grabs my waistband. She tugs my shorts over my hips until my cock springs free.

I push her shorts down over her hips. She quickly shifts and kicks out of them before she's back straddling my lap. She wraps her arms around my shoulders. I grab myself and run the head of my dick through her already slick folds before slowly lowering her over my length.

"Holy shit. Alex!" Her eyes roll back in her as her pussy pulses around my dick. She takes me further and further until I'm balls deep inside her.

"Holy… God…, baby." My head falls back against the couch.

"Mmm…" She clenches around me as she starts moving her hips back and forth.

And it's then I realize I'm not sheathed. "Fuck, baby. Condom. I don't have any down here."

She groans as her head falls against my shoulder. "Damn us for being responsible adults."

I laugh as I slowly pull out of her. She's so wet, I can hear every movement I make. I grin and kiss her neck as I replace my dick with two fingers. "Can't leave you all wet like that," I rumble against her.

"Oh my God. Yes…" She tangles her fingers in my hair as she starts riding my fingers as I thrust them deeply into her.

I groan at the sounds her pussy makes with each thrust as she coats my fingers with her essence. I can't help but look down at her pretty pussy and the way she takes my fingers like such a good girl. I love watching her lose control, and as I finger fuck her, I'm more than happy to be the only one who gets to see her lose it like this.

"Good girl," I say with a smirk as I thrust deeper and harder.

Her head falls back as she closes her eyes. "Fuck… Alex." Her hips move faster back and forth as she slams down on my fingers, meeting my thrusts.

I watch her tits bounce before I lean forward and start sucking her nipples, lavishing them both with all of the attention she deserves. I twist my fingers and crook them until she's writhing, moaning, and unable to form any kind of words.

"So, so beautiful." I kiss up her chest to her throat. "Come for me," I command with a low rumble. I kiss her throat. I nip and lick my way to her neck.

She clenches so tightly around me, I feel her squeezing my fingers. I wish like hell it was my dick. Fucking condoms. I curse myself for not having one down here or in my pocket. Fuck. Anywhere near us at all.

Jessa's pussy pulses uncontrollably around my fingers as her orgasm hits her. "Alex! Alex… Alex… Alex…" Her mouth falls open in a sexy smile as she rides out her orgasm. I thrust slower and slower, helping her through. "Mmm…" She falls against me and hugs me as I pull fingers gently out of her.

I suck her off my fingers with a grin. "Taste fucking good, too."

She buries her face in my neck with a giggle. Just as I'm about to beg her to let me come down her throat, my phone vibrates. I sigh as I take out my phone from the pocket of my shorts. Which are still pushed down my hips. My dick is still painfully hard. Whoever is ruining this moment better have a good reason.

Gavin.

I quickly read the text warning me that they're on their way up because Marissa is whining. They must have run into Damon or something when he left. Gavin would definitely try and distract Marissa long enough to give us alone time. But Marissa is too fucking self-absorbed to give a shit.

I roll my eyes. "Time to get dressed, baby. Gavin and Marissa are back."

Jessa sighs as she climbs off me. We quickly get dressed. Neither of us are too happy about me being in the state I'm in, but we don't have to worry. As soon as I see Marissa, the hard on will be gone. I'm not her biggest fan. I tolerate her because of Jessa and Gavin, who has seemingly forgiven and forgotten all of the shit they went through about his money.

I haven't. I still don't like her. I doubt I ever will.

We both watch in silence as Gavin and Marissa both laugh at something as they come inside. They wave to us and walk directly to the rooftop pool.

"So? Where did that come from? What happened?" Jessa asks after they are outside.

"You're fucking intuitive. You know that?" I grin and snuggle her closer to my side. She smiles, and I shake my head. "I didn't do any of that because anything happened. I just needed you. I wanted you. But… something did actually happen."

"What's wrong?"

"Damon is in some trouble. Well, not him exactly. His girlfriend. It's not bad. He got himself in some financial trouble helping out his girlfriend. He's in debt. It's not that I can't help him. And I will. Damon is family. But his girlfriend is getting evicted from her apartment. And if she can't get caught up with tuition, she's going to get kicked out of school."

"I remember him saying something about her being hurt. She was staying here for a bit while she recovered."

"Yeah. Same one. Tia. She quit stripping after that, but that was her income. She doesn't have another job. She's applied, but no one wants to hire a former stripper, so she's fallen pretty far behind."

"That's really dumb. If she has the skills, they should hire her based on that."

"Well, unfortunately a lot of people don't share your view, baby. I agree with you, but many employers are very judgemental."

"She'll have to stay here. There's plenty of room." She bites her lip. I know she's anxious about the other stuff and trying to figure out a way to solve the issue about school and the debt.

I hug her tighter to my side. "Don't worry. The debt will be dealt with. And we'll figure out her tuition."

"You mean, you'll pay her tuition. Because your heart is really big, and you know how much school means to her by the way she was talking about it before."

I chuckle and rub my hand up and down her arm. "Good thing about coming from a rich family who has a lot of disposable income."

She looks up at me with a soft smile. "But it won't come from your family. It will come from your trust fund because it's who you are. Family always comes first. And if Damon really cares for Tia, then it means you'll do whatever you need to in order to solve the problem for both of them."

I can't help but laugh. "You know me too well. I need to start putting up shields and walls or some shit."

She giggles. "I'd be able to see through it all."

I grin because I don't fucking doubt for a single second that she would.

✖✖✖

The next morning, Jessa stirs in my arms, and I pull her closer to me with a groan. After we talked to Damon and arranged for Tia to move in, we came to our bedroom and fucked around until we fell asleep because both of us needed it. I didn't think I'd be able to get hard for days after how many times my girl made me come, but I was wrong.

She giggles. "Alex…"

"Jessa…," I rumble into her hair.

"I'm starving."

I grin and run my hand up her stomach to cup her breast. "I can think of a few things to help out with that." I squeeze her tits and roll her nipples between my fingers.

She giggles again as she grinds her ass against me. "So hard already."

She turns to me, pressing her tits against my chest, and I wrap my arms around her. I lean down to kiss her when, suddenly, we hear a loud crash from downstairs followed by yelling. Jessa nearly jumps out of her skin. Adrenaline immediately courses through my veins.

I jump up from the bed, grabbing a pair of shorts and putting them on, as I run for the door. It's too early in the morning for Damon to be moving Tia in already. That crash and subsequent yelling sounds like someone is fighting.

"Wait!" Jessa nearly screams.

I turn to her mid-stride. She looks terrified as she grips the blanket to her chest. She looks like she's barely breathing. I can't leave her. "Grab a t-shirt. Hurry up," I say. She leaps out of bed and grabs my t-shirt off the floor. She puts it on, then plasters herself to me. "Stay behind me. Do what I say when I say it."

"O-okay."

I take her hand, and we very cautiously make our way down the stairs.

Jessa is shaking behind me. "Alex…" She's whispering as I stop and peek around a corner.

"Marissa is going to be pissed," Gavin says, his voice betraying a hint of fear.

135

"It was an accident. I'll pay for it," Damon says.

"Pay for it? That was a family heirloom. The one thing her parents didn't have the chance to take from her. She's going to go fucking supernova on you."

I see there's glass shattered all over the floor. "Shit," I say.

"Alex." I turn to Jessa and take her face in my hands. Tears are streaming down her face. She's hyperventilating.

"Honey, it's okay. Look at me, baby. It's okay."

"What..." She takes a few shaky breaths. "Hap... happened?"

"You're okay. It's okay." I kiss her, then pull her close to me, hugging her tightly.

"Jess? Are you okay? What happened?" Marissa looks up at me as she joins in my hug. Jessa is all out crying into my chest. I meet her eyes, and it's all she needs to understand Jessa is panicking.

Ever since Grant attacked her, Jessa's attacks are getting worse and worse. She refuses to acknowledge that she's having panic attacks and refuses to go in to the doctor. Her parents can't even get her to go.

That stops. This all stops. I'll drag her to Dr. Freeman if I have to.

Marissa presses herself to Jessa's back and runs her fingers through her hair. "Alex? What happened?" Marissa asks again.

"You need to talk to Gavin and Damon about that. I'm not getting involved," I say quietly. And I'm not. It was an accident, but I know damn well she won't see it that way. Of all of us, Marissa was the only one who seemed upset about Damon's girlfriend moving in.

Jessa starts to calm down the tighter we hold her. After a couple of minutes, she's taking deep breaths and breathing in my scent.

Marissa lets her go, and I wrap her tighter in my arms. "It's okay, baby. I got you. You're okay."

She nods as Marissa walks around the corner. She keeps her voice low and steady so as not to set Jessa off again. I make a mental note to thank her for that, even though I think she's a bitch. "Gavin? Why is my grandmother's glass painting laying shattered on the ground?"

"Uh...," Gavin starts. He lets out a breath.

"I...," Damon trails off.

"Seriously, Damon?" Tia's voice is shaky. I can tell she's upset about what happened, but given her voice is betraying a hint of fear, I'd guess Marissa is glaring at her, even though she's talking to the guys. Jessa pulls back and wipes her eyes as she sniffles.

"I don't know who you are, but I wasn't talking to you," Marissa says. "If you say one more word to me or anyone else in this house, I will drown you in the pool. Shut up."

"Marissa. That's uncalled for," Damon says.

"Fuck, Marissa. Stop it," Gavin growls.

"How dare you?" Tia asks, bewildered. "You don't even know me, and already you're threatening me?"

"Tia. Don't," Damon says in warning.

"But -" Tia begins.

"I said don't. It's okay. I got it. It's a misunderstanding. Marissa, I knocked it down. I apologize. I was carrying one too many boxes. I couldn't see. I set them down too close to the wall. I hit the frame, but I didn't realize it. I turned around, and the next thing we know, it had fallen and shattered," Damon explains. "The whole thing was my fault. You want to be pissed, you can be pissed with me. Tia had nothing to do with it. You threaten her again, she won't be the one being drowned in the fucking pool."

Jessa giggles and looks up at me. "I can't believe she threatened her like that."

"Damon obviously has it under control." I push her hair back. "You okay?"

She nods. "I'm sorry. I feel better now."

"Please let me call Doctor Freeman. He can help you."

"I'm not sick, Alex. I'm fine. Really."

"Baby, your attacks are getting worse. You can't control them anymore. You used to be able to at least keep them at bay."

"I don't get panic attacks. I was just really scared. I thought someone was breaking in. It just took me a second to catch my breath after I realized everything was okay." She runs her hand along my stubble and steps around me, but I grab her arm.

"Jess."

"I'm okay. Really." Her hand goes automatically to her chest as she walks into the living room.

I sigh and follow, gently grabbing her arm. "I didn't want to do this, but I can't stand here and know how badly you're struggling. You can be pissed at me if you want to, but I'm calling Dr. Freeman."

She watches me for a moment before she finally sighs and relents. She says nothing but gives me a nod at least. She wraps her arms around herself with her hand clutching her chest. To anyone else, it would look like she's just hugging herself. But I know the truth. I know her chest is hurting her.

I follow her the rest of the way into our living room. Marissa, trying not to cry, is kneeling next to the painting, picking up glass. Gavin and Damon are helping. Jessa kneels down to help. Tia, however, has folded herself into a corner away from everyone and looks miserable.

I stride to her when I see Marissa shooting her vicious glare after vicious glare through her tears. "That was a little intense, huh?" I say with a soft smile and gentle tone.

"It wasn't Damon," Tia says barely above a whisper and sniffling. "He was covering for me. I tripped. The box I was carrying went flying. I tried to catch it, but I was falling. I reached out and hit the painting as I was trying to catch myself."

I glance over my shoulder as they all finish picking up the glass. Damon looks at Tia, concerned, as he drops the bag he has near the garbage can in the kitchen. I turn back to her with a sigh when Marissa shoots her another glare.

I shake my head and wrap her in a hug when she starts crying. "Don't worry about her. She's pissed off. Gavin will calm her down."

"I d-didn't want to c-cause any trouble!" she sobs into my shirt.

"It's not your fault. It was an accident. Nothing more. It sucks. But there's nothing that can be done."

Damon appears at our side. I step back so he can wrap her in his arms. He sways gently with her as she clings to him and cries. "Shh…," he whispers against her neck. "We're going to take the pieces somewhere. We're pretty sure it can be restored. It's okay, baby. I promise."

After several moments, Tia's sobs begin to subside. Marissa looks significantly calmer. Jessa, though, is still hugging herself and clutching her chest. I make my way to her. Gavin and Marissa are talking quietly as Gavin rubs up and down Jessa's back. I take my girl in my arms and hug her close and tight.

"I just wish it hadn't happened," Marissa says with a sniffle. "I really hope it can be restored. This painting means everything to me."

"I know, baby," Gavin says as Damon and Tia make their way to us. "I know. The guy is the best. I'm confident he'll be able to fix it." He wraps his arms around her now that I have Jessa, and I can't help but feel pretty damn good that he put Jessa first. Maybe my concerns about Marissa are getting through his thick skull.

When Damon and Tia reach us, Tia puts a hand lightly on Marissa's arm. "I'm so sorry."

Marissa shakes her head, keeping her face buried in Gavin's chest. He hugs her tighter. Tia bites her lip and drops her hand, quickly turning into Damon's waiting arms when Marissa says nothing.

Jessa's tension begins to slowly ease out of her body. Her grip on herself begins to loosen until, finally, she puts her arms around me. She doesn't know it, but that one motion sets me at a lot more ease because I know she's coming out of the panic she was just fighting. The fist that had her heart in a vice-like grip finally lets go.

Fuck.

It's way past the time she should have seen someone. I shouldn't have waited so long to force this. I won't let her continue to hurt herself by denying what we all see.

Chapter Sixteen

☆ Alex ☆

(Two Days Later)

"Jess?" She doesn't answer, and I slowly open my blurry eyes. "Jessa?"

I'm both whining and whimpering, but I don't care. Damon's birthday party last night laid me out. My head is pounding, and the sound of her ringtone going off is like a freight train running through my head.

"Jess? I'm dying." I look up at the alarm clock. Four in the morning?

Every cell in my body screams in protest as I lift my head off my pillow and turn to Jessa's side of the bed. "Jess?"

Her phone has stopped ringing, but immediately restarts. Jessa isn't in the bed. "What the hell?" As soon as her phone stops again, mine starts ringing. I fight a wave of nausea and reach for my phone. It's a number I don't recognize but I answer it anyway. "What?"

"Hello, is this Alex Lang?" a slightly panicked female voice asks.

I look at my phone a second, unsure what to make of the voice. "Uh... Yeah. Who are you?"

"I know it's early, and I'm sorry to bother you. I got your number from Brian Holloway's phone. I'm Sergeant Gomez with the LAPD."

My heart leaps into my mouth. Brian Holloway. Jessa's father. "That leads to more questions."

"Yes, sir. I understand. You and Jessa Holloway are listed as ICE contacts in Mr. Holloway's phone. We contacted Jessa, but we got disconnected. Uh… her parents were in a car accident."

"Fuck." I leap off the bed, ignoring the pain in my head, and run for the bedroom door, grabbing a pair of jeans on the way and pulling them on. I already know what happened. I know my girl. "How long ago did you call her?"

"Maybe ten minutes? I've been trying to get her back for a few minutes now."

"What hospital are they at?" I open the door and run for the stairs.

"Sir, um. They…. they didn't make it. I got word they died on the way to Cedar. Jessa heard my radio, and we got disconnected."

"Shit!" I hit the bottom of the stairs, eyes peeled for Jessa. My suspicions have just been confirmed. "Thank you for the call, Sergeant, but that call over your radio caused Jessa to have a panic attack. You better get me a fucking escort to the hospital."

"Give me your address!"

I give it to her and then hang up. "Jessa! Where are you, baby?"

"Dude. What the fuck?" Gavin has both of his hands over his head like he's trying to keep it attached to his shoulders.

"Yeah, can you be any louder?" Damon whimpers.

"Snap the hell out of it! Jessa's parents just died in a car accident."

"Oh, my God!" Marissa appears next to Gavin and covers her mouth.

"You think it caused a panic attack," Damon says. He doesn't even need to think about it. Tia hovers hesitantly next to him. She still hasn't found her footing here. She walks on eggshells around Marissa, though the rest of us have tried to make her feel welcome.

"Yes, and I can't find her!" I nearly yell. My chest is on fucking fire. If this is how Jessa feels when she has a panic attack, I'm going to do all I can to keep them from happening because the pain is unbearable.

141

"Go get dressed. I'll call Doctor Freeman and have him meet us at Cedar. You can't go to the hospital like that," Gavin says, waving up and down my body. He's right. I'm not wearing shoes or a shirt.

"Marissa, look around the house. I'll check the parking garage," Damon commands.

"Um… do you… want me to check anywhere?" We all turn to Tia. I'm impressed she offered. She doesn't usually say a word if Marissa is around.

"Look around the pool. I have a police escort on the way. Anyone finds her before me, tell me," I order. We all split up. Gavin and Damon quickly get dressed as I'm running upstairs. Seconds later, I'm running back down the stairs.

"Doctor Freeman will meet you at Cedar," Gavin says.

"Alex! She's not down here!" Marissa flings herself at Gavin in hysterics. It's so overly dramatic, I'm convinced she's acting, but I have no time to think about that right now.

"She's not in the pool area," Tia says quietly.

"Christ!" I run for the door as the phone in my hand rings. I glance at it before quickly answering. "Damon?"

"I got her. Get down here. I'm by your car."

"Thank God. Thank fucking God!"

"Don't thank that fucker yet. I sent the elevator up. Get down here."

"I'll meet you down there," Tia says as she runs to hers and Damon's bedroom. It's then I notice she's only in one of Damon's shirts.

"Hurry," Gavin says as we all run to the elevator and pile in. As soon as it opens up into the parking garage, I sprint out of it, nearly knocking Marissa over. I run to my car, dropping next to Damon. He has Jessa in his lap and is holding her tightly. All she's wearing is the panties she fell asleep in .

"Jess?" I can feel tears prick my eyes as I run my hands through her hair. I'm shaky. I've never shown weakness. I don't panic. I don't tremble. But in this moment, I look at Damon. I don't even know what to say. What to do.

"I found her down here. She was lying face down on the ground. She's breathing, but her heart rate is out of fucking control."

"We have to get her to Cedar," Gavin says, taking the control I don't fucking have. "Damon, drive. Alex… you're gonna have to hold her in your lap, man."

It takes a second for my mind to clear. I take a deep breath and take out my phone, calling the cop who called me. I have to switch to boss mode. It's the only way to save her.

"Alex? I'm out front," Sergeant Gomez says to me.

"Come to the parking garage. Around back," I say as steadily as I can manage.

"On my way." I gently but quickly take Jessa and stand, covering her as best as I can by pressing her against me. "Follow. Close," I say to Damon. Damon nods, and I turn with Jessa in my arms and run to the garage entrance. Sergeant Gomez is waiting as she promised. I get into the back of the car. "Go. My guys are following. Take us to Cedar."

"I'll get another squad. And a blanket for her." She barks orders into her radio as she flips on her lights and sirens. She starts to step out of the car.

"No time. Just go… Come on, baby. Wake up. I'm here, Jessa." I'm whispering the words in her ear as I kiss her neck. Her carotid artery feels like it's going to burst under my lips. Sergeant Gomez closes her door and peels out. "Holy shit." I force myself to stay calm. I don't like not being in control, but Jessa needs me. Driving is out of the question. Gomez is driving like a fucking crazy person, but I have to trust her. I have no other choice. "You're okay, Jessa. I got you."

I rub her back and run my fingers through her hair, doing everything I've done in the past to get her to calm down.

"How's she doing, Alex?" Sergeant Gomez asks.

"Not good. Go faster." I feel her step on the gas. Two other officers have joined us as my crew chases after us.

"Almost there. Just hang on."

"Baby, come on. Stay with me. Please?" A few tears fall onto her neck. I hug her closer. As tightly as I can. "You're going to be okay. I promise. I'm not letting you go, baby."

"Pulling in. Where am I going?"

"The ER. Doctor Freeman should be there."

Sergeant Gomez skids to a stop in front of the ER. Doctor Freeman, waiting patiently for us, opens the backdoor to the squad.

"She's…" A sob escapes, and my arms are shaking. Doctor Freeman grabs a blanket from the stretcher, then reaches for her.

"Give her to me, Alex. Let me take care of her."

I nod as I release her slightly. Doctor Freeman wraps her in the blanket, picks her up, and puts her on a stretcher. I hurry out of the squad. "Doctor?"

"I've got her. You know you can trust me, Alex. Is she allergic to anything?"

"I… don't…" I shake my head. How could I not know? How could I not know something so fucking simple and important about the love of my life?

"Doc, go. Take care of her. We have him." Damon puts his arm over my shoulders.

I nearly collapse as Doctor Freeman takes Jessa away. Damon leads me back to the squad, and I drop to my knees. I've been trained from damn near birth to hide my emotions. Never show weakness. Never fucking cry.

Yet here I am on my knees. Sobs completely take over, and I'm an incoherent mess. Damon kneels in front of me. Gavin pulls Sergeant Gomez aside. I assume to get information on Jessa's parents.

"Hey. You did great. Bro, you got here. You held it together long enough to get her help. Just like she needed you to."

"What if…?" I can't finish the sentence. I nearly choke on my tears as I force myself up.

"Mr. Lang?" Sergeant Gomez grabs my arm, but I shake her off. I shake them all off.

"Alex," Damon says as he reaches for me. I dodge him and shake my head. I don't want to be touched. I want to know Jessa is okay.

"Don't. There's only one person that can talk him down right now. Let him go," Gavin says quietly.

He's right. There's only one person I can think of who might be able to calm me down. Make me think rationally again.

Josh.

Damon nods. He squeezes my shoulder as he walks by. "I'll get you a room." Damon hurries into the hospital, and I blindly follow, taking deep breaths.

After a few moments, he leads me to an office. He opens the door and closes it behind me, leaving me in the blissful quiet. I collapse on the chair and call Josh. I need him. I need him to bring me the fuck out of this because all I want is to storm back there and make certain she's going to be okay.

"Mmm… Alex? What's up?" His voice is sleep deprived, and I instantly remember he was on a mission. He probably just went to bed.

"Fuck. Josh. I forgot. I…" My voice cracks.

I'm fucking torn between the need to see my girl and the overwhelming sense of guilt I feel for not knowing if she's fucking allergic to anything. What the hell kind of man doesn't know that about his woman? How the fuck fucking selfish am I?

"What? Alex, what happened? Are you crying?"

"Jessa. She's…" I lose it again, putting my head on my arm on the desk.

"What about Jessa? What the hell happened?" His voice is filled with gravel and a protective edge for my girl. I knew I could count on him to help. I force a few deep breaths. He takes one of his own. "Alex. Hey, listen to me. Whatever happened, I got your back. But you have to calm down enough to talk to me."

"Her parents. They were killed in a car accident."

"Was Jess with them?"

"No. No. Thank God. She… got the call. She's in the hospital. Damon found her." I gulp in air.

"Alex, hey. What happened? She got the call and then what? Walk me through it. Like you make me do."

I nod and force myself to breathe. He's right. I have to focus. "I woke up to her phone ringing. I tried to wake her up. She wasn't in the bed. And then mine started ringing. I answered. It was the police. She told me Jessa's parents were in an accident. She'd been talking to Jess and got disconnected, so she tried calling her back. Jess didn't answer. And I just knew." I gulp in air again.

"Knew what?"

"I knew her parents didn't make it. The cop said Jessa heard over her radio that they died in the ambulance. I knew she was having a panic attack. I started to look for her. But she wasn't in the penthouse. Damon

145

found her in the parking garage next to my car. She passed out. Wasn't wearing anything but panties."

"Are you... joking? She just..."

"Wasn't thinking. All she was thinking about was getting to her parents. I couldn't wake her up, Josh."

"Are you at the hospital?"

"I got her here, yeah. Nothing I did helped. Nothing. Holding her. Telling her I'm here. She's okay. Nothing woke her up."

"She's in the best of care. She's where she needs to be."

"I was drunk. Hungover. Whatever. I didn't even feel her get out of bed. You know what a light sleeper I am."

"It's not your fault."

"It's -"

"Alex. It's... not... your... fault. You got her where she needed to be. You're getting her help. Now, maybe she'll understand she needs to take something for her anxiety."

I take another breath. "Yeah."

"That's what this is. You know that. She went into a full blown panic attack after hearing what she did about her parents. She's not like us. It's hard for her to control her emotions. With the anxiety and panic. You know that."

"You're right."

"I know I am. She's more in touch with her feelings than a normal person. You've said that yourself."

"I know. Because of her anxiety."

"I don't understand a lot of that shit. But I know you. I know you love her. I know you did all you could, and now you have to trust she'll be okay, and that they'll take care of her."

"You're right. It's all I can do."

"Do you want me to meet you there?"

"Truthfully, yeah. I do. But I haven't told her yet."

Josh is quiet a few moments. "You know I trust your judgment and support you, but you guys are really getting serious."

I rub my forehead. My headache is back full fucking force. "I know. I'll tell her. But not until after graduation. When you take over. That's always been the plan." I look up as Damon walks into the room. "I gotta go. Might have some news."

"Call or text me, okay? Let me know how she is."

"Yeah. Thanks, Josh. I love you, bro."

"Love you, too."

I hang up and Damon motions me out of the office. "Doc come out?"

"No. Not yet. I got her a private suite in VIP, and we have a private lounge." He leads me to the elevator bank and swipes a card. The elevator opens, and we step in. He hands me an ID badge.

"I'm sorry. Usually, I'm a lot more in control."

"This is different. And it's what you have a team for."

We're silent until we get up to the VIP floor. Damon nods to security, who waves us by. He leads us to the private lounge, and I sit in a chair.

"Shut the lights out. I'm fucked up enough over Jessa. I don't need fluorescent lights aggravating my hangover."

"Seconded," Gavin groans.

Tia shuts the light out and sits on the floor in a corner. She draws her knees up to her chest. Damon sits on the couch closest to her. Gavin lays on the other one and pulls Marissa down next to him.

"Tia, there's another chair. You don't need to sit on the floor," I say quietly.

"She must have been so scared when she got that call." I hear the tears in Tia's voice.

"Her anxiety isn't your fault. She's had it for longer than she's known you," I say. Over the past couple of days, I've learned quite a lot about her. She blames herself for everything.

"Tia, this has nothing to do with you. Stop crying," Marissa says, annoyed. I shoot a glare at her. She isn't helping.

"Marissa, for fuck's sake. Shut the fuck up," Damon growls. Marissa huffs. Gavin lets out a warning growl. Damon reaches down and pulls Tia into his lap. "Baby, come here. I didn't even see you down there."

"I...," She sniffles as she melts into him. "I ran to your room and grabbed her some clothes before I followed you all down to the garage...," she says to me. She wipes her eyes and gestures to the bag on the floor beside her. "If it were me, I wouldn't have been thinking about clothes if I was panicking about my parents. I wanted to make sure she had something when she woke up...," She trails off.

147

"That was a smart move, honey," Damon says, kissing her head.

"It was. Thank you," I say with a small smile. I'm grateful she thought of it. It didn't occur to me to take anything at all for her when I left. All I was thinking of was her.

She gives me a watery smile as she curls into Damon's chest.

It feels like hours go by before Doctor Freeman finally walks in the room. I nearly bolt out of my chair. "Doc?"

He holds up a hand. "She's okay. We didn't know her allergies, so we gave her Ativan, and she had an allergic reaction. We gave her Epinephrine. She's doing very well."

"Thank God. Can I see her?" I choke out.

"Yes. Absolutely. Come." Doctor Freeman leads me to Jessa's room. "I have her on Pexeva right now. I'll get her a prescription. I want to see her once a month for at least a year to make sure it's working. I'll also be checking the dosage. If it needs to be adjusted, we'll get it adjusted." He stops outside her door and turns to me, grabbing my arm. "This is important, Alex. She needs to make sure she takes this medication on schedule. She needs to take one pill every night. But if she has an attack, I'm going to give her another pill to help. She needs to keep that one with her at all times. Understand?"

"Yes, sir." I look anxiously towards the door.

"I know you're anxious, but we have to get through this before you go in there. She knows about her parents. Gavin briefed me. I wanted to tell her, so if she went into another attack, which she did, I could control it. She's distraught right now. She definitely needs you."

"Then let me in there."

"Hang on. You need to know a few things first. You've done well with her up until this point. Your scent and holding her. Making her breathe with you. Grounding her. If she has an attack, and you're with her, doing that is the best option. If it doesn't work, make sure she takes her pill, but don't let her go. Remember, holding her tightly is always the best option. That's not what all people with her condition need, but it's what she does. Sometimes, though, she'll need more. She needs to feel safe. Protected. When she has an attack, her mind will be going a million miles an hour."

"Doc, you explained that to me already."

"I know. But listen to me. When she has an attack like she did tonight, you'll have to learn how to help her. Sometimes, just hugging her isn't enough. You'll have to lay on top of her. She needs to feel you. Your weight. Almost like a weighted blanket. It'll force her to feel nothing but you. You'll have to force your breathing to be steady to steady hers. And you'll need to get her to take her pill."

"The pill. Will it help calm her heart? When I brought her in, her pulse was insane."

"You're right. It was off the charts. We got it under control, but that's why I told you what I did. If she ever gets to that point again, you need to lay on top of her. Again, that's not what everyone needs, but it's obvious it's what she does. Don't get up until she feels safe. And when she tells you she's okay, do it slow. Doing it too fast can cause her more panic. I can't stress enough, Alex. Make sure she keeps those pills with her. At all times." He opens the door to her room. "I'll get those prescriptions. I'll also talk to everyone in the lounge. We're keeping her here overnight. You are not to leave her side. If she falls asleep and wakes up without you, it can send her into another attack."

I nod as he lets me in the room, closing the door behind me. I rush to Jessa's side. "Jess?"

She looks up at me and gives me a sad smile. Her eyes fill with tears. "I'm sorry. I'm so, so sorry."

I shake my head and climb into her bed with her, pulling her close to me and wrapping her in my arms. She burrows her head into my chest and breathes me in. "Baby, shh. Just rest. Relax."

"My parents…"

"I know, Jess. I know. Shh. Just rest. Okay? I'm here. Please. Please just rest." She presses herself against me as close as she possibly can. I lovingly run my fingers through her hair.

She doesn't know it, but I need this as much as she does. I need to feel her in my arms. It's the only way I can convince myself that she's really okay.

Eventually, her breathing evens out, and I can tell she's asleep.

Over the next few hours, Jessa wakes up off and on, but the medication they gave her knocks her right back out. I doze eventually, refusing to let my girl go.

"Well, sweetheart? How do you feel?" Doctor Freeman sits on the other side of Jessa. She's laying on her back in the bed. I'm lying next to her, my hand resting on her stomach.

Jessa looks at me sadly, then at him. She shrugs and looks straight ahead. A tear escapes her eye. I lean in to kiss it away.

"Sad. I feel sad. Devastated. Empty." My stomach clenches. My heart breaks for her. Her parents were all the family she had. Other than me, Gavin, Damon, and even Marissa and Tia, she has no one. Doctor Freeman squeezes her hand as I kiss her shoulder.

Uncontrollable sobs wrack her body. I wrap my arms around her. "I'm so sorry, baby. It'll take time, honey. It'll take time to heal," I whisper in her ear.

"They left me! How could they leave me?"

She yells and screams into my chest and punches my arm. I hold her tighter as she sobs, soaking my t-shirt.

She beats on my back. I take every blow until she goes limp with her gut wrenching cries.

She bunches the fabric of my t-shirt in her hand. "How could they leave me alone, Alex? How?"

"You're not alone, Jessa." I hug her tightly, tangling my fingers in her hair. "You're not alone, baby. You have me. Us." I know she knows who I'm referring to.

I look at Doctor Freeman. For the second time in my entire fucking life, I don't know what to do. I don't know how to fix this. Doctor Freeman stands and pats me on the shoulder before he leaves the room. He doesn't need to tell me he's getting her paperwork. And he doesn't need to encourage me that I'm doing everything right. The simple gesture was all I needed.

Jessa cries the entire time Doctor Freeman is gone to get her discharge paperwork. It seems like hours, but I don't let her go. I won't.

Doctor Freeman finally comes back, and Tia follows. She's carrying my duffel bag that she threw some of Jessa's clothes in. I'm continuously grateful she thought of it. She even grabbed things for me so I could freshen up earlier.

"I brought you some clothes, sweetie," Tia says quietly.

Jessa sniffles and looks at her as she wipes her eyes. "Thank you."

"Honey, why don't you go get dressed? Let Tia help you." I kiss her lips softly. She quietly and slowly gets up. Tia leads her to the bathroom and closes the door. I sit up and run my hands over my face.

"You've been a champ through this whole thing," Doctor Freeman says quietly.

I nod. "Yeah. It hasn't been easy, but I'll do whatever she needs me to do to make it better."

"This is going to be an incredibly long road. She's really going to need your support. Her mind is going to be racing. You're going to have to take control. Get her to take things one step at a time."

"We've already decided she needs time. We're dropping classes this semester. We'll finish a semester late. Maybe even a year. Depending on what she needs."

"Wise." He hands me paperwork and her prescriptions. "Here's her discharge paperwork. It gives her direction on her prescriptions. Remember what I told you."

"I will."

Doctor Freeman nods as the bathroom door opens. He gives Jessa a soft smile. "You'll call me if you need anything, Jessa."

"Yes. I will."

Doctor Freeman turns back to me. "Take good care of her."

"Yes, sir." He turns and leaves the room. Jessa stands next to me as I stand. I cup her face in both of my hands. "Ready to go home?"

"Ready." She says the words softly as she takes my hand in hers.

We leave the hospital together. She squeezes my hand reassuringly several times. I have to chuckle because I'm supposed to be her strength. Not the other way around. But the simplistic gesture gives me confidence. She's going to be okay.

We're going to be okay.

Chapter Seventeen

☒ Josh ☒

(One Year and Eight Months Later)

"It's a problem for another day. The problem today is Alex." I stop outside my dad's partially cracked office door at the mention of my brother, making sure to stay out of sight. The fact that he just said Alex is a problem has me instantly on edge. Alex is perfect to him. The model son. In order for him to say Alex is a problem, something really bad must have happened. Something really big.

"Is this about the hot little bitch he's dating?" Keith, my dad's second in command, asks.

"She's keeping him from his duties, Keith. And you know how much that pisses me off."

I hold my breath. I know he's talking about Jessa. He's been researching her. He knows her parents died, though I question if the asshole had something to do with it. He knows she sold her father's company. Alex helped set her up with savings accounts with the money from the sale and helped her donate a large sum to a children's hospital.

Mostly, though, he knows they're together. He knows Alex is serious about her.

Alex knows that he knows they're dating. He's made it clear that she's not going anywhere and to not go anywhere near her. For some reason completely beyond my comprehension, he's followed Alex's orders. He's stayed away. I thought it was because he was counting on Alex to keep his word about taking over after he gets his degree. I guess I was wrong.

"What would you like to do?" Keith asks.

"I'll give him one chance to break it off. If he doesn't, we take both of them out. I've been patient. My patience is wearing thin with him. I'm damn near about to give Josh control. He's been doing really well."

"Thought you hated him."

"Oh, I do. I wanted to give him up, but Rebekkah refused. It's the one and only time I've ever listened to her. Won't make that mistake again."

I choke my anger down. It would be so easy to take out my gun and shoot him. But I would never make it out of this house alive. He has far too many loyal guards who would love to make me suffer. Ever since the night they beat me down, they've just been waiting for another chance. And they've gotten a few.

Instead, I shoot daggers at the door in front of me as I lean against the wall and cross my arms. I lean my head slightly to listen.

"So why give it to him?"

"Because he's my last hope. I may be forced to kill Alex and his hot little sex toy. Of course, I'll have a lot of fun with her first, and I'll make him watch. I'll have to make Josh my heir with some stipulations. He'll have to marry and have an heir of his own before I give him control. At least then I'll know the Lucinio Mafia will be in the family and safe for years to come."

"Let me know what you need. I need to get back out there. Alex's sexy bitch should be getting out of her first class soon. If you want her tailed, I gotta go."

"Another thing she fucked up. Alex should be taking control right now. He shouldn't be starting his last semester. He should have graduated already. Go."

"Yes, Mr. Lucinio."

I duck into a guest bathroom as Keith leaves the office. A few seconds later, my dad follows. I check to make sure the coast is clear before I sneak into his office. He never locks his door. He's too cocky to think anyone would dare do what I'm about to. That anyone would defy him. Betray him. He's never in his life ever had anyone dare try. What he doesn't know is I've been doing this for years. Everything he's tried to keep from me I've found.

I keep my ears in tune to anyone walking towards his office as I turn to his desk. Sitting right there is an open folder. Jessa's picture is on top. Part of me can't believe he didn't at least attempt to hide it. The other part of me knows his incredible arrogance far too well.

I leaf through the papers and photographs. There are tons. There's a daily log of her movements dating back two years.

"That's when she moved into the penthouse. What the fuck?" There's pictures of her and Alex in the rooftop pool at the penthouse. Most are focused on her. Some are close ups. There's pictures of her sleeping. Pictures of her changing. "Holy shit."

I find pictures of the night her parents died when Damon found her almost naked in the parking garage. He has close up pictures of her breasts, her panties. He has pictures of her completely naked and others of her coming out of class on campus. He has shots of her with friends.

I nearly throw up. He's obsessed. Fucking obsessed with her.

I force myself to dig further and find a picture of her and Alex on their couch in a heavy sex session. She's not wearing a shirt or anything but the panties. It's pretty obvious he's buried inside her. The picture is close enough that it's obvious her panties are see through. The picture itself is smeared with something. I look a little closer.

"Ahh… Fuck." I drop it and wipe my hands on my pants when I realize my dad was jacking off to a picture of Alex and Jessa fucking. His own fucking son and his son's girlfriend.

Who does that? Who the fuck does that? I know how messed up he is, but I never realized how fucking sick he is. I make my way out of the office and walk directly to my gym to think. I need a plan. A fool proof fucking plan. He thinks he's killing my brother or Jessa, he's got another thing coming.

"Come on, Josh. Think. You can do this. Alex tells you how fucking smart you are all the time. Time to prove him right and dad wrong."

I take off my shirt, lay on my weight bench and start lifting. I could always kill the old man. But it would cause unrest. All of his allies would come after me. And with his loyal guards, no way I'd get out of here still breathing and without being riddled with bullet holes.

No. I can't do that. It's a fucking suicide mission. His second in command, Keith, would take over and kill Jessa and Alex outright because he would want the power for himself.

Killing dad is out of the question. Without me and Alex, my mother would be left alone. No telling what the guys would do to her. Nothing would be solved.

I grunt as I put the weights back up and sit up. I need to go for a run. I step on the treadmill and start my warm up before breaking into a full run. The burn from the weights combined with the run is just what I needed to clear my head.

"Think about this, Josh. Keep that mind clear."

Would Alex tell me if the situations were reversed? If it were me with the girl? Me our father was threatening?

Probably. But I'm stronger than that. He says it all the time.

I need to deal with this myself.

"Not just Alex I need to worry about," I murmur as I run.

Jessa.

Sweet, naive Jessa. Thrown in the middle of this all because Alex fell in love and refuses to fucking tell her the truth. I never would've done that. She deserves better than that. She deserves to know the truth. To prepare. She doesn't deserve a future she only knows half of. It's too late for any of that, though. Now, my brother and an innocent girl are both in danger of being killed by a crazy old fucking man.

"Fuck!"

I really only see one way out of this. I hate what I'm about to do but it's the only way to save them. It's the only way to protect them. I drop my speed until I'm walking. Cooling down. I'm already sorry for this. Hopefully one day Alex will forgive me, and Jessa will understand.

I stop the track and jump off, stripping my pants and underwear on the way to the shower. I turn the water on and step under the hot spray. "Damn, I don't know what to do."

But I do. I know what has to be done. I'm just trying to think of any other way to achieve the same result without having to go to the depths I'm about to.

My mind races through option after option. Telling Alex. Telling him to take Jessa and run. But my father would find them. A life on the run isn't a life.

Let Alex kill my dad. Same end result. He'd be assassinated by some other boss of one of my dad's many allies. I'd die protecting him, and Jessa and my mother would be alone to fend for themselves. This mafia would be turned upside down and in utter chaos. Jessa and my mother would be sold to someone.

We could fake their deaths, but neither of them would really be able to follow their dreams. They'd still be looking over their shoulders all the time. And I'd never be able to see my brother again. Well, until my dad is gone, at least.

"Dammit!" I slam my hands against the shower wall and shut the water off. I grab a towel to dry off, then wrap it around my waist.

I walk through the gym, picking up clothing that I had stripped off along the way. I throw them in my hamper, then walk up to my bedroom in nothing but my towel.

I can hear my dad shuffling around in his office, but I avoid him and silently slip by on the way to the stairs. I take them two at a time. I close the door behind me and sit on my bed, grabbing my phone.

Josh: Hey. Any plans tonight?

I get dressed as I wait for my brother to text me back. I have no time to waste. This plan needs to get implemented immediately.

Alex: Nah. Jess is letting Marissa and Tia drag her to a club. She hasn't really been out in a while.

Josh: You aren't going? How's her anxiety?

Alex: She's fighting through it like a fucking solider. She's refusing to let it control her. Actually, the guys and I are going for pizza and beer. We're gonna watch the game. Come out with us.

156

Josh: What club are the girls going to? And what bar should I meet you guys at?

Alex: They're going to the Exchange. We'll be at Clayton's.

Josh: Good. I am glad you'll be close. Just in case she needs you.

While I am glad about that, I'm even more glad that she'll be close to make it easier for me to do what I have to do.

Alex: Yeah, with dad knowing about her, I don't really want her out of my sight.

Josh: Wish I could say you could do that. She has to be able to do things by herself, though. Live as normal of a life as possible.

Alex: Doesn't mean I have to like it. Kickoff is seven. Meet us there. We'll be at our table in the private lounge in the back. The one they always have available to us.

Josh: I'll be there.

That gives me an hour to get there. I grab my keys and hurry towards the garage.

"Josh! Get your ass in here."

Fuck.

I take a deep breath and step into the office, staying by the door. "What? I'm meeting my buddies for beer and pizza."

"Watching the game?"

"Yeah."

"I won't keep you. Your mother needs to know what you need from the store."

"Really? That's… it?" I stare at him, disbelieving.

He raises an eyebrow and laughs. "Contrary to what you may believe, son, I don't enjoy yelling at you all the time. You're a good kid. Too good for this."

What the hell is happening? Who the fuck is this guy? What's his game?

"Um… I… don't need anything from the store."

"Okay. Have a good night, son."

I leave the office confused as hell. In all of my twenty-three, nearly twenty-four years, my father has never called me son or been that nice to me. He's made yelling at me and belittling me into a fucking Olympic sport. He's never hidden how much he enjoys it.

I'm not fucking stupid, though. This has everything to do with his fucked up inheritance plan. I just don't know exactly what his play is. There is no love lost between the two of us. He can enact his stupid plan without being nice to me.

No. Something else is going on. I don't know what. But I intend to find out. But first, I have other plans that need to begin. I'm saving my brother and Jessa from his craziness if it's the last thing I do.

Unfortunately, the only option is to force a breakup. There's no way either of them will do it on their own, though. Their bond is too strong. I have no doubt Alex is going to ask her to marry him. So, I have to force it. I have to make them break up.

There's really only one way to do it, and I know both of them will probably hate me forever when they figure out what I've done. I really can't even say I care. All I care about is the two of them coming out of this alive.

If I have to sacrifice myself?

So be it.

Chapter Eighteen

✗ Jessa ✗

I sip my glass of wine as Marissa and Tia laugh at some of the dancers on the floor of the club.

"Oh my god! That guy is doing the worm! Jessa, look!" Marissa grabs my arm excitedly and points to a guy worming his way across the dance floor.

I laugh. "That's insane!"

"People are clapping and cheering him on. He's kinda cute!" Tia says. Marissa and I both laugh and shake our heads. Tia is one of my favorite people. Marissa is still a little snotty sometimes towards her, but she's starting to come around. Her and Damon are one of the cutest couples I've ever met.

"What is this? Our fifth?"

"Your fifth," I say with a smile. "You did say keep them coming!"

Marissa laughs. "I did! I definitely did!" Marissa downs her drink and stands, grabbing her fresh one the server just brought over. "Come on. Let's dance!" Marissa says as she pulls me and Tia up.

My eyes widen. "No way! I'm not going out there!"

"Yes! You are! Dance with me, Jess! Come on!" Marissa begs.

"Ugh! Fine." I grab the glass of wine I've been nursing the entire time we've been here and let Marissa drag me to the dance floor.

I'm a little light-headed, but I feel good. It's been so long since I've been able to let loose and have fun. There's no nerves tonight. Usually, when I get around a lot of people, I get anxious. I haven't been in a club in, well, ever because I'm afraid it could burn down. Or get shot up. The possibilities are truly endless.

Marissa leads me to the middle of the dance floor, and the three of us start dancing together, connected by our hands. The other people dancing next to us start to blur as Marissa spins me.

Right into someone's rock hard chest.

The contents of my glass splash out, and I can't help but look up laughing. "I'm so sorry! Oh my gosh!" I start trying to wipe the wine off his shirt, but he grabs my wrist and stops me. He takes the now empty glass from my hand and sets it on a nearby table before putting that hand at my waist to steady me as I lean into his chest.

"I'm Cole."

I giggle. "Jessa." Why do I feel like this? I've only had one glass of wine. Am I that much of a lightweight?

"I know. We have business law together. You sit behind me."

"Oh. Yeah. Sorry. I forgot." I look around for Marissa and find her dancing with Tia. Both are completely wasted. "I'm so sorry about your shirt!"

He leans in close, so I can hear him over the music. "Don't worry about it. Glad you're drinking white wine tonight. Red wine on a white T-shirt would have sucked."

I can't help but laugh as we dance. "Thank God! Otherwise it might look like you murdered someone!"

We both laugh as he pulls me a little closer. I smile and breathe him in. He smells like my spilled wine, but there's something very masculine about his spicy, woodsy scent. Protective. And he's definitely attractive. Tall and muscular.

He's steady.

I shake my head like I'm coming out of a daze and look up at him just as a pair of strong hands grip my arms. Hard. Tight. I nearly scream as I'm yanked away, slamming into a hard body. Harder than anything I've ever felt. So muscular, I'm not convinced it isn't steel.

"Hey, man! What the hell is your problem?" Cole takes my hand and tries to pull me back to him.

"My problem? My problem is your hands all over my girl. Back the fuck off if you know what's good for you."

"Alex?" I look up, gasping, and Alex's eyes are on fire. He's glaring at Cole and looks like he might actually punch him. I don't think I've ever seen him so angry. I quickly turn to him, fighting dizziness.

Oh God, what's wrong with me? My heart leaps into my throat, and I forget all about the dizziness. *Did he see me enjoying dancing with Cole so closely?*

I clear my throat. "Babe, it's okay. Really. Cole is just a friend. He's in our business law class."

"Looked more than friendly to me," Alex growls.

Cole looks at me, concern filling his features. I give him a soft smile, and he relaxes, but only slightly. "I'll see you in class Monday," he says tightly.

"I'll be there!" I say, trying to be as cheerful as possible. Cole glares once more at Alex before he turns and walks away.

Alex, still gripping my arm tightly, pulls me off the dance floor and outside to the alley. "Alex! Stop!" I yank myself free and rub my arm where his fingers were. "You're hurting me! What is the matter with you?"

"With me? Jess, that guy had his fucking hands all over you, and you're asking me what's the matter with me?" He backs me against the wall of the building. "I never want to see that again. Do you understand me?" His fingers dig into my hips as his eyes burn into mine.

"I…" I'm so confused. Alex has never acted like this before. Ever. Something is wrong. Tears sting my eyes as he pins me tightly between his body and the wall.

"Do you… understand me?"

"Alex, you're hurting me. Please let go." He loosens his grip on my waist but only slightly. He's still very much in control of me.

"Answer the question, Jessa."

"Yes! I understand, okay? I understand." He drops his hands completely and takes a step back as my chest tightens and I gasp for air. He reaches out to tuck my hair behind my ear. I flinch. Never ever have I flinched when Alex has touched me. Or tried to.

He drops his hand. "You shouldn't be drinking while you're taking anxiety pills anyway. It says it right on the damn bottle."

"I'm… sorry."

"Get your ass in there and tell the girls you want to go home. You've had enough to drink."

I look up at him, trying to understand what's going on, but I can't. The alcohol is taking effect, and I really do feel like I've had enough. Though, I still don't understand how one has fucked me up so much. Is it because of the anxiety pills? Is that why I'm not supposed to drink with them?

Alex turns and walks down the alley without a glance over his shoulder at me. "I mean it, Jessa. Go home." I watch him stuff his hands in his jeans pocket as his head drops and his shoulders droop.

The tears threatening to fall burst from my eyes like a damn. I hurt him. I was dancing with someone else. I can't even claim it was innocent. I liked having Cole's hands on me. They felt real. Like… like Alex's used to feel. Before things started changing between us. I don't even know what's happening, but I feel like there are just so many secrets he's keeping.

I furiously wipe my eyes and compose myself before I walk back into the club in search of Marissa and Tia.

I see Cole standing near our table looking more than a little concerned. "Jessa, are you okay?"

"Yeah, um…" I scan the dance floor for Marissa and Tia. "I'm just… ready to go home. I was looking for Tia and Marissa."

"The girls you were with just left. They saw your boyfriend, and I guess figured he'd take you home."

"Oh. Um…" My heart starts to beat a little faster and I close my eyes.

"Jessa? What happened? Are you okay? He seemed pissed."

I look up at him and force a smile. My head is more than a little hazy, and I'm starting to feel nauseated. "I just… I take medication for anxiety. I shouldn't have drank. Alex was upset about it. Rightfully so, because I feel like shit."

He looks like he doesn't believe me, but I don't care. I very suddenly need to leave. The nausea has turned to something else. Something far more urgent. I turn for the door and nearly run to it. I have to get out. My stomach is relocating into my mouth.

162

"Jessa?" Cole follows me as I flee. I barely make it outside before I'm suddenly losing what little contents are in my stomach all over a nearby bush. Cole holds my hair. "Christ, Jessa." After a few minutes, I shakily stand. Cole steadies me. "Why don't you call your boyfriend? Have him come get you?"

"I'll just take a cab. It's fine. They're watching the game. I don't want to bother them."

"Watching the game? Then he has to be close if he can just show up here, bitch at you, and then leave." He's angry and frustrated. I look up at him. He shakes his head. "Come on. I'll take you home."

"Cole, really. It's fine. I'll take a cab." I turn to hail a cab and stumble. Cole catches me before I fall.

"Jessa, please. Let me just make sure you get home safe. If you don't want to get in a car alone with me, fine. I'll hail a cab. But I am not going to just let you get in one by yourself and trust you to get home okay. I'll go with you. So, a cab, or my car. Your choice."

He looks so sincere and concerned as he looks down at me. "Okay. You can take me home."

"Cab or car?"

Everything around me looks so hazy. My head feels heavy. I feel like I'm going to pass out. "Car."

I lean heavily on him as he leads me to his car. He helps me in, then gets in himself. He starts driving. I give him my address, then lean against the glass and close my eyes.

Before I know it, Cole is gently shaking me awake. "Hey. You're home. Give me your phone. I want to put my number in it."

"Oh. Um…." I'm not sure what to say, so I bite my lip.

"Jessa, I just want to make sure you're okay. And that you have someone you can trust to contact if you need help. My major is Criminology. I'm trying to be a cop. You can trust me." I nod and hand him my phone. He quickly puts his number in and hands it back to me. "Do you want me to walk you to your apartment?"

I give him a soft smile as I look at him. "I'll be okay. The security is really good."

He smiles back, then gets out. He helps me out and walks me to the front door. "Text me, okay? Just so I know you got up there."

"Okay." I let myself in and stumble my way to the elevator.

"You okay, Ms. Holloway? Need an escort up?" the night security guard asks me.

"Um… yeah. Actually that might be wise. I'm… definitely not feeling well."

"Okay. Sure thing." The security guard grabs a key card and makes his way to me. He guides me to the elevator and helps me in. He swipes his card for the top floor, and the elevator begins moving. I groan and grab the railing. "Rough night?"

"Many mistakes were made. The first of which was going out at all. The second of which was drinking while on medication."

The elevator lurches to a stop, and I put a hand to my mouth as my stomach threatens to rebel again.

"Well, let's get you off this elevator. I would hate for it to be the reason you lose what's left of the alcohol in your system."

"And you'd prefer not being thrown up on."

We both laugh. "Going home with a clean uniform would be preferable." He smiles as he walks me to my door and waits as I let myself in. "Have a good night, Ms. Holloway."

I smile. "Thank you."

I make my way upstairs and take off my clothes, intending to take a shower. Only, I don't make it that far. The haziness impacting my vision finally overtakes me.

With what's left of my willpower to stay awake, I take out my phone to text Cole as I promised.

Jessa: I'm crawling into bed. Thank you for getting me home.

I crawl under the covers and sink into the soft mattress.

Cole: Good. Get some rest. Text me tomorrow.

I smile as my head hits my pillow. The events of the past few hours blur until they become nothing. I drift into an incredibly restless sleep.

Chapter Nineteen

⚔ Alex ⚔

When I wake up the next morning, I realize I forgot to shut the shades to our bedroom windows. The sun pouring through the floor to ceiling windows and beating against my eyes is a type of pain I'm not prepared to deal with.

"Fuck, I need to stop drinking." I keep my eyes squeezed tightly shut as I blindly reach for the remote for the blinds. Through squinted eyes, I find the button and push it. The shades close, plunging the room into a peaceful darkness.

I roll onto my side and drop my hand to Jessa's hip. I softly run my fingers just below her stomach and pull her close to me. She wiggles against me, and a soft moan leaves her lips.

I smile into her hair and drop my fingers lower along her smooth skin. She shaves. I've always loved that she shaves. She hates the feel of hair on her pussy. It makes her itch and feel dirty. Neither feeling is enjoyable for her.

"I'm really sorry for last night," she murmurs.

I smile into her hair and pull her closer. When I got home, she was laying on top of the blankets and whimpering in her sleep. She kept apologizing to me and said she felt like shit. She'd never drink with her anxiety medication again, and something about a kid in our Business Law class who was nice to her and took her home. I didn't understand a lot of what was happening because I was fucking drunk myself, but the part I did get was that she only had one drink and it made her feel like shit.

"It's done and over. Lesson learned," I tell her as I kiss her neck.

Jessa melts into me. Whatever tension she was feeling is gone. She pushes even more against me, spreading her legs just a little. I hiss because her ass is flush against my cock. I could move just slightly, and my dick would slide into her pussy.

I don't need to, though. Jessa moves and reaches between us, guiding me into her hot and wet as fuck center. My mind damn near blanks. My girl has never not told me what she needs, but this feels slightly different. She pushes back against me, silently begging for me to thrust.

But it's more than that.

As I give her what she wants, she's already trembling. It's like she's asking me to forgive her, but for what, I can't be sure. Fucking up and drinking while she's on medication? She doesn't drink. She hates the taste of alcohol. Even when we went out or had beer at the house, she always had something without alcohol in it. She doesn't even like champagne.

I don't know what possessed her to drink anything last night, but if forgiveness is what she needs, I'll gladly give it to her.

"I forgive you, baby. You don't need to worry. It's over." I hug her tighter and thrust harder, deeper, and faster.

She melts even more. I hold her with one arm and grip her thigh with my other hand, hooking it over mine. I pound in her pussy with the intensity she obviously needs from me. She grips my arms and arches. I nip, lick, and suck her neck as I slide my hand between her thighs, pressing my thumb against her clit and rubbing to the rhythm of my thrusts.

"Alex! Yes!" She screams and whimpers at the same time. It sounds so sexy, I can't help the low growl that comes from deep within.

"Fuck, Jess."

Her pussy clenches so tightly around me, my cock feels ten times bigger and thicker than it is. And I know I'm already twice the average size. Her erratic pulsing around me as I drive into her is hurling me closer and closer to a release we both desperately need. Her thighs tremble uncontrollably. I bite down on her neck and suck hard, leaving my mark on her with a possessive rumble.

"Alex!" She comes hard and without a lot of warning. Her walls collapse around me and squeeze tightly, almost wrenching my own orgasm from me.

That familiar pleasure jolts down my spine. My dick twitches. The sudden realization that I'm not wearing a condom races through my mind. Just before I spill everything I have into her sweet, tight pussy, I pull out and shoot stream after stream of my come over her ass and thighs with a low groan.

"Jessa. Jesus fuck, baby girl."

"Mmm…"

After several moments of catching our breath, I gently untangle myself from her and head for the bathroom. I quickly clean up and bring a warm cloth out for her. She smiles softly as I gently clean her up. When I finish, I head back to the bathroom and rinse the cloth. After hanging it next to the one I used, I bring out Aspirin and water.

I sit next to her and kiss her forehead. "Take these and drink the water."

She turns and sits up slowly, doing as I tell her. "Thank you."

I stand up and walk to our dresser. I grab a pair of boxer briefs for myself and put them on. I tuck myself away and grab a pair of panties for her. I toss them to her as she stares at me.

"Are you… not coming back to bed? It's so early."

I close my eyes. I want to tell her, but I can't. I have a meeting with my father regarding my future with the Lucinio mafia. He wants an answer on if I am going to break up with Jessa and take over or not. And he wants that answer by today.

First thing.

"I have a meeting, baby. I'm sorry. I'll be back in a few hours."

I don't look at her because if I do, I'll cave. I've kept this from her for way too long at this point. I need to tell her. She deserves to know the truth. She deserves to know the danger she's in. The threat from my dad.

But I have a plan to keep her safe. I always have a plan.

I've been thinking long and hard about everything, and I came up with a solution that I think my dad will go for.

Italy.

We have factions in Italy and legit businesses that could use some help organizing. With my new degree, or soon to be, I have incredible ideas. I also have a branch of Lucinio Tech there. It's my company. I can fully take it over and still have Ryan's guidance. I could make the branch in Italy the official corporate office.

I make my way to my car and jump in, driving to the house.

My plan is to get him to let Josh take over our US factions while I run the factions overseas. It would allow me to keep Jessa away from him. And when control is given to Josh completely, I can get totally out and give him absolute control. That was always the plan.

Of course that last part is something my dad doesn't need to know. Ever. When Josh takes over, he won't have any say on what happens anyway. It will all be Josh's call.

It only takes me about twenty minutes to get to the house. There's hardly any traffic at this hour on a Sunday in L.A. At least not enough to cause a traffic jam and piss me off even more than I already am.

When I walk in, I smell sizzling bacon and waffles. I walk directly to the kitchen and see my mom dancing around the counter. I can't help but laugh.

"Alex!" She rushes to me and throws her arms around me, squeezing me as tightly as she can.

"Mmm… mom. Can't breathe," I say with a grin as I hug her just as tightly.

She laughs and loosens her grip, but doesn't let go. "I'm making your favorite. Josh said you'd be here this morning for breakfast."

"I did. And see? I delivered!" I grin as Josh appears and joins in the hug, sandwiching our mom between us.

"My two babies. I couldn't ask for anything more." She melts into the two of us and enjoys the hug.

I pat Josh on the back. "You seem happy today."

"Incredibly."

After letting mom go, we each grab plates and silverware to set the table with. When we get to the dining room, I turn to Josh. "You take that pretty brunette we met at Clayton's last night home?"

He grins, and his eyes sparkle. It's all the answer I need. "We went to her place. She was amazing. Fucking wild."

I laugh as we set the table. "Son of a bitch. I knew you'd have fun with her."

"Best I ever had. Not kidding." He waggles his eyebrows, and I laugh. "Seriously, though. It was a good night. I had fun with everyone. I feel like I haven't seen you all in years."

He isn't wrong. We haven't been able to hang out as much as we'd like to, but we make as much time as we can to spend with each other. Josh is just as much family to Gavin and Damon as I am. They miss him as much as me sometimes. We both share a look of disgust and shut our mouths as our father walks in the room.

"What are you two talking about?" He grumbles as he sits. "Where the fuck's the coffee?"

"Coming. I'll grab it," Josh says, quickly darting back to the kitchen.

"I'll see if mom needs any help," I say, following him.

"Ungrateful fucking brats." He says it low in his throat, but we both hear it. We meet each other's eyes and shake our heads as we walk into the kitchen.

"What the hell is his problem today? He's in a fucking mood," I say.

"I don't know, but he seems more grumpy than usual. Funny, because he was being really nice to me yesterday."

"He was out doing surveillance until late last night. He didn't get home until after one in the morning," mom answers, keeping her voice low.

Josh looks as surprised as I feel. "What's happening?" he asks.

Mom says nothing as she takes the bacon and waffles. She scurries out of the room without another word. Josh and I both stand in the kitchen looking after her. After a few moments, I glance at him before taking the orange juice. He grabs the coffee pot and my dad's favorite cup.

"What the fuck? What am I about to walk into?" I ask Josh.

"Your guess is as good as mine. I had no idea he was doing surveillance last night. He didn't say shit to me about it, but it explains why the hell he was being so nice."

"He wanted to keep it away from you."

"If it's what I think it is, he probably knows I'd go to you."

Jessa.

I follow him out of the kitchen and take my place to the left of my father. I bite my tongue to keep from saying anything. I don't know what the hell is going on, but I have a feeling I'm not going to like it.

We all eat a few minutes in silence before my dad clears his throat. "Alex, there's a reason I asked you to break up with Jessa, and it's not for the reasons you think," he begins. I scoff, a forkful of waffle halfway to my mouth. I glare at him as I continue eating. Mom refuses to look at any of us. Josh is watching him cautiously. Dad slides a folder to me. "It was sent here. By an ally."

I take the folder, glancing at Josh. He gives me a small shrug, confusion written all over him. Whatever this is, he doesn't know about it. I look down and open it. There's pictures of Jessa walking to class, walking into our apartment, cleaning her parent's house.

"What the actual fuck? An ally? What the hell kind of ally, dad?" I ask. The anger that was simmering is quickly reaching my boiling point.

"I realize how it looks, but hear me out," dad says. "These were found by a guard they have undercover within a rival crew. The guard recognized you in one of the pictures and, thankfully, took the file. He gave it to his boss who gave it to me."

I stare at him incredulously. Josh looks like he's about to be sick. "You actually want me to believe that some random gang is after my girlfriend? Are you fucking crazy?" I start to stand, but he grabs my arm. I meet his eyes, mine on fire.

"No. I don't expect you to believe that. They're after you. And they'll go to any lengths to get to you." He looks at the file, then back up at me. "Including through her, Alex. Jessa is in danger. Serious danger."

I stare venomously at the file in front of me, trying to decide what the hell to do with the information. Part of me wants to believe this is some fucked up scheme. The other part almost believes it's true. I'm the heir to a powerful fucking mafia, as far as everyone in our world believes. This kind of shit is what happens. It's the exact reason I want fucking out.

"We have a team dealing with this, son, but this isn't the only time this is going to happen. People will be gunning for you just because of who you are. And they'll stop at nothing."

"It's... just something you need to be prepared for," my mom says quietly, speaking her first words since we sat down.

"And prepare her for," my father says quietly.

I hate that he's right. That I could've let this even happen. I need to be more vigilant. This shit can't happen again. It should have never fucking happened in the first place. I get up and start clearing the dishes without a word.

No goddamn way am I letting Jessa get hurt. No way am I ever getting caught off guard like this again. We only have a couple more months until we graduate. After that? I'm done with L.A. I'm taking Jessa away from all this bullshit. Somewhere I control the situation. Not my father. I take a deep breath and turn to head back to the dining room.

Dad is standing right behind me. "I know you're upset -"

"Italy."

"What?" he asks, and I relish in the fact that he's caught as off guard as I just was.

Fucking good. I look him directly in the eye, standing to my full height.

"Italy. I want Italy. I'll take over the overseas operation. You give Josh the US. That's the deal. You can take it, or I walk. I'll take Jessa with me, and you'll never see me again. We'll disappear and you'll have no choice but to give control of everything to Josh. You want my help? That's the fucking deal."

Dad watches me, but I don't flinch. It's a plan I've already told Josh. He's on board. I can see the calculation going on behind dad's eyes, but I know I've won. I know he knows I'm serious and this is the only way he'll get me to take any part of his precious mafia over.

"Fine."

"It means you stay the fuck away from her."

"Alex, for Christ sake. Do you honestly think I want anything bad to happen to her? When I told you she was going to get hurt, this…" He holds up the folder. "This is what I fucking meant. Okay? I know I've failed as your father, but I do care at least a little bit. An innocent girl doesn't deserve to be in this situation. And that's something you would have and need to fucking think through." He drops the folder on the counter and walks away.

After a couple of seconds, Josh walks in. "You know he has a plan," Josh says.

"Yeah."

"I'm sorry if you feel like I am failing you. I'm doing everything I can to run interference but...," He trails off as he turns back to the dining room. "You and I both know there's more going on here. Just... watch your back. Okay? " He disappears back to the dining room.

"Yeah. Always," I say to his retreating back. I grab the folder and stride out of the house. I've had enough of my father for one day.

I only have a couple more months before I can get her the hell out of here. And get her away from whatever mess my dad has her in. I'm not fucking stupid. I know these pictures weren't taken by some random gang. But some small part of me has to wonder if he's telling the truth.

My only hope right now is that Jessa will understand why I kept the truth from her for so long and come to Italy with me.

Marry me.

Because if she doesn't, all of this has been a waste of time.

Chapter Twenty

⚔ Josh ⚔

(One Month Later)

The past month has been absolute hell for me. I've been running myself into the ground trying to foil my dad's stupid plans and trying to get Jessa to break up with Alex. She's doing exactly what I want her to and running into the arms of some other guy. Her friend. Cole or something. I've done my research. He wants to be a cop. The hope is he can keep her away from the dark side of this world. The side Alex and I live in.

Truthfully, I know Jessa is happy with Alex. And I know Alex is in love with Jessa. But Jessa seems very content and relaxed with Cole. It doesn't take much to see it. He makes her laugh. She's carefree with him. I catch her looking at him out of the corner of my eye sometimes when I'm surveilling her. She blushes furiously when he turns to her and catches her in the act. He does exactly the same thing.

Above everything, though, I hate keeping this from Alex. He's my twin. I hate playing him and making him out to be an asshole. He's everything but. Alex would never do the things to Jessa that I have. All things that make my stomach turn. I keep telling myself it's for the best, but I hate every damn second of it. I probably don't have to do anything more. It's obvious she's falling for Cole. But I can't leave anything to chance. Especially something this important. She needs to be driven to him and crash. Hard.

I truly hope they forgive me someday. But this has to happen. Alex will never give Jessa up willingly. He doesn't understand that he has to. There is no other option. This is the only way to protect him. To protect both of them.

To Alex, dad has agreed to let him take over Italy. He agreed to let Alex and Jessa live happily ever after. Alex already bought the tickets and intends to surprise Jessa with the trip after graduation. While there, his plan is to come clean. He hopes she'll understand and forgive him and accept his marriage proposal.

What he doesn't know is that dad has other plans. Plans that involve Jessa. Plans that involve Alex's untimely demise. He wants Jessa for himself. And he's sick of Alex ruining his plans of making him take control. It doesn't matter if I tell Alex what I found out or not. It's not going to help either way. He'll never be able to simply disappear with her. He'll always be found. And he'll always need to be ready to run.

That is why my plan needs to go off perfectly. Alex needs to go to Italy without Jessa. Because if he brings Jessa, dad will follow and will kill him. In order to save them both, I have to separate them. I have to show my dad that Jessa is out of the picture. That Alex is living up to his end of their deal to take over all of the overseas operations. I have to make him see that Jessa is no longer in the middle. That she's gone.

If I have to go to extreme lengths to hide her, I'll do it. I'll do whatever I have to do to make sure they're both safe. Because I sincerely doubt my father won't still attempt to go after her. He just doesn't know I'll always be watching his every move. Alex and Jessa will be safe, but they need to be apart.

It's obvious to me why I'm so protective of Alex. He's my brother. My twin. The literal other half of me. He'd do the same for me. Go through the same extremes. Hell. He has. He's always protected me. Now, it's my turn.

What surprised the ever living fuck out of me was how much I suddenly started caring for Jessa. When I approached her at the club, my intention was to scare her. Make her think Alex has a temper. A side that he's never shown her. A controlling, rough, obsessive side.

What I didn't plan for is how much it would physically hurt me to see the pain on her face as I dug my fingers into her hips. The confusion. The hurt I had caused her. I didn't expect to feel anything at all. I didn't intend to get so close to her. I didn't intend for her scent to fill me and calm me as it fucking did.

"Goddammit." I scrub my hands over my face as I stay hidden in the shadows.

Jessa is with a study group in the library on UCLA's campus. I put a track on her phone, so I know where she is at all times. I've intercepted her a few times. Each time, my behavior as Alex has only gotten worse. I can tell she's becoming more and more fearful of him. Every time I try to touch her, she flinches.

The kisses, though. I shouldn't have kissed her the first time. It was so wrong, but I felt so bad for hurting her the way I did. I felt like I had to make it up to her in some way. I didn't think of anything more than that. I just crushed my lips to hers. Anything to make the tears I'd caused stop. To make my heart start beating again. Her pain slayed me.

Holy shit, the way she tasted. The way she felt against me. The way she responded. It took everything in me to stop.

I almost quit everything right then. I almost called Alex and both confessed my plan and what I had done, as well as told him everything about dad's plan.

I didn't because I know the end game. I have tried to talk to him many times about everything. But dad's flat out lies he feeds him daily further my conviction that I *am* doing the right thing. He's showed Alex several of the pictures he took of Jessa. He says they're from that gang and his ally's give them to him just to make it look like she's still in danger.

Such a fucking lie.

So, I'm continuing with my plan. And it's working like a damn charm. Not much longer and I truly believe Jessa will be ready to break up with Alex. It'll hurt both of them like hell, which will kill me, but this is the right thing to do. It has to be done.

I watch as Jessa laughs quietly and leans into Cole. It actually hurts a little to see her so comfortable with him. To see the subtle touches of their legs or feet under the table.

She lays her hand on his arm, like she's hugging him, just before she stands. She heads towards an aisle near me. This study group is for her Business Law class, so I made sure I'm near that section of the library. Alex is also in this class, but his study group is meeting at someone's house. I really lucked out that they were in two different groups working on two different projects. It made it far easier on me, and I silently thank their professor every day for doing pre-assigned groups.

I duck deeper into the shadows and walk along the backside of the library until I reach the aisle she's in. Stealthily, I walk up beside her and roughly grab her arm. She drops the book, but I catch it and drag her to a dark, quiet corner.

"Alex, you're hurting me." She whispers and whimpers and tries to pull away, but I grip her arm tighter and shove her against the wall. I hate hurting her. I hate that she fears me like this. "Alex, please. You're hurting me. What are you doing here?" she whispers.

"Do I need a reason to see my girlfriend? Looks like I got here just in time anyway."

"What? What are you talking about?"

"I thought I told you to stay away from fucking Cole?"

Her lip quivers and she bites it to keep from crying. "You know it's not my fault I have to be in this group with him." Her voice cracks.

My heart breaks for her, but this is for her own good. I steel myself against the tears forming in her eyes. They're like my kryptonite. I have to be tougher than that.

"Are you fucking him?" I growl in her ear.

"That's not fair. You know I've only ever been with you. Please let me go."

"Do I know that? You look pretty damn cozy with him. Touching his leg with yours. Playing fucking footsie under the table. You think I didn't see the hug?"

"Alex, please, please let me go. You're h-hurting me." She chokes down a sob.

I press my body harder against hers and let myself feel her. Feeling her is the only way I'm going to get through this because I feel more and more like an asshole every time I'm near her. I need her to remind me of the reason I'm doing this.

"Prove it. Prove I'm the only one you want." My lips are less than an inch from hers. Her hands are on my chest, and she pushes against me, but I don't move.

"Alex, please. I have to get back." She's still talking quietly, not wanting anyone to hear. I push harder against her, my lips brushing hers as I whisper to her. I see the tears she's been fighting start to fall. I fight hard to keep from gently kissing them away.

"So, you can get back to flirting? Letting him touch you?" I roughly grab her tits and inadvertently moan. I was absolutely not expecting her to feel that good underneath my palms.

Shit.

Holy shit.

My dick is instantly hard, and I push my hips into her.

I can't help it. I can't stop myself. It's been far too long since I had a woman under me. I haven't had time since the night of the game with Alex, Gavin, and Damon. The night I first started this dangerous game I'm playing. I run my hands down her sides to her ass and squeeze.

"Please... Please don't do this. There's nothing going on."

I force a glare instead of the want I know is shining in my eyes. I want her.

Part of me feels like a backstabbing asshole. Alex doesn't deserve this. Fuck. She doesn't either.

But that is not the part that's in control. It's the other part.

The part that needs to feel her lips.

Her body.

"Please don't."

I can't help it. My lips meet hers, and I kiss her long and hard until she melts into me. Until she whimpers and moans for me.

"Say you're mine." I need to hear those words. Even if they're a damn lie. I grind against her. My dick is so hard, I almost whip it out.

But she deserves better than that.

"Please, please stop..."

Tears are rolling down her face as she tries to push me off her. I continue squeezing her ass and pulling her into me. God, she feels so fucking good.

"Say it, Jessa. Or is it Cole you want? You want Cole to touch you like this? Is it him you want to fuck? His dick you want to touch?"

"No! No. You. I only want you."

"You're mine." I let her go because if I don't, I'm going to lose control. I already feel like I am. Like I'm not the man I am when I'm around her.

She drops to the floor in silent sobs. I shake my head, clearing the fog. I don't even know where that came from. Or why I suddenly have an intense as fuck headache. I look down at Jessa. She's trying so hard not to draw attention. I quietly thank her for that. In my mind, though, I'm kicking myself for hurting her like this. For putting her through this.

I kneel in front of her. "Fucking say it."

She hugs herself, her small hand clutching her throat. She gasps for air as she cries.

Fuck.

I went too far this time. My heart constricts. Like she's reached into my chest and is squeezing it with all of her strength. I didn't mean to cause a panic attack.

"I'm yours. Always yours," she whispers.

I pull her up and wipe her tears away, giving her a sweet kiss. I hug her and sway gently with her until I feel her breathing start to even out. I may need to act like an asshole to get her to break up with Alex, but not even I can let her suffer like this through a panic attack that I caused. I hold her, letting her feel me breathe to steady hers. I want to apologize, but I can't. Fuck I wish I could.

"Did you bring your pills?" I ask her quietly, keeping my grip tight. She nods into my chest. "Good." Thank fucking Hell for small favors.

"Jessa?"

Fucking Cole.

I fucking need him for her, but I don't have to like it for a damn minute. Jess jumps and looks up at me, pure terror in her eyes. She's silently asking me for permission to leave and go back to her study group. It's permission she should never need to ask for. But if I'm going to make this work, I have to be the borderline abusive, absolutely overly possessive dickhead I'm portraying.

I give her a smile, making sure my eyes portray warning and danger if she disobeys me and gets too close. "Go. Remember what I said. You're fucking mine. Go take your pill."

She nods and wipes her eyes as she hurries towards Cole's voice. I follow but duck into a different aisle. I have to at least make sure she's okay.

I rub my temples as I listen and fight a wave of nausea. I push back the jealousy I feel for my brother. Jealousy that never used to be there and has no fucking place in my life. I have nothing to be jealous about.

"Hey. Are you okay? What happened?" Cole asks her quietly.

"I… just had a panic attack. I don't know why. It was dark back here. My mind just went haywire a second. I'm so sorry."

"Hey. No. Don't be. Let's get you out of here, okay? I'll take you home."

"Really?"

"Of course, sweetie. Go to my car, so they don't see you like this. I'll grab your stuff and get you a cup of water for your pill."

"Thank you, Cole."

"No need. That's what friends are for. Now go. Hurry up."

I hate myself for what I just did to her. I feel like such a dick. But I have to remember that if I don't do this, both her and my brother will be killed. This is for the best.

I take a deep breath and head to my car. No matter how wrong it is, I can't stop thinking of the way she feels against me. Her mouth moving against mine is like nothing I've ever felt. The way she melts into me when I kiss her is such a turn on.

I'm betraying my brother right now, but I can't help it. Jessa is intoxicating. I can't get enough of her. Jessa is sweet, beautiful, sexy, smart. She's truly the entire package. I can see why Alex loves her. He's lucky. He's so fucking lucky.

I can't help but wonder where I would be if our roles had been reversed. What if I had been the first born? Would it be me dad had been training to take over? Would I have wanted to break away and go to college? Me with Jessa?

Alex has always had everything so easy. He's always had everything handed to him on a diamond fucking platter. He didn't grow up with a silver spoon. He's been given the entire damn collection.

I've never hated my brother. I've never been jealous of him. But fuck, it's hard sometimes. Especially lately. I know it's not even his fault, but all I feel recently is this dark jealousy.

Anger.

All emotions I've never felt before towards my brother.

"I have to get the hell out of my head," I whisper as I sneak out of the library. I know just how false everything I'm thinking is. There's no room for anger, jealousy, or resentment towards my brother. None at all.

I decide to head to the cliffs. A jump will set me straight. Clear my head. I need that right now. My job is to protect Alex and Jessa. That's it. I shouldn't be doing something stupid like having feelings I shouldn't be. Or catching feelings for a woman I have no business feeling anything for.

Even though I do.

Fuck me. I'm fucked. So fucked.

I park my car and quickly strip down to my underwear. Before I even allow myself to think anymore, I take a running start and leap off the cliff. I soar through the air and close my eyes right before I hit the water.

"Fuck, yes. This is exactly what I needed." I flip to my back and backstroke leisurely to the shore. I growl as my thoughts war with each other, though, because that's the point of the jump. To stop this shit. And then they land on Jessa like she's honey, and they're the bees.

I want Jessa like I've never wanted another woman before. Her scent is intoxicating. Her moans are addictive. Her body is downright sinful. I want it all.

But I hate the fact that I'm betraying my brother to keep them safe. I hate that I barely see my brother. I really fucking hate that my brother, my fucking twin brother, plans on abandoning me.

Fucking hell. I growl as I dive back into the water. I stay under until I have to come up for air.

I have no idea how I really feel about any of this anymore. How un-confident I am in my own fucking plan.

And that lack of confidence is what scares the hell out of me.

Chapter Twenty One

✗✗ Jessa ✗✗

What's happening? What the hell is going on with Alex? He's never been like this! He's always so sweet and protective. He's never rough with me or hurtful. He's never jealous! He told me to stay away from Cole, but after we talked about it, he seemed fine with it. He even talks to him in class.

I start sobbing uncontrollably. I can't hold it back anymore. I'm so confused. I don't understand what's happening to him. To us!

I nearly jump out of my body when Cole opens the driver's side door and slides in.

"Jesus Christ, Jessa. What the fuck happened to you?"

I can only shake my head as I try to catch my breath. I vigorously wipe at my tears, but they keep falling.

"Jessa, look at me. Please?"

I gulp in air, but I can't get enough. I need more.

Cole gently takes my hand with one of his and puts the other on my cheek, softly turning my face so that I'm looking at him. "Jessa. Honey, talk to me. Tell me what you need from me."

"My pill." I squeeze my eyes shut, praying for this to end or for a swift death.

Cole reaches for my purse on the floor and digs for my pills. I let out another strained cry and throw my head back on the seat. I don't understand. I just don't.

Cole takes one of my hands and holds it tightly while putting my pill in the other hand. I shakily bring it to my mouth. He hands me a small, plastic cup of water that he had put into the cup holder. I bring it to my lips, but my hand is shaking so badly, some of it sloshes onto my lap.

Cole puts his hand over mine to steady me and helps with the water. When I finally get the pill down, he takes the cup from my hand and tosses it into the back seat.

"Sweetie, what the fuck happened?"

I look at him. I see the very moment he sees how scared I am, how panicked, reflected in his eyes. He takes a deep, calming breath before bringing both of my hands to his chest. He forces my fingers to splay over his heart, then puts his hands over mine so that I can feel his breathing and his heartbeat.

"Close your eyes, Jessa. Focus on this. My heartbeat."

I close my eyes. On top of my hands, his fingers tap out the rhythm of his heartbeat. After a few more agonizing minutes, my heart rate begins to match the steady rhythm of his. The trembling and shaking subside. My throat feels like it's opening. My lungs inflate.

"Thank you, Cole." I whisper the words and slowly open my eyes.

"You feel okay enough for me to let go?"

I nod. He slowly lets go of my hands, and I quietly put my hands in my lap. He continues to look at me, though. I know he wants an answer.

"Sweetheart, what happened? Was it another fight with Alex?"

I nod and look down at my hands. Cole has been the only person I've been able to talk to about Alex. Marissa thinks I'm crazy, and Gavin and Damon are like brothers to him. Tia told me that I could always talk to Damon about this. But there's no way they'd listen to anything I have to say about him. I told her that I would talk to him just so she would drop the subject. She hasn't mentioned it again, so I think she believed me. I know she doesn't believe that Alex would do anything he has been either. I don't even believe it.

"He's just crazy jealous of you, Cole."

"He seems cool with me in class."

I shrug. "I thought he was. But he got so angry when he saw me in there with you."

"What? He was in there? Where? I thought he was with his own study group."

"So did I. But he said he came to check on me. And saw me touch you." I don't tell him how violent he got with me. The way he grabbed me. Instead, I look out the window.

"Jess, come to my place tonight. I don't want you around him if he's that pissed off. And he had to have been if he scared you as badly as he did."

I shake my head. "Just take me home."

"Jessa... I've seen you have panic attacks. This one was bad. Please just come home with me, so I know you're safe."

"Please, Cole. I just need to be home right now."

I blink away a fresh wave of tears as he sighs and pulls out of the parking place he's in. What he doesn't know is that I do want to go to his house. I'm scared right now. He's safety. The safety Alex used to be.

We drive in silence back to the penthouse. I know he understands I need the quiet to organize my thoughts. I'm grateful to him for not trying to talk.

When we finally arrive, I open my door and start to step out. Cole opens his and meets me at mine, taking my hand. He walks with me to the secured door, then pulls me in front of him. He reaches up and tucks my hair behind my ear before he pulls me close to him and hugs me tightly.

"Please, please call me if you need me, Jessa. I'll be right here. I promise."

His grip tightens on me, and he kisses me on top of the head before he lets me go. I nod and force a smile of understanding before I turn away from him and let myself in. I can feel his eyes on my back until I turn the corner to the elevators, and he can't see me anymore.

The elevator ride up seems to take longer than usual. When I finally let myself into the penthouse, no one is home.

"Thank God," I whisper.

I make my way upstairs and get ready for a long, hot shower to wash the sting and pain of my run in with Alex away. I let the tears fall until I'm too exhausted to cry and the water has turned cold.

I step out and get ready for bed. Thankfully, Alex isn't home yet.

(One Month Later - Graduation)

"Jesus Christ, Jessa. What the fuck is wrong with you? I'm not going to fucking hurt you!" Alex yells.

For I don't know how many days in a row, Alex and I are fighting. Ever since the night at the library, it's all we do.

Today is graduation, and we just got home from the ceremony. Almost immediately the argument started, and I am cowering on the couch crying.

"Alex, please. I don't want to fight."

He stalks towards me and kneels in front of me. I involuntarily shiver in fear. He's so angry. His eyes flash with barely controlled rage. I hug myself as I shrink into the couch. He doesn't touch me, though he's right in front of me.

"You've known me for over four years. I've never hurt you. I've never yelled at you. Yet for the past month, every fucking time I touch you, you flinch. You won't talk to me. You won't sleep in the same fucking bed with me. So, if this is what you want, fucking walk. Because I'm sick and tired of you acting like I've done something to make you fear me." His eyes flash.

I stare at him like he's lost his mind. Does he honestly think that shoving me against a wall in the library wouldn't make me fear him? That screaming at me about my friendship with Cole wouldn't upset me? That threatening to kill Cole, like he did just last night, wouldn't terrify me? I don't even know what to say. I can't say anything. Instead, I cover my face and burst into tears.

"Yep. There they are. The fucking tears to make me feel bad, right?" He stands up and walks towards the door. He pauses and looks back at me. "You have two choices, Jessa, because I can't fucking live like this anymore. Either you get the fuck over whatever is going on or leave. Your choice."

He grabs his keys and leaves. I sit staring at the wall for several minutes trying to decide what to do. Finally, I stand up and head towards the bedroom. Our bedroom. No. It's just his now. It hasn't been ours in a long time. I make it as far as the bed before I start crying again.

My relationship is over. There's no denying it. My perfect relationship with the most perfect and amazing man has fallen apart at the seams because he wasn't as perfect as he seemed. Maybe it was all an act.

I thought I would marry him. My first real boyfriend. My first real kiss. I experienced so many firsts with him. My first orgasm. Everything. Everything with him was my first. I lost my virginity to him. My entire heart.

I love him so much that it physically hurts me to be away from him. Seeing him so angry and hurt when he left tore me to pieces. I feel like he ripped my heart out and took it with him. But I'm so scared of him that I don't know what to do. Maybe it was never love. Maybe it was infatuation. Maybe... Maybe... Maybe...

If it was never love, would I feel like this? Like a piece of me is gone? If it was love, would I feel attracted to someone else? Would I trust him more than I trust the man I thought I'd spend my life with? Maybe... Maybe... Maybe... So many maybes...

Not knowing what else to do or who I can turn to, I call Cole. He's the only person I know I can trust right now.

"Hey, there. What's up? Happy graduation, lucky. I still have another semester."

I sob into the phone, gripping my chest with my other hand. It burns. It hurts so bad that it burns. Like my chest is on fire and could burst into an inferno at any moment. My head feels like it's going to explode. My arm feels numb. I'm not even sure I'm actually holding my phone.

"Cole."

"Jessa? Honey, what happened? Where are you?"

"Home." Another sob is ripped from my stomach, and the cry that escapes is guttural.

"I'm on my way, Jess. Stay on the phone with me, okay? I'm not far away."

"Okay." Security. I have to call security. They have to let him in. "I... have to... let security know."

"Can you call down there without hanging up?" I get up and slowly make my way into the hallway. "Jessa, don't go silent on me. You need to keep talking."

I place my hand on the wall and walk slowly down the hallway to the stairs. I feel so shaky and weak. Like I could collapse at any second.

"I feel like..." I lean against the wall and squeeze my eyes shut as I clench my chest.

"Jessa? Come on. Keep talking to me."

"My chest. It hurts."

"Honey, listen to me. Listen to my voice. Can you hear me?"

"Yes..."

"Take a deep breath, Jessa." His voice is so calming. Soothing. Like Alex's used to be. I try to take a deep breath but sob instead. I can't breathe. "Fuck, sweetheart. I'm close. I'm almost there."

"Security..."

"Get them to let me up, honey."

Focus.

Come on.

I can do this. I have to.

My mind is racing. What if Alex came back? What if he tries to hurt me? Would he hurt me? Really hurt me? Has what he's done really been all he's capable of? Would he resort to more? Could he kill me? Would he?

"Jessa, please. Please talk to me. Tell me what you're doing."

I reach the stairs and start to walk down them. I'm shaking. Violently. "The stairs. I'm walking... down the stairs."

"Good. Good, honey. Keep talking for me, okay? What are you wearing?"

"What?" His question throws me off.

He laughs. "I'm trying to distract you. I'm wearing jeans and a red t-shirt. What are you wearing?"

"Um... jean shorts and... a t-shirt." I reach the bottom of the stairs and start heading for the door, trying to focus on my breathing. It hurts. It hurts so much. My vision is blurring, and I'm trying not to succumb to the darkness. "I feel... like I'm going... to pass out."

"Not happening, Jessa. I'm here, sweetie. Call down and tell them to let me up."

I finally reach the speaker box and call security.

"Security. How can I help?"

"Um... Cole. He's a... friend. Please let him up."

"Ms. Holloway? Are you okay? Would you like me to call Mr. Lang?" the security guard asks.

"No! Please, no!" I start crying again and gasping for air.

"Jessa? I'm here. Are they letting me up?" Cole asks.

I collapse on the wall clutching the phone tightly. "Cole, please. I need you. I... I'm going to pass out."

"Are you Cole?" I hear the security guard ask. I don't know if it's over the intercom in our apartment or the phone.

"Yes! Look, you have to let me up. Jessa is having a panic attack. She needs help."

"Is she on the phone? She's not answering her speaker box. Fuck it. Don't worry about check-in. Follow me!"

"Jessa? Jessa! Answer me, honey!" Cole shouts.

I can't. I try, but my throat feels like it's closing up. "Cole...," I choke out. The tears stream down my face.

"Fuck, Jessa. Hang on, honey."

I'm weak. My arms are so heavy. I close my eyes. My heart feels like it's expanded into my throat and is going to come out of my mouth.

The door bursts open. My eyes fling open. I scream as I start to crawl away, thinking it's Alex.

I'm very suddenly swept into a pair of strong arms that squeeze me so tightly I feel like I am in a cocoon.

Not Alex.

Different smell.

Cole. It's Cole. I sink into him.

"I'll call 9-1-1," the guard says.

"Don't worry about them yet!" Cole barks. "Just bring me her purse! It's on the counter. I saw it when we came in. Get a glass of water, too." Cole pulls me into his lap and squeezes me close to him. I burrow into his chest. I'm shivering. "I got you, Jessa. I'm right here, okay? You're okay now."

"Water and her purse," the guard says.

"She has a prescription bottle in there. Take it out and give her a pill. I can't let her go. If I do, she could pass out from fear. Her mind is telling her to fight. Her body wants to run. She's at war with herself."

I'm so glad that I opened up to Cole about the anxiety and everything I need when I have a panic attack. We've only known each other for a few months, but I honestly felt so safe and comfortable with him. I quickly started to trust him, and I'm so happy I did because I need him right now. I need someone who doesn't think I'm crazy.

"Sweetie, take your pill for me, please?" Cole coaxes.

I turn my head and take the pill from the security guard's hand, shakily drinking some water before giving him the glass back.

Cole continues to hug me tightly, and I force myself to breathe, concentrating on the steady rise and fall of his chest. He sends the security guard away with orders to call up here if Alex is on his way.

The mention of Alex's name sends me into near hysterics. Cole keeps his grip tight and whispers in my ear. "Shh... I got you, Jessa. I'm not going anywhere. You're okay. I'm right here."

What feels like hours go by, and he doesn't let me go. He keeps whispering in my ear and sits with me on the floor. He doesn't judge me. He just holds me close to him.

Like Alex *used* to do.

I finally look up at Cole as I pull away. He keeps his arms tightly around me. "Thank you. For... everything."

"That's what friends are for." He loosens his grip slightly, and I give him a weak smile. "You okay for me to let go?"

I bite my lip and look down at my hands. I'm okay enough for him to let go, but I don't want him to. Being like this with him feels... good. "Slowly?" He does as I ask until his arms are at his sides. I take a deep breath and slowly stand up, but I miss the warmth of him. He follows, staying close. Thankfully. "I need to pack my stuff."

"What?" I head for the stairs. Cole quickly takes my hand, forcing me to pause. "Hey, wait a sec. What happened?"

I continue up the stairs, pulling him with me. Cole has no choice but to follow. "We had another fight. Alex left. I can't stay here anymore. He's changed so much."

I enter our bedroom and walk to the closet where we keep all of our luggage. I take mine and my duffel bags. I'm glad I kept a few boxes from my parent's house when we cleaned it out. Alex teased me when I broke them down and put them behind the dresser.

"Jess, stop." He takes my hand again. I take a deep breath as he makes me turn around to look at him. "I'll support whatever you want, but did you think this through? You and Alex have been together for so long."

I close my eyes a moment before looking him in the eyes. "We've done nothing but argue for a month straight. And over the past few months, he's changed so much. He's always been secretive, but it's different now. One minute, he's so sweet and loving. The next, he's crazy jealous, hurtful, and mean. How is that fair?" I rub my chest as I start taking all of my luggage and putting it on the bed. "I hate it, but there's nothing left to do. This isn't an easy decision for me."

He starts helping me pack things. "I know, Jess. You think. Overanalyze. I just want to make sure this is what you want."

I shrug sadly and very conflicted. "Of course it isn't. I don't want my life to fall apart. I never asked for this. But I've tried talking to him. Every time I think things are okay again, he flies off the handle." We pack in silence for a few minutes. "Remember when you asked me what happened at the library? I told you Alex and I fought?"

"Yeah. I remember."

I take another deep breath as I look down at a framed photograph of my parents. I hug it to my chest. I miss them. So much.

"He pretty much attacked me. He shoved me against the wall. It's not that he's never touched me or kissed me. Just never like that. He was rough. Hard. It was really scary. And it wasn't him. Not my Alex. Not who I fell in love with." I kiss the picture of my parents and put it on top of my clothes before I close the suitcase and zip it. I turn and look at Cole. "I don't deserve this. And neither does he. I don't know what happened. What went wrong. I don't know what he's into. But I deserve a life better than with someone I can trust. Someone like you."

He sighs. "Jess, why didn't you tell me? I could've done something." He shakes his head. "I knew it. I never should've taken you here. I should've followed my fucking instincts and taken you with me to my place."

"I couldn't really believe what happened. Even though it wasn't the first time and wouldn't be the last."

"What? Jessa, are you kidding?" He scrubs his hands over his face. "Why didn't you say anything? You've been suffering in an abusive relationship for how long? I could've helped you."

"It started at the club when he saw me with you."

After throwing more things in suitcases and boxes, Cole sighs. He says nothing, though, as he picks up a couple suitcases and heads for the door. I grab the smaller ones and follow.

He looks pissed.

"Did I say something wrong to make you angry?" I ask quietly. Maybe this was a bad decision.

"No, honey. I just want you the hell out of here. We can talk about this shit later. How are you feeling after that attack?"

"Not really well. Tired." He leads me into the elevator, and I lean against the wall and close my eyes. "Sore. And I feel like an idiot. Like a little girl who can't control her emotions."

"Jessa, is that how he makes you feel when you have an attack? Jesus Christ."

I shake my head. "No. Lately? He ignores them. He walks away, and I have to fight through them on my own. He promised he'd never do that to me." I open my eyes and look at him. "But it's not totally his fault. I inadvertently cower whenever he's near me." I look down.

"Fuck. Inadvertently? He attacked you. Multiple times from what I'm gathering. It's not inadvertent." The doors open, and we take everything out to his car.

After a few more trips, all of my things are in Cole's vehicle. I left my key card on the kitchen counter with a note for Alex. I'm not sure how I'm supposed to feel. Heartbroken? Conflicted? Why don't I feel completely lost?

"You can just take me to a hotel."

"You're coming home with me. We'll get your car tomorrow. I'm not fucking ignoring myself this time." He puts the car in drive and pulls away from the curb.

The buildings and cars go by in a blur of bright colors.

I lean my head against the glass and watch them all as we pass. I should feel sad. Devastated. A relationship I've been in for over four years has ended in quite a drastic measure. I should feel my heart breaking in my chest. Shattering.

So, why do I feel hurt, but like my life is just about to begin? Why do I feel hope?

Chapter Twenty Two

✗ Alex ✗

I storm out of the house with keys in hand and jam the button for the elevator. I impatiently keep pressing it until the doors finally open. Once inside and behind closed doors, I punch the wall of the elevator.

"Fuck! What the fuck is wrong with her?"

For the past couple of months, Jessa has completely changed. She went from this beautiful, confident, amazing woman to this scared, fearful girl that I don't even recognize. She jumps at the slightest noise. She hasn't been sleeping well, but since last week, I don't think she's slept at all. But how the fuck would I know? She won't sleep in the same fucking bed as me anyway!

The doors open in the parking garage, and I briskly walk to my car. I slam the door closed and peel out. I need to go for a drive. I have to clear my fucking head and figure out what the hell is going on with her.

The girl back there crying on the fucking couch isn't the person I fell in love with. She cowers when I look at her. She fucking shrinks into herself when I try to fucking touch her! I raise my voice even slightly, and she flinches like I'm going to slap her.

Fuck, what the fuck?!

Speeding down the freeway, I see an exit for West Century Drive. "Ryan. I wonder if he's around." Dialing his number, I take the exit.

"Hey, Alex. What's up?"

"You in LA?"

"Actually, I'm just about to leave. I had a business meeting. Why?"

"You at your penthouse?"

"For the next two minutes."

"At the risk of sounding like a whiny kid, stick around. I need my big brother."

I would usually go to Josh for this, but I know how much stress he's under. And for the past few weeks, every time I mention Jessa, he gets weird. After I told him how she's changed, he suggested a fucking break up. It's like everyone has gone fucking insane.

"Okay. You have access to all my buildings. Just come up. I'll wait."

I chuckle. "Of course you fucking own the building."

"Best way to keep my ass safe."

Ryan has become exponentially more powerful than even my family's mafia over the past few years. My dad hates him for it, but not even his crazy ass would go up against the Crane Mafia. Maybe before, but definitely not now. Not too shabby for someone who just turned twenty-seven.

"I'm about to pull in. See you in a couple minutes."

I hang up and head for the parking ramp. The good thing about having access to his buildings is that I don't need to go through the layers upon layers of security his buildings have. It also means if anyone is ever after my ass, I can run to one of his buildings and not have to worry about being killed in the middle of L.A. It probably would happen, but it's nice to have that extra layer of security.

I get to his penthouse floor and knock. He opens it moments later, and a flood of relief washes over me.

"You look like shit. Get in here. Sit. I'll get you a beer." He waves me in and heads for the kitchen.

"Thanks." I mumble and trudge into his penthouse, closing the door behind me. Where mine cost seventy five grand a month, Ryan's is easily in the millions. The curiosity actually makes me smile a little as I sit on the couch. "This place is fucking gorgeous. That view. It's better than the other one you had."

"It's peaceful. Good place to clear my head if I need to. Far more security. The elevator doesn't open right into my living room."

"You have a lot more square footage than me. Must cost a hell of a lot."

He laughs. "I bought the building, remember? Cost me about five hundred million."

I nearly choke as I look back at him. He's leaning against the kitchen counter removing the bottle tops from the beer. Imported. Christ. Only Ryan fucking Crane. "Fuck. Seriously?"

He laughs again as he walks across the room. "This penthouse costs thirty five million to buy." He nods towards the balcony. "Let's sit outside." He hands me a beer as I stand, and I follow him outside.

"I don't think I'll ever get sick of the sun setting over this city. Something I'll miss." I sit in a chair and bring the bottle to my lips. The cold, fizzy liquid slides smoothly down my throat, but I say nothing else.

Ryan sits next to me. "Well, that was fucking cryptic."

I spare him a glance before I start peeling the label from the bottle, focusing all of my attention on it. "I think Jess and I are done, Ry." A sob threatens to escape, but I swallow it down. I won't fucking cry.

"Why? What happened? Another fight?"

I shrug. "She's terrified of me. I tried pushing some hair out of her eyes today, and she literally folded herself onto the couch and started shaking."

Ryan sighs and takes a long sip of his beer. "Do you think maybe she figured out who you are?"

I look at him and swallow the lump in my throat. "I don't know."

"It would make sense, don't you think?"

I shrug and continue peeling the label from the bottle, looking out over the city. I love L.A. It's really too bad that I'll have to leave it. "You really think that could be it?"

"I really don't know, Alex. But I did tell you a long time ago that you need to tell her the truth."

"Yeah. Fuck. You did. Okay? Happy?"

"No."

I glare at him and take another long drink of the beer, downing it completely.

The truth is, he's right. Abso-fucking-lutely right. I should've been up front and honest with Jessa from the very beginning. Especially after I realized that I was in love with her. Am I in love with her? Fuck, I don't even know. It was all so damn quick.

Ryan stands up and grabs my bottle. He walks back into the penthouse, leaving me to my thoughts.

Could she have found out who I am? Who my family is? Is that why she's suddenly become so afraid of me? Did she try to give it a chance? Maybe her anxiety got the best of her. Maybe she decided there's no way she could ever be involved with the mafia. Maybe her fear of the mafia made her fear me.

Ryan returns to the balcony with two empty glasses and a bottle. He sets the glasses down and fills them both with a deep amber liquid. "Thought you could use something a little stronger."

"What is it?" I ask cautiously.

"Something that will burn going down, and you'll regret in the morning."

"Sounds like my kind of drink." I pick it up and slam it. He's right. It's like the hottest of flames are burning their way down my throat. "Shit. Holy shit." I squint against it and try not to cough.

"Told you." He says with a grin as he refills my glass. "So, what are you going to do?"

I shrug and down my drink again. "I'm not nearly fucked up enough to answer that question." I grab the bottle and fill my glass a third time, then a fourth, followed by a fifth. "I don't know what to do, Ry. I fucked up this past week. Hell. The past few months. Our whole relationship. I let this lie go on. And then I let her fear take over. I didn't even try. And now it's too late. I told her to get over it or leave."

"It's not too late if you love her."

"Yeah, it is. I made her feel like shit. Every panic attack she had over the past few weeks, and there were a lot, I walked away. I fucking walked away. I let her fight alone. I swore to her I'd never let her fight alone." I fill my glass a sixth time.

"You intend on drinking yourself to death?"

"The fact that I know this is my sixth means I'm nowhere near fucked up enough to care about alcohol poisoning." I down the glass and Ryan fills his as he shakes his head. "I was planning on taking her to Italy with me."

I reach into my pocket and pull out the surprise I've been carrying around for months for Jessa and put it on the table.

"Jesus… Christ…."

I stare at the ring as I fill my glass again. Eight? Ten? Who fucking cares? " I'd been trying to find a time to ask her to marry me, but the timing was never right." I down the drink, no longer feeling the liquid burning its way down my throat. "I thought I'd tell her in Italy, and if she stuck around, I'd ask her."

"Why Italy?"

Hadn't I told him? I don't even fucking remember. "To get my dad off my back. I told him I'd run overseas. Josh could run the US operation." My words are starting to slur, but I pour another drink anyway. The last of the bottle.

"And that new company in Italy needs help. You have a branch of Lucinio Tech there, too. So, you decided there."

I nod and immediately get dizzy. I down the drink and rub my head. I'm starting to lose focus now. Fucking good. "I need to go." I stand up too quickly and stumble, knocking over my chair. Ryan grabs me before I fall. "Shit. Sorry."

"Don't worry about it. I got you."

"I'm fine. I can hold my liquor." I take a few steps on my own before I crash into the door frame. My vision blurs even more, and Ryan catches me again before I fall. "Damn."

"I don't think you're going anywhere."

"I have to get out of here. Sooner I get to Italy the better."

"You're not in any condition to drive."

"Then take me."

"No."

"Fuck you. So bossy."

"That's what brothers do. You need to sleep this off."

"I need to go." I reach into my pocket for my keys. The penthouse starts spinning, and I close my eyes. "Fuck, bro. You didn't tell me you could make this place spin. Shut it off."

Ryan chuckles as he slings my arm over his shoulders. He steadies me with an arm around my waist and starts slowly walking. "I'll get right on that. In the meantime, let's get you to a guest room, huh?"

"Does it spin?" I'm silently begging him to say no.

"Maybe. Guess we have to see."

"Asshole."

He gets me into a room and helps me into bed. He starts taking off my shoes, but I don't know if he finishes because I'm out as soon as I roll on my side.

I groan as I slowly open my eyes. I don't recognize my surroundings in the slightest.

"Where the fuck am I?"

I don't dare move. The pounding in my head proves I definitely made the right choice to stay still. I close my eyes and groan again, turning my face into my pillow.

The bed shifts next to me as someone sits on it.

"If you aren't a five feet three inch brunette with a perfect ass and sexy as hell tits that fit in the palm of my hand, then go the fuck away."

"I'm six feet five. Don't have tits, and if you touch my ass, I'll break you."

I grin, even though I don't want to. "You're such a dick. What do you want?"

"Take these. Drink this," he commands. I open my eyes as he sets two pills and orange juice on the nightstand. "Take a shower. There's a change of clothes for you on the bed. When you're done, I'll have my famous hangover breakfast ready for you."

"Does that mean Cinnabon and bacon?"

"Fuck you. Cinnabon. Who the hell do you think you're talking to?"

"A dead man if you don't get out right now."

"You couldn't take me if you tried." He stands up and leaves.

I take the Aspirin and drink the orange juice before I even attempt to get up. When I'm finished, I head to the shower, turning on the cold water. Steeling myself for the frigid temperature I'm about to subject myself to, I take a deep breath and step under the spray.

The events of last night are hazy at best, but I vividly remember every word I said to Jessa. Every action. Every stupid thing I did. Every lie I told her since I met her.

"So fucking stupid, Alex."

I quickly wash up and step out of the shower. After I'm dressed, I head to the kitchen and find Ryan. He's pulling fresh cinnamon rolls out of the oven. Ryan is a man of many talents, but cooking may be his most well-hidden. If you aren't close to him, you'd never know.

I sit at the counter and wait for him to finish plating everything. My mouth waters at the smell of both the bacon and the cinnamon rolls. Finally, Ryan turns and puts everything on the counter. He hands me a plate, and I look at him, silently asking permission to dig in.

Ryan laughs. "Go ahead. But you call my cinnamon rolls Cinnabons again, and I'll cut you off. Forever."

"Deal." I don't wait any longer. My stomach hurts, but I don't know if it's because I'm starving, or because of the alcohol.

"Just take it easy. You eat too fast, you'll puke."

I know he's right, but I take a huge bite of the warm, gooey roll anyway. I close my eyes and moan in pleasure. "This is better than sex."

"Damn. You must not be getting enough if you think these rolls are better than sex."

I actually grin and laugh but it all quickly vanishes, and I shake my head. "I really fucked up."

"Then fix it."

I nod and finish my breakfast in silence. Ryan grabs the dishes and puts them in the dishwasher before he turns back to me. He puts my keys and Jessa's ring on the counter. Tears sting my eyes, and I take a deep breath as my eyes fall on the ring.

"Fuck," I whisper.

"Go home. Talk to her. Tell her everything."

"You're right."

"Usually am."

I take my keys and put the ring in my pocket as I head for the door. Before I leave, I turn back to Ryan. "Thank you. For everything."

He shrugs. "I'm your brother. Maybe not by blood, but by heart. The bond is stronger. I'm here for you. Either way this goes."

I nod and turn to leave, more than thankful for the millionth time in my life that I have him.

"Alex," he says. I turn back. "I mean that. I'll be here to cheer you on, or I'll be with you on the flight to Italy drinking ourselves into oblivion. Whatever happens, let me know."

"I will." I leave and hurry to my car. I speed home and practically run to the elevator. I wait impatiently for it to arrive, then wait even more impatiently as it takes me up to the top floor. I let myself into the penthouse and stop in my tracks.

It's quiet.

Too quiet.

"Jess?" I glance around and notice Jessa's framed picture of her with her parents isn't on the table where we put our keys. My heart quickens. "Jessa?"

I start heading for the stairs when a note that's folded like a card catches my eye. I walk towards the kitchen counter praying that it's from Marissa to Gavin or some shit.

My heart stops beating when I see a key card sitting on the counter with Jessa's building ID card.

"Fuck." With a shaky hand, I reach for the note.

My Dearest Alex,

Writing this is the hardest thing I have ever had to do. And that includes my parent's death and fighting through my panic attacks alone.

A tear I don't bother stopping falls onto the paper. I don't wipe it off.

I never believed it possible to fall so far in love with someone as amazing as you only to have my heart completely broken by that same person. But it happened. It happened, and I don't know where it went wrong.

"God, baby. I'm so fucking sorry."

You told me tonight to either figure this out or leave because you can't live like this anymore. With me fearing you. And you're right. It's not fair to you. It's not fair to me. To us. This whole thing isn't fair.

I don't understand what happened. But maybe it's for the best. Maybe now isn't the time for us. Maybe we were in love with the idea of each other more than each other.

I sink to the kitchen floor, barely seeing the words on the paper.

I decided it's best to leave. It's the most fair to you. Me. I'm so sorry. You'll always hold a special place in my heart, but I'll be okay. I want you to know that. And I want you to find someone who can make you happy. I want you to find someone who will love you like you need to be loved. I'll do the same.

I guess I don't know if you will, but please don't worry about me. I promise I really will be okay.

Jessa

I clutch the note to my chest as I take out my phone.

"Hey, bro. How'd it go?" Ryan asks. I know he already knows. I can hear it in his voice.

"Italy." I can barely get the word out.

"Shit."

"She's gone. I fucked up."

"I'll be right there, man."

"Fucking hurry."

He hangs up. I stay on the floor. I couldn't force myself up even if I wanted to. The pain of losing her is so unbearable that I can't even think straight. I can't see straight. The roar in my ears from my breaking heart overpowers all else.

I fucked up. I didn't try to figure out what was going on, and I lost her. Her words seemed so final. Like her decision was made. There's no going back. Not this time. This is finished. The final nail in the coffin.

What seems like hours go by, but Ryan finally gets here. He hauls me up and takes me to his car. We arrive at the airport and board his plane. No words are said. I'm numb now. I don't even feel us taking off. I don't feel the ascent. I don't feel us level out.

I don't even know if Ryan has said anything to me. I haven't heard him. I haven't heard a fucking word anyone has said since I read Jessa's letter, which is still clutched in my hand.

I've read it over and over again, and it still won't sink in. How could this be over? How could I let the woman I love go? I grab the phone on the plane and dial Jessa's number. Maybe we can talk this out.

"Hey! It's Jessa! Leave a message after the beeeeeep! Ha! Just playing!" The phone beeps, and I take a deep breath, my heart sinking.

"Jess, it's me. I…" I choke back the lump in my throat and close my eyes. "I'm sorry. I'm so fucking sorry. I'm sorry I hurt you." I feel Ryan's hand on my shoulder. A show of support. Comfort. "Call me back. Please? Let's talk this out. At least try to."

I hang up and let my head fall back. I just left my entire life behind. My heart. I'll never get that back.

It belongs to her.

Chapter Twenty Three

✕ Jessa ✕

(One Year Later)

It's been a whole year since Alex and I broke up. Each day is better than the previous one. I don't have a near breakdown when something reminds me of him anymore.

At first, it was Christmas. Christmas came and went, but it reminded me of our first Christmas together, and all the ones that came after. Then it was New Year's. I thought about all the years that he kissed me at midnight. Like kissing me was all he wanted. Then it was Cole drinking orange juice. It reminded me of how much Alex loves his orange juice. So many little things would make me think of him. And it would bring a fresh wave of confusion all over again. Even a little pain.

I truly believed that Alex and I would never break up. He was my first love and will always hold a special place within my heart and soul. I thought we would spend our lives together. I still can't believe how wrong I was about him. How stupid and blind. I can't believe I made excuses for his behavior towards me. For our entire relationship, I ignored all of the lies. Shadiness. The disappearing in the middle of the night and not saying a word about why.

I lost everything when he left. I lost Marissa. She refuses to talk to me because she doesn't believe any of the things Alex did. She thinks I'm a liar. I haven't tried to contact Gavin or Damon. I don't see the point. Neither of them would side with me over Alex. I haven't even reached out to Tia. She tried to get me to talk to Damon after the breakup, but I refused to. We haven't spoken since.

I realized far too late that my life revolved around Alex. My friends were his. I lived in his penthouse. Besides my clothing and few belongings, I had nothing. Everything was Alex's. Alex was my entire life. The center of my whole world.

"Hey." Cole kisses me on the forehead.

I smile up at him. Cole and I slowly went from friends to something a little more. One night, we took our relationship to the next level. We realized very quickly that we are much better friends than anything more. The attraction is there, but that's all it ever was and will be between us. We're happy as friends.

Best friends.

He sits next to me. "I should've known I'd find you here. Hunkered down and lost in thought."

I love this window seat. It's my favorite place in Cole's apartment. It's like my own little nook. When he helped me pack and leave the penthouse and took me to his place that night, he begged me to stay a few days. A few days turned into a few weeks. Every time I thought of getting my own place, I had a panic attack.

Now, this is home. And not just because I'm afraid of being on my own. I'm not. It's just that I really love this place. I love the neighborhood. I love how people wave to me when I go out to get the mail. Everyone knows my name, and I know theirs. I feel... content.

"How was your day?" I ask him. He became a police officer with the LAPD right out of school. It was his dream, and he's so good at it.

He smiles and leans back against the window. He's still in his uniform, but it looks a little less crisp than it did when he left last night for his shift. "I got to help out on this traffic stop. Huge drug bust." He grins.

My eyes widen. "On a traffic stop?" I ask in disbelief. "How?"

Cole laughs and leans forward. "They were pulled over for running a stop sign. When they ran the plate, the car came back to a nice older gentleman, but that isn't who was driving. I was in the area so I stopped to help out. We got halfway to the car when we smelled weed. In the backseat, I noticed a blanket covering some stuff, but it wasn't pulled down all the way. They were plain as day bricks of weed. Obviously selling."

I wrinkle my nose. "People are incredibly stupid."

"Not even the worst of it. We searched the car and found bricks of heroin in the trunk. The kid said he knew nothing about it. He was going to pick up his girlfriend for a date. He said the car belonged to his dad. Guess who his dad is?"

I furrow my brows. "Uh. Someone important? Oh! A judge."

Cole laughs again, his eyes crinkling at the sides. "Not too far off. The nice older gentleman it belonged to is none other than our Chief."

I nearly choke. "Oh my God! The Chief's son?"

Cole nods. "Yep. He wasn't too happy having his ass woken up at three in the morning by a rookie cop who should have been on his way home."

I laugh. "How did that go? Did he read his kid the riot act?"

"He told us he isn't coming down. Tow the car. Arrest him. Throw the fucking book at him. So, we did as the boss said."

"That's fantastic!" I laugh again.

After a few moments, Cole sobers. "So, have you slept?"

I bite my lip and look down at my hands. I haven't been sleeping well. Even with the pill I was prescribed to help me sleep. It's not even that I dream of Alex or anything. I really am moving on and getting over him. It's more that I have so much stuff running through my head that sleep is almost impossible. Sometimes, if Cole isn't here, I don't sleep at all. We've found I sleep a lot better if he's around me, so if he's working, it's unlikely I'll sleep. I'm sort of on his schedule.

I shake my head. "Not really. Maybe I dozed a few minutes. I was reading for a while. And then I was putting the finishing touches on my drawing."

"Jess…," Cole rumbles with a sigh. "This isn't healthy. Sleep is a vital necessity. Your body can't function without it."

I let out a huff as I shift and stand from the nook. "I know, Cole." I make my way to the kitchen. My body is tired. I feel almost numb. "I wish I could sleep. I do. It's just -"

"I know, Jess. Your mind gets out of control, and you don't sleep well if I'm not here."

I open the refrigerator and pull out a bottle of water. "Yep."

"Well, guess what? It's time for bed, then."

Suddenly, Cole's arms are around my waist, and I'm being spun around. I let out a squeak just before I'm thrown over his shoulder. I have no idea where my water went, but I start giggling like a child as he walks down the hall.

"I can walk, you know," I say with a huge smile.

"I'm sure you can. But this is much more fun." He walks into his room and drops me on the bed.

"Your room? Why your room? It smells like a gym in here." I teasingly wrinkle my nose.

He cracks up as he heads to his shower. "Lies! I happen to know that it doesn't because you refuse to allow it!" He closes his bathroom door as I laugh.

I kind of love mornings like this. With Cole, there's no pressure. I love that I can be who I am, and he expects nothing in return. We can just be friends and have tons of fun together. Talk. Be honest and open. I can be completely goofy and dance around the kitchen if I want to. Cole will join right in. It's so fun and easy with him. I'm so happy we decided to stay friends after realizing we definitely didn't love each other as more than that. Friends. Family.

I jump out of bed and quickly find a movie. Cole loves the Jurassic Park movies. New and classic. It doesn't matter to him. I grab Jurassic World, then make us both toast. While it's toasting, I pour us both a bowl of our favorite cereal. Trix. It's absolutely not just for kids. As the toast is popping up, I hear Cole's shower stop. I smile and grab butter and our favorite jam. Strawberry. There's no other option.

When I'm finished, I balance everything in my arms and make my way back to Cole's bedroom. I set everything on the nightstand next to his bed and put the movie in the DVD slot on his sixty inch TV that's mounted to his wall. When I'm finished, I grab his remote and crawl under the blankets. I snuggle down and wait for him to come out while I queue up the movie.

After a few more moments, Cole comes out dressed in boxers and a t-shirt and practically dives into the bed. "Tell me we're watching Jurassic Park."

I shake my head and giggle. "Nope!"

"Fast and Furious?"

I shake my head with a giggle and hand him his bowl and toast. "Nope!"

He groans as he takes his cereal and toast. "Don't subject me to Twilight. I beg you."

I laugh. "Does the intro music sound like Twilight?" I nod to the screen as I smile at him over my own bowl.

He raises an eyebrow and takes a bite of the cereal. "No. Thank God." He's quiet for a few moments before he laughs. "It is Jurassic Park! I guessed that. You said no!"

"Because it's not Jurassic Park. It's Jurassic World." I try to keep a straight face as I blink at him.

He laughs again. "You're a brat." He takes a piece of toast and dips it into milk in his cereal.

I wrinkle my nose. "Eew. Why? Why do you do that?"

He grins and takes a big bite. "Because it's really fucking good. Wanna try?" He dips the rest of his toast in the bowl.

"No. No, I do not." I shake my head.

He grins and eats it. I just laugh and go back to my cereal. When we both finish, Cole takes our dishes to the kitchen. I yawn and burrow into the covers, finally feeling like I can sleep. I don't know what it is, but Cole makes everything easier. He quiets my mind and cuts through the chaos. And neither of us really understand how he does it.

It takes only seconds after Cole comes back and lays down with me that I'm fast asleep.

Chapter Twenty Four

⚔ Alex ⚔

It's been a year since I let Jessa walk away from me. I still don't really know what I was thinking. I've never interfered with her choices before, though. If she felt like she needed to leave, I'll always respect her wishes.

Ryan and I have spent countless hours talking, and the only conclusion that makes sense to us is that she found out who my family is. She found out my family is one of the largest mafias in the world, and she got scared. I can't blame her. Especially with all of the secrets I kept and lies I told her to keep my identity a secret.

I truly wish that she'd given me a chance to explain. I'd called both her and her friend, Cole, every day for at least two weeks. Neither answered and neither returned my calls. Eventually, I decided there was nothing left for me to do. I can't make her talk to me. I won't come off as obsessive and make her fear me more.

No. Jessa has to make the decision to come to me. She has to be the one to call me. It has to be on her own terms. Just like our entire relationship. It was all on her terms. Everything. I respected her enough to keep it that way. I'd never do anything to hurt her or push her into something she didn't want. I still won't. I still respect her.

It hurt me more than words can describe to know that I hurt her by keeping the truth of my family from her. Looking back, all I wanted to do was protect her. I wanted to keep everything separate. I wanted it all. But life doesn't work like that. Life is a fickle fucking bitch who plays by her own damn rules. Not mine or anyone else's.

"Hey."

I look up as Gavin walks into my office. Books line the walls behind my cherry wood desk. I smile a little. Gavin and Marissa came to Italy with me and are engaged to be married. I might still have my own doubts about her, but I can't deny Gavin is more content than I have ever seen him. I wouldn't say he is the happiest engaged man I've ever seen, but he seems happy enough.

"What's up?" I ask.

"Looks busy as shit for you." He nods to my desk with a raised eyebrow.

I look down at the pile of paperwork, and my small smile turns into a huge shit-eating grin. "I'm fucking enjoying it. Does that make me psychotic?"

"Yep! It absolutely does."

I laugh. Gavin has been great about getting me out of my head. "Honestly, taking over Lucinio Tech was the best decision I've ever made. I truly enjoy this. The numbers. The decisions. Everything."

"Marissa certainly enjoys her position. Art is literally her life."

"She's good at what she does. I'll give her that."

"She loves waking up, walking outside, and painting whatever comes to her."

I chuckle and lean back in my chair. "So what does my COO need?" I ask.

"I'll be honest, when you offered me the Chief Operating Officer position, I was pretty sure you lost your damn mind, but this actually is pretty fucking great."

I grin as I put my pen down. "Second best decision I ever made. Even though your dad wants to kick my ass."

"I'm surprised that fucker didn't freeze all your accounts after you stole me away."

I laugh. "I think your engagement to Marissa helped me out a little. You never would've met her without me, and they seem to like her a lot."

"She's a good girl." He smiles but it falters slightly. He clears his throat. "Hey. The reason I came in is because I know for a damn fact where we're hemorrhaging our money from."

I raise an eyebrow. "You found our leak?"

"Yep. The old CFO."

I look at him in bewilderment. "I fired all of the top managers. Chief Financial Officer included."

"Account numbers were never changed. Mr. Donovan still has access, and is skimming off the top."

"How the fuck did I miss something so fucking easy?" I start leafing through a pile of account withdrawals and comparing them to another stack of deposits. Gavin finds my account numbers as well as old account numbers. "Where the fuck is my highlighter?" I mumble looking for the stupid thing. I've managed to lose it more times than I can count.

And that's just today.

"Here." Gavin plucks it off the floor and hands it to me, trying to follow my thought process. "What do you see?"

"You said accounts. There are deposits and withdrawals over the past four years that all have the same account number. I made a mental note to track the account number to see where the fuck everything is going." I highlight a few lines. "See? Same day every week."

I move aside just a little as Gavin looks over my shoulder. "Automatic withdrawals. See? EFT. Electronic Funds Transfer."

"Makes no sense, though. These same deposits end up here. Look." I highlight the same deposit totals on the same day to another account.

"This account isn't ours. This is the account I saw that has all of these deposits."

"What?"

"Look. This account number matches none of these accounts." He puts a list of account numbers in front of me. He's right. It doesn't match any of them. "This is an offshore account number, Alex. See the withdrawals on this account?"

"Yeah. I see it. I didn't know it was offshore. I sort of thought my dad was laundering money somehow through it."

"This is your company. This isn't your dad. I checked to see if he had his hands in it at all. Just to make sure. None of the money tracks to him or any of his offshore accounts. It looks like Ryan has kept him out while he was controlling it for you. And the amount behind pulled is definitely lower than anything your dad would dream of."

He's not wrong. The amount is ten grand a week. My dad would be taking ten million. "I need to track these accounts."

"Already called Lance."

I smile. Lance had only joined my team a few years ago, but he quickly fit right in. He did what I asked without fail. Became pretty fast friends with Damon. Damon stayed back in the U.S. I offered him the CFO position, and he took it, but he loves L.A. so he works from home. He couldn't bring himself to leave permanently. He's not with Tia anymore, but they're still very close friends. He does fly out here whenever I need him to, though.

"Okay. So how does this go back to Donavan?" I ask.

"Check this out." Gavin grabs my highlighter and starts highlighting a shit ton of withdrawals. All different amounts and smaller than the ten grand. All on different days of the week.

"Holy shit."

"Not done. I'm just sorry it took months to find it." He starts highlighting deposits that match the amounts of the withdrawals. They all go to the same account number.

"Son of a bitch. I bet that account belongs to Donovan."

"Your bet would make you a lot of money, Mr. Lucinio. Lance is tracking the money that went to the offshore account, but he did get me this." Gavin hands me another stack of papers. It's every single small withdrawal deposited into Kristof Donovan's account.

I grin like an idiot. I haven't been on a mission in a long time, but this seems like the perfect opportunity. "What do you say to a mission?"

Gavin grins. The devilish glint in his eye matches my own. "You don't want to take this to the authorities? Do it legal?"

"Maybe some part of me. But fuck. I'm a mafia boss, right? Forced into the role. Maybe it's time I start acting like one. Get a team together."

He grins even wider. He's missed this shit just as much as I have. "I'll get a surveillance team. Observe a couple days. Give you a chance to change your mind."

I laugh. He knows as well as I do that I'm not changing my mind. Maybe this is exactly what I fucking need to get back into the game.

XXX

(Two Days Later)

A couple of days later, Gavin and I are sitting hidden staring at the second largest villa I've ever seen. The first one is, of course, mine. I'm a mafia boss. CEO of a huge fucking tech company. I have an image to uphold.

The villa in front of us is three stories. The lawn is perfectly manicured and, thankfully, not very wide open. There is a fountain in the middle of the property, but it's not that large. At least not like mine. I chuckle arrogantly to myself. My property is wide open and covered with security. Kristof Donovan's property leaves a lot to be desired and provides a lot of places to hide, which my team is doing quite well.

"You sure about doing this in broad daylight?" Gavin asks.

"He's too cocky to have security," I smirk. "We don't have to worry about that. And I told you. His wife is off limits. She gets home at six every night. We need to be in and out by then. That gives us ten hours."

"And you want the kill to not take place on the property. That's not like you."

"I don't want this to touch the wife or his family. They have nothing to do with it. I want the money back, him gone, and the family taken care of."

"Which is why even though he's stolen millions, you're still giving her a package worth millions."

"You saw the shit he did with the money. The family didn't benefit at all. His house in Greece; all his trips. They have no idea. So we make it look like he disappeared. Took everything."

"And you step in looking like a damn hero." Gavin grins.

I grin back. "Makes me feel a little better about doing exactly what I said I didn't want anything to do with."

"Only until your dad gives up control."

"He doesn't seem too keen on that idea."

"Fucking seriously?" Gavin looks at me in astonishment.

"Pretty sure he thinks he won when I took over overseas and left Josh the U.S. He thinks if I took over this much, I'll take it all."

"He's not going to give it up, is he?"

"Fuck if I know."

"How's Josh? I haven't talked to him much. He seems to always be busy."

"Seems to be okay. Says dad has been more open with the day to day operations with him. He keeps saying dad is going to give him control soon."

"What do you think?"

"That he's still holding out hope I'll take over, and that he has some stupid as fuck plan up his sleeve. I think he's going to disappoint my brother yet again."

I can tell me leaving my brother has been weighing on him. He was barely holding it together before. Every day gets harder and harder for him to stay strong and stand up against our crazy father. I feel as bad about leaving him just as much as I feel guilty for fucking things up with Jessa. But Josh has to learn how to do things on his own. I may not always be there. He's snapped at me a few times when I've called. I hate that he feels like I abandoned him. But maybe it's what he needs to stand up and be the strong as fuck man that I know he is.

"Alright men. Everyone read me?" There's a chorus of 'yes, sir's' over my earpiece. "Good. Teams. Storm the house, and enter on my count. Three... two... one!"

My team that's surrounding the house leap into action in perfect unison. We're all wearing black tactical gear and facemasks so Donovan has no idea who we are. At least not until I want him to. We're all carrying high-powered, semi-automatic rifles because I want to scare the fuck out of this asshole. We all still have our handguns strapped to us, mine on my thigh and shoulder, as usual.

We enter the house and stealthily head for the kitchen where my team said the scumbag was.

"Donovan is on the move! Heading right for Team One!" one of my guards says into our earpieces.

"Where?" I growl. I raise my rifle as I slowly move forward.

"Coming around the corner to your left," the guard says. Me, Gavin, and the rest of my team freeze and point our rifles at the hallway to our left. Donovan runs around the corner right into us.

"Shit!" Kristoff Donovan yells. He quickly turns right and directly into the second half of my team.

"I wouldn't do that if I were you." I say dangerously.

"Who are you?" he asks, glaring at me.

"Your worst fucking nightmare," I answer, returning his glare. "Cuff him."

"On it." Gavin flips the safety on his rifle and lets his gun fall to his side. He takes out a pair of cuffs. "You planning on making this hard for me? I'd hate for your pretty little wife to see your brains splattered all over her wall."

"Leave my wife out of this," Donovan says through gritted teeth. I'm impressed at the guy's English. Heavily accented, but damn good, nonetheless.

"I plan to," I say. "What you've done doesn't concern her. But she'll be well provided for after your very untimely disappearance."

"Don't fucking touch her," he growls.

"Didn't he just say he wasn't going to?" Gavin laughs. "Cooperation is in your best interest right now."

"Or maybe I'll reconsider and fuck your wife right up against that wall. Bet you I can satisfy her better," I say darkly.

My entire team laughs sinisterly. It's not something I would ever do. But anything to get this fucker to cooperate. I don't want to do this in the house. My team will clean it up, but I don't like to taint an entire family when all I have a problem with is one person. This guy's wife lives with him. His teenage daughter and son are both away at boarding school, but they live here, too. His family doesn't deserve to live in a tainted house.

Donovan glares at me.

I glare right back. "I'll let one of my partners here fuck your daughter right there on those stairs while your son watches. You want to test me, or you want to man up and face the consequences for all your fucking sins?"

"You swear to all the God's that you'll leave my wife and family alone?" he asks me.

"My problem isn't with them. It's with you."

213

"Swear," he manages to get out over the emotion that's overcome him.

I roll my eyes. "Fine. I swear. I will not touch your family."

All of the fight leaves him as he turns around and puts his hands behind his back. Gavin snaps the cuffs on and we lead him outside to my SUV. Gavin sits in the back with Mr. Donovan, and another guard takes his place up front. I jump in the driver's seat and take off. I drive about an hour outside the city to a secluded area where no one can hear anything.

Screams.

Gunshots.

Gavin pulls him out of the vehicle when I finally stop. The rest of my kill team pulls up behind me. We all take off our masks. Gavin removes the cuffs and throws Donovan to the ground.

"Kristoff Donovan," I begin. "Previous CFO of Lucinio Tech. Skimming off the top ever since you took the position." I kneel next to him. "What I don't understand is why in all the Hells did you think that was a good idea?" He turns his head towards me, spitting out dirt. As soon as he recognizes me, his eyes go wide. I grin sardonically. "Didn't expect me, did you?"

"Mr. Lucinio! Sir, I'm sorry. I'm so sorry! I'll stop. I swear I will. I'll pay everything back! I have all of the money in different accounts. I'll give it all back!"

"Oh, you definitely will." I stand and aim my Glock at his head.

"Mr. Lucinio! I won't ever do this again!" He starts bawling like a baby. I close my eyes and sigh as Gavin starts laughing.

"Jesus fucking Christ," I say. "Shut up and listen." I open my eyes and shake my head. He takes a few deep breaths, and the sobbing subsides. "Your wife and family will be provided for. They have nothing to do with your bullshit. You, on the other hand. You live an entire other life! A house in Greece. You've gone places you've never taken your wife. Trust me when I say she'll be a lot better on her own."

He swallows. Hard. He closes his eyes and lets out a breath before opening them again. "Please, Mr. Lucinio. Let me explain." He meets my eyes.

I have no idea why I do it, but I raise an eyebrow and nod. "Talk."

He lets out an audibly relieved sigh. "What I did was wrong. I'll be the first to admit that. I have another family in Greece. But it's not what you think. My wife knows about them. They're…" He trails off and looks down.

After a few moments I let out my own sigh. Only it's impatient. I'm not in the fucking mood. "They're…?" I prompt.

He looks up at me once more. "They're her brother's family. He was killed by the Italian mob for fuck only knows what."

I lower my gun and glance at Gavin before looking back at him. "Get up. On your knees. Tell me about the money."

He does as I tell him to. "I took it to pay them off. I don't know when they'll come for her, but I know they will. I wanted to have the money sitting there for when they come. I shouldn't have done it, but that's why I took it. I bought a house. A yacht. I made sure her kids are going to a private school. Everything I have here, I made sure she has there. Things to make her look to everyone that she's a widowed mother taking care of her familia. Family."

"You think you can get me names of the people who went after your wife's brother? Help me out with that, I'll make sure you're protected and your sister-in-law is as well."

He watches me for such a long time, I'm wondering if he's gone into shock. Finally, he opens his mouth. "Who are you?"

I chuckle. "I guess your knight in shining fucking armor."

He takes several shaky breaths as he nods. "What about the money?"

I put the gun in my hand back in my holster. "It belongs to the company. You're giving it back. But I will take care of you and your family. I'll take you back at Lucinio Tech. I'll give you your old salary. The person I have in place now really wants to do something else with his life. But the money you took goes back. You'll be watched very closely. Be good and be on my side, I'll be your best friend. Fuck me over, and I won't hesitate to go back to my mafia roots and shoot you. Understand?"

His eyes widen when he realizes just how big of an opportunity I'm giving him. How thick of an olive branch. He doesn't attempt to get off his knees, but he does nod enthusiastically. "Yes, sir!"

I hold out a hand. He takes it, and I help him to his feet. "I mean every word, Mr. Donovan."

"I understand, sir. I won't let you down."

"We'll come up with a plan on the way back to your house. You start back at the company on Monday."

He nods. We all pile back into the SUVs, Gavin in the front next to me this time.

"Feel better?" Gavin asks as I start driving.

"Surprisingly. It kind of felt good. Getting back to my roots."

"Not having to hide who you truly are?"

"I mean, I'm not my father. I don't want to pressure people into paying me for my protection or taking control of half their business to use for money laundering. I don't give a fuck about drugs or weapons. That's all a bunch of shit. I care about good people not having to deal with bad ones."

"Sounds about right. Like you."

I chuckle. I want to take after Ryan. Not my father. Protect the innocent while making the guilty pay. Donovan isn't guilty. But the ones who are will wish they never fucked with him. Because now they'll have to deal with me.

A long while later, I pull into the driveway of my villa. It's only two stories, but it's spread across my property. It's modern with a touch of the old Italian style. My property is open with a few trees for shade. The pool out back is Olympic size with a fountain in the middle. It's the center of my property.

As Gavin and I grab our gear and head inside, I have to smile. It's nice getting back to who I am. The real me. The protector. And as I get ready for my date tonight, I realize something I haven't really thought of in a long time...

I'm happy.

Chapter Twenty Five

✗ Josh ✗

An entire fucking year since Alex fucking abandoned me. My father still hasn't given me control like he told Alex he would, but it doesn't surprise me at all. I don't think he intends to give me control. I think he's stringing me along. Dangling the prize in front of my face like I'm a damn dog.

That all changes today.

Alex has always been the strong one. He's always stood up to our dad. But he's not here. He left. It's time for me to stand up and fight for what I want.

I'm just about to storm into my dad's office when I stop in my tracks at the door. It's cracked so I lean against the wall. I've been doing this a lot lately. It's how I get all of my information.

"I don't get it," Keith says. "I thought you wanted Jessa killed for what she did to Alex. Taking him away from this."

"Are you questioning me?" my dad asks.

"No, sir. Absolutely not. I wouldn't dream of questioning you, sir. Just trying to understand."

"Your job isn't to understand. Your job is to do what I fucking say. But in the interest of getting this done right, that was before."

"Before?"

"Before my surveillance of her. She's beautiful. She's sexy. She's every man's daydream. I can't get her out of my head. I fantasize about her. I want her. For myself. She'll give me the heir I want. One who won't defy me at every damn turn. I need the perfect fucking leader, or this mafia goes down with me."

Keith is completely silent, and I nearly gag. My father's obsession with Jessa is sick and bordering on psychotic. I knew he was still surveying her. I've seen the pictures. But he's going too far. The pictures he's taken are of her mostly naked. Like when she's changing. I don't know how the fuck he even gets them. Her bedroom is upstairs. What the fuck? Does he climb a tree? I've seen the smudges all over the pictures. I know he's getting off to her. Fucking gross.

I've been keeping an eye on it in case I need to step in. Until today, I hadn't felt the need to. As long as he got off to the pictures and didn't try to touch her, I didn't think a confrontation over it was the best option.

Ever since Alex left, I haven't gone near Jessa. I haven't needed to. My goal was to break them up. The problem is my feelings for her haven't gone away. For a while, I thought I only had them because of my proximity to her. The truth is, they've blossomed. I honestly care about her. I hate all I had to do to protect her and my brother, but I've been questioning if I even made the right choice with that.

I got what I wanted. The immediate goal was reached. Alex went to Italy without Jessa, ensuring his safety. The ultimate goal, however, wasn't. Alex took over the overseas factions. I was supposed to get the US. As soon as that happened, Alex was going to give me overseas. I'd be running all of the mafia. And there wasn't a fuck of a thing our father could do about it. Alex would get what he wanted, to be away from all of this, and Jessa would always be safe.

And she was safe. For the most part. I can deal with jacking off on pictures of her. I can't deal with this entire fucking scheme. My father isn't touching her. Not a single hair on her pretty little head.

"Tell me what you need," Keith finally says.

"Her habits. I know her home habits. I need her schedule. From when she wakes up to when she goes to bed. Go," my dad orders.

I shake my head and smirk, still leaning against the wall. My arms folded across my chest. He's fucking crazy. If he thinks I'm letting this shit slide, he has another thing coming. Alex might play to him, but not me. This ends right now.

"Close the door behind you," dad growls.

Keith walks out of the office and closes the door. He looks at me. "Your dad's lost his damn mind." He keeps his voice low.

What my dad doesn't know is that Keith has become more my second in command than his. My dad's recent crazy antics had nearly gotten Keith killed more than once. Keith is starting to understand why Alex and I are such fucking problem children.

"Do what he says," I whisper. "I have a plan."

Keith raises his eyebrows. I motion for him to follow me. We head to the garage. "You aren't going to let him do this." I can hear the desperation in his voice.

"I'm going to let him think I am. But no. I'm not. I'm going after Jess myself."

"What? She's not even a part of this anymore! I mean, I have little conscience, but even I draw a line where innocents are concerned."

I grin and put a calming hand on his shoulder as I shake my head. "Alex never told her that he has a twin. That's how I got them to break up. I pretended to be Alex and acted like a possessive, jealous, asshole."

"Wait. You had a hand in that?"

"You think I'd let him kill my fucking brother?"

He gives me a relieved smile. "So, what's the plan, boss?"

"Simple. I'll pretend to be Alex. Win her back. That way I can keep her safe, and my dad can stay the fuck away from her."

"But Alex is in Italy."

"Jessa doesn't know that. As far as she knows, they just broke up and Alex has stayed away. She's never been here. Never met the family. She has no fucking idea who he really is. He never even told her his true last name. He used an alias."

"He really didn't want her near this."

"Nope. But things will be different this time. I won't tell her the whole truth. Nothing about the mafia. I'll keep Alex's alias. But I will introduce her to the family."

"What? They'll call you Josh and ruin everything."

I smile, becoming more and more confident in my plan as I talk. "By that time, I'll have told her that my middle name is Joshua. My parents call me Josh. The full name of Alex's alias is Alexander Joshua Lang."

"That is his name, though. Minus the last name.

"Yep. That's what makes them so perfect. We don't really have to lie about who we are except for that last time."

Keith grins. "You're fucking smart, kid."

I grin back and shrug. "It goes back to when we were kids. We'd play bank robbers. We had a whole fucking identity and everything. Mine is Joshua Alexander Lang. I still use it to this day. Same initials and everything, but no one has a fucking clue who we really are or who our family is. We have ID's with that information and everything."

Keith laughs. "Fucking clever."

"Anyway, listen. In all honesty, I caught fucking feelings for her when I was getting them to break up. I wouldn't let my father near her anyway, but certainly not when I have strong feelings for her. She doesn't deserve any of this."

Keith raises an eyebrow at my confession. "I had a feeling. Go get your girl, boss." Keith turns back for the house but pauses. "What about surveillance? If you're going after her, should I leave you out of the photos?"

I give him a cocky smirk. "Fuck no. Let him see. Let's see what he says. Remember, you're still working for him. Let him keep thinking you hate me as much as he does. He doesn't need to know you report to me."

Keith laughs as he turns away and continues into the house. I get into my car and take off. I need to get to Jessa before he does. Maybe this could be a way to make up for everything she's been through. As much as I hate that I had to hurt her like that, I know it was necessary. It was the only way to get her to walk away from Alex.

But what the hell kind of man would I be if I allowed a psycho to continue to violate her privacy like my father is? Who the hell would I be if I allowed him to hurt her? If I didn't protect her?

It doesn't stop me from feeling worlds of guilt, though. I put her through a lot in the name of protection. I've thought about it over and over again. Would things have differed if I'd told them both the truth?

I rub my temples and follow my GPS to a flower shop. If I am going to do this, I have to do it right. Flowers. Candy. Whatever I need to.

I have a lot of groveling to do with her. Things are going to go a lot differently this time. I can't just show up and tell her who I really am. Alex, the fucking idiot he is, ruined that for me.

What the fuck? I shake my head to rid the thoughts. Alex isn't an idiot. He knew what he was doing. I may not have agreed, but I understand the reasoning. And I can't be pissed at him leaving. He did exactly what I wanted him to.

I pull over in front of a flower shop. Thoughts of how pissed off Alex would be if he knew what I was doing creep into my mind. He'd probably never talk to me again. I lean my head back against the headrest and growl at myself for letting the negative thoughts creep in again.

No. He wouldn't be. He'd understand my reasoning. I'm doing this to protect Jessa. He might be pissed that I have feelings for her, but he'd get over it and understand. He has realized over the past year that he didn't love her as much as he thought he did. He's told me that on the rare occasions I get to talk to him.

Between the rare moments I'm not insanely jealous of him, that is. Fuck. Alex is in Italy, and our father still dotes on him like he's God's fucking gift. He even calls me Alex sometimes. He's never done that before. Not until Alex left us.

Fucking Hell. Stop it. Alex isn't the fucking enemy here. You have a job to do. Protect Jessa. Get over yourself and focus.

After the miniscule pep talk, I walk my ass into the Empty Vase Flower Shop. My eyes nearly pop out of my head. So… much… pink. Pink lights. Pink vases. Pink flowers. Pink curtains. Pink. Everything is pink.

"Jesus," I say under my breath. I hear a throaty laugh come from somewhere to my side. I don't bother to look. I just roll my eyes. I already know what's coming.

"Hi. I'm Desi. I'm a florist here."

I barely spare her a glance. She's slim. Leggy. Average height. Barely there tits. Red heads aren't my thing. They're nothing more than a fun couple of hours to me. But just like so many other women of all types, I apparently give off a 'fuck me' attitude because they flock to me.

"I'm here for something pretty and understated without looking understated." I realize my mistake as soon as the words are out of my mouth and fight the urge to groan. I'm not in the mood.

Desi sidles to my side and puts her hand lightly on my arm. I've never had an issue getting women to fall into bed with me. Usually, all they need is a look before they're dying to unzip my pants. I guess Desi only needs to hear my voice.

"Is that so?" Her soft voice is an octave too low and gets directly onto my nerves.

I lightly brush her off and take a step back. She's not the one I want. Doesn't even compare to the woman running her way through my mind. The woman who has been on my mind ever since I first brushed my lips against hers.

I smirk. Playing a bit with this girl might be satisfying, though. "Flowers, Desi. And chocolate covered strawberries. If you have them." I know Jessa has a fondness for strawberries. Add white chocolate to them, and, according to Alex anyway, she'll fall at my feet.

Desi looks slightly confused. It doesn't seem like she's used to getting rejected. She clears her throat. "Sure. We only have one box left of a special shipment. We don't usually have them, but we wanted to try something new." She leads me to a small refrigerator covered with all different types of flowers and one single box. She unties the tie and lifts the lid.

I raise an eyebrow. "Silver? I've never seen silver on strawberries before."

"Special ordered. Like I said. They're edible, though." She closes the lid and re-ties the bow.

"Fine. I'll take them." Not the white chocolate I wanted, but silver is kind of cool. It's my favorite color.

She nods as she looks up at me through her lashes. My cock doesn't even twitch, but I have the overwhelming urge to fuck around with her. She puts the strawberries on the counter, and I back her into it. Her ass hits the counter and she lets out a little gasp.

I put my hands on each side of the counter, pinning her. "Are we alone?" I let my voice drop a little.

"Y-yes…"

I step closer so my cock is against her and grind into her. She moans, and I give her a sexy smile, dipping my head low. "You like that?"

"Yes… yes…"

I'm not at all turned on by this girl, but I can't deny the sadistic part of me is enjoying it. Redheads are the exact opposite of the type of girl I truly enjoy in my bed. But I do like messing with them. I like watching their disappointment when they realize that all of their flirting doesn't faze me. Giving them a little taste and pulling back is one of my favorite things to do. Pretty fucked up, but what just turned twenty-five year old man would give a shit?

I lean down, and she closes her eyes. I ghost my lips across hers as I hear the door to the shop open. I keep her pinned as I move to her ear and whisper. "Carnations."

Her eyes fly open as I step back. "What?"

"I need carnations. Pretty ones. Something that says, 'I'm sorry. I love you.'" It takes a second for my words to sink in. She visibly shakes her head, like she's coming out of a daze. "You also have customers," I whisper as I watch her.

That gets her to snap out of her lust filled daze. She hurries over to the other customers, and I turn my intense glare on her back. I lean against the counter, arms over my chest. After she greets them and they begin looking around, she slinks back to me. I visibly let my eyes rake over her body. She's too thin. She has no curves, no ass. She's model thin. A stick. Too tall.

I keep a soft smile on my face when she touches my abs and steps closer to me. Her hand is the only thing touching me, but she's so close that I can feel the heat from her body. I have no doubt that if I grabbed her between her legs, she'd be soaking wet for me. I fight the curiosity to see if I'm right; if I turn her on as much as I think I do.

"What kind of an arrangement would you like?" she asks, her voice husky.

I don't move. Instead, I stay in the very position I am and watch her. "She likes pink. It's her favorite color. Dark pink. She likes carnations. She's beautiful, but she's understated. She doesn't try at all, and is still a knockout. You think you can make me an arrangement that says all of that? Something that compares to her while still telling her I'm sorry for fucking things up?"

I gain satisfaction as I watch her begin to realize that I won't be taking her to the backroom and fucking her on the table she uses to make the flower arrangements. She takes a step back, disappointment radiating off of her. She nods slightly and bites her lip to keep herself from turning thirty shades of embarrassed.

"Um…Yeah. I have something."

"Good. Don't worry about the cost. I don't care if you come back here with a million dollar bouquet. I don't have much time."

I make a point of looking at my watch as she scurries away. I chuckle deep from within my chest as she hurries around the store. She grabs a vase and several flowers. She takes everything to the backroom, avoiding eye contact with me. I walk around the shop, looking for anything else to help me with Jessa.

My eye lands on a stuffed piglet. I grin as I pick it up. One of the days I cornered her, she was alone in the library on campus. Before I dragged her to a dark, quiet corner, I saw the stickers and drawings she had all over her notebook. She loves piglets.

"Perfect."

I carry it with me to the counter as Desi walks out from the back with the arrangement I requested. She puts it on the counter next to the piglet and the box of strawberries. The pink and white carnations are full and mixed in with a few fire and ice ones. There's baby's breath and fern, giving the arrangement that special something extra I was looking for while still remaining beautifully simple.

"What do you think?" she asks quietly.

I grin. "Fucking perfect." I pay for everything and head out without a backwards glance, even though I can feel her watching me.

I jump in my car and head for Jessa's apartment that she shares with Cole. Through my dad's surveillance that I sneakily search through on a daily basis, I know Cole is a cop for the LAPD, but he's in some kind of training event in San Francisco. I have five days alone with her to make her mine.

I also know that Jessa just started a job as a project manager at a small architecture firm. She took time off after she graduated. I don't know if it was because of how much the breakup fucked her up, or if she just wanted time to figure out what she truly wanted. Lucky for me, the firm is a startup and doesn't have a building yet. That means Jessa is able to work from home, giving me more time to truly fix what I fucked up.

After one more quick stop, I pull up in front of her building and gather everything. Thanks to that same surveillance, I know which apartment she lives in and everything. My disgusting father was good for something at least. Foiling his fucked up plans is going to be a lot easier. And using his own bullshit against him makes it so much sweeter for me.

I enter the building and head up to her floor. I quickly find the apartment and set the pig on the floor out of her sight. I want that to be a surprise. Well, more than everything else, but mostly more than me showing up here.

Alex. I have to remember I'm portraying him right now. At least long enough to fix all of this and get her to marry me.

Taking a deep breath, I knock on the door. My heart beats faster, and I realize that despite all of the fucked up shit that happened, I miss her. She wasn't afraid of me every time I saw her. And even when she was, her kisses were still the best I've ever experienced. Her body's response to me, even through her fear, was nothing if not hot as hell.

"Just a sec!"

I hold my breath and try to compose myself. I'm doing this to protect her. I shake my head as my mind starts to cloud. Again. I put a hand against the doorframe to steady myself. Fuck. Not now. I need to think clearly. Not succumb to whatever the hell happens to me after a beatdown. Like the one I got a couple of weeks ago. At least I'm not sick anymore and dry heaving in the fucking toilet. Still get dizzy as hell, though. And my thought process isn't always clear for a long while afterwards.

I hear the lock on the door being worked, and, moments later, Jessa opens it. It's like the fog falls away. Like she's the answer to make it all stop. She's wearing short jean shorts that show off her perfectly tan legs, and a blue tank top that shows just a little bit of her midriff. It shows no cleavage, but her tits are on full display. It's hard to hide double Ds.

I swallow. Hard. This. Her. She's the perfect fucking woman. Perfect curves. Her petite height. Her ass. Damn. She looks even better now than she did a year ago. And she was fucking perfect then. But it's not all about her looks. She's truly sweet and incredibly smart. Jessa is everything. Fucking everything.

"Jessa," I manage to get out. It's not my fault my voice sounds so deep. Even to my own years. It's a miracle I was able to even speak at all.

Her vivid blue eyes widen in fear.

But also something else. Something I wasn't expecting.

Love.

She still loves Alex. At least some part of her.

I don't know if that pisses me off. Hell, I don't even know what the fuck I'm feeling right now. There's really only one thing I know for sure.

And that is her feelings for my brother will make things a whole hell of a lot easier on me right now.

Chapter Twenty Six

⚔ Jessa ⚔

I stare in open-mouthed shock at the man standing in front of me. He looks taller. More muscular somehow. His jeans ride low on his hips. His red t-shirt clings to every single one of his hard ridges.

I don't know whether to scream, run, jump in his arms and hug him, or cry. Or if I should simply give in to the sudden urge I have to pass out.

"Alex…" I feel my hands start to shake, and I suddenly can't breathe. I take a couple steps back. I think my body is making the decision for me. Everything around me starts to blur.

"Jess?" Alex is looking at me with his brows creased in concern. He slowly kneels to the ground.

Or maybe he doesn't. I don't really know because suddenly, the ground seems to swallow me as everything goes black.

I slowly open my eyes and feel something wet against my cheeks and forehead. Tears?

No. Something else.

I reach up and touch my forehead.

"Hey, I got it, beautiful."

I sit up quickly at the sound of a voice I never thought I'd hear again and immediately regret the decision. "Oh, God. No." I snap my eyes closed and hold my head in my hands. I'm instantly dizzy and nauseated.

"You hit your head when you fell, baby. I saw it coming, and I caught you before you hit the floor, but I didn't know there was a table next to you. You smacked the side of your head." His hand cups my cheek, and he gently turns my head. "It looks good, though. How do you feel?"

"Sick." I take a deep breath and plunge forward. May as well get everything out. Word vomit. He should be used to that. "Nauseous. Scared. Confused. Angry. Upset. Frustrated. Most of all? I hate that I don't know what the hell to feel."

"I have a lot of apologizing to do. Hours upon hours of groveling. But first thing's first. All I care about right now is how you are. Physically. We can deal with the rest later."

I take another deep breath, trying to steady my racing heart, and slowly open my eyes again. I'm laying on the couch with my head in Alex's lap, but I'm not sure how I got into this position. I thought I sat up.

Alex is smoothing my hair back from my face and looking at me with so much love and regret that it overwhelms me. It's like I'm looking into the eyes of the Alex that I fell in love with. I don't know what to think.

"What happened? Between us?" I ask quietly.

It's a question I've wanted to ask him for a long time. If for no other reason than to ease my own mind. Get answers to questions I've asked myself over and over again, but never could actually find peace in.

Pain crosses Alex's entire face, and he tenses. I'm immediately on edge, and I flinch when his hand brushes hair off my neck. My flinch causes him to wince.

"I'm sorry," I say, immediately feeling bad for flinching in the first place.

"For what? I caused this," he says quietly. I sniffle and close my eyes. Alex caresses my cheek. His thumb brushes across my bottom lip, and I can't help but lean into him. "Things were so fucked up for me a year ago, baby. Fuck. They have been for a long time. So many crazy things were going on at home. My dad was causing a lot of problems with my mom. I took it out on you, Jessa. I'm sorry. I know I shouldn't have."

His voice. I've always loved how calm and soothing his voice is. How deep it is. I love the cologne he wears. I love how amazing he looks without even trying. But most of all, I love who he is as a person. Or was. Is?

I sit up again. "What the hell am I doing?" I sit up again and whimper.

Alex immediately has an arm around my waist. "Hey. I know you're pissed off, and a lot of shit is going on in your pretty little head, but you took a nasty fall not that long ago, honey. You have to be careful with the way you move right now." He kisses my neck, like it's the most natural thing to him, like he's still allowed to, and then stands. He puts a couple of pillows behind me and helps me lay back down.

"Maybe I should call Doctor Freeman." I've seen him a few times, even without Alex in my life, and he's always available to me when I need him.

"Want me to call him?" He kneels next to me and puts his hand on my stomach. I may be completely befuddled right now about everything, but there is one thing I don't doubt. One thing I trust. Even though he had gotten pissed off and sometimes violent, Alex would never endanger my life.

"What do you think? Do you think I'll be okay, or do you think I should be looked at?"

He smiles softly and leans down. He brushes his lips against mine, and I close my eyes. I missed him. So much. I have to be crazy. After everything, how is it possible to miss him so much? To want him as much as I do? Does it make me crazy to both wish he'd wrap me in his arms and never let me go while simultaneously wanting to punch him?

"I think you'll be okay. But we'll keep an eye on you." He stands and walks to the kitchen counter.

After a moment, he comes back and sits on the coffee table in front of me, hiding something quickly behind his back. I watch him, both curiously and cautiously. It doesn't make sense that he's here after this long. Nothing about any of this makes sense.

I'm probably dreaming. Or having a nightmare, depending on how this goes.

"I came here to tell you how sorry I am. I know I messed up everything with you. I let everything going on get to me, and I wasn't honest with you. The one person in my life that was good, and I took all of my pent up anger and frustration out on you. That was wrong of me, baby," he nearly whispers. I stay quiet as he presents me with the most beautiful bouquet of pink and white carnations I have ever seen. "I know how much you love carnations. I had this designed especially for you. To show you how sorry I am. To show you how much I still love you. How much I'll always love you. How badly I miss you, and how much I want you back."

The bouquet says everything he described to me. The love. The apology. How much he still cares. It brings tears to my eyes. He takes a box from beside him. It's perfectly wrapped and so pretty that I hate the idea of unwrapping it.

The wrapping is pink and silver and looks like a Japanese flower. I want to weep at its beauty.

"I stopped and had that rewrapped. The original wrapping just didn't do you justice," he says quietly as he watches me.

"It's beautiful." I slowly try to sit up, so I can see everything better. Alex puts the box on the table and helps me.

"I got you, baby." He very sweetly and gently helps me to sit. He adjusts the pillows behind me once more before he sits in front of me again.

"Thank you," I say softly. He smiles and puts the box in my lap. "You really didn't have to do this."

"Yes, I did. I have a lot to prove and apologize for."

I look down at the box, still so confused. I still have no idea what's happening. I don't know how to feel. I take a deep breath. My heart is still racing, and I am desperately trying to calm it down. I slowly open the box. Revealed to me are a set of beautiful silver colored strawberries. My mouth falls open.

"Alex...."

"I remembered your fondness for strawberries. They're chocolate covered. I know they aren't white, like you like. You can eat them."

I look at him in wonder, and he laughs. He takes a strawberry and holds it up to his mouth. He takes a bite as he watches me, and his face breaks out into a charming Alex-like grin. I can't help but laugh with him.

"Good?" I ask, grinning.

"Fucking amazing. Here."

He holds the rest of it up to my mouth and pulls it slightly back as I am about to bite into it. He grins and puts it back. I eye him suspiciously and attempt to bite again. He pulls it back slightly once more.

"Alex!" He chuckles, and I grab his hand, so I can bite into the strawberry as he laughs. My eyes widen in happy delight. "Oh my God, I'm going to have a foodgasm."

Alex looks at me and blinks. "A… food… gasm?"

I laugh. "It's when something is so good that nothing compares."

"I don't think I've ever heard that."

"Well, now you have."

He grins and quickly swipes the box. I gasp and then groan sadly, reaching for it. He holds it out of my reach and gives me a quick peck on my lips. "I think I'd prefer to be the one to give you your orgasms." He winks.

I turn crimson and look down, thinking of just how many of them he'd given me; how enjoyable they were. I don't understand how he can have such an effect on me after everything that happened between us. How can such a quick kiss make electricity shoot through every part of my being? How can I still be so insanely attracted to him despite being terrified of his intentions?

Of him.

I shake my head. "Alex, what are you doing? What are you doing *here*?" I don't look at him. I can't. I can feel how hurt he is. I can feel it because I feel the same way.

"Can I ask you something?" he asks me. I bite my lip and force my eyes to his. "Do you still think about me?"

"That's not fair…," I whisper.

"Jessa. No. I didn't ask you about fair. I asked how you feel. This has nothing to do with anything else. It has to do with us."

I look in his beautiful blue eyes and see everything I'm feeling reflected back at me. The uncertainty. The overpowering love. The fear of what's to come. I feel the tears sting my eyes, and before I can stop them, they start to fall. Alex thumbs them away. Like magic, everything I feel comes flying out of my mouth.

Word vomit.

"I love you so much it hurts sometimes! I can't stop thinking about you. Even when I think I'm okay, and that I've forgotten about you, something reminds me of you. Okay? Are you happy?" I'm fully sobbing at this point. "I don't want to get over you no matter how hard I try, and I feel like such a stupid, horrible person. I hate myself for how I feel about you! I thought I was okay! I thought I moved on! But then it always ended up right back with you!"

"Baby -" Alex tries to hug me, but I push him away. He looks so hurt that it completely crushes my heart.

But I carry on. "I'm terrified of you! How could you hurt me and scare me like you did, and then pretend you didn't do anything to me? How could you leave me alone when I needed you? You promised I'd never have to fight through my attacks alone!"

My sobbing turns hysterical. I don't even recognize the sounds coming out of my mouth. I don't recognize myself.

Alex just sits in front of me with his elbows on his knees as I let everything I've been bottling up finally go. Everything over the last year spill out of me like lava.

"You promised you'd never leave me! You promised me! You promised me you'd never hurt me! You said you loved me!" I'm shaking and hyperventilating and I can't calm down. I sob even more uncontrollably. "You promised you'd never let me fight alone!"

"I'm so sorry, Jessa. So fucking sorry."

I can barely see him or hear him over the thundering of my own heart; the animal sounds coming from me. He gingerly touches my arm, but I furiously pull away.

I want to hit him. I want to pound on his chest. Scream. Cry. Rage.

"Please let me help you through this," he says calmly. So calmly, it pisses me off. How can he be so calm? "I know how bad I fucked up, Jessa, but I still know you. I still know what you need, and I know it's me. I know Cole, as your lover or friend, or whatever the fuck he is to you right now, can't calm you down the way I can. As quickly as me. Let me help you. Let me at least keep a promise I made to you and help you through this. Not let you fight alone. After that, I'll leave if that's what you want from me. Even if it is the last fucking thing I want."

My chest is physically hurting me because of my erratic heartbeat and uncontrollable sobs. All I can do is nod my head because he's right. I need him right now, but I don't know how I feel about it. I hate that he's the cause of this, but he's the only solution to getting me out of it.

Alex sits next to me on the couch and gently pulls me into his lap, letting me do most of the work. Giving me the option. Letting me make the decision and control the pace.

"I want you to feel comfortable and safe. Just tell me what you need if I'm not doing enough for you, okay?" Always so calm.

I curl up into him and lay my head on his chest, gripping his shirt. He wraps me in his arms. He runs his fingers through my hair and hugs me tightly to him as I soak his shirt with my tears. Tears that I've fought so hard for so long.

I don't know how long he sits with me, but he doesn't say anything. He lets me cry it out while he holds me tightly and rocks me gently. He keeps his breathing steady, even though I can feel how hard it is for him. The more heart-wrenching my cries are, the tighter he holds me.

He begins to whisper to me over and over how sorry he is. He repeats again and again how much he loves me. How badly he fucked up.

Eventually, I can't cry anymore. There's nothing left in me, but I don't want him to let me go. Being with him feels so natural. So right. Perfect. He's everything I've ever wanted. This year without him has felt like a part of my soul is missing. I haven't felt whole without him. I've done my best to move on, and I've done well. One day at a time. But there was always a piece of me that was just gone.

"All I want is for everything to be better. I want to fix us and be like we were before," I whisper into his chest. "How wrong is that? How fucked up does that make me?"

"Baby, it doesn't. It will take time to repair the damage I caused. I'm not going to rush you, but I'm also not giving up. It's always been you and me. It always will be. I'm just sorry it took me a whole fucking year to realize it." He swallows, hard, as he leans forward. He keeps me tightly against him, but takes something off the table. He sets it in my lap.

I look at it and then him, a huge smile breaking out across my tear-stained face. "You got me a stuffed piglet?"

He smiles and runs his hand up my arm to my face. He wipes my tears away and leans forward to place a light kiss on the corner of my mouth. "My hope is that you'll think of me whenever you see it." He smiles. I hug him and relish the feeling of his body against mine. He kisses my neck.

"I should go. Before your boyfriend comes back." He grimaces. I don't know why, but the thought of him leaving makes my heart break into a billion pieces. "I put my new number in your phone. If you need me, call. I'll be right here."

I look up at him, trying to focus on the words that just left his mouth. My mind is still on the fact that he remembers so much about me. Like how much I love baby pigs. But the fact that he just said he plans on leaving makes my heart sick.

"Why don't I want you to leave?"

He smiles and squeezes my hip. "Say the word, baby. I don't expect you to forgive me or trust me right away. I won't force anything with you. But if you ask me to stay, I'd never be able to turn you down."

I watch him, looking for any sign of deception or anger. Any sign that he might hurt me again. I see nothing but love and devotion. The same love and devotion that always shone from Alex's eyes whenever he looked at me.

I reach up and touch his face. He turns and kisses my wrist. "Is this really real? Am I dreaming? Are you really willing to give us a chance again?" I ask, unsure.

"You're not dreaming. It's real. And yes. I want to give us a chance again, baby. More than anything. Just one big difference." I watch him, waiting for him to continue. "No more lies. On my part. No more accusations of you cheating. No more jealousy. I know you love me. All that shit before was me lashing out because of the stuff going on at home. Never again. This time, you and I are partners."

I bite my lip, watching him for a few moments before nodding. "I'd like that."

He smiles so hard that my face hurts for him. "Jess, I'm not gonna lie to you. If you don't let me kiss you, I'm going to lose my fucking mind. I miss you. Your taste. Your touch. The way you feel when you come for me."

I blush as his hand drops to my ass, and he squeezes. My eyes widen as immediate heat pools between my legs. I gasp, but force myself to stay strong. "Slower this time. We have to work back up to that," I whisper. He groans. "But… if you want to kiss me…"

It's all the permission he needs. His lips crash to mine. The kiss is familiar and all-consuming. I bunch his shirt into my fists as his tongue slips between my lips and fights mine for a dominance I'd always give to him. I whimper when he stands with me in his arms and starts walking down the hall.

"Where's your room?" he growls against my mouth.

"First one," I answer breathlessly.

Our lips crash together again and again. My fingers run through his hair, and I tug slightly. He kicks the door shut behind us and drops me on the bed. He climbs in with me and pulls me close to him as the kiss continues.

After a few moments, he pulls away. I whimper again. I missed everything with him. The way he makes me feel is only a small part of it, but right now, it's everything. I want to feel worshiped in the way only Alex knows how to do.

He smiles as he nips my lower lip. "Patience." He glances over his shoulder. "Do you always sleep with your shades open?"

"Oh. Uh… yes. Usually. I like the lights."

"Aren't you afraid someone could watch you?"

I glance towards the window. "I guess I never thought about it. I thought I was high enough up." I lean in and try to kiss him again. I've missed his lips on mine. I didn't know how much until now.

He leans back and smiles. "Shades closed from now on. You never know the lengths people will go when it comes to gorgeous women."

I realize just how right he is and how stupid I've been. "Oh. Okay. I'm sorry. I'll close them."

He smiles and gives me the kiss I want. "I got it. Go get ready for bed. I'll grab something for us to eat, and then we can watch a movie or something."

I smile back and kiss him again. "What about you?"

"What about me?"

"You hate wearing the same clothes the next day."

He grins and his eyes twinkle. "Are you asking me to stay?"

I look away shyly and bite my lip. "Is that wrong?"

"No. We were together for four years. We know how much we missed each other. We know we belong together. We know where this is going, no matter the pace. My only concern is Cole."

Why does he keep bringing up Cole? Is he… Oh my God! He thinks I'm with him. "Cole is at some kind of training convention in San Francisco. But we're not dating. I mean, we tried, but Cole and I are just friends. Best friends, but that's all."

He gives me a sly smile before he kisses me again and stands up. He walks to the window and stands by it a few moments like he's scanning for any threats to my safety before he closes the shades. He turns towards me and winks as he strides to the door.

"Get comfortable, baby."

I smile and jump out of the bed, quickly stripping off my shorts and tank top as well as my bra, leaving only my panties. I search through my drawers looking for something to wear and still haven't decided when Alex comes back.

"I made a couple sand-" He cuts himself off as soon as he sees me. I spin around. His eyes rake over my body. They're on fire, and I forget completely that I am standing in front of him nearly naked.

He gives me a wolfish grin as he shakes his head and puts the sandwiches on the bed. He takes off his shirt and tosses it to me. "Put this on before my dick gets so hard it fucking falls off."

I lick my lips as my eyes drop to his cock. I can see my effect on him quite clearly. He laughs as I put the shirt on. He takes off his jeans and pulls the covers back. He crawls in, and I crawl in next to him. We find a movie and watch it as we eat.

We talk like no time has passed between us. Like everything bad that happened never did. We find a second movie and curl up together.

Wrapped tightly in Alex's arms, I feel myself starting to relax. To trust that he means what he says. I believe his apology, even though there are a lot of questions in the back of my head about his intentions.

The biggest one is that I'm not sure if I'm making a mistake. I don't know if I'm following my heart or my head. I can't tell if the two are at war or in agreement. I don't know which of them to follow since neither of them really know what's happening.

If I'm dreaming.

But as I start to drift off, I feel calm. For the first time since Alex and I broke up, I feel normal. Like myself. I feel like the world is right. I feel like I'm right where I need to be. Where I'm supposed to be. In Alex's arms.

Where I've always and will always belong.

Chapter Twenty Seven

 Josh

(One Year Later)

This year with Jessa has been the best I've ever had. I love getting to know her more than just what my brother shared with me while they were together. I love kissing her. Touching her sets my whole body on fire.

Getting involved in my dad's psychotic plan was the smartest thing I ever did. I understand his obsession. She's fucking beautiful. She feels like Heaven in my arms, and she tastes like nothing I could have fathomed.

Even if I'm not near her, I can taste her on my lips. She wears this cake batter lip gloss, and I can't get enough. She's the best damn cake I've ever had.

I've spent almost every night with Jessa since I showed up on her doorstep. I'm not so sure Cole trusts me, but I don't care about him. Jessa is all that matters. And she's made it clear I'm the one she wants because she didn't move into a house with Cole when he bought one. She stayed here, in this apartment. Ours.

I need to make an appearance at my parents' house tonight. I haven't considered it home in a long time, but certainly not now. Jessa has become my home. Wherever she goes, I go. I'm not in my right mind without her by my side.

Which is why I hate that our morning together is about to be ruined. Besides the mandatory appearance I need to make in front of my asshole father, Jessa has to meet her boss at some fucking coffee shop to talk detail of her next project. She deserves better than some fucking start-up. She's far more talented than small time shit that isn't going to go anywhere. It's been a whole damn year. They still don't have an office.

Jessa stirs in my arms, and I grin into her hair. I dislike mornings. I spend so many nights spying on my father, or running missions, that I rarely ever see a morning. I usually sleep right through them. If I end up getting woken up, it wrecks my entire day.

But having Jessa in my arms damn near every morning is quickly changing my mind. She's so fucking perfect and makes my mornings worth it.

"Good morning, handsome." Her sexy, throaty morning voice against my chest vibrates through my entire being. She looks up at me and smiles when I lean down to kiss her.

"Good morning, gorgeous."

She pulls herself closer to me, and I groan. All I can think of is her hands on me.

"Thank you," she whispers against my lips.

"For what?"

"Everything."

I smile because I know what she's getting at. She's told me a lot over the past year that everything between us is better than before. And fuck if that doesn't make me feel incredible. She gets me out of my head when everything is so fucked up. I haven't gotten any beatdowns recently, but that hasn't stopped me from waking up and not knowing what the fuck happened sometimes.

And it definitely hasn't stopped me from going more and more back and forth about Alex. The problem is that it's a lot less back and a fuck of a lot more forth. I'm more and more bitter with him as the days go by.

Two years. And he hasn't come back once. He knows what it's like with our father. He knew what would happen without him. He knew our father would never give me control. Which means he has a plan. Alex always has a plan. It's pretty damn obvious whatever it is doesn't include me. As far as I'm concerned, I'm on my own. He has our entire family, Gavin and Damon included, on his side.

Which means mine won't include them anymore. None of them. My plans include me, Jessa, and taking over this mafia. That's it.

Jessa kisses my chest and starts to get up. I tighten my grip. I'm not ready to let her go. She cuts through the bullshit in my head and makes me feel normal. When she's not around, things are a lot less fucking chaotic.

"Alex, I have that meeting."

"Five minutes. Please?"

"I can't be late… This meeting is important."

"I'll drive you there myself."

I lock her in my arms and pull her on top of me. She giggles as I tangle my fingers in her hair and bring her mouth to mine. The familiar taste of her soft lips sends all the blood straight to my head. And not the one comfortably attached to my shoulders.

I groan as she wiggles against me and slide my hands down to her hips. I can't help myself. I push her down on top of me and let her feel what she's doing.

"Mmm…" She grinds into me.

"God you're gonna kill me."

She wraps her arms around my shoulders and deepens our kiss. I rub against her while letting my fingertips slip underneath her panty line to her ass. I rub in slow circles. She rocks her hips against me in the same slow rhythm that I'm rubbing her.

Her tongue finds mine, and I glide my hands up her back underneath my t-shirt that she's wearing. Fucking hot as hell. She presses herself harder down onto me and whimpers into the kiss. I smile and grab the hem of the t-shirt, slowly lifting it over her head as I sit up with her straddling me.

"You're making this very hard," she whispers, already trembling for me.

I grin. "You're beautiful in nothing but panties." I lean forward and kiss her neck.

She tastes so sweet. It's something unique to just her because I've seen her body wash. Tahitian Escape. It's cheap and smells just okay, but

240

on her? It's like she's transporting us to her very own island. Somewhere only the two of us exist.

"I really should go. I don't want to be late, but I really want you." Her fingers tangle in my short hair when I bury my face in her tits and start nipping and licking them.

"Then give me five minutes. Five minutes to show you how much you mean to me," I rumble against her mounds before taking one of her nipples in my mouth. I roll my tongue over her nipple and lightly scrape it with my teeth just before I suck. Hard.

"Oh…," she moans.

My other hand snakes up her side, to her stomach, and stops just under her other perfect breast. As she always does when I touch her, she arches into me. Like I'm the only thing in the world that matters to her. The only man in the world who can make her feel.

Fuck if that doesn't do things to me no woman has ever managed to. Jessa is, by far, the best I've ever had. Now that I've had a taste of her, I don't want anyone else. I never will.

Finally giving into her silent demand, I take her other breast in my palm. I roll the nipple between my thumb and forefinger and pull while I tug her other one into my mouth again. I lavish it with my tongue before switching and doing exactly the same to her other.

"Oh, Alex. That feels so good." Her voice is breathy, like she can't decide if she wants to whisper or scream.

Holy shit, my name on her lips. It's like the most dangerous fucking addiction that I'll never attempt to recover from.

Her quiet moans make me so hard it hurts. She's arching into me; grinding down on me, and I nearly fucking die. I need release. I can't take any more. I'm about to make a mess. I'd much prefer that mess to be on her thighs, her stomach. Fuck, even her face. Anywhere but my underwear.

I pull her down on top of me and release my dick from the confines of its prison. I grab it and rub it against her panties. She cries out when I hit her clit.

"There it is. There's my girl." I nearly growl the words as I shove my dick against her clit and start thrusting. I kiss her neck as she meets my thrusts. "Fuck, Jessa. I need to feel you. I need to feel your pussy."

"Alex! Alex, please!" She shifts slightly, still plastered against me. She kisses my neck and digs her nails into my shoulders.

I tug her hair until she's looking at me. My lips meet hers in a fevered kiss as I reach down between her legs. I push her panties aside and slam my cock into her with a groan. She moans into my mouth and starts riding me so hard and fast, I know I'm not going to last.

"I'm so close. So close, baby," I say shakily. I want nothing more than to destroy her pussy with my come, but I have a plan. A plan that doesn't include an heir until after she meets me at the end of the aisle and becomes mine in all senses of the word.

"Me, too…" Her thighs start shaking. Her stomach tightens. But Jessa's pussy keeps clenching my dick tight and sucking me into her as she slams herself down onto me.

I love when she loses control. I love the way our skin slapping together feels. I love the way her pussy feels as it gets wetter and wetter while I pound into it, meeting each and every single one of her thrusts with a hard one of my own.

My stomach starts quivering against hers. Jessa grips me tighter as she shivers and trembles. Her pussy clamps around me each time I bury my dick inside her. She glides over me and moves as erratically as her pussy is pulsing. I love when my girl rides me, but I love even more when she gives up control and submits to me.

I grip her hips and hold her tighter as I flip us both over, keeping myself deep inside her warm walls. She wraps her legs around me and meets my thrusts when I once again start pounding her pussy as she screams. Our lips crash together. Our tongues tangle together and ignite into a fucking explosion of desire. Electricity shoots down my spine straight to my dick.

"Fuck, Jess. Come for me, baby. Come all over my cock," I command against her lips.

She throws her head back and screams again, this time, my name. "Alex!" Her pussy grips me so tightly that moving my cock would be impossible. I bury myself in her, relishing in her release, as her hips buck against me. With each pulse of her pussy, she squeezes me tighter and tighter until holding back is completely out of the question.

I quickly shift to my knees as I pull out, even though my dick screams at me not to. I grip and stroke it as I watch her sex-induced haze wash over her. She watches me as I twist my wrist and beat my cock until my own orgasm hits me. Stream after stream of hot come hit her stomach and tits as I let my head fall back.

"Holy fuck, Jessa!" My hips jerk in time to my strokes as I mark her with all of me. I look down at her. She keeps watching me as my strokes slow until I stop coming.

So beautiful. And mine. Fucking mine.

After a few more moments of both of us staring at each other with soft smiles on our faces, I force myself to stand. I grip her feet and tug her to the edge of the bed as she giggles. Christ, I love that sound. Her happy. And me being the man who gives that to her. I help her to her feet as I kiss her.

"We need a shower," I say with a grin against her lips.

She giggles again. "Yes. But the last time we took a shower together, you made me late for a conference call." She slips by me as she giggles again. "So, you get to take one on your own!" she calls over her shoulder .

I laugh and grin as I watch her naked ass as she disappears into her bathroom. "Anything for you, my sweet girl."

✗✗✗

After dropping Jessa off at her meeting, as promised, I start driving home. I'm not looking forward to the conversation I'm about to have with my father. He hasn't said anything to me for too long. No phone calls or texts since the last beating.

I know he's surveying her still. Both of us. Since I told him my plan over a year ago, he's said he'll quit. He hasn't. Not only has Keith told me, but I've gotten the feeling we're being watched. Every time I close the shades at night, I pose by the window just so he can see me and what I'm doing. So he knows he's not going to get a fucking glimpse at her.

I've intentionally made out with Jessa on the window seat she loves so much. It's within perfect view of where I found out he's set up in an apartment he's rented in the building across from hers. I'm lucky she likes kissing me as much as I like kissing her. I hope dad enjoys watching my tongue in her mouth because it will never be fucking his touching her.

I pull my car into the garage and step out. Before I even reach the door to the house, Keith pops his head out and steps into the garage.

"We have a huge fucking problem," he hisses.

"Yeah? What's new?" I raise an eyebrow.

Keith speaks quietly. "He's pissed about this plan. He said it's taking too long. He's beyond livid. He's talking about leverage against you."

I furrow my brows. He has nothing on me. What the fuck is he talking about? "Leverage?"

"Your mom. He's threatening your mom."

My breath catches. My mom and Jessa are my world. I'd do anything for them. My dad knows that. He knows how to manipulate me. I should've known he'd go for her. I failed. I got cocky in my foolproof and underestimated him.

"Josh?"

I shake my head. That single word snaps me completely out of whatever the fuck alternate universe I was just in. The Heaven that Jessa takes me to is suddenly a distant memory. Abruptly, I'm not the favorite son anymore. I'm not the golden child. Remembering Jessa calling me Alex as I was fucking her immediately cuts through my heart. It's like my mind is made of glass. And it just fucking shattered into a million tiny shards.

I'm not Alex.

I'll never be Alex.

I'll never be the leader as long as he gives our father hope that he'll take over.

Nope. I'm Josh. And this whole fucking game is getting harder and harder to play.

"What did he do?" I growl.

"Nothing yet, boss. But you need to be careful in there. He wants me in there for this meeting. You know what that means."

Full well. It means I am about to suffer a hell of a beating. The fog starts to clear a little more. Fog I really didn't even know I was under until my name tumbled out of his mouth.

"Nothing I haven't handled before, Keith," I say after clearing my throat.

He watches me for a few moments before he sighs. He slumps slightly, as if his body is reading and acting out just how defeated I feel. "What do you want me to do? I'll defy his orders if you tell me to."

"You can't." I shrug with a deep breath. It's like his words bring me crashing into reality. "He needs to give me control willingly. You know that. If he doesn't, and I take over with force, I'll be dead by the end of the week. You know how the mafia works."

"I could defy him, Josh." There's that world again. Josh. Everything becomes clearer and clearer. "It would save you another beating."

I have to smile at the worry in his eyes. "He'll kill you. You have a family. Just stay out of it. Let him call in the other guards. You stay back. Have a doctor on call. If I'm still unconscious by seven, text Jessa. I'm supposed to call her. Tell her I got caught up, and I'll text her as soon as I can."

"What if he goes after her?"

My heart physically skips several beats. I don't even want to think about what would happen to her if I'm unconscious. I have to trust Keith to help me out here. He's all I have. "Then defy him. Don't let him touch her. Get to her first. Bring her to my room. Lock her in."

He watches me for a few moments before he sighs and nods. "He sent me out here to get you. Bring you directly to his office."

"Then let's go." We walk to my dad's office in silence. I stay slightly in front of Keith, like he's herding me to my father.

When we reach the door, Keith turns to me. "I don't like this," Keith whispers.

"Your orders are Jessa," I command just as quietly as he spoke.

He looks at me again a couple of moments before he shakes his head and opens the door. For show and his cover, he shoves me inside the office in front of him. I stumble because that's what I'm supposed to do. Look weak in front of the big bad mafia boss.

"Josh. Sit. Explain what the fuck you think you're doing with Jessa Holloway. The plan was for you to marry her and give me my fucking heir," my dad says, glaring at me. His voice is deadly calm.

I already know this isn't going to go well for me. I take a deep breath and sit down. "Jessa and I are taking things slow," I say, just as coldly as him because I refuse to show that much weakness. "You know

Alex fucked her up. I have a long road ahead of me to get her to truly trust again."

His eyes narrow into slits. "Bullshit. What's your game plan? I know Alex didn't do that much of a fucking number on her. He's not the fucking stupid one."

Ignoring the pain those words cause, I think quickly. Coming up with shit on the fly is one of my best qualities. And this time will be no different. I decide to use his own plan against him, the one he has no fucking clue I know anything about. "Fine. You really want to know?"

"Would've I have fucking asked? You're such a fucking petulant child."

I do my best to ignore him, but the words sting. Especially after he just called me stupid. I shake it off. "I don't think you plan to ever give me control. At least not until you know how serious I am. So, I decided the only way to do that is to do what you did. Settle down. Get married. Have an heir. You think it's just about Jessa with me, but it isn't. I'm doing all of this for me. Not her. But I won't stray from my plan. In order for all of this to work, she has to trust me. When she does, fully, I'll marry her. Then, and only then, will she ever learn the truth of all of this. Because if I'm honest and tell her now, she'll walk. I'll be forced to make her bend to my will, and Alex will come after me. And since he's stronger and smarter, he'll win. I don't want to lose this mafia, this family, or my damn life. Not at the hands of my brother. You know damn well, when he finds out, he'll take Jessa and run. No heir. No one to take over. You'll be back to where you started. With no chance of an heir."

I don't blink. I don't swallow. I barely breathe. I just look him square in the eyes and pray to God that he falls for it. It's the biggest lie I've ever told him. None of what I said is the truth. I'm doing this all to protect Jessa from his crazy ass. I'm in love with her. I won't let him or anyone else have her. Including fucking Alex.

After the longest stare off of my life, he finally breaks the silence. "Why Jessa?"

I take a second and focus on more than just the anger, so I don't glare at him and spew the truth. "Because of Alex. He talked so much about her that I felt like I knew her. I wanted to see if we had a connection like they did. So, I tracked her down and showed up at her apartment. She thought I was him. She kept calling me Alex. Alex spent their entire

246

relationship lying to her and never told her he had a brother. She didn't even know his real last name. She practically threw herself at me, and the kiss was like nothing I ever felt. I know it's wrong to not be honest, but…" I shrug, trying to keep my face neutral. He has to believe I love her enough to fight for her, but not enough to let her fuck up my chances of taking over. He needs to believe I won't make the same mistake as Alex. "But the sex is fucking fantastic."

I give him a devilish and challenging look, not willing to give anything away, but still playing to his lust of her. The lust he has no damn clue I know anything about.

He grins. "I bet it is!" He claps me on the shoulder, then pulls me in for a hug.

What the fuck?

I look at Keith. He's quietly leaning against the wall. He shrugs, looking as confused as I feel. My dad pushes me back, still grinning widely.

"We'll stick to the plan. You're right. Keep pretending to be Alex. Woo her. Get her to marry you, then we'll tell her the truth. She'll be stuck then," my dad says excitedly.

In the mafia, the only exit from marriage is through death. If Jessa marries me, which she will, no one can touch her. Not my father. Not Alex. No one. She'll be mine forever. That's the reason I plan to tell her the truth after we get married. It wouldn't matter what she thinks then.

For the first time, I'll be better than my brother.

"I'm damn proud of you, boy!" He nods to Keith, and I raise an eyebrow. Keith gives me an apologetic look and leaves the room.

"Really?" I ask, my eyes narrowing as I cross my arms over my chest. What the fuck made me think I'd get out of this unscathed?

He completely ignores me. "You need to be more serious than Alex was. Bring her home. Introduce her to your family."

I panic slightly. I don't want her anywhere near my dad. I already covered myself if either him or my mother call me Josh.

But I don't want him to touch her.

Dad sits down behind his desk and glares at me. "You still fucked up."

I shoot daggers at him. "Bullshit I did. I talked to you about all of this a long time ago."

247

"You did. But it's taking too damn long. And you didn't talk to me about all of it. The trust. The marrying. The timeframe. And there are consequences for that. One day, you will learn to stop fucking defying me."

He gives the guards a look. I watch Keith look down sadly. The guards surround me, and I take a deep breath, preparing myself. I know the look in my dad's eyes. He has a plan. And judging from the lustful way he's looking at a picture of Jessa on his desk, my bet is that it has to do with her.

I clear my throat and meet Keith's eyes when he looks up. I give him a slight flick of my head, imperceptible to anyone else, so he looks at the desk and sees what I do.

Keith flicks his eyes only towards my father, then back to me. He nods as I clench my fists. He's starting to back out the door just as the first guard attacks. Keith slips out to get to Jessa as my fight begins.

As is their usual method, they grab my arms, but everyone forgets that I have feet, muscle, weight, and my height. As soon as I feel their hands on me, I use all of my strengths to my advantage. I'm fast. I pull away quickly and punch one of them in the face. He falls back against my father's desk, holding his nose.

I turn and kick the legs out from another one. His momentum sends him flying into my forearm. It's an effective move. If I gave all of my strength, which I do, I could break someone's windpipe. When the fucker falls into a chair with wide eyes that are unseeing, I know I succeeded.

One down. Fuck only knows how many to go.

And just like that, all of them come after me. I take blow after blow, kick after kick. I fight as hard as I can for as long as I can before I can no longer stand up. The guards are all worse for the wear, but I definitely got the short end of the stick. The numbers game. It almost always wins the battle in the end.

But I'll never let them win the fucking war. They may have beat me this time, but fuck them all if they think they'll ever be able to keep me down.

With one of their arms snuggly around my neck just waiting for me to fight so they can snap my neck, my dad kneels in front of me. I'd probably still fight them because I know I can beat them, but one of the assholes has a gun to my head. Even if I got out of the hold, I'd never walk away.

My dad chuckles. "When will this rebellion stop, Josh?"

I glare, letting out a low growl. Dangerous. "When you give me fucking control of what I deserve."

"Then maybe you should start thinking about becoming more compliant. Doing what I say. Stop trying to defy me and do things your own damn way. Be more like your brother. I like you much better when you listen. And you will. Even if it fucking kills you in the end."

I see my dad's fist flying towards my face, but I refuse to close my eyes. I can take another hit. He connects with my jaw. I spit out blood as my head snaps to my right.

But no way in all of the Hells am I going to let him be the one to knock me out. My vision might be blurred, but I fight through it as I slowly turn my head back to him. My own fury is reflected in his eyes, but I don't fucking flinch.

"Hold him down," dad growls, not taking his eyes off mine.

I prepare myself for whatever the fuck he has coming. I expect more hits. Kicks. Yelling. Screaming. Stomping.

I don't expect the prick to the side of my neck. My head jerks. I'm instantly nauseous and dizzy. Weak. Numb. The blurred vision quickly intensifies to total blindness. Everything goes black as I'm forcefully pulled to my feet.

"Get that asshole out of my sight. Upstairs to his room," dad commands.

But his voice sounds like it's in slow motion and little more than an echo. The pain I feel throughout my entire body is immense. I tense just before I seemingly erupt in flames. I'm being stung by thousands of bees all at the same time. My blood is burning, but I can't even scream. It's like I'm locked inside a cage in my own mind watching myself die and being unable to help myself.

My last conscious thought before I succumb to the darkness is at least Jessa will be safe.

Chapter Twenty Eight

⚔ Jessa ⚔

I decide to enjoy the warm day after my meeting and walk home. It'll give me a moment to organize my thoughts about this new project. It's going to be fairly large. The biggest one we've had since the company started. We're building a large condo near the Pacific Ocean. The clients are requesting balconies off every condo and luxurious, state of the art rooms. I'm so incredibly excited to start drawing it out that I feel like bursting with excitement. I can't wait to tell Alex.

I smile with the thought of Alex. I had such a hard time the first couple of weeks trying to believe that he was really back and wanting to try again. Last night, I got so anxious about this meeting today that I had a panic attack. It was the first one I've had for quite a while. Like since he came back last year. Alex got me through it. He didn't complain or make me feel small and weak. Instead, he kept whispering in my ear about how strong I am, and how much he loves me. He wrapped me tightly in his arms just like he used to.

I had texted Cole over the course of that first week. Initially he was nervous about Alex being back considering how he had treated me before. He almost said fuck his training and came home. After we talked, though, he started to be okay with it. He understood better than I thought he would and really helped me to be okay.

I was afraid that he wouldn't agree with the decision to give things another shot. Even though my heart told me that I needed to try. He told me over and over that just because he wasn't sure he'd agreed with me didn't mean we wouldn't always be friends. But he did go all protective and tell me he'll always be looking out for me.

I took so much comfort in all of that because I don't ever want a life without Cole in it. I may not love him anywhere near the way I love Alex, but I do love him. He means so much to me. He's honestly my best friend.

I smile as I near my apartment. I truly love Alex. More than I ever thought was possible. This last year has been amazing. Having him back means the world to me. Learning to love each other again has caused much deeper and stronger feelings to develop. I really think we're in such a good place. Way better than we were before. We're starting on a much more solid ground.

"Ms. Holloway?" I look up at the deep voice in front of me. He seems to be somewhere in his thirties. He's fairly tall and muscular and seems kind. Not intimidating.

"Yes? Do I know you?" I smile softly, still on guard. I really don't do well with strangers.

"No. I'm sorry to bother you. I was sent by Alex's family. My name is Keith."

My heart skips several beats as I take a shaky breath. Alex. "Is… everything okay?"

"I'm so sorry, but no. There's been an accident. "I put my hand against the building to steady myself. Just when things are going well, the rug is pulled from under me. "Ms. Holloway, Alex has been hurt. I can take you to him if you'll come with me."

"Of course. Yes." I'd follow him wherever he wanted me to, as long as he's bringing me to Alex.

He leads me to his car and opens the door for me. He closes it behind me and gets in the driver's side. I try to stay calm. Strong. But way too many scenarios are racing through my mind. At the back of it, the very deep dark part, is the thought that maybe I'm being kidnapped. Maybe Alex is really okay.

Unfortunately, that isn't the part of me that's in control of the rest of me. One day when Alex was really down, he mentioned that it's possible one of his family's friends might come for me someday if he ever got hurt. I can't help but wonder if maybe one of the many arguments he has with his father about his mother has finally turned violent.

"Ms. Holloway, I have to warn you. What you're about to see…. it's not good. He's in bad shape."

I swallow and focus on the traffic in front of us. "What happened?"

"Uh… he was… jumped. Outside the property. We've been having a little violence in the area with a gang. Considering the area we live in, that's unusual. He was able to get home. We had a doctor look at him. I… I'm not sure how he is, Ms. Holloway. Just that he needs you. As soon as I got the doctor to him, I came directly to you."

I can feel myself starting to slip. His story seems logical, but given that Alex warned me this day would come, I find myself with questions. I refuse to give in to the distrust, though. I won't. Alex needs me. Besides the year we were apart and a little while at the end of our relationship, Alex has always been there for me. It's my turn now. I won't let him down. It's his turn to need me.

"Thank you for telling me. Just get me to him."

"Yes, ma'am." He speeds up and weaves through traffic until he reaches an incredibly nice neighborhood.

"Pacific Palisades? Shit…," I breathe. I look around the luxurious houses sprawling in front of me, my mouth agape.

"Like I said, you wouldn't think he'd be jumped in this type of neighborhood."

I frown as he turns into the driveway of the largest house I've ever seen. "Jesus."

"I'm really sorry, but we'll be going in the back way. I don't want anyone stopping us on the way to Alex."

"Stopping us?"

"His dad. I don't want him to stop us and introduce himself. It's a waste of time. There will be time for that later."

He parks the car, and we get out. I don't understand why his father wouldn't be with him, but I don't press it. If it were me in his shoes, I wouldn't leave his side.

I follow him into the house. He looks around and takes my hand, pulling me through a maze of hallways until we finally reach stairs. He holds my hand tightly and pulls me up the stairs. I nearly trip a few times trying to keep up.

He finally reaches a room and quickly opens it, pulling me in. "Alex is on the bed, Ms. Holloway. His mom just left. She didn't have a choice. There's a bathroom right over there." He points to my right, and I nod as he takes a deep breath. "I'm sorry, Jessa. Truly. I am."

There's a strange edge to his voice. And something I can't quite understand. Guilt? And why did his mom not have a choice? He steps to the side, and I see Alex laying in the bed. Bruises cover his body. I gasp as I rush to his side. I barely acknowledge the door closing behind Keith as he leaves.

"Oh my God! Baby! Alex? Can you hear me?"

I glance to the bathroom and decide I have to get a washcloth to clean him up. It looks like someone has already, but I have to do something. If I don't, I'll succumb to my own darkness. I fight the rising panic and focus on helping him. At least he had his mom here. He wasn't alone.

Tears overwhelm me, and I let out a strangled sob as I wet the cloth down. Alex's face is swollen and bruised. His eyes are closed as he sleeps, but one of his eyes is puffy. I don't think he'll be able to open it. His arms and chest are red and bruised. I haven't looked the rest of him over, but I'm terrified to.

I hurry back to him and start gently dabbing the cloth over the parts I can see that are swollen. A few minutes later, after I'm nearly done, Alex's eyes begin to flutter open. I was right about the one. He can barely open it.

"Mom?" he whispers. He sounds so weak. I force myself to stay strong for him, even though I feel like I'm falling apart.

My voice comes out a whisper as I lean down closer to him. "It's me, baby. Jessa. I'm right here."

"Jess…" He grits his teeth when he says my name like he's fighting off some kind of pain. I immediately back away, thinking I hurt him. "No…," he pleads as he shivers and tenses. "Stay with me."

I bite my lip and choke down the sob. I won't fall apart. I won't let myself. "I won't leave." I drop the cloth onto the floor and climb into his bed with him. I mold myself to his side and hold him as hard as I dare. I know he's fighting through something. I can feel it in every fiber of my being.

"Don't leave me," he says even more weakly than he had when he first woke up.

"Never, my love. I'm not going anywhere."

Me being close to him must comfort him because he slowly untenses and falls back to sleep, seemingly content.

I don't sleep at all.

XXX

The sun begins to rise the next morning, and I still haven't slept. I haven't left Alex's side. His parents haven't come to check on him at all. At least not that I have seen. I can't fathom that. Both of my parents wouldn't have left my side. He's always there for his mom. So many nights that she needed him, he never hesitated. It's baffling that she hasn't come up here.

Alex stirs, and I press myself closer to him. He's woken up a few times. Each time, he asks for his mom. It's taken him several minutes to come back to himself and remember who I am. I don't want him to feel panicked or feel like he's alone when he wakes up. I want him to know that he has someone. Anyone. That I'm here. That I'm not going anywhere.

"Jess?" Alex whispers. It's the first time my name has come out of his mouth when he's woken. It both breaks my heart and puts it back together.

"I'm here, babe. I'm right here."

He's quiet for a long time. "You didn't leave me," he whispers.

"Never, Alex. Jesus. Never." I kiss his arm and fight back tears I wasn't even aware I could still cry.

He groans and tries to get up. I leap off the bed to help him. "Maybe you shouldn't be moving…"

He chuckles low and deep. "Gotta piss sometimes, baby."

I chew my lip and carefully help him up, making sure he's steady on his feet. "Well, take it slow."

"Fuck. I feel like I got hit by a train," he groans. He stays still and closes his eyes as I support him as best I can.

"Keith said you were jumped outside the property, but you made it into the house where he found you."

Alex is quiet. Instead, he slowly lets me help him to the bathroom. He's limping. It's obvious how much pain he's in. When he woke up, he was doing a lot of grimacing and groaning. He was holding his stomach and chest. He was never awake that long before he passed out again. I noticed some kind of a mark on his neck. It looks like a bee sting or something. It's a little swollen around the injection area. I was keeping an eye on it, but it's pretty much gone now. There's no swelling or anything anymore. I can barely even see the injection mark.

"I'm sorry, Alex. We don't have to talk about it," I say quietly.

"Good. I don't want to talk about it." He limps his way into the bathroom, leaving me at the door.

I can't blame him. I wouldn't want to talk about it either. "Are you sure you're going to be okay?" I ask worriedly as he uses the counter for support on his way to the toilet. "Do you need help?"

He grins, but winces at the pain. "Why? Wanna help me in the shower?"

He's teasing me, even though I'm trying to be serious. I love him for that, but I bite my lip. "If you need me to," I tell him with a sniffle I don't mean. I hate seeing him like this. He's so strong, but all the bruises and cuts are jarring to see under the light.

I step back and lean against the wall as he uses the bathroom. I close my eyes and wait until I hear the water stop before I open them and take a deep breath. I move back and lean against the doorframe. He makes his way closer to me and lovingly cups my face in his palm when he reaches me. I lean into him as he lifts my chin, so I'm looking him in the eyes. He leans down to kiss me. I kiss him softly because I don't want to hurt him.

He smiles against my lips. "Don't worry about breaking me. I'm pretty tough."

I can't help but laugh. "I love you."

"I love you, too. I promise if I need help, I'll call for you."

I love how well he can read me. "That's all I ask."

I walk back to the bed and after a few minutes, Alex limps back out with nothing but a towel around his waist. I watch a water droplet glide down his perfect V and disappear underneath the towel. I lick my lips.

Alex laughs as he stops in front of me. "See something you like?"

"God, yes." I don't hide the fact that I can't keep my eyes off him. "Even with…" I sniffle as I reach up and softly touch his chest. It's like everything comes crashing back to me. How hurt he is.

He smiles softly and leans on the bed with his hands on either side of me. He pushes me back a little, and his lips meet mine with a controlled intensity that I love feeling with him.

"Look at me," he whispers against my lips. The dominance behind the words leaves no room for argument.

I look up at him, but my lip quivers. "You're really beat up. It's scary to see."

"I know how it looks. But I'll be okay, baby. You've seen me with a few bumps and bruises."

"Yeah, but that's different! Kickboxing and… this…" I reach up and wipe my eyes.

He kisses the silent tears. "Jess. Baby, you make everything better for me." He kisses me softly again and stands slowly. He drops the towel and tosses onto a chair. "Lose the clothes, honey."

I watch him in utter fascination and wonder. "Alex."

"Jessa."

"You -"

"I want to feel you next to me, baby. That's all. I don't want clothes between us. I'm fucking tired. I'm sore. I just want my girl. I want to hold you. I want to talk to you. I want you to soothe me. Make my mind right again. Fucking calm it, so I don't go to a dark place I might not get out of. I know that's a lot to put on you, baby, but I need you."

I quickly scurry out of the bed. "Okay, but can I at least change the sheets? You… were… sweating so bad at one point… I want you to be comfortable."

He smiles as he nods towards the bathroom. "Why don't you freshen yourself up, since I doubt you've left my side."

I glance towards it, then look up at him. But the silent command I see in his eyes is really all I need. He doesn't leave room for negotiation, so I head for the bathroom and quickly take a shower of my own.

When I come back out with a towel wrapped around me and another wrapped around my hair, a petite, almost frail woman with dark hair is slipping out of his bedroom. Josh looks after her with a haunted expression on his face. His towel is back around his waist again and he's sitting on his bed with his head down.

I sit down next to him and put an arm around his waist. I kiss his arm and lean my head against it. "Doing okay…?"

He sighs and looks at me. There's so much pain floating around in his eyes that I'm taken aback. I press closer to him, wanting to do all I can to fix whatever is broken. Heal him from the inside out. Anything I can to calm the raging storm.

"I don't feel anything, baby. I'm okay."

I furrow my brows. "What do you mean?"

He smiles and kisses my forehead. He drops the towel again and crawls into bed, waiting for me to follow. I watch him curiously as I drop my own towels. I pick them all up and bring them to the basket near his door. He watches my every move, making me blush, until I'm settled against his body.

He wraps his arms around me and tucks me into him, then leans down and kisses me so long and sweetly that I nearly forgot my name. "You make everything better, Jessa. I'm okay because of you."

He kisses me again and again until both of us are completely exhausted. He doesn't know it, but he's eased my mind so much. I'm so happy and content to be in his arms that the entire world fades away, which I think is his intention.

After he puts a movie in and we settle in to watch it, him spooning me on the bed and wrapped so tightly around me that he's engulfing me, I feel he's at peace. Calm. It makes the fear and heartbreak I feel for what happened to him fade away.

With his arms locked around me, nothing matters but us.

Chapter Twenty Nine

⚔ Josh ⚔

(Three Years later)

"Your little plan needs to start moving forward. I'm not fucking telling you again," my dad growls to me.

It's been a total of four years since I walked back into Jessa's life pretending to be Alex, and I'm truly conflicted on how I feel about this entire situation. I feel like I've fallen head over heels in love with her. But then I start blaming her for everything I've had to do over the past few years to protect her. I'm pissed that I've basically lost my brother, and I hate being anywhere near her.

I also don't like lying to her, but I can't tell her the truth. I'm still trying to protect her. My reasoning for doing this hasn't changed. My father is obsessed with her, and I won't let him hurt her. But I know I'm using her to get what I want, which makes me feel worse. And then I got back to being pissed with her all over again.

That doesn't mean my frustration with all of this bullshit hasn't grown exponentially. Especially lately. My father has made it clear that the only way for me to take over is to get her pregnant with my heir. The issue is that while we're ready to get married, neither one of us are ready for kids. She's super talented and has a fucking hell of a career in front of her. She's not ready to give up on her dreams, and while she would never have to do that with a kid in the picture, she feels like she would have to because she doesn't know how to juggle both.

I'm not ready for kids because I'm not even sure I'm in love. I'm not like my father. I can't just marry someone and have a kid for the sake of this mafia. I could never allow a woman to be forced to stay in this life because I've seen how it's affected my mom. And forcing a child to be raised in that type of an environment would never kill the cycle Alex and I grew up in.

But it all goes back to the fact that I want this. I want to take over. Some days I really feel like I would do anything to make that happen. Including marrying her under false pretenses and throwing her directly into the lion's den. Those days are becoming more and more frequent and getting longer and longer.

It all scares the fucking hell out of me. It's like I'm turning into a whole other person. Fucking bitter. Vicious. Uncaring. No morals. Someone like my father, and I swore my entire life, I'd never be like him. I'd be better. I fucking will.

"I'm working on it," I say as steadily as possible. "She's not ready." It's only a partial lie. It's both of us who aren't. And I'm trying to find a way out of this shit.

"Not…. not ready?" My dad laughs. Manically. I watch him. "Not ready!" He continues to laugh, and I narrow my eyes. Finally, he stops. I shake my head as I keep my eyes on him. "Force her, you fucking useless piece of shit. It's what I did with your mother."

I close my eyes against the insult. I try hard to not let it, but it fucking stings. It hurts. And they are getting more and more frequent. Everyday I hear another one. I'm a piece of shit. Not good enough. Insolent. Idiotic. Stupid as fuck. Useless. That one is my favorite. That one takes a lot longer to recover from. A lot more to ignore.

I take a deep breath as I open them again. I'll never be like him. Fucking never.

"Alex never would've made me wait this long. Why the fuck can't you just be more like him?"

Right. Alex. *Perfect fucking Alex.* The one who left me. Abandoned me. His own brother. Abandoned his own girlfriend, who he was supposed to love so much. Left it all on my shoulders. Because he couldn't just take responsibility. Live up to his destiny. Take over and give me fucking control like he promised. Tell Jessa the damn truth. None of this would have happened if he'd just told her the fucking truth and did what he said he would.

It was never as hard as he made it out to be. He could've just stayed and helped me. Helped protect me against our father like he always had. Like he fucking promised he would! Helped me stand up against him and protect me from the constant beatings I took. The constant berating. He could've lived up to his promises instead of leaving me to fight on my own!

He promised it would always be us together. Us against the world. But no. First, he left me for Jessa. Then he left because of Jessa. I'm so fucking pissed at them both for putting me in this position. But mostly at Alex. Jessa has no damn clue what's going on behind closed doors. She'd never do what I need her to if she did. Fuck, maybe it's time for me to tell her the truth.

But I can't. Alex made it that way. This is all his fault.

"This is Jessa's fault. She's made you go soft. She's made you into this coward you've turned into."

I force myself to stay calm, but it's hard. I want to argue with him. I want to defend her, but I can't. Defending her takes a lot out of me because part of me blames her just as damn much as Alex and my father. I sigh.

Fuck it all. I don't need Alex. I don't need my father. I don't need Jessa. I have Keith. Keith can help out. Maybe help me take the old man out. Make it look like a rival. Give me an excuse to take another leader of another mafia down. Then Jessa can make her own decision. Be with me or not. At least she'd be able to make her own choice.

"Just give me some time," I breathe. "I'm close. Okay?"

"Fucking imbecile. You're such a complete moron. I don't know how the hell you walk and talk at the same damn time."

He nods to the two guards behind me, and I steel myself for yet another beating. He's gotten good. He makes sure my face isn't bruised anymore so Jessa isn't suspicious when I show up after I fight through the day of pain and nausea. I just leave my shirt on after beatings now. I heal quickly. I always have. But she asks questions. She loves my chest and abs and questions me when I don't take off the shirt.

Jessa and I still share her apartment for the most part. She wants us to be our own people with our own lives. It was a mistake she wanted to fix from the first time around. I was totally on board because it means keeping her away from all of this until I can figure out what to do is easier. But the longer this goes on, the worse my frustration gets. My father is right. I need to make a move. I need control so I can make sure she's safe from him. Jessa is the only way that's happening.

The two guards yank me to my feet. One of them kicks me behind the knee, and I drop. Just as I'm about to start fighting, I watch as another guard brings a man inside the office. The man has a black mask on and is handcuffed. The guard shoves him to his knees.

I furrow my eyebrows as my heart stops beating. My dad grins like fucking Satan and yanks the mask off.

I try to breathe, as soon as my worst fucking fears are confirmed. "No. Holy shit, no. Keith!"

I try to get loose, but during my alarm and shock, my arms have been cuffed behind my back. A fourth guard disarms me and is standing behind me with my very own gun to my temple.

"Move, and he shoots," my dad smirks at me. He's enjoying every second.

I panic. My heart rate shoots into outer space. "What the fuck are you doing? Let him go!"

"I don't like when people betray me, Josh," My dad says with a vicious glare. I'd return it, but my eyes are focused on the gun he's holding to Keith's neck. "I don't like when people plan behind my back. Especially when that man is my friend. My second. And the person he's conspiring with is my own fucking son." My dad raises the gun to Keith's temple. His eyes never leave mine. "This is on you. You remember that. His blood is on your hands."

Tears fall from my eyes as Keith's eyes meet mine. He tries to stay brave. He gives me a small smile and nod and closes his eyes. He doesn't cry. He's trying to tell me that he regrets nothing. That he'd do what he did all over again.

But my dad is right. I never should have let him work with me. His life is about to be taken because of me.

"Let him go! Dad! Fuck! Let him go! He has a family!" I scream.

I pull against the guards, not giving a shit that one of them might actually shoot me. If I can just get to him in time. Maybe my dad will shoot me instead. Let Keith live. My life for his. He doesn't deserve this. Any of it. It's my fault he's here.

The guards hold me tighter, yanking me back against them.

Dad shoots. The noise is deafening. His gun doesn't have a silencer on it today, and I know it's intentional. I know he wants me to hear the shot. He wants to make sure I know Keith's life being taken is my fault. All fucking mine. My decisions cost him his life.

Keith falls to the ground. Blood instantly pools around him.

"No! Noooo!" My screams are animalistic; unrecognizable to my own fucking ears. My cheeks are wet with tears. "How the fuck could you do that to him?"

The guards shove me to the ground, but I barely feel myself falling.

Keith.

It's my fault.

His family lost him because of me.

I really am worthless. I can't do anything right. I'm a fucking loser. Stupid. Just like my father always tells me.

"Fuck him. Get off him. Uncuff him. He's not worth the effort," my dad says so nonchalantly that my heart physically shatters. The pieces scatter on the ground next to Keith.

The guards uncuff me, and I crawl to Keith's side. I hold him in my lap and cradle his head to my chest as I cry. I don't even care that his blood is seeping into my clothes. It's already stained my soul.

I lost Alex.

I lost Keith.

All I have is Jessa.

Jessa. I need to get to my girl. And that's the lost conscious thought I have before I feel something sharp against the side of my neck. My vision blurs just before I fade into the darkness.

I scrub my hands down my face before unlocking the apartment door. I'm pissed off at myself that Keith was killed because of me. I'm seething that I lost two days of my life afterwards. And I'm even more viciously angry that there are no fucking bruises anywhere on my body, yet I was out for two days writhing in excruciating agony. Like my fucking blood was made of glass or something and tearing my veins apart as it coursed through my damn body.

I miss Jessa. I don't remember getting a text out to her over the past couple of days, but apparently I did. Or someone did because there is a text that tells her I'll be home in a couple of days and needed to help out my dad on a business trip. My bet is on my mother. There's no fucking way I was thinking clearly enough to shoot a text to Jessa so she wouldn't worry.

I take a deep breath as I open the door. Something smells delicious. It makes me smile, despite how incredibly upset I am. I've thought of ways to kill my father the entire way over here. It all comes back to the same damn conclusion, though. I won't make out alive. My mother and Jessa would be left defenseless.

Jessa smiles at me from the kitchen as I close the door. "You're just in time."

My eyes fall on the plates she has in front of her. "Holy shit. That looks delicious. What is that?"

"Portabella mushroom steak with grilled asparagus and roasted potatoes."

"It smells incredible." I sit down at the table as she brings the plates over. I'm starving and immediately dig in. I haven't eaten in two days. I just wanted to get the fuck out of there as soon as I was lucid enough to leave. The rare steak melts in my mouth. I moan. "I needed this. It's fucking incredible."

She gives me a small smile, and I'm struck by her beauty. I really needed this. I needed all of it, but mostly her. All I can think of right now is how much I hate Alex and my father for putting me in this position.

Despite the fact that my mood is lifting, though, Jessa doesn't seem like herself. In fact, I've noticed the past couple of months she doesn't seem as bubbly as she is typically. Not as happy. It's like something is weighing on her mind.

By the time I finish eating, Jessa has only managed to get down about a quarter of her food. I put my fork down and look at her. "Baby, what's wrong? You seem upset about something. And you've barely touched your dinner."

She sighs and puts her fork down. She looks up at me. Her eyes are filled with more sadness than I know what to do with. She's chewing her lip. It's then I noticed that her lip is chapped and bitten up. I already know I'm not in the mood for what she's about to say.

"Do… you… think this…" she gestures between the two of us. My eyes fall to her hand before finding her face again. My heart sinks.

"Jess. Don't." I shake my head. The fog I fought so hard through sets back in again. I rub my temples.

"Alex," she whispers.

Alex. Always fucking Alex. He fucking has it all. My father wants me to be him. Fine. If that's what everyone wants, I'll start being like perfect fucking Alex. I shake my head. Nausea accompanies the headache suddenly raining down on me. Pins and needles prick my skin. Fucking Alex.

I chuckle. This isn't happening. None of it. "Don't, Jessa," I growl low as my eyes meet hers. I can feel the fury slowly seeping into me. I've lost everything. I won't fucking lose her, too.

"I'm just being honest," she says quietly. "I just… don't… feel like I used to." She bites her lip again as her eyes fall to her plate. She folds her hands in her lap and shakes her head. "The love is gone, Alex. We can't pretend it isn't."

It's all the words I need to make me snap. "Don't fucking do this to me, Jessa."

"Alex." She looks back up at me and flinches when she sees the rage careening to the surface.

I stand quickly and flip the table. "We're not fucking doing this!"

"Ah!" she screams as she covers her head and rears back, falling to the floor.

Food flies everywhere. Our plates crash to the ground and shatter. I have to chuckle internally because it's the perfect symbolism of my entire life. I reach down and grab her around the waist as she scrambles away from me. She screams again.

I haul her against my chest. "This isn't over," I growl against her neck. "You're mine."

"Let me go!" She screams and flails against me.

I drop her on the couch. "I'm sick of the fucking games. You fucking owe me!" I yell. And she does. She owes me her goddamn life. She wouldn't be breathing if it wasn't for me. She'd have been used and killed long ago. I reach down and grab her hair to pull her back to me.

"Get away from me!" She screams and sobs as she kicks both of her feet out. One connects with my stomach, the other with my dick.

I stumble backwards against the coffee table and crash over it and to the ground. "Fuck! You fucking bitch!" I cup my cock and moan in pain. I can't focus on anything but the fact that my balls feel like they're in my mouth. Jessa runs out the door.

First Alex leaves me.

Keith gets killed because of me.

My mother is fucking terrified to be seen anywhere in my presence.

Now Jessa abandons me when I need her the most.

This is all her fucking fault. Her and Alex are fucking made for each other.

Little does she know that I'm not giving up that easily.

She's mine. No one else's. Fucking mine. I need her in order to get what I want.

I'll never let her go.

✗✗✗

(One Month Later)

One month since Jessa walked out on me. One fucking month. Of course she ran directly to Cole.. He turned her against me so fast I didn't have a damn chance. Before I knew what was happening, she had filed a restraining order against me. Well, against Alex. She quit her job. She moved. She changed her phone number, her email. She severed all contact with me.

But it didn't take long to track her. I hired a hacker and gave him her social security number. I'm not as stupid as my father and brother seem to believe. I know that social security numbers can get me any information I need. He found her so fast that I hadn't left his apartment before he was telling me he was done.

I showed up at her office building, the start up finally got a building, and tried to get her to talk to me. She saw me and ran. I couldn't follow because she ran right to her office. The building is secured. She had security and everything after me. Ten minutes later, Cole showed up in his damn squad car. Took her from me.

She quit that very day, but she started a job somewhere else. My hacker found her, and I decided to be smarter. I had my hacker track her. Instead of just trying to talk to her, I followed her. I learned her routine. She always left the building through the employee stairwell, so I waited for her. I grabbed her and tried to get her to talk to me, but she screamed so loud it echoed through the whole fucking building. I slapped her. Hard. Before I could drag her out, though, security came for her.

I got away, but cops showed up at my house to arrest me. My good for nothing father proved Alex was in Italy, and that whoever attacked Jessa couldn't possibly have been him. She caused me to get one hell of a beating, but I didn't care. I'm so used to them, they don't even faze me anymore.

What does faze me is my father. Without Jessa, I'm nothing more than a worm to him. Nothing more than an insignificant bug that he could just swat away. That he could squish. I told him I could get an heir. I could find anyone to get pregnant. And I could. I could walk into a bar and pick up anyone.

I didn't matter to him, though. It's Jessa or no one. If I can't get Jessa, it means that Alex is the better brother. I need something he doesn't have. Her. I need her to prove to my dad that Alex can never compare to me.

She disappeared again after the stairwell incident, but she still lives with Cole. She even changed her damn number again and quit her job. She'd only been there a couple of weeks. But my hacker got me her new phone number and even tracked it. I know where she is at all times. She never leaves her house.

And that brings us to today. I just left another meeting with my father. He called me a bunch of names like he usually does and for some reason, it hurt a lot more than it usually does. I don't understand why he can't just be proud of me like he is of Alex. Alex isn't even here, but our father can't stop singing his praises. Can't stop telling me I'll never measure up.

Jessa is the only hope now. My only hope to make my father see that I *am* worth it. That I have the one thing Alex doesn't. I have the girl he let get away. She'll be my wife. I'll be the one with the heir. My father can't deny it then. He can't deny me. He can't tell me I'm the worthless one when I have everything he wants Alex to have.

My mind starts to fog. I close my eyes. It's happening more and more. I'm sure it's too many hits and kicks to the head. I call Brandon, my best friend and hacker. He's the only one who knows everything. I didn't have to tell him, but I felt like I needed to.

After losing Keith, I needed someone else I could confide in. After Brandon did what I told him to without hesitation and kept doing it, I decided I could trust him. And if he betrayed me, I would just kill him. Lucky for me, Brandon turned out to be one hell of a guy.

"Hey, J. What's up?" Brandon asks when he answers.

"I'm ready to grab Jess. I need her location. I'm sure she's probably home, but I don't know when Cole will be back."

"Cole works until three in the morning. That's his shift. Jessa looks like she's home. Give me a sec." I hear him tapping at some keys. "She's home, man."

I look up at Cole's house. It looks quiet. There's a window seat next to a huge bay window. Jessa loves sitting there. But she's not there, and the house is dark.

"Are you sure? House looks empty. I haven't seen much the past thirty minutes I've been here."

"Unless she left her phone, she's home."

I look up at the house again and sigh. "Alright. Thanks, man."

"Call me later. I want to know how it goes."

"You got it."

I hang up and make my way to the house. As soon as I get to the front door, I look around. No one seems to be watching me, so I knock and wait for my girl to answer. I don't care if she doesn't believe it. She belongs to me.

After a couple moments, the lock on the door unlocks. I'd put my finger against the peephole and turned my back to the window at the side of the door, so she couldn't see me. Interestingly, she didn't even bother with the window. She must feel pretty safe here.

As soon as she sees me, her eyes widen in terror. My eyes harden. I'm not the one she should be terrified of. I'm the one trying to protect her. It's my father who's stalking her. Threatening her. If it weren't for me, she'd be dead.

"Jessa," I say huskily.

"A-Alex…" She tries to slam the door in my face. I stop it and shove it open as I step inside.

"Knock it off. We need to talk." I shove her back and shut the door. Her eyes are wild, and I know she's looking for an escape. "I'm bigger and faster than you are, Jessa. You're not getting away from me this time." I glare as I grab her arm. She flinches and tries to pull away. I fling her onto the couch and sit next to her. "You're mine, Jessa. You always have been. You always will be."

"Please Alex. Please. Don't."

I need her to cooperate, but if she doesn't, I'll just make her. After all the beatings I have taken because of her, she doesn't get a say. She belongs to me. End of fucking story. When I walk her through that door, my dad will be proud of me again. Like he used to be when she was being a good girl and playing by the rules. Before she left and fucked everything up.

Not again. I'll marry her. Tonight. I'll get someone to perform the ceremony. She can't escape me then. Dad will love that. He'll love the control I exude over her. He'll be proud of me. More proud of me than Alex because I'll have Jessa.

"I miss you, baby." She tries to stand up, but I pull her back down. "Come on. I'm not doing this. I'm not going to hurt you." I lean in, shoving her against the back of the couch, and kiss her. Her lips are stiff under mine, and my eyes narrow even more. I back off and stand up, pulling her with me. "Get your stuff. We're going home."

She whimpers and cries as she shakes her head. I glare, barely containing my anger. "No. Alex, please. Please go."

"Go? Sure. Get your stuff. And then we'll go. Move it. Do as you're told." I push her in front of me toward the hall I assume her room is down. Her lip quivers. Her eyes dart to the door. I grab her other arm and force her to look at me. "You belong to me, Jessa. You're going to do what I say, when I say it. No options."

I shove her towards the hall. She stumbles, but darts for the back of the house where I know another door is. I grab a fistful of her hair and pull her back to me. She screams as she hits my chest. I pull her back to the living room, and she flings herself from my arms. She lands hard on the floor and starts to crawl towards the door.

"Jessa, stop!" I grab her around the waist and pull her up. She's feather light. She weighs practically nothing. She's no match for me.

"No!"

Tears are streaming down her face. She's out of breath, and I can tell she's starting to panic. Good. It will help me out. As soon as I get her home, my dad can call someone to deal with her attack. I'll marry her and end this ridiculous shit.

Jessa keeps struggling against me. She flails, and her elbow connects with my rips. I flinch just enough for her to get out of my hold. She turns and slaps me across the face, stunning me, before she flees for the door.

"Bitch!" I chase her and reach her just as she gets to the door and flings it open. I haul her back against me and slam the door. She screams as I throw her against the wall. I slap her, and she falls to the ground.

"Stop! Stop, please! Please!" she pleads.

I kick her, and she crumples into a crying heap. I grab her hair and pull her up. "You honestly think you can hit me and get away with it? After the amount of beatings I've taken for you? Fuck no!" I throw her into a glass table. It shatters around her, and she cries harder. She tries to get up, but I kick her again.

She screams and sobs harder, holding her stomach and sides. "Please...," she begs.

"You think you can embarrass me? Leave me? You fucking belong to me! You're never going to forget that again!" I grab her hair again and yank her back up, forcing her to look at me. "Are you?" I snarl at her as she tries to get away.

"Please… Please!"

I slap her once more, and she falls against a chair, slamming her head against an end table before she hits the floor. "Are you?!" I yell.

She belongs to me. When I walk her into that house, everyone will know it. Everyone will know that I belong leading the Lucinio Mafia. My father will be proud of me. I'll finally be better than Alex! Finally get everything I deserve!

I don't even care that I don't fucking love her anymore. I don't care that I hate her. That she disgusts me. She'll have no choice but to do as she's told. I'm the boss. I'm the one in control. She and everyone else needs to open their eyes and see it just as clearly as me!

Jessa doesn't move from where she fell on the floor.

"Get up!" It's a command. I'm not asking her anymore.

I own her.

She's fucking mine. She needs to do what I say, and right now I need her to prove to my dad that I'm not a fuck up.

Jessa still doesn't move, so I scream at her as I kick her again in the stomach. "I said get the fuck up! Now!" I kick her again, but she stays motionless.

I kneel next to her and grab her hair, intending to pull her back to me. Suddenly, I hear sirens approaching. I look out the window just as someone bursts through the door.

"Jessa?"

My eyes meet the eyes of someone I used to consider a brother as I stand up.

Gavin.

"What the fuck are you doing here?" My voice betrays my surprise, but still exudes the anger I feel. "I thought you were in Italy?"

"Get the fuck away from her," Gavin growls threateningly.

He rushes to Jessa and kneels next to her, turning his back to me. He's cocky. Always has been. He doesn't think anyone can touch him. That no one would dare try. He thinks I'm weak. Just like Alex does. That I needed protection.

Not anymore.

"You aren't fucking taking what's mine."

I punch Gavin, but he dodges me and spins. He punches at me as he stands, but misses when I sidestep him. I went through just as much training as him. We're as evenly matched as I am with Alex and everyone else in this mafia.

"Back the fuck off, Josh!" Gavin snarls at me. "Can't you see she needs to get to the fucking hospital? What the hell did you do?"

I glare and rush him, sending us both crashing against the couch and flipping it. I fall on top of him and punch just as he's punching up at me. We both connect with each other's jaws. I fall backwards, but I'm not letting him beat me. I'm not letting him take Jessa from me. She's mine to take care of. Mine.

"What the fuck are you even doing here? Came to rub my failures in my face for my dear brother?"

Gavin and I both jump to our feet and rush each other again. This time, though, Gavin has the advantage. He shoves me against the wall and has his forearm against my neck so quickly, I don't have time to counter him.

"What the fuck are you talking about? What the hell is going on? You just beat the shit out of someone!"

"You don't get to come back here after abandoning me, leaving me to deal with the fallout, and start asking fucking questions!" I knee him in the balls as hard as possible. He slumps but doesn't let go of my neck. "It's none of your goddamn business!" The sirens are getting closer. I have to get out. I deliver another knee to his dick.

"Fuck!" Gavin lets me go and doubles over.

I deliver an uppercut to his jaw followed by an immediate kick to his stomach. He flies backwards and slams against the wall, cracking his head and slumping against it. He groans as his eyes flutter closed.

I hear a car squealing to a stop outside and look towards the door. Way too fucking close. "Shit." I can't take her. I have to get out. I won't get a second chance at getting away. "Fuck!"

I stand and run out the back door, my mind already churning with a new plan.

I will get her. Jessa is mine.

She can't run forever.

Chapter Thirty

⚔ Alex ⚔

Four years ago, I left L.A. and Jessa behind. I ran to Italy to protect her and because I didn't know what the fuck happened to us. I was so incredibly hurt and angry that she left. I wasn't thinking straight. I just had to get away and think.

The problem is when I finally came out of my funk, it was too late to go back. There was no way I could just walk back into her life after so long. It wasn't fair to her. It wasn't fair to me. I owed it to both of us to allow each other to move on.

I took a page from my brother's book instead. He finally found a woman that he liked enough to actually spend more than a night with. He told me he introduced her to our parents. Our father even seemed genuinely happy for him.

I never found what I had with Jessa. I never found anyone I wanted to give more than a night to. I was with a girl on an actual date when I got the call. I hadn't been on a date since Jessa, but this girl was beautiful. She was fun to talk to. For a little while, she made me forget. Nothing will come of it, though, because when I jumped on a plane, I didn't miss her.

Lance, my hacker, got information on my alias, Alex Lang. Jessa had gotten a restraining order. He sent me the order, and I was confused as all fuck. It said I hit her. I threw her into a nightstand. I hurt her. There was a damn warrant for my arrest, which he got rid of. Thankfully.

He called as soon as he saw it, and I flew out immediately. Gavin took care of getting me a place to stay. Under no circumstances is my family to know I'm home. Not even my mother, though I miss her like crazy.

It took me time to figure out what was going on, and a little more time after that to believe it. I was so pissed I didn't figure it out before, and so fucking betrayed when I had. I'm still pissed off and feel even more fucking betrayed than before.

My brother.

My own fucking brother. How could he do this to me? I wouldn't put it past my father. He's a sick son of a bitch. But Josh. How could Josh do this? Why the fuck would he even think this was the right fucking thing to do?

I was even pissed at Jessa. Did Josh act so much like me that she couldn't tell? From what I know, she was with him for four years. Same as me. How could she not tell how fucking different he is from me?

But I realized a few things. Everything had spiraled completely out of control without me. My father was right all along. Josh isn't ready to take control. I've come to the conclusion that Josh is being controlled by our father.

If he could be controlled that easily, no fucking way he can lead. If he can be convinced that fucking easily to hurt someone and play with her fucking emotions, no way he's ready to take over. If he can't be his own man without my guidance, he can't lead.

I hate thinking any of that because I know he's capable of it. He's fucking done it. I always let him take the lead on missions we were on. But somehow, my father got his claws into him. Twisted his mind completely from who he is, and molded him into someone in his image.

Even knowing all of that, I can't help but feel guilty. The first year after I left, he would snap at me for abandoning him when I called. He stopped after a while, but I know my leaving hurt him. I left him alone in that house knowing what my father is like. Knowing exactly how he treated Josh. We all left. Me. Gavin. Damon. Everyone he considered family was gone in the blink of an eye.

After hearing about Keith's death, I knew why Josh snapped completely. Why he had lost total control. Josh had always prided himself on his self-control. It seems to be non-existent now. Josh had no one to turn to. No one to lean on.

I did that to him.

I left him alone.

I made him feel like he couldn't come to me. I had always been there for him to lean on. I always protected him from our father. I made sure he knew he could come to me night or day. But when I left, I took that away from him. I don't think I'll ever forgive myself for that.

After figuring everything out, I sent Gavin to watch Jessa. I didn't want it to be me because I didn't want to scare her. And she technically has a restraining order against me. She's living with Cole. I don't know, but I'm pretty sure they're together. I'll never interfere in that. Especially if it means she's safe.

The problem is she isn't safe. Josh walked right through the restraining order several times now, including tonight. I got a call from Gavin saying that he lost Jessa while he was following her. She had some kind of an appointment at a doctor's office. One Doctor Freeman doesn't work for and isn't associated with.

Gavin got stuck in traffic. He had Lance track her phone and found out she was home. He rushed there, but when he got there, he saw Josh in the window. He called the police first, then me. Then he went after her. I haven't heard from him since.

I slam on my brakes as I get to Cole's house. My car skids as I fly into the driveway. I can hear sirens and hope to hell that they're coming here. I jump out of the car just as Damon and Lance pull up behind me. We all run into the house. Jessa is laying on the ground covered in glass. Gavin is slumped against the wall groaning and holding his head. I hear the back door close and look at Damon and Lance.

"We got it," Damon says. The two take off, and I kneel down next to Gavin.

"What the hell?" he grunts. He pushes himself up to his knees.

"You okay?" I ask, keeping my eye on the unmoving girl in the center of the room. She's breathing. I can see her back rising and falling.

"Yeah. Fuck. Get Jessa." He waves me off.

I move to Jessa. "Peanut? Hey, honey, can you hear me?" I gently move her hair out of her face and touch her neck just to confirm what my eyes see. She is breathing.

"He was throwing her around like a fucking ragdoll," Gavin says as he crawls to us. He touches her neck himself. "Thank fuck," he says, relieved. Jessa's breathing is incredibly shallow, and I force myself to stay calm as I check her for injuries. "I'll call Doctor Freeman. He can meet us at Cedar. You need to get out of here. She technically has a restraining order against you, man."

I shake my head as I continue to check her. "I don't care." I hear the squads pull up and doors closing. Voices as they run to the house. "Forget it," I say, choking up at seeing Jessa like this. "I never should have fucking left."

"What? Alex, you're going to get arrested! Let me take care of her. You need to go."

I shake my head. "She's what matters now. You can bail me out. We'll straighten it out. I fucked up once leaving her here. I'm not fucking leaving her now." Several cops come through the door, but I don't move as I look up. I won't leave her side.

"Alex?" Cole says in complete bewilderment.

"Look, Cole. There's an explanation," I start. "Just get her to a hospital and take me in if you have to. I'll explain." I look up at him. Guns are trained on me, but I look Cole directly in the eyes. Gavin has his hands up in surrender and is barely breathing as he watches my every move. I keep my hand on Jessa's neck, making sure she's still breathing. I try to stay calm. "Cole, she's -"

"What's her nickname?" Cole asks, his eyes never leaving mine.

"What?" I shake my head incredulously. "She doesn't have time -"

"Answer the fucking question! What is the nickname you call her?"

His gun doesn't move from my head. His hands aren't shaking. He's in complete control. His partners look as confused as I feel. But his eyes. Something in his eyes. The rest of the cops look fucking bewildered. Not him. He's determined. Confident. Cole's eyes show me something else. Something like... understanding? Like he knows something no one else does.

"Peanut. I call her peanut," I finally answer.

"What's her favorite movie?" he asks me. The rest of the cops go from bewilderment to astonishment.

Not him.

"That's a… trick question. Twilight. All of them. But also the Fast and Furious series. Except the second one. She hates it."

"Last question. Her favorite animal."

I smile a little, thinking of all her drawings. Everything I bought for her over the years to show her what she means to me. "Dragons and baby pigs. But she also has a fondness for wolves. One she hasn't really told many people."

Cole lowers his gun and signals for everyone else to do the same. Gavin shakily puts his hands down, not taking his eyes off me. He waits for my move.

"Fuck. Thank fuck it's really you," Cole says.

I look at Gavin. "Call Doctor Freeman." Without a word, he takes out his phone and does as I say.

"EMS is on the way," Cole says. I look up at Cole, my hand not moving from Jessa's neck.

"How did you know?" I ask him.

"I don't know everything. But there are a few things that never made sense to me. She'd tell me how amazing you were. She thought you were going to propose. But then it was like a switch was flipped. At first, I thought you were just a typical domestic abuser. Woo. Get her to trust. Trap her. Then the fists start flying."

"I'd never hurt her."

"I know. She lived with me for a while. We dated a little bit, but realized we were better friends and wanted to stay that way. I learned a lot about you. After you came back -"

"I just came back. A month ago."

He nods. "When the restraining order was filed," he says like another piece of the puzzle clicks into place.

"Yeah."

"About a year after you left, Alex, someone pretending to be you walked into her life. I met him. I couldn't tell the difference. But there were things that were off. She responded to him like she did you."

I wince. I didn't want to hear that.

It means Josh is really good at pretending to be me.

Cole sighs. "But he didn't know her favorite movie. Her favorite actor. Favorite food. Colors. Things I knew after knowing her only a couple years. One day, she was a little upset with him. They were fighting. She said he never calls her by her nickname."

"Peanut."

"I started digging a couple days ago, after talking with Jess about something that happened after her parents died. Something about you not leaving her side. Something just struck me. Didn't sit right. And I was right. You're a fucking ghost. Other than the restraining order. Not a hell of a lot. So, I started with the college. Alex Lang was never enrolled at UCLA."

I hear more sirens closing in on us. The ambulance. Jessa's pulse is holding steady, but she isn't waking up.

"But Alex Lucinio was," he continues.

I nod. "She doesn't know. And for good reason. I'll explain, but please get her to the hospital."

The sirens stop and moments later, two paramedics run in with a stretcher. The house is overrun with people in uniform, but Cole is holding his own in directing the scene.

After Jessa is loaded up, Cole looks at me. "What hospital? Where's your doctor?"

"Doctor Freeman. Cedar Sinai. He'll be waiting at the ER entrance."

"You following?"

I look at him. I honestly don't know if I should.

"They'll follow. Gavin, go with Alex. Lance will take your car. We'll deal with the house," Damon says. I hadn't noticed him and Lance come back, but thank God for my team. Always able to jump in when I freeze up.

Gavin and I follow the paramedics out. We jump into Gavin's car and take off after Cole and the ambulance.

"What's the plan?" Gavin asks.

"We know how he keeps finding her. And we know he has to have help. So we stop him."

"How?"

"Lance. He's really fucking good. He's about to earn all that money I pay him. He needs to mask her. Everything. Social security. Accounts. Anything that comes up anywhere. Her name comes up on the internet in a news article, I want it gone."

"Dude, that might not be possible."

"Make it possible."

"Alex -"

I glare at him, and he immediately shuts up. "From now on, Jessa Holloway doesn't exist. She's a fucking phantom. We protect her in that hospital. We do it secretly. And when she's released, we erase her. We block him from ever finding her again." I turn back to the road as Gavin drives.

Finally, he nods. "I'll call Lance and Damon when we get to the hospital."

I nod and chew on the inside of my cheek. This can't all be Josh. Josh isn't a cold, calculating, criminal mastermind like our father. Dad has to be the one pulling the strings.

Josh's strings.

"I want a track on Josh. I want one on my father. If they so much as think about Jessa, I want to know about it."

"You got it, boss," Gavin says. I drum my fingers on the door as we near Cedar. "What about you? Are you going to talk to her? Explain everything?"

I'm quiet for a long moment as I think. Finally, I sigh. "No. She's going to walk away from this. And she isn't going to look back. She's going to start a new life, free of the pain and fucking chaos my family has thrown at her. But you damn fucking better well believe that I'm never letting my family touch her again."

Gavin nods as I slam on my brakes. He may not agree, but he won't question me. We both jump out of the car and run to the back of the ambulance as the paramedics take her out. Cole and Doctor Freeman meet us.

"Alex?" Doctor Freeman asks. Last he knew, I was in Italy. I gave him strict orders to always be there whenever Jessa needed him. I had no fucking clue she was seeing another doctor.

I meet his eyes. "It was Josh."

Doctor Freeman nods. "I'll take care of her. I promise." I nod, and he takes off with Jessa and the paramedics. "Alex! Room 9600!" he calls back to me.

"Thanks!" I head into the hospital as Gavin parks my car.

Cole follows me. "Explain the rest, man. Tell me what I'm missing."

"You've heard of the Lucinio Mafia?"

"Yep. Your dad is the leader. You're supposed to take over."

I nod. "I don't want it. Never did. Being with Jessa solidified that for me. But my twin brother? He lives for it. Long story short, my dad wants me to take over. Not Josh, my twin brother. He's spent the last twenty-eight years tearing Josh down. He plays on Josh's weakness to please him. Josh's jealousy of me. I would bet my fucking fortune that thanks to him, Josh is so fucked up right now, he doesn't even know what end is fucking up."

We get to the VIP wing and check in. We get to Jessa's room, and I collapse.

"What does any of this have to do with Jessa?" Cole asks.

"It has everything to do with her. My dad is obsessed. I didn't realize how much until I got back here and started figuring everything out. He's so obsessed that he somehow convinced Josh that the only way to protect her from whatever the fuck was to pretend to be me. I haven't worked that part out yet. But I know my dad is fucked up, and I know he's fucking up my brother. Josh never would've done something like this if he had some semblance of control. It's obvious he doesn't."

"He fucking hospitalized her. I'd say he has no control. When I fucking find him…"

"You'll do nothing," I say as he trails off. "I found out my father killed Josh's best friend. It caused him to snap. To lose control. If you knew him, you would know just how big a deal that is. Josh prides himself on his self-control. Right now, he's pure chaos. You wouldn't stand a chance against him. I'll warn you now, Cole. My dad has a lot of people in his pocket. Josh won't get charged with this."

"The fuck he won't."

"He won't. Trust me. You can have an airtight case. Call in Gavin. Have him testify it was Josh. Have him testify to what he saw. But any good defense attorney, and he'll have the best, will say that it could've been me. All a jury needs is reasonable doubt." I shrug. Cole glares at the wall. "Can I ask *you* something now?"

"I guess." He doesn't look at me. Instead he continues glaring at the wall and chewing on his lip.

We both look up as Gavin comes in. "Damon and Lance couldn't find Josh. He vanished. Lance is on masking Jessa. Cole, your house is being set to right again." Gavin sits.

Cole looks at him. He shakes his head as his brows knit together. "What?" he asks. "Put to right?"

"It's part of what we do," I say to him. "Clean up."

"Fine. Whatever. What do you want to ask?" He meets my eyes.

"You love her?"

"Who? Jessa? Sure. Like my best friend. Nothing more. But since I'm not fucking stupid and know what you're getting at, hell yes. I'd do anything for her. Anything to make sure she's safe."

"Even if it means lying to her? Keeping me out of it? Pretending I don't exist, even though you'll be working closer with me and my team than with anyone you've ever worked with before?"

"Does it mean keeping her safe?"

"Absolutely."

He doesn't hesitate for a second as he nods, and my respect for the guy goes up a little bit. The true test, trusting him, is yet to come. "I'll do what it takes," he says.

"What if it's not entirely legal? Toes the line?"

"If Jessa is safe, I don't care what I have to do."

I nod. Trust level has gone up a little bit more. "Okay. I have one of my guys masking her social security number. That's how Josh found her. Where she worked and everything. We'll be working to hide her and keep her hidden. Whatever it takes. I want her away from this. I loved her enough once to walk away, and I love her enough still to stay away. She's better than this. She deserves better than this."

"Damn right she does."

"I told Josh a lot of shit, but one thing I never told him is that her ultimate dream in life is to work for a big property or architecture firm as a project manager in New York City or Manhattan. She's always loved New York. She's in love with Manhattan. The architecture. Buildings. All of it.

I'm praying to every God that I don't believe exists that she never told him that."

"She didn't," he says quietly. I watch him as he takes a deep breath. "I was with her one night watching movies. We did it once a week, depending on my schedule. Al - uh… your brother dropped by one night. It was unexpected. Jessa seemed pretty surprised he showed up. He seemed pissed. I offered to take off, but he told me to stay. We finished the movie, then all sat down to talk. He asked her some pretty weird questions. It was another thing that made me suspicious."

"What kind of questions?" Gavin asks.

"Questions like he was fishing for information. Things he should've known after being with her for so long. Things I knew after knowing her less than a month. I guess you would've been with her around seven years at that point. I would think if someone was with someone for seven years, they would know things like their favorite fruit."

"Favorite… fruit?"

"Yep. And then he asked us both our dreams and aspirations. He asked Jessa if she dreamed of going anywhere else, or if L.A. was it."

"Tell me she lied," Gavin growls.

"Yeah. She did. Took me by surprise because she told me she'd love to live in New York. But I didn't say a word because she had this weird look in her eye when she looked at me. Like she was silently pleading with me to stay quiet. Your brother kind of pushed it. Asked if she ever thought of Minneapolis or Dallas or New York. Chicago or Memphis. She said no. She told him she likes the weather here. Loves the ocean and could never ever leave here."

I smile. Good. Good fucking girl.

"I need you to convince her she needs a fresh start," I begin. "Go with her. Help set her up. I don't care what you have to do to make her leave. Do it. Get her set up wherever she wants. She has the money. I have Lance masking her accounts. I'll get her new debit cards, so we can mask those. She's about to become a ghost."

"Good," Cole says.

"But I can't be the one to do it. I want her away from my family. I want her to completely start over. Have a new life. I don't want her to know I have anything to do with this. My family has hurt her enough, and she deserves more. I'll do what I have to do to make that happen."

"You sure you don't want to explain to her what happened?" Gavin asks me.

"No. I know Jessa. She'll forgive me. She'll forgive Josh. She'll channel her anger at my father. Right where it should be."

"How is that a bad thing?" Cole asks me.

"Because my family is powerful. My dad won't quit. I'll have a fuck of a time keeping her hidden as it is, but it will be a hell of a lot easier if she's across the country. Away from it. I might not be in love with her any more, but I still love her. I want her to be happy. She deserves that."

I don't tell him that Ryan is in Manhattan, and that if I asked, he'd have twenty guards on Jessa with a snap of his finger. My feelings might have changed towards her, but I will always love her. She was my first love.

"I'm with you. New life," Cole says.

Doctor Freeman steps into the room and quietly closes the door. "She's awake." We all breathe a sigh of relief. "But she's in bad shape. She has several broken ribs, a shattered calf. She's got a broken wrist and torn rotator cuff."

I get angrier and angrier at the words coming out of his mouth.

Fucking Josh. I'm so torn. What he did to her is un-fucking-speakable. It's unreal. But I also know that this is completely my father's fault. He did things to Josh that I can't even fathom and still can't believe. The beatdowns and the constant brainwashing. Things that he was saying to him while I was here had to have gotten worse without me to stop it. Shit he experienced because I wasn't here. Because I left him in my fathers hands.

Alone.

I shake my head to banish the thoughts. That isn't important right now. Jessa is.

"She had some internal bleeding that we were able to stop," Doctor Freeman continues. "She has some chest bruising and both of her lungs are bruised."

"Fucking Christ," Gavin says.

"That's not the worst of it," Doctor Freeman says. "He also must have either kicked her in the back or slammed her into things. Jessa is paralyzed from the waist down."

"What?" I growl. I can't stop the tears that instantly sting my eyes.

"No. Jesus. No," Cole whispers.

"I think it's temporary," Doctor Freeman sighs. "I really do. I have to have someone look to be absolutely certain there's nothing I'm missing, but I think she'll get through this. It is going to be a long road and will involve rehab, but I truly believe Jessa will make a full recovery."

"I want her here, doc," I say. "Full security. Full surveillance. No rehab facility. Do it all here. On this floor. No one gets to her except you, her team of doctors, and Cole."

"Couldn't agree more, but I noticed you didn't mention yourself or your team," Doctor Freeman says.

"You're right. Because as far as she's concerned, we were never here," Gavin says.

Doctor Freeman looks at me, perplexed.

"She can't know," I say. "I'll pay all of her hospital bills, but this is for her safety. The only outside person allowed to see her is Cole. If she says anything about bills, tell her it's taken care of. If she pushes it, tell her Cole and the department have come together to deal with all of it. She'll be concerned about the financing because she gave a lot of the money she got from her parent's estate to the children's hospital. She didn't want it. Didn't think she needed it."

"She's saved a lot of her income living with me, but you're right. She doesn't have a lot. She invested some, but they're in retirement accounts she won't touch. I want a detail on her room at all times," Cole says. "I'll give you a list daily of the officers I'll have posted outside her door, and the times they will be here."

"If they aren't on his list, I don't give a shit if they give you all of the credentials for a L.A.P.D. cop. They don't get in," I say.

"I'll get you pictures of Josh and both of their parents," Gavin says. "His mother isn't bad, but she could be used as a decoy or some bullshit."

"Wouldn't put it past my father," I say. "They for sure don't get in, though."

"Okay," Doctor Freeman says. "I'll make it happen. Jessa will be up shortly, and then I have a list of tests she'll need for tomorrow."

I look at Cole. "You won't be leaving her fucking side. You accompany her to every fucking test Doctor Freeman needs. Every rehab session. Make arrangements. Take a leave. I'll pay you for your time, so you don't lose income. I want you with her until she's set up safely."

"Definitely don't have to tell me," Cole says.

I nod and stand. I give him my contact information as well as the contact information for my entire team. "You need anything, call," I say. "I'll send the entire fucking mafia if it means keeping her safe."

"Much obliged," Cole responds.

Gavin and I leave. I don't know how the hell I feel right now, but at least I know she'll be safe.

I might blame Josh for his actions, but the person behind the curtain is my father.

I'm going to kill him.

Chapter Thirty One

 Jessa

(One Month Later)

It's been a little over a month since Alex attacked me. Five weeks of being in this damn hospital. I'm sick of it. I'm sick of the nurses. I'm sick of the doctors. I'm sick of the food. But most of all, I'm sick of the rehab. I'm sick of everyone treating me like a porcelain doll. I'm not going to break for Christ sake.

"Getting tired?" Cole asks me. I look up at him. Part of the rehab is walking. I've walked this entire floor five times today. Mostly to work off my aggression at being treated like a fragile piece of glass.

"More angry, actually." I glare at the floor.

Cole chuckles. "You're doing really well. You've defied all of their expectations."

"Not all of us," Doctor Freeman offers. "I had every confidence you'd do great."

I smile. Doctor Freeman and Cole have been my literal rocks. They pushed me when I needed pushing, and let me scream and cry when I was frustrated. I should have never decided to not see Doctor Freeman anymore. He has no contact with Alex. He assured me of that and even proved it by letting me scroll through his phone.

Cole is the absolute best friend I could ever ask for. He's never left my side. He took time off work and spent the entire five weeks with me in the hospital. He never went home. He had one of his friends take his dirty clothes and launder them and bring him clean stuff.

We get back to my room, and I sit in the chair, sighing heavily.

"I know this is frustrating, sweetie, but it's necessary," Cole says as he sits on the edge of my bed.

"Actually, Jess. You're really doing well," Doctor Freeman says as he pulls a chair up near me. "I think that you're close to being ready to be released.

I perk up. "Really?"

"Really. You'll have to watch your lifting. I know you'll be moving damn near immediately," Doctor Freeman says.

"Immediately. She's already got her apartment. But no worries about packing and lifting," Cole says.

I smile at Cole. "Cole got a few of his friends to drive out there in a moving van and get me set up."

"Good. That's good. Cole, when I release her, I'd like for someone to stay with her for at least four weeks. We need to make sure that we don't have any problems."

"No relapses. Make sure she can do everything on her own." Cole smiles softly at me.

"Exactly. If anything, and I mean anything happens, I will be on the first flight."

I blush. "Thank you, Doctor Freeman. You've always taken such good care of me."

"It's been my pleasure, Jessa. Please keep in touch with me. I want to know how you're doing."

I smile. The next few minutes are spent finding out how I'm progressing and feeling after today's walks and workout. After he's satisfied, he leaves me alone with Cole.

"Okay. We know you're physically good. How are you otherwise?" he asks.

"I'm frustrated. Angry. I'm just ready to get out of here. I don't want to leave you behind, but I hate L.A."

"I don't think anyone could ever blame you for that. And don't worry about me. I'll always only ever be a phone call or a text away. If you ever need anything, I'll be on the next flight."

I smile and hold out my arms. He laughs as he gets up, He bends to hug me.

There's no way I could've gotten through without him.

I hug him tighter as I think of what lays ahead for me.

(One Week Later)

Cole holds open the door for me to my new apartment and follows me inside. Other than online pictures and pictures I was sent by the realtor, this is my first time seeing it. It's an open floor plan and spacious. It has wooden floors and white walls. The floor to ceiling windows overlook Manhattan.

"Oh wow… It's perfect." I lightly brush my fingertips across the soft fabric of the couch. "Who got the furniture? I expected I'd have to order it."

Cole hesitates. "Um… I guess we all kind of just went in on everything. The department."

"Cole… I can afford my own stuff. I saved enough from my income, and I had some left from the sale of my parent's estate. I don't have it all in retirement accounts." I look up at him and give him a soft smile.

He pushes my hair behind my ear and hugs me. "I know. But I want everything to be smooth for you. The transition is going to be hard enough. This way, everything is set up and you can adjust easier."

"Thank you." I breathe in his fresh and familiar scent a moment before I pull slightly away.

He grins and takes my hand, leading me down the hallway. "Your bedroom looked bigger in the photos, but I actually think it's a pretty good size. Not as big, but still good." He opens the door.

I gasp as I walk in. There are floor to ceiling windows that open onto a balcony. I'm surrounded by bright lights and the breathtaking beauty of the city I'm about to call home.

"Damn. The pictures just didn't do it justice," I say, awestruck.

"I made sure to get you blackout shades. I know you like mine. The remote for the shades is on the desk."

I smile again as I turn to him. "I don't know how to thank you. For everything. For being such a good friend. For taking care of me. Never giving up on me, or turning your back on me. For all of this." I gesture around the bedroom.

"I'll never give up on you, Jess. I'll always be here for you. You never have to worry about me not being your friend."

✘✘✘

(One Month Later)

Almost an entire month has gone by since I moved to Manhattan, and I am so deeply in love with it that I can't envision ever living anywhere else. I love the architecture. I love the skyscrapers that defy all laws of gravity.

Moving was the absolute best decision I have ever made. I'm so glad Cole suggested and supported me so much on making it a reality. The opportunity to start over and make my own life was everything I have ever wanted.

I can't even tell anymore how injured I'd been. It's almost like I'm a real life phoenix. I've risen from the ash ruins of my life and blossomed into this strong beautiful being. This being that has risen from the destruction and now soars high above what was.

"Holy shit. That's a high fucking building," Cole says.

I smile as we look up at the building we just arrived at. He's right. It soars into the sky and stands out among all the other buildings in the area. It's modern. Sleek. Intimidating.

"It's so beautiful," I whisper next to him. Cole puts an arm around my shoulders and turns me towards him so I'm looking up at him. He's always been able to sense my nervousness.

"You got this. This is your dream job. Everything you've ever wanted."

I take a deep breath and turn towards Crane Enterprises, the largest property development firm in the world. I would be lying if I said I didn't feel intimidated. Walking into this firm with such little experience is by far the craziest thing I've ever done.

"Maybe I should work on getting more experience before I walk in there."

"Jessa. You got this. You've always believed in fate. Dreams. That everything happens for a reason. It's literally what you stand on. This position being posted just as you were starting to look for jobs was fate. You were meant for this job. No. I take that back. This job? It was made for you, sweetheart."

I can't help but laugh as I hug him. When I pull away, I smooth down my black pant-suit and look at him. "How do I look?"

Cole looks me up and down, then reaches out to adjust my jacket. "Like a fierce as fuck go-getter who is going to completely crush this interview and be the best Project Manager this world has ever seen."

I beam at him as I take another deep breath. "Here goes nothing."

I put on my best and brightest smile as I turn and step through the doors of Crane Enterprises. I confidently stride up to the security counter and give the guy behind the counter my most self-assured grin.

He smiles back. "Hey. I'm Nick. How can I help you?"

"Hi. I'm Jessa Holloway here to see Mr. Crane. I have an interview with him."

"Right. Yeah, I have you right here." He smiles again as he types something into his computer before he stands. "I'll escort you up."

He leads me to an elevator and swipes a card. I briefly flashback to the penthouse I shared with Alex. I needed a keycard to access our floor. I close my eyes to the memory as the doors to the elevator close. I press myself into a corner and take a deep breath, forcing my eyes open. I hate elevators.

"You know, you must be something special. Jason Crane doesn't do interviews with anyone."

I look at him, slightly surprised. "Really? I guess I sort of thought this was the way he worked."

"Well, he approves everyone that works here. But interviewing them is another story. The only person he's ever interviewed on his own is his Executive Assistant. Well, I guess a few more."

"I get the Executive Assistant because that's going to be someone who works closely with him. But really? Hardly anyone else?"

He laughs. "Damn. I already like you. I hope he hires you! To answer you, he hired higher ups. People he works closely with. Executives. Accountants. Jason prefers to focus on the business. He doesn't like interviewing unless he has to. Project Managers, like you're interviewing for, would be done by the head of that department. Jason interviewing you means you must be something special."

"Jason. You must be really close if you don't call him Mr. Crane."

He laughs again. "Don't miss much, do you?"

"I've had to learn not to."

He gives me a look as he nods. "Yes. We're very close. Jason is my brother."

I smile as the doors finally open on the top floor. Nick steps out, and I follow him to the desk in the large lobby. "Now it all makes sense."

"Nancy. This is Jessa Holloway," Nick says to the woman behind the counter. She has kind eyes. She doesn't look too old. Close to what my mother would be, if she were still alive.

"Ms. Holloway! It's nice to meet you." She smiles at me and eases my nerves. Nick gives me one last smile and a wink as he heads back to the elevator. Nancy stands. "Just follow me, please."

She leads me to a conference room, and I immediately take a seat and gawk. The room exudes power and control, but doesn't intimidate me. It's large, but not large enough to make me feel small or unimportant.

"Mr. Crane will be here in a moment, Ms. Holloway." She leaves the room, and I lean forward slightly, taking a closer look at the design.

"Wow. This is incredible," I whisper, noticing all of the small details most people would probably miss.

"Thank you," a deep voice rumbles behind me.

I quickly stand and turn around. Leaning against the doorframe with his arms folded over his chest is one of the most attractive men I have ever seen. He's tall, built of pure steel, and has the most piercing blue eyes.

Even more piercing than Alex's, and I never thought that was a possibility. His day old scruff is the perfect length to make him look rugged, yet clean. Powerful and dangerous, yet confident and professional.

"Uh… s-sorry. I don't usually talk to myself," I stammer.

"Can't say I minded the compliment. I designed the room myself."

My mouth goes dry and waters at the same time as he strides assertively into the room. How is it possible for a mouth to be just as dry as it is wet? He sits, and I am forced to lick my suddenly dry lips as

I clear my throat. Is it hot in here? It's like a hundred degrees. "It's an incredible room. The lines are incredible."

He raises an eyebrow as he sets out a folder. "Lines?"

"Oh… um… yes." I stand and walk to the other side of the room. He watches me. "This wall. The way it comes out from the rest of the room. A lot of people think it makes the room smaller. Intimidating. But this actually brings comfort to people, while still maintaining a controlling type of environment. It says you, being the CEO, are in complete control of the meetings that are in here, but the people you are meeting with don't feel that way. They feel like equals." I smile softly as I take my seat near him. He's sitting at the head of the table.

"You got all of that from the design of a wall? Impressive."

I keep my eyes on his, but I struggle to understand how. All I can think of is his very kissable lips on mine. I watch his eyes drop to my mouth, and I can't help the little flutter in my chest as I bite my lip. I look down at my hands clasped tightly on the tabletop. No one has had this effect on me. Not since Alex.

Mr. Crane clears his throat. "As I'm sure you're aware, Ms. Holloway, I'm Jason Crane."

I shake his extended hand, and a jolt of electricity shoots through my fingertips all the way to my toes. He holds my small hand in his large one a little longer than necessary before he abruptly lets go and clears his throat again.

He flips open the folder. "You've been involved with one major project in L.A. Three smaller ones. You've been with two different firms. You quit both without notice and haven't worked at all for a couple of months. That doesn't make you look very reliable."

I swallow. Hard. "U-um… L.A. was… not where I belonged." I look up and meet his eyes, refusing to allow anything from my past dictate my future. "I know how it looks, but if you check with all of them, they'll all give me glowing references. My work speaks for itself. If you look at the rest, you'll see numerous examples -"

"I looked at your samples, Ms. Holloway. I checked your references. You wouldn't have gotten this interview if I hadn't. Your work does speak for itself. You're really good. But this is a huge firm. We have projects going all over the world. You'll be required to work on more than one thing at once. And you're required to be a leader. Your position would put you in control of a team. You have no experience leading."

"My major at UCLA -"

"I know what you majored in, Ms. Holloway. But majoring and doing are two very different things."

"I have every confidence -"

"I appreciate the confidence, but I have no room for a junior project lead. I need someone who can lead now. I have no time to train anyone."

He closes the file, and I stare at him, completely baffled at what just happened. My chest begins to constrict. I take a deep breath as I nod and stand, gathering my things.

"I see. I apologize for wasting your time, Mr. Crane."

I turn to leave. I've done my research, and I know that Jason Crane is self-made. I know how difficult he can be. How intimidating and ruthless. I also know that he respects people who fight for themselves.

So, I do just that. I close my eyes as I reach the door, calming my nerves before opening my eyes and turning back to him. He's already gathering my file as he stands up.

"Mr. Crane, I realize I am not experienced. I'm not what you would typically look for in an employee. But I take pride in my work," I say as confidently as I can. He watches me with calculating eyes, but a small smile forms on his lips. "I have every confidence that I will not only succeed here, but that I'll help you take your company in new and exciting directions. I know I'm talented. I know my worth. I know that if you allow me to walk out that door, you'll regret your decision because you'll never find someone who can take this company to the level I can. I hope that you'll give me the opportunity. I can assure you that it will be the best decision you ever make." I turn towards the door and then turn back once more.

He's watching me still. He raises an eyebrow. "Yes, Ms. Holloway?"

I take another breath. "I've done my research, Mr. Crane. I know you're one of the youngest people in the world to become a billionaire. I know you started this company on your own and worked your ass off to get where you are. You had to take a lot of risks to get to the point you are today. Some calculated. Some not. In that, you and I are a lot alike. I'll get a position with another company and take that company to new levels because I'm passionate and determined. I just want a chance to work for the best." I give him a small shrug. His smile has grown a little bigger as he crosses his powerful arms over his muscular chest. His suit jacket strains at the movement. "You're the best, Mr. Crane."

I turn once more and leave the room. I walk with purpose to the elevator, refusing to cry until the doors are safely closed behind me. Before I can push the button, I feel an incredibly broad and hard chest against my back. I hold my breath. The heat radiating off him melts me. As soon as his large hand touches my arm, I forget my name.

"You're hired."

His breath against my ear forces my eyes to close, and his woodsy, spicy scent turns my legs to mush. I have no idea how it's possible. I truly believed Alex was the love of my life, but my reaction to Mr Crane is so much more intense than anything Alex ever brought out of me.

The first day of the rest of my life starts today with this man. This powerful, intimidating man who has the entire world in the palm of his hand. I know he's going to change the world one beautiful development at a time.

And I can't wait to help him do it.

The End

Next In The Crane Family Series

The dark and sexy Crane Family Series continues in **Billion Dollar Love Story**.

Last year, the girl of my dreams walked into my office for an interview. I haven't been able to get her out of my head since.

Jessa Halloway is beautiful, quiet, and mysterious. Ever since I saw her, I haven't been able to stop thinking about making her mine. Problem is, I'm the CEO of Crane Enterprises.

Her boss.

When Jessa doesn't show up to work one day, my protective instincts go into overdrive. She's a creature of habit. Never been late.

I wasn't expecting the danger lurking in the shadows. I'll be damned if I let them get their hands on her. Not with the allies I have at my side.

Defending her means admitting I love her and diving back into the dangerous, dark as midnight world I fought so hard to leave. I'll do anything to keep her safe.

Even if it costs me everything.

~ This book is a steamy CEO/Mafia Romance that has dark and violent themes, mental health themes, emotional abuse, mental abuse, physical abuse, physical assault, and strong language that may not be suitable for all readers. ~

Order **Billion Dollar Love Story** now!

The Crane Family Series

Available Now

The Reluctant Mafia King
Sweet Lies
Billion Dollar Love Story
Be Mine
Protecting Her
Dangerously Forbidden Love
His Heart
Love In The Dark

Box Sets Available

The Crane Family Series

Other Books By Melony Ann
The Beautiful Dream Series

Available Now

Loving You
My Love, My Heart
Softening Lyric
Undercover Temptations
Captain Charming
Breaking Boundaries
Crashing Into You
Tactical Inferno
Ravishing Our Queen
Cherished By The Texan
Unveiling Our Passions

Box Sets Available

The Beautiful Dream Series: Box Set: Part 1
The Beautiful Dream Series: Box Set: Part 2

The Deimos Trilogy

Available Now

Connor's Legacy
Aryan's Alpha
Kade's Redemption

Box Sets Available

The Deimos Trilogy

The Forbidden Temptation Series

Available Now

The Detective's Forbidden Temptation
The Running Back's Forbidden Temptation

The Lucinio Family Series

Available Now

Rising From The Ashes
The Player's Rebel
Encrypting My Heart

Multi Author Series
Piper Falls: Firehouse 49

Available Now

Ignite My Fire by Melony Ann
Regain My Fire by Kindra White
Playing With My Fire by D.L. Howe
Fight My Fire by Darley Collins
Against My Fire by Anneke Boshoff
Relight My Fire by Louise Murchie
Harness My Fire by Ayana Lisbet
Quench My Fire by Havana Wilder

Let's Be Friends

Follow me on

Bookbub

Facebook

Goodreads

Instagram

Tik Tok

Visit my website
www.melonyannauthor.com

Subscribe to my newsletter and get a FREE never-seen-before NOVELLA
just for subscribers!
https://www.melonyannauthor.com/exclusive-content

Join my Facebook Reader Group!
Jason's and Melony's Sizzling Book Nook

The official Crane Family Series Playlist on YouTube
https://youtube.com/playlist?list=PLGEiD5wbQmDc78K7gNeODh-janqmlFiie

Dedication

You're the sweetest of all the sweets in the world. And you're all ours.

Acknowledgements

Brad - I don't know where I would be without you. When everything fell apart, you were the one who kept me from breaking. You were the one who guided me. You were the one who fixed me. You've never doubted me or my talent. You never let me give up. You loved me. You keep loving me. You're my heart. I love you.

Laura – I truly love you. More than I could ever express. When my world came crashing down with a spectacular showing of sparks and colors, you were right there to hold me together and make sure I didn't break. My love for you is never ending.

Jay - For a long time, you were my only rock. You lifted me up when I felt like I couldn't do it. You talked me down when I was freaking out. You dropped everything for me on so many occasions, just to make sure I was okay. Even when your life got chaotic, you never abandoned me like so many others did. You've always been my best friend, and now you're so much more. I love you beyond all logic.

Ayana - Thank you for being family and such a great PA. I love you so much!

Anneke - I can't wait until you're stateside, love! Love you so much!

Jason - I'm always in complete awe of your talent, but I think I'm even more in awe of you. You're honestly the most sincere and honest person I think I've ever met.

To the Bookstagram Community.

To my family.

To all of those who believe in me and support me.

To all of those who don't.

Cover by: Carter Cover Designs

Edited by: Alyssa Skaggs

About Melony Ann

Melony Ann began writing short stories and poetry as a child. She continued honing her craft over the years until she took the plunge and began publishing her work, despite having severe anxiety.

Melony writes contemporary romance stories that are full of suspense and a lot of steam.

When she isn't writing, she is loving her family and working to make her life something she deserves.

Melony believes that if her writing can inspire just one person, then all of her hard work is worth it.

Her hope is that her writing allows each and every one of her readers to escape for a little while. To dive into a different world one book at a time.